The Rebel Doc

LOUISA GEORGE
SUSAN CARLISLE
JOANNA NEIL

MILLS & BOON

First Published in Great Britain 2019
by Mills & Boon, an imprint of HarperCollins*Publishers*
1 London Bridge Street, London, SE1 9GF

ISBN: 978-0-263-27474-5

0119

MIX
Paper from
responsible sources
FSC™ C007454

This book is produced from independently certified FSC™ paper to ensure responsible forest management.

For more information visit: www.harpercollins.co.uk/green

Printed and bound in Spain
by CPI, Barcelona

TEMPTED BY HER ITALIAN SURGEON

LOUISA GEORGE

CHAPTER ONE

'WHAT ON EARTH...?' Ivy Leigh blinked at the image downloading to her inbox, pixel by tiny pixel.

A...bottom?

A beautiful perfectly formed, tanned, bare bottom. Two toned thighs, a sculpted back...a naked male body, in what looked like a men's locker room. A tagline next to the pert backside read: *Dr Delicious. As perfect as a peach. Go on...take a bite.*

She swallowed. And again. Fanned her hot cheeks. She might have imposed a strict dating hiatus but she still had an appreciation of what was fine when she saw it. But why on earth would her work computer be the recipient of such a thing?

Maybe the spam screens on the hospital intranet server weren't up to scratch. Adding a new note to her smartphone to-do list—*Call IT*—she let out a heat-infused sigh that had nothing to do with sexual frustration and everything to do with this new job. Two weeks in and yet another department she needed to pull into order. Still, she'd been employed here to drag this hospital into the twenty-first century and that was what she was going to do, no matter how many toes she trod on.

Twisting in her chair to hide the offending but not remotely offensive bottom from anyone who might walk past her open office door, she sneaked a closer look at the image, her gaze landing on a pile of what looked like discarded clothes on a bench. No, not clothes as such…

Scrubs?

Please, no.

Dark green scrubs bearing the embroidered name of St Carmen's Hospital. She gasped, and whatever vague interest she'd had dissolved into a puddle of professional anxiety…her bordering-on-average day was fast turning bad.

So who? What? Why? *Why me?*

She slammed her eyelids shut and refused to look at the accompanying email message.

Okay, big girls' pants.

Opening one eye, she took a deep breath and read.

From Albert Pinkney. St Carmen's Hospital Chairman. His formidable perfectly English pronunciation shone through his words. 'Miss Leigh, what in heaven's name is this? Our new marketing campaign? Since when did St Carmen's turn into some sort of smutty cabaret show? This is all over the internet like a rash and is not synonymous with the image we want to present. The benefactors are baying for blood. We are a children's hospital. You're the lawyer—do something. Make it disappear. Fix it.'

Because she was probably the only person who could solve this—when all else failed call in the lawyer to shut it down, or drag some antiquated law out and hit the offender with it.

And, damn it, fix it she would. Although making it disappear would be a little harder. Didn't Pinkney know that once something was out on the net, it was there for ever? Clearly he was another candidate to add to her social media awareness classes.

First, find out who this…specimen belonged to. Now, that was going to be an interesting task. 'Becca! Becca!'

'Yes, Miss Leigh?' Her legal assistant arrived in the doorway and flashed her usual over-enthusiastic grin. 'What can I help you with?'

'Delicate issue… You've been here a while and have your ear to the ground. You must know pretty much all of the staff by now. Have you any idea who this…might belong to?' Ivy twisted away and made a *ta-da* motion with her hands towards her computer screen.

'Oh, my…' Becca fanned her face with the stack of manila folders in her hand. 'Take a bite? I'm suddenly very hungry.'

Me, too. 'That is so not the point. Can you see our logo? Right there. We can't have this sort of thing happening, it's very bad for our reputation.'

'Not unless we're trying to attract a whole tranche of new nurses… No? Wrong response? Sorry.' Becca gave a little shrug that said she wasn't sorry at all and that, in fact, she was really quite impressed. 'It's very nice. It is kind of perfect. And it says it belongs to a doctor so we can narrow it down. We could do one of those police line-ups, get the main suspects against the wall and…' She looked back at the picture, her voice breathy and high-pitched. 'I'm happy to organise that.'

'Get in line.' But, seriously, how many years at law school? For this? This was what she'd studied so hard for? This was why she'd hibernated away from any kind of social life? Her plan had always been to get into a position where she could safeguard others from what she'd had to endure, to prevent mistakes that cost people their happiness. Not chastise a naked man about impropriety. Still, no one could say her job didn't have variety. 'I don't want to narrow it down, Becca, I want it gone. We need to send out a stack of take-down notices, get the PR team onto damage limitation. And whoever put this out there is going to learn what it's like to feel the wrath of Ivy Leigh.'

It was late. The cadaver transplant he'd just finished on a ten-year-old boy had been difficult and long, but successful, with a good prognosis. He had a planned surgery list lined up for tomorrow and a lot of prep to work up. A ward round. And now this—an urgent summons to a part of the hospital he had not even known existed. Or, for that matter, cared about. The legal team? At six-thirty in the evening? Wouldn't all the pen-pushers have gone home? Matteo Finelli's mood was fading fast. He rapped on the closed door. Didn't wait to hear a response, and walked right in. 'You wanted to see me?'

'Yes.' The woman in front of him sat up straight behind an expensive-looking wide mahogany desk that was flanked by two filing cabinets. Beyond that a large window gave a view over the busy central London street. It was sunny out there and he imagined sitting in a small bar or café with the sun on his back as he downed a cold beer. Instead of being in here, doing this.

Apart from a calendar on the desk there was nothing else anywhere in the room. Nothing personalised, no photos, no pens, stapler...anything. She either had a bad case of OCD or had just moved in. Which would explain why he had not heard of her or seen her around. She ran a hand through short blonde hair that made her look younger than he'd imagined she must be to have achieved such a status and such a large office.

Cool green eyes stared at him. The blouse she wore was a similar colour—and why he'd even noticed he couldn't say. Her mouth, although some would say was pretty, was in a tight thin line. She looked buttoned-up and tautly wound and as if she had never had a moment of pleasure in her life. She met his anger with equal force. 'Mr Finelli, I presume? Please, take a seat.'

He didn't. 'I have not time. I was told you needed to see me immediately… What is the problem?'

'Okay, no pleasantries. Fine by me. I'll cut to the chase. Tell me…' The eyes narrowed a little. Her throat jumped as she swallowed. Emerald-tipped fingers tapped on a keyboard and an image flickered onto the screen. 'Is this you?'

There was no point in concealing his laugh. Whoever had taken the photo had held the lens at a damned fine angle. He looked good. More than good. He whistled on an out breath. 'You like it?'

'That's not the point.' But her pupils flared and heat hit her cheeks.

'You do like it? It is impressive, yes? And you summoned me all the way to the other side of the hospital for a slide show of naked bodies…interesting.' He turned to go. 'Now, I can leave? I have work to do.'

'Not so fast, Mr Finelli.'

Ma che diavolo? 'Call me Matteo, please.'

The woman blinked. 'Mr Finelli, why did you post this picture on the internet? Were you hoping for it to go completely viral, because, congratulations, it did. It seems that cyberspace can't get enough of your…assets. Have you any idea what damage you have caused the hospital by posing for this with the St Carmen's logo available for the world to see?'

'Everybody calls me Matteo, I do not answer to Mr Finelli—too formal. Too…English. I did not post that picture anywhere. And with all due respect, Miss…' His eyes roved over her face—which was turning from a quite attractive pink to a dark shade of red—then to her name badge. Her left hand. No wedding band. Definitely Miss. 'Miss Ivy Leigh. I was not posing.'

'Do you deny this is your bott...er...*gluteus maximus*?'

It wasn't fair to smile again. But he did. 'Of course I don't deny it. I've already agreed that it is mine. But clearly I did not take the picture and I did not pose. It looks to me like I'd had a shower, I was stretching to get my clothes out of the locker, with my back to the lens, you cannot see my face. I can't take a photo of the back of my head from that distance, can I? Besides which I am a very busy doctor and I do not have time to sit around playing on the internet like some people.' *Like you*, he thought. But he let that accusation hover in the silence. 'I don't know for sure who took the picture, but I can guess.'

'Oh? Who?' She leant forward, her eyes fixed on his face, eyebrows arched. In another lifetime it might have been fun to play a little more with her. To see where her soft edges were, if she had any. But not in this life.

'Ged Peterson.' *Touché, my man. You win this round.* 'My registrar, he loves playing pranks.'

'Peterson. Peterson. Ged? Short for Gerard?' Those green-tipped fingers tapped into some database on the computer. 'He doesn't work here.'

'No. But he did. Until last month when he went to work in Australia. He said he was going to give me a leaving present. I didn't realise it would be this.' Matteo stepped back, primed to leave. 'And now we have solved the mystery I must go.'

'Absolutely not. Stay right there.'

That got his attention. No woman had ever spoken to him like that before. It was...well, it was interesting. 'Why?'

'Again, I ask you; have you any idea of the damage you have caused? Lady Margaret has withdrawn her funding for the new family rooms in protest already. Parents are complaining that this is not what they expect from an institution responsible for their children's lives. Surgeons who complain about being overworked and underpaid and yet have time to flaunt their bodies make us look ridiculous. It's not professional.'

'Everyone needs to stop overreacting. It is nothing.'

With a disdainful look that suggested he was in way over his pretty little head, she shook hers. 'Image is everything, Mr Finelli. In this technological age it's all about the message we send out to gain trust and respect. We need people on side to volunteer, raise funds, hit targets. We do not need some jumped-up surgeon flashing his backside with our logo in the picture.'

He strode forward and leaned towards her, pointing at the picture getting a nose full of honeysuckle scent in the process. Overly officious she might be, but she smelt damned good. He edged away from the perfume because it was strangely addictive and he didn't need any more distractions today. This was enough and he still had a few hours' work ahead of him. 'If you are worried about funding I have an idea...why not take another eleven pictures of me and make some calendars you hospital administrators all seem to love so much? Sell me?'

'I am a lawyer.' As if that explained anything. Actually, it explained a lot. With one brother already qualified and another working his way through college, Matteo knew that law school was just as rigorous as med school. That those dark shadows under her eyes weren't from late nights drinking in bars but from studying into the early hours. That this woman had worked diligently amidst strong competition. Along with her English-rose complexion and porcelain skin, it also explained that she'd probably spent the best part of her life cooped up indoors with her nose in a book, not exploring the world, not simply lying in the last rays of a relaxing afternoon letting the sun heat your skin. It explained why she was so damned coiled.

She shook her head. 'The money you've already lost us is in the thousands, possibly hundreds of thousands, Mr Finelli. Calendars only make a few pounds per copy.'

'With my backside on them it would make a lot more.'

'You really do have a high opinion of yourself, don't you?' Her voice had deepened and he got the feeling she was trying very hard to be calm.

Good, because that meant he was niggling her, probably not as much as she was niggling him…but, well, he had more important things to do. Like go check on the transplant patient. 'Sure. Why not?'

In what he could only describe as a power play she stood up and walked around the desk. If he wasn't mistaken it took her a moment to steady herself, then she grabbed a file from a filing cabinet and slammed it shut with finesse and flair. She sat back down again, but not before he'd taken a good long look at the cinched-in waist, curve-enhancing, slim-legged trousers and wedge heels.

Even more interesting…

Opening what he now realised was his employment file, she gave him a cold stare. 'Look, Mr Finelli, it's obvious you are not taking this issue seriously. I need to make sure you are aware of the consequences of having your naked body sprawled over the internet with our name and logo on it. I have discussed the issue with the HR department and the chairman and we are all in agreement that we need to instigate some courses for the staff on the whys and wherefores of social media etiquette. These will be mandatory for every—'

'Because of this? I did nothing wrong.'

'Because of this. Because we can't run risks with people's lives, or be distracted from our true purpose as a hospital. Because we can't make mistakes. Distraction causes death or damage.' This was clearly very important to her—personal, maybe, judging by the passion in her eyes and the slight shake in her hands.

She took a sip of water from a glass next to her elbow. And didn't, he noticed, offer him anything to drink. She waited a moment and seemed to settle herself before continuing. 'We have to control how we are seen, and this episode has just cemented my point. I ran the classes very successfully at my last place of employment and am starting them here on Thursday. You will be required to attend.'

No way. 'I operate on Thursdays.'

'And Tuesdays and Fridays. I know. There are only four sessions. You will be expected to attend them all, like every other person in this hospital, then no more will be said about the matter.'

Dio santo. She was serious. 'Have you any idea how precious operating theatre time is to a surgeon?'

She looked away and her eyes flickered closed for a moment. Then she gathered herself together. 'I have some understanding, yes.'

'And if I refuse?'

She tapped his folder. 'You will have to face a disciplinary hearing. Then there will be no operating time at all. It will be time-consuming and messy. There may even be a stand-down period. Who can say?'

Now the niggling descended into outright anger. 'On what grounds?'

'Bringing the organisation into disrepute. Refusing mandatory training. It's all quite clear in the employment contract...expected behaviour, training requirements, dress code, et cetera. Mr Finelli, many hospital boards don't allow their physicians to have a public face on social media. We are not unusual in wanting to protect ourselves.'

Round one to Ivy Leigh. Ivy...wasn't there a plant...poison ivy? *Sommaco velenoso*. It described her perfectly. He just needed a counter argument to bring Poison Ivy down a peg or two. 'Perhaps I could sue you too.'

Now her eyes widened with a flicker of nervousness. 'What the hell for?'

'Breach of my privacy. I could suggest that I did not give my permission for my body to be used in such a poorly contrived advert.'

She laughed and it was surprisingly soft and feminine. 'Go on and indulge yourself in any fantasy you like. But you and I both know this was not an advert. You have no grounds, but I do. In fact, section three of the Workplace—'

'Forget it. I'm not listening any more. I will not attend your sessions.'

'Okay. Your choice.' She reminded him of his younger sister, Liliana, who would not give up. Ever. Arguing with her was like arguing with a brick wall. 'Then I will have to invite you to attend a meeting with our human relations director first thing tomorrow morning.'

'No.' Take more time out of his work schedule?

Maybe Mike would swap his cardiac roster from a Wednesday for one week just to make this insufferable woman go away?

'Mr Finelli, we are both on the same side.'

'Like hell we are.' But he did not have any more time to waste on this. Better to get it over and done with. 'You leave me with no choice. I'll do the four sessions.'

'Then it's sorted. After that you won't hear anything more from me on this matter. Thank you for your time.' She put out her hand and, grimly, he shook it. It was warm and firm and confident. And a little something reverberated through his body at her touch—which he steadfastly ignored. Clearly she felt none of it as her voice remained calm and cool, like her eyes. 'I'm sure you'll find the sessions most interesting.'

'I'm sure I won't. Now I need to rearrange my day. Four sessions shouldn't take up much time. I will be free from what time? Lunch?'

Amusement flashed across her features, as if she'd won a well-fought victory. 'Oh, sorry, didn't I make myself clear? By four sessions I meant four days.'

'Four days? No. No way. I'm not doing it.'

'But you agreed. And we shook hands. Is an Italian man's word as good as his honour?'

He held her gaze. His honour was fine and intact, unlike others he could name. He would never betray anyone the way he had once been betrayed. 'It is. But I have one condition.'

'Oh, yes?' Her expression told him she thought he was not well placed to be making conditions.

'For every minute I have to spend in your ridiculous class you have to spend an equal amount of time with me, doing my work. The work this hospital is so famous for doing. Saving lives. Then perhaps you'll see just how badly you have wasted my time.' He held her gaze. Saw the flicker of anxiety stamped down by determined resolve as she nodded.

'Okay.' Her smile was like condensed milk—way too sweet. 'Seeing as I'm new to the hospital, I have to familiarise myself with each department anyway. And it'll give me invaluable insights into the specific kind of legal issues that could arise there and a chance to review policy. This way I'll be killing two birds with one stone.'

How had he thought it might be fun to play with her? Fun was over. This was war. 'Believe me, Miss Leigh, the only killing going on in my OR is of your determination to make a damned fool of me. Goodbye.'

CHAPTER TWO

HE WASN'T GOING to come.

Ivy surveyed the conference room filled with porters, nursing staff, ward clerks and doctors, all chattering and drinking copious cups of coffee before the first session started in less than two minutes. And why the heck, with a room full of attendees who looked interested and invested in learning about social media, she was shamefully disappointed that she couldn't see Mr Finelli's famous backside in the foray, she couldn't fathom. Only that she now appeared to be locked in some sort of battle of wills with the doctor and she'd been looking forward to showcasing her side and proving her very valid points. The man may have been infuriatingly narcissistic but she'd believed him a worthy adversary. Clearly not. Typical that he hadn't bothered to turn up.

Mind you, with those dark Mediterranean eyes, that proud haughty jaw and thoughts of what was under those scrubs, it was probably a good thing. And it would be hard to concentrate on her talk with that glower searing a hole in her soul.

'Okay, Miss Leigh...' Becca handed her the folders of hand-outs for the participants. 'One each and a few to spare. Morning tea's at ten-thirty. Catering will deliver at about ten-fifteen.'

'And lunch? You know how these things go. If they don't get regularly fed and watered they get grouchy.'

'One o'clock. In the Steadman Room. Oh, and the laptop's all set up with the projector, you're good to go. Good luck.'

Excellent. Everything was running perfectly, apart from a niggle of a headache. 'Thanks, and, Becca, please, please, drop the formality and call me Ivy. I know the last incumbent had you calling him sir, but I do things differently.'

'Okay. If you're su…' Her assistant's face grew a deep shade of puce as her gaze fixed on something over Ivy's shoulder. 'Oh… Just, oh.'

'Are you okay?'

'Oh, yes. Just *peachy.* Such a shame he's a break-your-heart bad boy.' Becca grinned, and moved forward as if levitated and as if breaking your heart was some kind of spectator sport and he was the *numero uno* world champion title-holder. Which he probably was. 'Mr Finelli, please grab a coffee first and then take a seat. Let me show you where the cups are.'

Great. For some reason Ivy's heart jigged a little. First-time nerves, probably. She was always jittery at the beginning of a workshop. There was so much to think about… technology not working, correct air-conditioning levels—too hot and everyone fell asleep, too cold and no one could concentrate—snacks arriving on time, holding everyone's attention, keeping track…

Suddenly he was walking towards her. She imagined Becca would think him hot, all brooding chocolate-fudge eyes and unruly dark hair. But Ivy had switched off her sexy radar years ago when she'd learned that men wanted their women perfect, and that she didn't fit that bill. Since then she'd watched her flatmates have their hearts broken and her mother reduced…just less, diminished somehow…

because of a man—and Ivy had decided she wasn't going there. Give her books and her career any day. There was something perfect about a beginning, a middle and an end of a novel—a whole. Complete. And, truth be told, reading was just about all she had the energy to do after a day's work.

Unlike the other consultants, he'd adopted informal dress—no suit and tie for Dr Delicious of peachy-bottom fame. Just a white T-shirt over formidable shoulders, with dark jeans hugging slender hips. The same uniform she'd seen on every youth in Florence when she'd been there on a weekend break. She imagined him with dark aviator sunglasses on, perched on a moped like something out of a nineteen-fifties movie. Then her mind wandered back to that picture of him naked, and the knowledge of exactly what was under that uniform made her feel strangely uncomfortable. Heat shimmied through her. It was unseasonably warm in here—a spring heatwave, perhaps? Too many bodies in such a small room? She must ask someone to fiddle with the air-con at once.

Where was she? Ah, yes, keeping…what? Keeping track. *Focus.*

'Good morning, Miss Leigh. And so it begins.' Oh…and then there was the accent. Kind of cute, she supposed. If you were Becca and easily taken in by deep honeyed tones melting over your skin. She let it wash right over her, along with the irritated vibe that emanated from his every pore.

'Mr Finelli, glad you could eventually join us. I hear you kicked up a bit of a fuss about it all, though.'

A frown appeared underneath the dark curls that fell over his forehead. 'The HR director is as enthusiastic about this as you are, it seems. Does no one in this hospital have any common sense, Miss Leigh?'

'That is exactly what I'm trying to engender with this

course, but some of our staff seem to want to flaunt themselves at every opportunity. And, please, call me Ivy.'

'Ivy, ah, yes. But only if you call me Matteo. Or if you can't manage that, Matt will do. *Ivy.*' He smiled as if something other than this conversation was amusing him. He took a sip of black coffee and winced. '*Dio,* more poison. Why is coffee so bad here?'

More poison? What in hell did that mean.? Uh-oh, she could guess. 'Poison ivy? Really? Is that the best you can do? I've been hearing that since I was in kindergarten. I expected better…more…from you, Mr Finelli. Oh, sorry, Matteo. Please, do try harder.'

He put the cup into his saucer, clearly much more insulted by his drink than her words. 'I was just seeing what it would take to wind you up—not a lot, it seems.'

She played it cool, ignoring the fluster in her gut. 'Oh, make no mistake, I'm not wound up. Just disappointed by your performance so far.'

The smile he gave her was wicked and it tickled her deep inside. 'Oh, trust me, Miss Leigh, no woman has ever been disappointed by my performance.'

Heat hit her cheeks as she realised she'd been drawn in and chewed up—worse, he was flirting and she could barely admit to herself that she was a little intrigued by someone so sure of himself. Her heart beat wildly in her chest and she willed it to slow. This sort of battleground tactic was way out of her league—flirting wasn't something she was used to. A cold, hard stare and feigned disinterest had always been enough to keep any potential lovers at bay, that and her refusal to undress in anything other than darkness. Plus a side helping of reservation had helped, and a desire to not end up like her mother.

No way would she let a man have any kind of effect on

her…no way would she let *this* man have any kind of effect on her.

What she needed was to put him on side and a little off balance. She looked at his cup and wondered…maybe if she let him in on her little coffee secret he might just be so taken aback he'd sit quietly at the back of the class and listen, instead of— She could only imagine what he had in store. Creating merry hell about her subject matter. What better way to derail him than by being friendly? She leaned a little closer and whispered, 'There's a coffee shop down the road on the corner, Enrico's, great coffee. I always make sure I get one on my way into work, it keeps me going. I don't like to offend the catering staff here so I decant it into one of their cups.'

'And now we have a secret shared. Me, too. And who would have thought you could be so subversive? Maybe there is more to you than I thought.' His eyes widened and then he winked. 'Enrico's a friend, and, yes, his coffee is the best this side of the English Channel. Although that isn't hard.'

'No. I guess not.' Subversive? *Subversive?* And to her chagrin that thought made her feel damned good. Although it was a stretch even for her imagination—she'd spent the better part of her life working hard and toeing every line she found. Her gaze roved over his face, all swarthy and handsome…no, beautiful, if you were the sort to get carried away by tall, dark and breathtaking. She wasn't.

Then she caught his eye. For a second, or two, maybe more, he looked at her, those dark brown eyes reaching into her soul and tugging a little. There was something about him that was deeper than she'd imagined…something more… She was caught by the hints of honey and gold in his irises, his scent of cleanness and man, and out of the two of them she realised that she was the one a little off balance. So not the plan.

The chatter in the room seemed to dull a little and he turned away, the connection broken. Ivy took a breath. For a moment he'd almost seemed human. But then he turned back, all trace of the friendliness she'd thought she'd seen wiped clear.

His voice lowered. 'So, I am keeping my side of the bargain and here I am. I'm losing valuable operating hours so you'd better blow my damned socks off with this. I'm looking forward to you joining us tomorrow. We have a double whammy for you. In theatre one we have a live donor retrieval. And next door, in theatre two, we will be performing, for your delight and delectation, a renal—*that means kidney*—transplant on a twelve-year-old girl. I hope you've got stamina as well as balls because you're going to need it. It's going to be a long day.'

He thought she had balls? Was that a compliment? Or did he just see her as an equally worthy opponent? She hoped so. 'I am well aware of what renal means, and cardio, hepatology and orthopaedic… Throw me a word, Mr Finelli, and I'm pretty sure I'd be able to translate from medico to legal to layman and back again—I aced Latin and my mother's a GP. I won my high school creative writing prize five years in a row and my favourite subject was Classics, so I think I cover all linguistic challenges. And I've got a lot more stamina than most.' She just wasn't going to mention the teeny-weeny little fact that she was also a fully paid-up member of the hemophobia club. One speck of blood and she was on her back.

So far in her hospital career she'd been able to avoid any incidents by making sure she was never in the wrong place at the wrong time—or always getting out quickly. No way would she admit to being nervous or in any way intimidated at the prospect of watching an operation—no, two operations. A real baptism of fire. 'Actually, I'm looking forward to it.'

'Me, too.' His mouth curled into a smile that was at once mesmerising and irritating. Heat swirled in her chest and she felt an unfamiliar prickling over her skin. Maybe her sexy radar had flickered back into life?

She brushed that thought away immediately. She had more important things to deal with than wayward, unsatisfied hormones.

Because somehow between now and tomorrow she was going to have to overcome her fear of blood. Maybe a quick phone call to Mum for some anti-anxiety drugs? Hypnotherapy? Although she'd heard the best way to deal with phobias was immersion therapy, she just hadn't ever put her hand up for it.

She also had to work out how she was going to stand for eight hours straight when her doctors had distinctly advised her against doing any such thing. Never mind. That was tomorrow. Today she had another hurdle to jump.

Stepping away from him, she nodded across the room to Becca, who rang a bell, drawing everyone's attention.

'Good morning, everyone.' Ivy made sure the room was silent before she continued and stepped up to the raised area. 'Thank you so much for coming today. I have what I hope will be an enlightening presentation that will entertain you as well as teach you something. I hope you don't mind if I take a seat every now and then up here on the stage—it means you get to see the slides and informative videos and not me, which I'm sure you'll all agree is preferable.'

In keeping with the presentations skills she'd honed over the years she ensured she made eye contact with as many people as possible. When her gaze landed on Matteo he looked straight back at her from his front-row seat, teasing and daring lighting up his eyes, but she had no idea what was going through his mind. She had no way of reading him, but she got the distinct impression he was weighing her up, his scrutinising gaze making her catch her breath.

Bring it on, Matteo Finelli, she tried to tell him right back. She was ready for this. *Bring it on.*

This was just the beginning.

'To recap, we have a social media policy for three main reasons: protecting patient confidentiality; protecting and promoting our brand; and protecting our staff. Be very sure that what you say is how you want to be seen, and remember that if something you put up on networking sites can be connected with St Carmen's or our patients in any way then that may result in disciplinary action. There is a lot of chatter out there and how we present ourselves is extremely important; it's very hard to erase a message or a footprint once it's out. These things have a habit of coming back to bite us in the proverbial behind.'

Matteo watched as Ivy's eyes flicked to him and he felt the sting of her retort. Okay, so having his behind out there for all the world to see hadn't been the wisest idea his friend had had, and Matteo was starting to understand a little of the ruckus it had caused. St Carmen's had a solid reputation for putting children first and he could see that having a connection with a naked man may well have done some damage. But, really, four sessions to get that message across? What in hell could next week's workshop be about?

Poison Ivy was certainly passionate about her job, he'd give her that. And her presentation skills had been first rate. He got the impression that public speaking was something she could do with finesse but that she didn't exactly love it. Her voice was endlessly enthusiastic, and he caught a hint of an accent…although not being native to England he couldn't quite place it. She certainly looked the part with another smart dark trouser suit and silk blouse—today it was a deep cobalt blue that had him reminiscing about the summer skies back home. And he felt another sting—sharp enough to remind him of the folly of thinking too hard and investing too much. And that love, in its many forms, could cut deeply.

But Ivy's ballsy forthrightness coupled with the curve-enhancing trousers and form-fitting blouse had piqued his imagination. Although why, he didn't know, she was the exact opposite of everything he usually liked in a woman. He went for tall women, and she was petite. He had a track record of tousled brunettes, and she was blonde with a... what was it? Yes, a pixie cut. He liked to entertain and enthral and she showed nothing but disinterest bordering on contempt. He wasn't usually spurned—spurning was his role. Ah, no—he never led a woman to believe he would give any more than a good time. Until the good times became more one-sidedly meaningful—and that was the signal to get out.

Putting this sudden interest down to the thrill of the chase, he nodded to her, raising his eyebrows. *Do go on.*

She gave him a disinterested smile and looked at someone else. 'I hope you've all enjoyed our journey into cyberspace and an overview of social media opportunities—as you can see, they are many and varied and more are exploding onto our screens and into our homes every day. Now that we've highlighted our hospital policy, I hope you can see how and when mistakes can be made, even from the comfort of your own sofa when you think you're engaging in a private conversation. Nothing is ever private on the internet. Next week we'll be talking about the good, the bad and the very ugly of social networking sites. In the meantime, in the words of someone much wiser than me...when it comes to the World Wide Web, don't be that person with the smartphone making dumb mistakes.'

And everyone around him seemed to have enjoyed themselves immensely. She gave a shy smile at their applause and then concentrated on logging off the laptop and clearing away her papers.

He followed the queue to the door but before he'd made it out he heard her voice. 'Mr Finelli?'

'Yes?'

She stepped down from the small stage and walked towards him, trying hard but not quite managing to hide the limp that now, at the end of a day when she'd mostly been standing, clearly gave her pain. 'I hope that was insightful?'

'It could have been a lot quicker.'

'Not everyone is as quick thinking as you.' She bit her bottom lip as if trying to hold back a smile. 'Besides, we have some very recalcitrant staff members who insist they know better than we do on these matters. I need to make sure I hammer out our message loud and clear.'

Remembering her barb, he gave her a smile back. 'I felt the hammer.'

'Good. My job here is done. I hope in future you'll be contemplating how to send positive messages that reflect the nature of our business. Or, indeed, not sending messages at all.'

'The only positive messages I need to send are in the numbers of children I and the renal department save. And in how many families don't have to endure suffering or loss of life.'

She studied him. 'Well, maybe a bit of help in drumming up support for your unit is in order? You could harness the wave, do some awareness campaigns and get…what? What is on your wish list?'

He didn't need to think twice about this—the same thing

every transplant unit across the world wanted. 'More organ donors, more people willing to sign up to donate when they die. More dialysis machines. More research.'

'So put your thinking hat on and see if you can come up with a way of reaching out to people across the internet. Without taking your clothes off? There are plenty of people here in London wanting to help a good cause…but many more reaching out across the internet. Just imagine… Well, have a good evening, I'll see you in the morning. Bright and breezy.' Then she gave him a real smile. An honest to God, big smile that lit up her face. And, *Mio Dio*, the green in her eyes was intense and mesmerising. Her mouth an impish curl that invited him to join her in whatever had amused her. And something in his chest tugged. It was unbalancing and yet steadying at the same time.

'Where are you from?' For some reason his longing-to-leave brain had been outsmarted by his wanting-to-stay mouth.

Her smile melted away. 'I'm sorry?'

'Your accent. I'm not used to all the different ones yet. Other people say Landan…you say Lundun.'

Gathering all her gear together, she shovelled folders under one arm and carried a laptop in her hand. With a hitch of her shoulder she switched the lights out and then indicated for him to leave the conference room ahead of her while she pressed numbers into a keypad that sent the area into lockdown. 'York. I'm from York, it's in the north. A long way away. Three and a half hours' drive—on a good day.'

'Of course I have heard of it.' He noticed a slight narrowing of her eyes and her voice had dropped a little. 'And that makes you sad, being away from family?'

She shrugged. 'No. Well…yes, I suppose. You know how it is. You do miss the familiar.'

'I suppose you do.' Maybe others did. He hadn't been able to leave quickly enough and trips back home had been sporadic. Betrayal and hurt could do that to a man.

They neared the elevators and she paused, put her bag on the floor and pressed the 'up' button. 'And you? You must feel a long way from home. Which is?'

'A small village near Siena. Nothing special.'

Her eyebrows rose. 'You're joking, right? Every Tuscan village is special.'

His village was. The inhabitants, on the other hand, not so much. 'How do you know? Have you visited there?'

'Florence, that's all, just a quick weekend trip. It was lovely.' Her ribcage twisted as she tried to hitch the now falling papers back under her arm.

He reached for them, his hand brushing against her blouse, sending a shiver through his gut. Strange how his body was reacting to her. Very strange. 'Let me take those papers from you.'

'I can manage.' She stopped short and shook her head with determination and resolve, obviously trying to be strong when she didn't need to be. He got the feeling that Ivy Leigh put a brave face on a lot—to hide what? Some perceived weakness? Something that was more than a problem with her foot.

'I know you can manage. But you have too many things to carry and I have nothing. Let me take them.' Without waiting for her to answer, he took the folders and slipped them under his arm, wondering what the hell the point of this was. She was on the other side—the annoying, bureaucratic, meddling middle-men side.

Talking with the enemy, helping the enemy, whatever next? Sleeping with the enemy? Pah! As if he would do anything so foolish.

And she obviously had a full appreciation of that. 'I

know what you're doing, Matteo. You're trying to get me on side and then you're going to strike. Pounce…or something. Try to catch me unawares, try to convince me to set you free from my course and then hit me where it hurts.'

'Never. I would never hit anyone.' There had been a few times when he'd come close—okay, once when he'd stepped over that line and with good reason. But never again.

She looked confused. 'Don't panic, it's a turn of phrase. I didn't mean you'd really hit me. I know you wouldn't do that.'

'Good. And, actually, I was just being nice.'

'Well, that is unexpected. Who knew you could be?'

The fleeting anger at the memories melted into humour. Ivy Leigh was good at sparring. He admired that. Always good to respect the enemy. Laughter bubbled from his chest. 'Strange, yes, considering we are on opposite sides. The next thing we know we'll be doing something ridiculous like going for a drink.'

'Oh, no. I can't do that.' She jabbed the lift button again and tsked. 'I never mix business with pleasure.'

'I'm intrigued that you think having a drink with me would be pleasurable?'

Again there was a smile, but it belied a look in her eyes that was…half wistful, half anxious. 'I'm sure the *drink* would be very pleasurable indeed. I'm very partial to a decent red. But, as I say, it's not something I do.'

'Neither do I.'

'Then I'm glad that we agree on something.' But that wistful look remained, until she turned away.

There was no one else around. The place was silent. The conference area had all closed down for the night so it was just him and her and a buzz in the air between them that was so fierce it was almost tangible. 'And you are going where now?'

She shrugged. 'Back to the fifth floor, if this lift ever arrives. I have work to do.'

'After five o'clock? All the other paper-pushers have long gone.'

Her lips curled into a smirk. 'Pen. It's pen-pushers not paper-pushers.'

'I know, I know. I apologise. I'm still getting used to your idioms.' And she was stunning when she smiled. Which, it appeared, made him tongue-tied too. Really? What in hell was wrong with him?

'Where the hell is this lift?' Jab-jab on the button with those emerald fingernails. 'I don't think about the time I put in. I just do what's needed, and if that keeps me here all hours then so be it. Like most lawyers, I expect to work hard.'

'Then you'd make a fine doctor too.'

'Believe me, I wouldn't.' She gave a visible shudder and he wondered whether she'd been hurt at some point. Maybe a doctor had broken that well-protected heart of hers. And, again, why that was remotely relevant to anything, he didn't know.

'You don't like doctors? A hospital is a strange place to work, then.'

'Most doctors are fine. In fact, my mum's one.' Finally the lift arrived with a jolt and the doors swished open. Taking the folders from his hand, she fixed her gaze on him. 'Only a few of them ruin the reputation for the majority…'

What? As she stepped into the lift he put a hand out to stop the doors from closing. 'You mean me? *I* have a reputation?' He laughed. 'Good to know. Let me guess how that goes… I am too outspoken. I am a maverick. I am too committed to my job. Worse, I leave broken hearts in my wake…'

'Apparently so.' Her fingers tapped against the cold steel

of the wall panel. 'And a lot more that I couldn't possibly say...'

'I am also very attentive to detail. Some would say passionate. I have a sense of humour. I play very hard indeed...' His gaze drifted over her face. The detail there was stunning. The eyes that gave away her emotions regardless of how hard she tried to keep them locked away. That mouth, the keeper of barbs and insults and a perfect smile. Those lips... How would it feel if he were to kiss her? How would Miss Prim and Proper react then? Would she let him see a little of what was under that hard surface? Because, dammit, he knew there was more to her. A softer side—a passionate side. Just waiting to be set free. Lucky man who ever achieved that.

The door jolted against his back, reminding him that this was neither the time nor the place to be kissing Ivy Leigh. And yet...he reached a hand to her cheek and he could have sworn he saw heat flicker across her eyes, just enough to mist them and to tell him that he was not the only one struggling with this wildly strange scenario. Her mouth opened a little, he could see her breathing had quickened, and her eyes fluttered closed for a micro-second. Enough to show he had an effect on her...and she liked it. Didn't want it, not at all, but she liked it.

She pulled away. 'So. I'll see you tomorrow. Show me what you've got, Mr Finelli, I'm expecting to be very impressed.'

He felt strongly that he could show Miss Leigh a thing or two and she'd be very impressed indeed. *Work. Work.* Reminding himself of what was truly the most important thing in his life, he took a step back too. *Che stupido.* 'Do not bring me back to that issue again. Those damned workshops. This social media thing. Miss Leigh, you make my blood boil sometimes.'

'I try my best. All part of the service.'

With that she gave him a very satisfied smile that he imagined would grace her lips at the end of a particularly heavy lovemaking session. For a fleeting second he imagined her naked and on his sheets. Spent and glowing.

'Goodbye, Mr Finelli.'

He watched the lift door swish closed, thanking the god of good timing that she'd had the good sense to put a stop to whatever dangerous game had been about to play out. She made his blood boil indeed, the heat between them had been off the scale. No woman had made him so infuriated and so turned on at the same time. He spoke to the metal doors as the lift lurched upwards. 'Goodbye, Ivy.'

Then he turned to walk up the stairs and back to the surgical suite. A ward round beckoned, then some prep, allaying the fears of his patients and their parents…then a quick gym session, a decent meal, some sleep.

He needed to be ready for tomorrow, for Ivy and for round two.

CHAPTER THREE

THIS IS YOUR JOB, for goodness' sake. Pull yourself together.

As long as Ivy focused on that she'd be fine. She'd put everything on the line for her job her whole adult life and had got exactly where she wanted to be: Director of Legal at a fabulous, age-old and well-respected institution. So this was just another hurdle. Just an incy-wincy hurdle that she would jump with ease.

If only for two little things…

Shut up. Blood and a bloody-minded man would not get to her. She dragged the scrubs top over her head and straightened it, leaned in to the mirror and watched her hands shake as she slid the paper hairnet hat thing over her hair, squashing her fringe in the process. *Great look, girlfriend.*

Then she took a little more notice of her surroundings. The scrubs with the St Carmen's logo and the locker room reminded her of the photo… Would she be for ever condemned to remember that image for as long as she lived?

Half of her hoped so. The other half tried to blot it from her mind.

'Hey, Miss Leigh, are you ready?' Nancy, the OR assistant, called through the door. 'We're going in now, the surgeon's here.'

And she so hadn't needed to hear that. 'Just a second,

I'm almost there.' *Okay. Breathe. Deeply. In. Out. In. Out. You can do this.* It was just a case of mind over matter. She was in control of this.

She didn't know what she was dreading most: the red stuff or the man she'd had the dirtiest dream about last night. The man she'd almost grabbed in the lift and planted a kiss on those too smug lips of his. Who she'd spent an hour trying to describe to her flatmate and had ended up with *annoyingly sexy.*

So, yes, she thought he was sexy. Just as Becca did, and, frankly, the same as all the women in the hospital did. So she was just proving she had working hormones—*nothing else to see here, move right along.* The man who was out to make her look a fool but, God knew, he might not need to try too hard, because if things didn't go as planned she'd be managing that quite well all on her own.

Popping two more herbal rescue sweets into her mouth and sucking for all she was worth, she took a couple of extra-long deep breaths and steadied her rampaging heart. Give her a sticky mediation case, two ornery barristers and an angry, justice-seeking client any day. Words…that was her thing. Words, debate, the power of vocabulary. Not medicine. Not blood. Not internal stuff. Exactly why she hadn't followed in her mother's footsteps.

Here we go.

The smell hit her first. Sharp, tangy and clinical, filling her nostrils, and she thought it might have something to do with the brown stuff a man in scrubs and face mask was painting onto the abdomen of an anaesthetised woman. Then the bright white light of the room hit her, the noise. She'd thought it would be silent—remembered only a quiet efficiency from those endless surgeries, but someone had put classical music on the speakers. It was the only soothing thing in the place.

So much for the rescue sweets. Her heart bumped along, merrily oblivious to the discomfort it was causing her, and now her hands were starting to sweat too. Someone sat at the head of the woman and fiddled with tubes. The anaesthetist, Ivy knew. She had enough experience to be able to identify most of the people in here. Another woman smiled at her and bustled past with a tray of instruments that looked like torture devices…hooks and clamps. Ivy shuddered and hovered on the periphery, not knowing what to do and feeling more and more like a spare part. Should she stand closer? But that would mean she'd get a bird's-eye view of the action.

The man painting the brown stuff raised his head and she realised it was Matteo. Matteo—she'd got to thinking of him like that. Not Mr Finelli. Not something over there and out of reach. But someone here…someone personal. Matteo. Someone she'd almost kissed, for the first time in what felt like a thousand years. All she could see of his face were those eyes, piercing, dark and direct as he looked at her. 'Ah. Miss Leigh. You're here. Come closer, please. Glad you could tear yourself away from your paper pushing.'

'Good to be here.' *Liar.*

'Nancy got you some scrubs. Good. We don't want to get your lovely office suits messed up with bodily fluids. Do come and get a better view of the procedure, my team will make space for you. I'm sorry we didn't reserve the gold-tier seating. And it's a little crowded as I need to teach as well as operate. Perhaps one day you'll be able to help us raise money for a decent viewing room? That would make all of our lives easier.'

She gave him a sarcastic smile, which she knew he couldn't see behind her mask so she stuck her tongue out instead. Then levelled her voice. 'You know very well that

I'm a lawyer, not a fundraiser. However, I'll add it to your wish-list. Which is getting longer by the day.'

'I know. We surgeons are so demanding, yes? You'd think we were wanting to save lives or something.' For a moment he regarded her with humour, but it was gentle and not rude, and then he became very focused and professional. 'Okay. This patient is Emily. She's donating her left kidney to her daughter, who is twelve years old and suffers from polycystic kidney disease. Emily is a perfect match in tissue type and blood type. She's a very active lady with no medical history of any note. With one kidney she is giving her daughter the chance to have a normal life. That is, of course, as long as her body doesn't reject it, although live donors are generally better tolerated than cadaver ones. Once the kidney has been removed, I, and a team of other surgeons, will…' He paused and looked over at Ivy. 'Are you okay, standing there?'

'Yes, thanks. I'm fine.' Shifting the weight from her left foot, she eased more heavily onto her right. And then realised he was still watching her.

His eyes flicked to her feet and then back to her face. 'This is a long procedure—in fact, it's going to be a long day. Would…er…anyone like a seat?' His voice, she noted, had softened, the jokey teasing quite gone. Which was not what she wanted or expected from him. He must have noticed her limp. Goddamn. When had that been? She didn't want anyone's pity; she could hold her own as well as the next person. He called out to the orderly, 'Eric…? Do we have any chairs?'

And look weak in front of all these people. In front of her colleagues? Him? No way. She shook her head vehemently.

Matteo paused with a large green sheet in his hand. 'If you're sure? Everyone?' But she knew he meant just her.

'This is your last chance. We're going to start imminently and then we all need to concentrate.'

Oh, God. *Objection!* she wanted to shout. *Stop!* But instead she fisted her fingers into her palms, dug deep to distract herself from her raging heartbeat. 'I'm fine. Please, just do the operation.'

'As you like.' He nodded to her, the scalpel now in his hand catching the light and glinting ominously. 'Here we go, everyone. One laparoscopic donor nephrectomy begins.'

An hour later and Ivy had run out of places to look other than at the patient and risk the chance of seeing blood. She knew the right-hand corner of the room intimately now and could have recited the words on the warning sign above the electrical sockets blindfolded. The ECG monitoring machine bleeped and she focused once again on the LED display. Lots of squiggly lines and numbers. A niggly pain lodged in her lower back and her legs were starting to ache. She didn't even have anything to lean against—that would have been helpful. So she stood rooted to the spot, trying to blot out the chatter, the music, the smell. Words like tubular...renal ligament...haemo...blood. She knew that. And sorely wished she didn't.

But while her heartbeat was jigging off the scale it was clear that Matteo's wasn't. As he worked three probes jutting out from the woman's abdomen while watching his handiwork on a large TV screen, his voice was measured and calm. For all his macho Italian remonstrating, the man was a damned fine surgeon, she'd give him that. He was also a decent teacher, taking time to explain to everyone exactly what he was doing—which really was amazing. Keyhole surgery was detailed, precise and very, very clever.

Okay, so she'd misjudged him. He was not narcissistic when it mattered, he was giving of himself to his patients and to the assistants. But he was still annoying. And sexy.

And had she mentioned annoying? 'We need to divide the adrenal vein so it is the optimal length for transplantation...'

She focused on the music because his running commentary was making her feel slightly woozy. Or maybe it was the heat in the room. Her gaze drifted over to him again, down his mask-covered face to his throat. The V of skin visible on his broad chest was suntanned, his forearm muscles contracting and stretching as he worked.

He stopped and arched his back, checked the screen, and, as he dipped his head to resume his work, he caught her eye. She could tell by the crinkles at his temples that he was smiling—what kind of a smile it was, she didn't know. She didn't want to. Just one look at those eyes made her gut contract in a sizzling, heat-filled clutch. She wondered what it would be like to wake up to those eyes, that skin... Or what would have happened in that lift yesterday if she hadn't pulled away.

She was darned glad she had pulled away...frustrated, but glad.

But what if she hadn't? Would he have kissed her? And why? Why her when there were so many beautiful women for him to kiss?

My God. Her mouth dried. She couldn't be thinking like that. She couldn't be imagining what it would be like to have Matteo touch her. To kiss him... Not when someone's life was on the line—although, thank goodness, not in her hands.

Not at all. She wasn't the kind of girl to have flings and she didn't want anything else. Didn't even want a fling... unless...

No. Not a fling. Not with Matteo damned Finelli.

She felt her cheeks heat, shook her head to clear her mind and realised it took longer than normal for her vision to catch up. Nausea ripped through her, rising up her gut. She focused on his hands. Hands that were red with blood now. Thick and red…and… The heat in the room was toxic…and she felt cold and hot…and she could feel the blood drain from her face…

'So you are with us again? That is good.' Matteo tapped Ivy's hand with as little force as he dared muster, but enough that she'd at least open her eyes. She looked so pale, so young lying on the trolley covered with a blanket. And as she was his responsibility in the OR he'd deemed it only right to check on her. That's what he told himself anyway as she stared at him, her cheeks reddening. She started to sit up but he coaxed her back down. 'Lie still. Your blood pressure dropped and you fainted. Are you feeling okay?'

'Oh, I'm so sorry. Please, go in and finish the operation. Leave me here.' Her eyelids fluttered closed, more, he figured, out of embarrassment than feeling faint again.

People fainted in the OR on a regular basis. Nothing extraordinary. Except that this time had been the first and only time he'd felt a need to barge in and carry the victim out. But even though he had stood there helplessly as she'd fallen to the floor he'd known that he was not in a position to run to her—no matter what. His patient was his first priority. 'It is all done—it takes more than a vaso-vagal to make me leave someone on the table. You were well cared for by the recovery nurses?'

She gave him a smile. 'Yes. And I'm so sorry I took up their valuable time. It wasn't necessary and neither is this visit. You're busy.'

'Nonsense. I have ten minutes before I go into the transplant. I thought I'd better check on my unexpected patient.'

She twisted to sit up, ignoring any attempt to keep her

out of harm's way. 'You didn't need to. Honestly. No one should have looked after me. I'd have been fine.'

'Oh, yes, we always leave the sick ones scattered across the OR floor like the battlefield wounded. We just step over them, like little human hurdles whenever we need to move around the room. Did you have breakfast this morning?'

'Yes.' Which was contrary to what he'd assumed and didn't explain why a strong woman like Ivy would faint. 'A little.'

'So you fell over. Why?'

She shrugged. 'It was hot.'

'We were all hot, it gets like that. The air-conditioning is faulty—just another thing to add to my wish-list.' Maybe it had had something to do with her leg. Maybe she'd been in pain? *Pazzo*, he berated himself. Idiot. There he'd been playing games with her and she'd been unable to stand for so long. Physically unable to, for whatever reason. And he didn't want to pry into something that wasn't his business. But… 'It was something more, I think.'

She looked like she was debating how to answer. 'Okay. Yes.'

He waited for her to elucidate. 'And…?'

'I think I overdosed on rescue sweets.'

'What?' He had not been expecting that. He held back a laugh because he could see she was serious. 'Rescue sweets? Really? You were nervous about the operation? And be honest. You have the kind of face that gives away all your emotions.'

'That is not what someone of my profession wants to hear.' She seemed to fold a little. 'It's not my usual work-place, is it?'

'Which isn't an admission of nerves, just a statement of fact.' Ever the lawyer. 'Were you scared?'

'No comment.' But her eyes dipped down and he knew he had her answer.

'So yes. What of?'

'No comment.'

'Which might work in the courts, Ivy, but won't stop me asking the questions. This is my domain now, not yours. You have a phobia? Needles? Blood? People?' *Me?* That thought made him smile even more. Because he had no doubt that Ivy believed him to be her equal. Maybe it was the buzz between them that she was afraid of. Of what that might lead to unless they both held themselves in check.

The way she pursed her lips reminded him of his sister Liliana again—reluctant to admit any kind of weakness. She'd started to look less fragile, stronger, back to her fighting self. Almost—but was that a little humility there too? 'Okay, if you must know, yes, I get a little woozy with blood…'

'Aha, so you are afraid of something. Interesting…' He'd found a weak spot. Excellent. Although seeing a young woman so pale wasn't excellent at all. Fainting in front of a group of colleagues was pretty embarrassing too, and made anyone feel washed out and often came with a thumping headache. And now he felt compelled to help her. Again. It was becoming a habit. An unusual habit that he needed to shake off. 'Okay, we'll talk about it later. I may have some suggestions to help you with that. Now, I must go and see my next client.'

'Wait. Matteo. Please.' She reached a hand to his arm and a thousand jolts rattled through him. He knew exactly what that was. Chemistry. Physics. And basic biology. There was a connection between them that overrode sense. That ignored his brain and went beyond any interest he'd felt for a woman before. What was it about Ivy Leigh that had him reacting so strongly? Why did he want to help her? What was going on with his body that this attraction was so intense, so fierce?

He wanted answers so he could stop it and get back to normal. He'd never become so interested in a woman that he'd thought about snatching a kiss at work, in an elevator. That was the stuff of romance books and definitely not for a sane, level-headed scientist like himself. He liked to have control in who he kissed…not some sort of urgent, frenzied need. Because he knew exactly where that kind of wild, irrational love got a man. And he wasn't going there ever again.

Her smile broadened. 'Thank you for your concern. But what about the transplant? I'd like to watch…from a safe distance.'

Drawing his arm away from her touch, he shook his head. 'You have nothing to prove, really. But you have to be able to hold your own in there, otherwise you become a liability, and perhaps today is a little soon for you to try to conquer your fears. So, no. You can't come in and watch. I need to make sure you are strong enough—'

'Strong? Of course I am…I was just a little overcome.'

'We don't need that kind of distraction in there. Try again next week?' By which time he'd have this snagging interest in her under control. 'I'll try to find something less intrusive for you to watch.'

Jolting upright, she fixed him with those dark green eyes. 'Damn it, I can do this.'

'Not today and that decision is final.'

Shaking her head, she lay back down on the trolley and covered her eyes with her forearm. 'So you won in the end.' She sounded disappointed but retaliatory.

'This round, yes.' Although there was less satisfaction in that fact than he'd imagined there would be.

Nancy arrived and handed Ivy a plastic cup filled with

water. 'You're fine to get up now, Miss Leigh. Your blood pressure is back to normal. Why don't you have a drink first, then pop along to the locker rooms and get changed.' His OR assistant turned to him. 'Matteo, I'm sorry to interrupt, but just wanted to remind you we're having Friday night drinks tonight. Will you be coming along?'

'Of course.'

Nancy's eyes flicked over to Ivy. 'Oh, and Miss Leigh, of course. You must come too.'

Matteo guessed Nancy was playing the polite card because generally the department was pretty tight, but it would be rude not to ask her when this conversation was going on within her earshot. He ignored a little leap in his stomach at the thought of seeing her again. If that was how his body was reacting then maybe he wouldn't go tonight if she was going to be there. It was better not to fuel this attraction any further. Bad enough she'd been the first thing he'd thought about when he'd woken up this morning.

'Why does everyone insist on calling me Miss Leigh? It makes me feel like I'm a ninety-year-old spinster. Please, it's Ivy…' Ivy shook her head vehemently. 'And thanks for the offer but, no. I can't come tonight.'

Nancy chipped in. 'But we all go, every Friday, across the road to the Dragon, straight after work. It's tradition. If you work in OR it's mandatory…'

Matteo added with a grin, remembering how forceful Poison Ivy had been about attending her ridiculous course, 'And we all know what that means. No getting out of it.'

Ivy swung her legs over the edge of the trolley and straightened her scrubs, her blonde hair stuck up in little tufts, and she looked very far from the sophisticated, competent lawyer. In fact, she looked pretty damned cute all mussed up. 'But I didn't exactly do any work here, I just made a fool of myself.'

'And now you have me feeling sorry for you all over again.' He leaned closer. Big mistake—a nose full of her fresh scent had his senses zapping into full-on alert. He stepped back again. 'Let me tell you a secret...the first day in Theatre as a medical student, I vomited.'

'In the theatre?' Both Nancy and Ivy asked at the same time.

He shrugged. 'No, in a bin outside. I managed to leave just in time. A coronary bypass—messy. It takes a bit of getting used to. There's a lot of smells and noise and the blood...and looking inside... It's something you learn to live with. You can't expect to be okay with seeing these things on the first day. Luckily, you have another three chances to get up close and personal.'

'Yay. Three.' Ivy's cheeks blazed as she drained the cup and popped it on the table next to the trolley. 'Er...well, yes. Hypnotherapy's good, I hear. Drugs. Total avoidance has been working really well for me for years. But I really do need to apologise to everyone for inconveniencing them.'

'What better place to do it than at the pub?' He couldn't believe he was convincing her to come. 'You said you needed to get to know the departments. People will chat to you more freely with alcohol in their bellies.'

'Yes,' Nancy chimed in. 'Come on, it's usually a good crowd. And if you do come I promise not to let anyone make fun of you.'

Matteo sniffed. 'Apart from me, obviously.'

'Of course, Matteo. Whatever.' With a shake of her head Nancy jabbed him in the ribs and winked at Ivy. 'Don't be taken in by him. He's just a softie really.'

'Nancy, how could you ruin my reputation?'

'Your reputation's already in tatters, my boy. We've all seen the picture... *Bite me*? Yes...oh, yes. Wouldn't we all love to do that.' Laughing, Nancy ducked away down the corridor. Leaving just him and a bed-ready Ivy, who was laughing and not making any attempt to hide it.

He gave her a smile. 'Now I definitely need you to come out tonight to fight my corner, tell them what penance I've had to serve for that damned picture. They'll be merciless.'

'This I have got to see.' Ivy patted his hand and he felt a comforting warmth that, as he looked into her sparkling eyes, transformed into a sizzle running through him. He wanted to kiss her. Right there. To see what that mouth tasted like, how it felt slammed against his. This was a struggle he was already losing. He wanted her. As he watched her she stopped laughing, but the smile remained. 'Sorry, Matteo, it's no more than you deserve. This is one battle you'll have to fight on your own. And I don't think you'll have a hope in hell of winning.'

CHAPTER FOUR

WITH AN UNEXPECTEDLY free afternoon to attack her to-do list, Ivy felt on top of her work for the first time since she'd taken the job. Wanting to purge the embarrassment burning through her, she'd hit the tasks with gusto and now had a new to-do list that contained *complete projects*, as opposed to, *Go through the masses of unfinished stuff the useless last guy left, find out what the outstanding projects are and then complete.*

Now she had a clear idea of where she was headed—until, of course, the next crisis occurred. Because she had no doubt that it would. She could only hope it wasn't more naked photos…because that scenario appeared to get her into hotter water than she wanted to be.

She buzzed through to the next office. 'Becca, would it be possible for you to line up some interviews for me for next week?'

'Sure. Hang on, I'll come through.' Becca appeared in her office, pencil poised and notepad at the ready, as if she was about to take dictation. 'Who, what, why and when? And, please, please, let it be more bottoms to identify… peachy ones, of course.'

Ivy tried to frown, but the thought of that… *Work, girl.* 'You are incorrigible. It's proper work. You remember that? The stuff we get paid to do? Look through my diary—any time apart from Thursday and Friday. I need to take a brief on the Partridge case. So, I need to speak to…' She scanned down the list of names on the paper in front of her. 'Maggie Taylor and Leslie Anderson from Ward Three.'

Becca tapped her pad. 'That's the med negligence case, right? The feeding tube that became dislodged?'

'Yes. That hearing's coming up in a couple of weeks and I need to be apprised of all the facts.'

'Certainly. I'll organise that for you.' Becca nodded. 'But, you know, we always win anyway. Or we settle beforehand if we don't think we'll win in court.'

'Yes. I know very well how the system works.' Ivy had personal experience on both sides, but that didn't mean she liked it. Not if it meant mistakes were still being made, mistakes that could be avoided.

With this job she'd found herself in a strange place ethically—on the one hand she wanted to ensure the hospital was a safe place for all, and on the other hand she was responsible to the hospital board. Sometimes it was exciting and technically challenging, and other times she just felt stuck between a rock and a hard place. But she loved it nevertheless. There was still a lot to do here, and she'd always been up for a challenge.

She looked at a pile of employment contracts and a thick file regarding a sexual harassment complaint against a catering manager, all ready for her review. Bedtime reading. Geez, bedtimes had never been such fun.

And why, oh, why did an image of a naked Matteo suddenly flit into her head at the mention of bedtimes? It was impossible these days to think of anything without him straying into her thoughts.

She was not going to go to the pub. She was going to stay here and work. Neither was she going to indulge any fantasies about him touching her or kissing her or undressing her in a lift…which was her most recent one…or perhaps something in the on-call room. She'd heard many a tale about that kind of thing happening in hospitals. But, no—it was all out of bounds.

When she eventually looked up again she realised her assistant was watching her while dragging on a coat. 'Yes, Becca?'

'I don't know where your head was right then, but it wasn't here. Maggie's coming in on Monday at two, Leslie will come straight after her shift on Tuesday at three-thirty.' Becca smiled. 'So, you never did tell me why you came back from Theatre so early. Weren't you supposed to be with Dr Delicious all afternoon, you lucky thing?'

Oh. That. The hospital grapevine was alive and kicking and the news was bound to spread fast. She might as well front up to it, take the ribbing and move on. 'You have to promise not to tell a soul. Or laugh. Or anything, at any point.'

With a very serious look on her face Becca drew a cross over her chest. 'My word is my honour.'

'I fainted.'

Becca bit her lips together to hold in a laugh. 'Aha. Hmm. Okay. Understandable.'

'Really? You think? Honestly?' Ivy breathed out a sigh of relief. It seemed the legal personnel had the same approach to bodies as she did. Preferring to look at them from the outside rather than the inside. 'I can't tell you how much better that makes me feel. I was standing up for such a long time and it was very hot in there.'

'Well, he definitely makes me all hot and bothered too.'

'What?' She might have known Becca's answer would be hormone-related. 'Oh, for goodness' sake, I didn't faint because of him, I fainted because the air-conditioning was broken and all my blood was in my feet and, well, I…don't like seeing inside bodies much. Mr Finelli is just a man. He's nothing special. No need to get all giddy.'

'Tell that to your face, Ivy. It's all red and blotchy.'

Ivy threw her assistant a smile. 'You know, I preferred you when you were meek and polite.'

'Sorry. Overstepping a little?'

'Yes. Kind of.' But, truly, Ivy needed some people on her side. After the stuffy atmosphere in the board meetings and the heavy, long hours, which she really deep down didn't mind, sometimes it was nice to have a little girl time. Usually by the time she got home after a long day her flatmate had either gone to bed or had hit the town with her boyfriend. They had a great flatmate arrangement, it worked well and they didn't get under each other's feet, probably because they rarely spent more than an hour a week together. Which meant that Ivy would find herself alone most evenings. Which was fine, given she had so much work to keep her occupied, but sometimes… 'Are you heading off now? Have a good weekend.'

Becca shook her head. 'Actually, I'm heading over to the pub. Everyone goes there on a Friday night. It's—'

As her heart fell Ivy interrupted, 'Oh, you too? Let me guess, tradition, right?'

'Tradition. Yes, most of the admin and support staff go—in fact, a lot of the hospital workers go. It's always good fun and there's karaoke later.'

'All the more reason for me to stay here, then.' Shuffling bits of paper on a Friday night, looking across the road at the lights in the pub. Listening to the laughter. God, she could have her own pity party right here.

Becca frowned right back. 'It's fun. Really. You should come. You don't have to sing.'

It wasn't the singing. It was the company. Certain company that she didn't want to face again today. 'No can do. I'm busy.'

'It'll wait. Turn your computer off.' With a dramatic flourish Becca stepped forward, stacked the files on the desk into a large pile and handed them over. She grinned, with no hint of apology. 'I know…overstepping again, but it's Friday. Take your folders home and read all weekend if you like, but tonight you're coming for a drink. We never did get to celebrate your arrival here. And it's about time we did. I can't tell you what a breath of fresh air you've been in here.'

'But… I… Wait…' To refuse would be rude. But to tell the truth would be embarrassing and refute what she'd just said about Matteo being nothing special. Because, really, he was a teensy bit set apart from other men she'd dated in her dim and distant past. He was attentive and could be gentle and funny in a macho kind of way. Plus, he made her heart skip just a bit. And she was intrigued by him, by a man who could hold her attention longer than any other had. And by that body, which had her pulse racing at the strangest and most inappropriate moments.

Which was exactly why she had no intention of stepping over the threshold of that pub door.

'Really. No. I can't. I'm just going to head right on home.'

'Seriously, you've got this far, don't be embarrassed. You'll be fine, honestly. I bet it happens all the time anyway. People faint, get over it. Come on.' Becca tugged on Ivy's arm as she had been doing almost every step through the hospital corridors in an attempt to bring her down here to the pub, despite every excuse Ivy could think of. In the end she'd had to give in because, it appeared, no one was listening. 'Last one at the bar buys the round.'

'Fine. Just give me a moment.' Ivy watched her assistant's back disappear into the pub and took a deep breath. If she didn't look at him she'd be fine. He'd be in the middle of a group, she'd shimmy past out of eye contact and hide in a dark corner with the rest of the admin staff. *No problemo.*

Taking another breath, she pushed the heavy door open and stepped in. The noise was bearable, people sat in groups and she could make out some familiar faces in the far corner, but as the door swung closed behind her everyone stopped what they were doing and stared at her.

Huh-huh. This was her idea of hell. Even though no one spoke she could almost read their thoughts. *She's the one who fainted. Top lawyer who's deep-down weak.*

But at least Matteo was nowhere to be seen.

At the bar Becca was talking to the barman, and beckoned Ivy over. 'Seeing as you're paying, I'm having the biggest cocktail they do. A jug of Cancun margarita, I think. What would you like, Ivy?'

'A glass of wine, please. Red.' *Make it a big one.*

'They do a nice merlot. Oh, look…' Becca pointed across to the admin crowd, who were grinning and waving back. 'Everyone's so pleased to see you.'

'Or they're laughing at me.'

'So, Miss Ivy Leigh, you decided to brave it out after all?' *Great.* Matteo's voice behind her thrilled down her spine. She couldn't see him but every tiny hair on her body was standing to attention in some sort of annoying hormonal salute to his arrival. Maybe the admin crowd hadn't been waving at her at all, maybe they'd all been giggling and flirting and fluttering their eyelashes at him.

As she turned she controlled her breathing. She would not be impressed. She would not be impressed. She would not… *Wow.* Every time she looked at him his eyes pierced her—so dark and intense. And right now they were sparkling with mischief. The shadows and dips of his cheekbones seemed more acute today and he certainly rocked the swarthy tall, dark and handsome cliché. In a collared black shirt that showed off his broad chest and snug jeans that hugged his legs he looked dangerous and sinful and so out of her league. Not that she had a league or even wanted to be in one. But, it was safe to say, if she did, he would be stratospherically out of it.

'Good evening, Mr Finelli. Yes, I'm here. My assistant insisted and it looks like the whole hospital is here too, so that's good, I'll get the humiliation over and done with in one clean swoop. I'm just showing my face, having a quick drink and then…' She lifted her overloaded workbag, the zipper almost splitting with the contents. 'Work.'

'Ah, yes. It never stops.' Shoving a hand in his pocket, he pulled out a wad of notes and gave them to the barman. 'I'll get these.'

Becca grinned her starstruck thanks and went to join the group in the far corner. *Double great. Thanks a bunch. Leave me here with him, why don't you? Traitor.* Ivy picked up her glass and nodded to him. 'Thanks. I owe you one.' Then she took a step towards her crowd.

'Not so fast.'

'Sorry?' Ignoring the flustered feeling in her chest, she turned back to him, wondering what the Italian for cold shoulder was. Because that was what she intended on giving him. *Freddo shouldero, matey.* 'I'm on my way over to Becca…'

But he didn't take the hint. Instead, he smiled. For a fleeting moment it was almost genuine. 'How are you feeling, Ivy? No ill effects? No more fainting episodes?'

'I'm fine, thanks. Absolutely hunky dory. I'll see you… Thursday? For my workshop?' *Round two.*

'Again with this.' His voice was grim, but his smile was infectious as he took her arm and gently steered her away from the busy bar to a quieter corner. And, to her chagrin, she went with him. Was it her imagination or could she feel everyone's eyes on her back? 'We're away from work now on neutral ground, and it's the weekend. People just want to relax and have a good evening, me included. How about we drop our guard a little?'

This could be interesting. 'This is where you lull me into a false sense of security then you pounce, right?'

He shrugged. 'I don't need to do that. We could just have a conversation and see where we get to?'

Nancy squeezed past them to get to the bathrooms. 'Hey, Ivy. How are you feeling? Okay? Is Matteo giving you some tips?' She winked. 'He's very good.'

Ivy looked at the curve of his mouth and imagined a million things he'd be good at. Then ignored the flare of heat circling in her gut. 'I'll bet he is.'

'With fainting cures, that is…'

'Obviously.'

As Nancy disappeared into the bathroom Ivy put her bag on the floor, took a long drink and felt the warmth of the wine suffuse her throat. 'She's a stirrer.'

'She's a joker, but she has a good point.' Matteo's smile hadn't dropped. 'How on earth are we going to get you ready to face the scalpel again next week?'

Aha. Plan A. 'I'll be fine. I was going to start by watching a few videos online. Type "kidney transplant" into a search engine and there are hundreds of operations right there to pick from. You get a bird's-eye view, too, and commentary. It's almost as if you're actually there in the room, without all the smells or noises or…' *Without you*, she thought, all large and looming and stealing her breath. So it would be videos all the way until she was inured to the gore, with the sound turned to mute and a decent bottle of wine for Dutch courage. Anything not to lose face again next week.

'Ah, yes. The joys of the web. Amazing what you can find.' His smile glittered teasingly.

She ignored that, too, knowing damned well he was referring to his glorious backside. Which she did not want to see. Or think about. At all. 'Like I told you, some people do actually put useful things up there. It can be very educational.'

'And you are not at work now, so you don't need to give me the chat.' He emphasised *chat* with a sarcastic twitch of his fingers. 'Enjoy whatever you find on the internet… but make sure you take your hands away from your face first. And that you're sitting…no, lying down. You'll have less far to fall.'

'Ha-ha. You really are enjoying this.'

'What's not to like?' he said, in a voice filled with smugness, like the cat that had got the grappa-laced cream. 'But I'm glad you want to come back and see the wager through. You have strength. You have this hard outer shell, but underneath there is a softer side to you. A side you don't always want other people to see.'

That touched a raw nerve. She was only protecting herself, something she'd learnt to do because of experiences with men like him. She'd already lost enough to a selfish, inadequate man who'd wanted to play God, so she intended to keep herself whole and had no desire to fall prey to any guy's wishes. Plus, she'd seen her mother curl up in a ball and weep over someone who she'd given a part of herself to. Watched her crumble until she'd thought she couldn't live without him, couldn't put one step in front of another. Couldn't function. Ivy had no intention of crumbling. 'Don't we all keep a side of us private? I imagine there's more to you than what you show, too, Matteo. It's just how we project ourselves to the world, that's all. We don't have to show all our sides to everyone.'

He looked at her for a moment, his eyebrows raised, then shook his head, clearly perplexed. 'I am me. This is it.'

'Sure it is.' All annoying and smug and profound Italian with raw sex appeal and, she decided, probably not a lot of substance.

He shrugged as if he was reading her mind and he didn't give a jot what she thought. He probably didn't. 'Okay, whatever you think. You have your mind made up, I don't intend wasting my time trying to convince you otherwise. But, seriously, take a few small steps. Watch a video or two and concentrate on your body's response. Make sure you even out your breathing. Make sure it's deep and slow and regular, not jumpy, like it is right now.'

Ivy took a long slow breath in, felt a thump of palpitation in her chest as she willed her heart to slow. 'My breathing is fine.'

'Really? Could have fooled me. Because right now I'd say you were about to hyperventilate.' He reached a hand to her earlobe and checked out her silver hoop earring, ran a finger across the sensitive part of her neck. 'See. When I do that…up it goes. You need to be aware of that.'

Hello, I am very aware. Too aware. Her heart jittered, her hand started to shake again as she rubbed the spot he'd touched. 'I'll bear that in mind.' And, for the record, if she was to have a *thing* with anyone, it wouldn't be with a sexed-up macho surgeon. She would choose someone interested in the kind of things she liked, art, literature, someone with class and sophistication.

Not just a nice ass. And nice hands. And a devastating smile.

The smile spoke. 'And relax. Know your body well enough that you can identify signs of tension and consciously relax. Or, another method if you start to feel light-headed, tense your arms and legs and get the blood flowing well. Wiggle your toes to make sure your venous return is sufficient.'

'Yup. Thanks.'

'And why not just start with watching someone take blood first...move on up to renal transplants in a day or so? You don't want to run before you walk. Yes?'

'No. Yes. Whatever. Thanks for the pep talk.' She tried, but failed, to keep the sarcasm out of her voice. 'You trained in psychology as well as medicine?'

'No.' His eyebrows rose. 'But I had to get back into that theatre on day two somehow.'

'Oh. You were serious earlier about being sick in the OR? I thought you were just saying that to make me feel better.' Something really had rattled the great Dr Delicious once upon a time? 'And even after that you went on and trained to be a surgeon? Why? Why didn't you go into something less gory if it made you throw up?'

'Because that wasn't my dream. My dream was to be a renal surgeon. I don't like to do second best.'

She didn't doubt that or that he'd fight tooth and nail for what he wanted. He was the kind of guy who always got what he wanted and was used to snapping out orders—and having them followed. 'Why renal surgery? Why not orthopaedics or plastics, or something else?'

He took a drink from his beer bottle and for a moment looked pensive. 'My sister needed a kidney when she was eleven. She got one, in the end, although it took some time. And I could see the immediate change in her. I got my little sister back, with no pain and a future and so much energy. It was like a miracle. They saved her life. It seemed such a fabulous thing to do that I set my heart on it.'

Again with the surprise. The man could do serious and

personal. This was the side of him she'd thought he hid. But he'd been right—he was up-front and honest. In an irritatingly candid way. Maybe she just hadn't asked him the right questions.

And maybe she'd be better joining Becca right now. But hell if her feet didn't root themselves to the spot. 'Knowing how much demand there is for kidneys, I'd say she was very lucky. You have just the one sister?'

'No. Two sisters and three brothers. Yes, I know. It's a huge family by most standards. Even by Italian standards.'

'Wow. That must have been busy. Are they all like you? Your poor mother.'

'It was challenging, I think. In lots of ways it was hard for her.' His face almost dipped into serious, then he broke out into a smile. 'I am the oldest. I know what you're thinking, yes, they hated me. I'm bossy and organised and like being in charge. There isn't any insult you could call me that I haven't already been called.'

'I don't know, I'm sure I could think of a few.'

'Don't think too hard.' He took another drink. 'And you?'

'Me? No. Not many people have insulted me.' Actually, that was a lie, but it had been the pitying looks that had cut the deepest. No amount of physiotherapy and practice could cut the limp out completely. And with that thought the pain came shooting back up her leg, tripping across the scars. She instinctively shifted her weight, wishing she could change out of her work shoes into something more comfortable.

Matteo looked at her as if waiting for her to explain her sudden reverie. 'Ivy?'

'What?'

'I meant family,' he explained. 'You have brothers and sisters?'

'I'm an only child. I did have a stepbrother once, for a few years, and then there was a divorce—make that the second out of three—and they moved away.' She tilted her head a little to one side and found a smile to try to tell him she was fine with it. Still, it had been nice being part of something bigger. More than nice. And the fallout when Sam had left had been huge in so many ways, losing her stepbrother, Taylor, just one of them. *He's not your real brother, so stop whingeing. Imagine how I feel without my husband. How will I cope without him? How will I survive?* 'Largely it's been just me and my mum.' And a string of unsuccessful relationships.

'The doctor. And you didn't want to follow in her footsteps?' He grinned. 'Ah, no, of course, the fainting thing.'

'That and the fact that I hated hospitals for a long, long time.' And now she'd said too much. Looking for an out, she turned to look over at a commotion on the stage. 'What's happening over there?'

Again he looked at her with a quizzical expression. 'Why did you hate hospitals?'

'Look, I really should go.'

'I'm sorry, I asked you something you didn't want to answer.' His voice softened a little and she was startled and humbled by his honest, straightforward approach. Yes, he had asked. And, no, she didn't want to talk about it and see his pity and later his revulsion. But he continued chatting, undeterred, 'It's charity karaoke. The bar manager lets us have fifty percent of the proceeds if we get the crowd started. Every penny counts. We're fundraising for a new dialysis machine. We're always fundraising for a new dialysis machine. We will never have enough. We can only do so much to make our own miracles.' He picked up her bag and started to walk towards the stage. 'Come watch?'

'Er...will I have to sing?'

'If you want to help us raise money. And you said you did.'

Despite the endless irritation he instilled in her, the thought of spending more time with Matteo really appealed. Really, truly, and she knew it was nothing to do with helping him raise money. Panic took over from the pain in her foot. She could not want to spend more time with Matteo.

She shook her head. 'This wasn't what I had in mind. There's lots of other, bigger ways we can help. Besides, I've already made a fool of myself once today, thank you very much. Singing is definitely not going to help my cause of winning over the hearts and minds of the staff.' She checked her watch. 'I'm going home.'

'Matteo! Matteo!' A guy called over. 'Come on, mate, stop chatting up the ladies and get that famous peach of a backside over here. We're starting.'

Matteo grimaced and raised a finger. 'Give me a minute, Steve.' Then he turned to her and she could have sworn his eyes flicked towards her feet and then back to her face. 'I'm never going to live that picture down. Now, how are you getting home? I'll walk you to the door and get you a cab. Or walk you to the car park.'

'It's fine. My bus stop's just over the road. I can walk across the pub on my own, and, believe me, it'll be a damned sight easier than walking in.'

'But you did it, and no one has said anything at all. Except me. And I have kept you all to myself.' Taking her glass from her hand, he gave her another warm smile. No—not warm. It was possessive. Hot. His hand brushed against hers and heat rippled through her. She tried to shake it off, but it stayed, curling into her, making her hot too. His voice was deeper when he spoke again, and it caressed her insides. 'Ivy, do you have to get back for the boyfriend? The husband?'

'No. I told you, I have work to do. I really do.' *Please, don't ask anything...more.* There was something about him that was different from other men, that connected with her on another level. Something about him… Her gaze slammed up against his, the warm tease now a molten heat. She wanted to…do so many things she'd promised herself not to do again. She didn't want to be beholden to a man. To fall too deeply in love with someone who would have a hold over her emotions and actions. She wanted to stay whole. To be herself, and so much more.

He shook his head. 'Okay. I know I'm going to regret this, but I'll let you go this time. Next week I might not be so lenient.' Was it her imagination or was he flirting again? She didn't know. Panic and heat rose in her gut. The heat overriding the panic, squashing it. No. This was not how she wanted to feel—she didn't want to lose control with him. Knew that if that happened she'd be on a spiral to disaster. She didn't need that in her life, not when she'd finally got where she'd wanted to be. His hand touched her arm. 'You're going to leave me to sing to these people, and I'll end up looking like a fool—as always—but it's worth it for the money. Don't work too hard, Ivy. Enjoy the videos.'

'I will.' *Another lie.* Breathing a huge sigh of relief, she pushed the door open and inhaled the late spring evening air. Thank God for that. What was happening to her insides she did not know, or want to even think about. But she knew she had to put some distance between her and Dr Delicious. Wrapping her coat around her, she began to walk towards the bus stop and realised…

My bag. Damn.

Without it her evening, her whole weekend, would be lost. Besides, those files held confidential information that she could not lose on any account.

Twirling back round towards the pub, she slammed hard

into a wall of muscle. A dark collared shirt. Brooding eyes. A hand holding out her bag. 'Ivy.'

'Oh.' But now she was touching him she didn't want to let go. Should have but didn't. Underneath the soft linen of his shirt she could feel every nuance of muscle, every ripple of movement. And there, underneath her fingers, his heart beat strong and regular. Steady. 'Matteo—'

'Hush.' The bag fell to the ground. Then he placed his palm to the back of her neck, pulled her towards him, and pressed his lips against hers.

It took a moment to register that this was Matteo, this was a kiss—so unexpected, and yet everything that their conversations had been leading up to. His mouth was playful as he nipped across her bottom lip and she could feel his smile against her own. Then she stopped thinking altogether—because thinking would throw up too many barriers, and just for once in her life she wanted to be free, to take what she wanted instead of holding back. To open herself up to...*this*. He tasted exotic, of spice and man, and it set her gut on fire.

Wrapping his arm around her waist and drawing her closer, he set the tone, and took control. His tongue slipped into her mouth and danced a fierce dance with hers. She gripped his shirt, pressed her body against his, took everything he gave her and gave it right back to him. All the fighting and the humiliation and the anger and the deep sexual need she'd experienced since she'd crossed paths with him was in that kiss. So too was a longing and heat that she'd never experienced before.

This was bad.

This was good.

This was the biggest mistake she'd ever made. As reality seeped into her brain she stopped. Fighting for breath, she pulled away. 'My God, Matteo. What the hell was that for?'

'You looked like you needed kissing.' And he was all bravado and outward calm but she could see the slight tremor in his body as he inhaled a breath. So it had been an instinctive unthought-out action and had taken him by surprise too. 'And I was right, you did. Kissing suits you. You should do it more often. Look at you now—alive. Vibrant. No words.'

She daren't imagine how she looked, but that was the least of her problems. 'Well, that's not the way I do things. And now I'm going home.' *Don't even think of asking to come with me.*

'Okay. If you insist.' As he appeared to get used to the idea that smile was back on his mouth. A mouth she'd actually, really, truly just kissed, in the street like a…an out-of-control teenager.

Kissing Matteo! She swiped a hand across her lips to remove all trace of him. What the hell had she been thinking? He was all mouth and smug and… Oh, my God, he was good. And she couldn't find an inch of her body that didn't want to do it again—but her conscience, oh, dear, her conscience was very unhappy with such a strange and unexpected turn of events.

'My bag? Please.' She reached for it.

'Sure. Here you go. Sweet dreams, Ivy.' With that he handed her bag over, turned and disappeared back inside the pub, leaving her breathless and hot and shaking.

Sweet dreams? Not if they were going to be filled with him. *Please, no.* Thanks goodness her bag was stuffed to the gills with papers that would keep her occupied into the early hours, because somehow she was going to have to keep her mind on her work and not on a peachy backside, startling eyes and smug mouth.

Good luck with that.

CHAPTER FIVE

'SERIOUSLY, I HAVE to sit in a circle and discuss hypothetical scenarios? Really? When there are real ones happening two floors down in ER...and an empty OR across the hospital?' Matteo looked around at the other members of the group in disbelief. Two doctors, a ward clerk and a phlebotomist. They were okay with this?

'Okay, then.' Ivy was hovering around them, going from group to group checking on progress, a smile plastered to her face. A smile, he could see, that wasn't comfortable every time her eyes settled on him. 'Why don't you share with everyone what the specific problems are for your department? We could do a brainstorm and set something in motion. It could be a true test of the skills you're learning here on the course.'

Marjorie, the ward clerk from ward three, nodded in agreement, her gaze homing in on Matteo. 'Okay, big-shot bottom, tell us what you need.'

He smothered a grin. That photo had certainly been one way of getting attention, unwanted but nevertheless—people certainly knew him now. 'I need, in simple terms, a new dialysis machine, or funds to buy one.'

'Ball park?' Ivy again.

'Around thirty thousand.'

'That's a lot of calendars you'd have to sell, Mr Finelli.

How about you approach a fund starter website? That would be a great place to start. Some people are seeing amazing results…' Ivy certainly got impassioned and enthusiastic about some things. 'Set up an account and get people to pledge money. Those kinds of forums work because it's a little more personal than just donating. You could have giveaways with each level of pledge—say, a plaque for a platinum sponsor. Plus a brochure and a personalised photograph or something…'

'We've already got a perfect picture for that, eh, Matteo?' It was Marjorie again. His backside had certainly gone viral.

Ivy rolled her eyes. 'That's enough about that picture, please. I am so over it. Really. As I've already explained to Mr Finelli, that's not the sort of image we want associated with St Carmen's—as we can clearly see it distracts us from our purpose. Still, great work. Brainstorming certainly helps.'

One of the other doctors chipped in, 'How about a charity run or a bike ride? A run might work better—around one of the parks? Hyde Park would be good. I know they allow a certain number of small events like that. Or Regent's? Or a skydive?'

Ivy beamed and shot an *I told you so* look at Matteo. 'All of these things can catch the public's eye—given enough warning, they would embrace it. We could get the message out via our usual social media outlets—contact radio stations directly, and get their followers to get involved—it's a chain reaction. A personal message in a public forum often gets huge hits and a better positive response. Something like *Want to fly high for St Carmen's? Charity fundraising skydiving event—have fun and do some good! DM us back for details…* Or something. That's off the top of my head, and you'd need to do it in conjunction with marketing.'

Matteo nodded, impressed with the enthusiasm, although daunted by the amount of time it would need to do all this. 'It sounds like a lot of work.'

'And we're not afraid of that.' Ivy tapped her marker pen against her mouth as she thought. 'It would be a team effort, anyway. Small amounts of time and energy spent efficiently, in the right ways.'

He preferred it, he mused to himself, when that mouth was not talking. When it was kissing him. Who would have thought that was how the evening would pan out? It had been a surprise even to him. More so, the way she'd kissed him back with such hunger had stoked a fierce heat inside him, one that had him wanting more from her in a way that he hadn't wanted someone in a very long time.

Which was warning enough. No more kissing.

The afternoon crawled along and eventually the workshops came to a close, and he wasn't sure whether it was such a coincidence that he was, once again, the last person to be leaving the room. His feet seemed to have started a revolution and were taking their time in walking towards the door.

'Mr Finelli. May I, please, have a word?' She sounded like a schoolteacher. Which made him grin to himself. That kiss had shaken her. And it had probably been wrong of him to have done it—but, *Dio mio*, she had looked so uptight and uncomfortable and after the kiss it had been like looking at a different woman. Her hair had become messed a little and her lips had swollen, her cheeks pink, but her eyes—man, her eyes had been alive. That intense green flecked with gold, and sparkling. Just sparkling.

Despite that, he knew bone deep that it had been a crazy thing to do. He had no business kissing Miss Poison Ivy. They were poles apart in everything, not least that he was a one-night-stand man and she looked, as far as he could see, like a one-man-only woman. No—it wasn't going to happen again.

He turned, but made sure he stayed where he was at the door—all the better to make a quick exit before any more kissing happened. 'Sure. What can I do for you?'

'Nothing. That's exactly it. I don't want you to do anything else. Ever.' She walked towards him, her mouth fixed and determined. Her gait, as always, just the tiniest bit off balance. 'No touching. No kissing. Nothing.'

'The kiss? You want to talk about it? I thought you would almost burn up with the heat. It was good, yes?' Just thinking about it again sent hot, sharp need rippling through him.

She shook her head, holding her workbag against her chest. 'That's not the point.'

'You say that a lot.'

'Say what?'

'"That's not the point."' He removed his hand from the doorhandle and tried not to touch her. 'When you deny how you're feeling, or what you're thinking, you close off a corner of yourself.' And he should learn a lesson from his own words—but, hell, he'd learnt to close himself off to attaching any kind of sentiment to a kiss. It was just human nature. It was lust. It was natural desire, that was all. This time he was in control and calling the shots and, besides, he had no intention of taking it any further. He just couldn't. 'It is exactly *my* point. It is a simple answer, yes? Or no? You liked the kiss?'

'Is not the poi— Oh…' she frowned and he thought for a moment she would stamp her foot in irritation, but instead she gave him a haughty smile. 'You are insufferable.'

'Hey, come on, I was there. I know that you liked it. Try to be honest, Ivy. Your eyes give you away anyway. You liked the kiss and you want to do it again, but you won't.

You have a very strong resolve and kissing won't get you where you want to be. Is that right?'

'Yes. Absolutely.'

'But still you liked it.'

Now she looked like she was trying not to laugh, that pretty mouth curling at the edges, light in the green eyes. 'You are very annoying, Matteo. Okay. If I say yes, will you shut up?'

'Perhaps. Take a chance and see.' He raised his eyebrows and waited. And waited some more as the silence in the room became amplified and the lack of anyone else there became more and more obvious. They were alone and if kissing was on the agenda it could happen here. Now. And no one apart from them would ever know. He perched on the edge of one of the tables. 'And…?'

She glared at him, all humour and frustration and tight-lipped. And eventually she shook her head and tsked. 'God, will you never give up? I liked the kiss, okay?'

As he'd thought. 'Good. You said it and nothing bad happened, so it wasn't so hard to be honest and open, was it? I liked it too, but it wasn't a sensible move.'

'No. It wasn't.'

'And if we do it again?' What was it about her that made him so rash? He wanted to say things to her that he'd never said to anyone else. 'You will slap me with a sexual harassment complaint?'

'Oh, no. I wouldn't do that. I fully acknowledge my part in it.' The smile gave way to a frown. 'It is mighty tempting.'

Indeed it was. Achingly so. And a lesser man might well have tried it again. But Matteo knew the score, he had nothing but respect for her and would not step over a line that she drew. But that didn't mean he couldn't be friends with her, somehow.

Friends? What the hell? A debate began to rage in his head. A man could have female friends, couldn't he? But friends with the woman he'd locked horns with last week? With the woman who enraged and entranced him? He'd find being friends with her very hard indeed. It would have to be work colleagues or nothing. 'So, we won't do it again. But for a moment last week I had a glimpse of what you could be like. You let me see a tiny chink of who the real you is. And then, bam, it was gone, all hidden behind the designer suit and the frumpy blouse.'

Her voice rose as she looked down at her top. 'It is not frumpy. It was exclusive—'

'And you are always so antagonistic, always fighting. Why did you have to learn to be like that?' His chest tightened a little, because he knew damned well that no one was born like that, knew that slamming up defences and fighting your corner was a learnt response. He'd been through that and out the other side, learning to withhold his need to fight back. Because, in the end, all that did was make situations worse.

Except, of course, when it was to do with a mandatory training course. He'd keep on fighting against that.

'I didn't realise. Oh.' Two hot spots blossomed on her cheeks. 'Is that how I come across? Antagonistic?'

Her frown deepened and he immediately regretted what he'd said. 'Maybe only to me.'

'I'm ambitious, I want to do well,' she railed at him. 'And I've earned my stripes, so in certain situations I get to call the shots.'

'I understand.'

She glanced at him as she dragged the door open with her free hand and held it open, leaning against it. 'Do you? Really? You understand how hard it was for someone like me to have achieved what I have?'

'Someone like you? What does that mean?'

'Oh, nothing. Forget it.' With that she stalked out of the room, favouring her left foot as always, and walked down the corridor.

'No. Tell me.' He caught her arm. There was a dare in her, a level that he connected with that was fresh and new and challenging and he liked it. A lot. She had depth, layers. Layers he'd like to unwrap. So, what the hell, he was never one to flinch from a challenge. 'I want to know.'

Her shoulders hitched nonchalantly as she slowed to a halt, surprise lacing her eyes as she looked first at his hand on her arm and then at his face. She was hiding behind bravado that was flimsy and fragile.

'Let's just say I didn't exactly have the most conventional route to getting to where I am now. At times it was a struggle and I had to fight very hard, to push myself. I have high expectations and I expect everyone to have the same. Sadly, they don't. I don't like to call it fighting or antagonistic, I prefer determined. Gutsy. And damned hard work. But, whatever it is, I learnt that to get anywhere you have to be prepared to go further than anyone else. And you always have to do it on your own. Because, in the end, you're the only person you can rely on.'

So, somewhere along the line she had been hurt. He got that now. And a dark feral anger shook through him, the ferocity of it shocking him so much he took a step backwards. But he shook it off. Not his problem. Not his fight. He never allowed himself to get swept up in a woman's dramas.

So he was startled by his reaction, his need to fight on her behalf. To protect her. And by the rush of something that clutched at his chest as he saw the pain in her eyes, and the fight. He dropped his hand from her arm but followed her, picking up her pace. 'They certainly picked the right person for the job here, then. I love St Carmen's but they do need to be brought into the twenty-first century. You'll have a challenge on your hands to do that.'

Once again they found themselves at the lift and she pressed the button. No jab-jab-jab this time; she didn't appear to be in such a hurry to get away from him. 'At least we agree on something. For sure, they do. I don't know when the employee contracts were last brought into line with the most recent laws, or the sexual harassment policies, not to mention the complaints procedures, but it wasn't this side of the millennium. So it's a hard enough job as it is, without having to be sidetracked by some jumped-up surgeon's bottom.'

'Touché, Ivy. Touché.' He leaned forward and whispered, 'That's not Italian for "You can touch it," by the way.'

'Ha! In your dreams, Finelli.' She flung him a disdainful sideways glance and shook her head. But he could see, as she hit the lift call button again, that her hands had a tremor. She was all talk of ballsy and brave, but underneath she was bubbling and boiling. 'Now, you must have something more important to be doing?'

More important, undoubtedly, but not as interesting. 'Yes.'

She nodded, all businesslike, as a queue began to form behind them for the lift. 'So, I'll see you tomorrow morning.'

'On Ward Four. Seven-thirty. We'll meet there.'

'Be prepared, Finelli. I've been doing my homework.'

Prepared? Sure. He kept trying to be, but just when he thought he'd got everything under control Ivy Leigh knocked him backwards or sideways or just plain upside down.

As Ivy stepped onto Ward Four she was consumed by the memories, the smell, the rush-rush of the nurses as they bustled by. The fear. That was it, the place smelt of fear. And no doubt that had not been the intention of the interior designer who'd recently been appointed to cheer the place up. Sure, they'd done a great job with the bright primary-coloured walls and the jungle-animal theme.

But it still smelt of fear.

Or maybe that was just her impression. Surely it was, because the kids she could see were cheerful and smiling and the parents too. It was just her and her memories. Of learning to walk again. Of the pain. And the loss. Of not knowing who was going to turn up to take her home. If, indeed, she had a home to go to.

Brushing those memories away, she fixed on a smile and headed towards the huddle of medics standing around a bed. As she closed in on them she heard Matteo's voice, soft and soothing, chatting to a little boy who was wearing Spiderman pyjamas and sitting up in front of a giraffe mural, with more tubes coming out of him than she'd ever seen.

Matteo stroked the kid's blond hair back from his eyes. Eyes that were dark and sunken and ringed and skin that was tinged with the grey pallor of sickness. 'So, Joey, what's so special about Spiderman? I mean, he can jump a bit, right? But that's all.'

'*Fly*. He can fly, silly. And he saves everyone. The whole world.' The boy's face was animated as he spoke, but depleted of energy, like a deflated balloon. 'He's very cool.'

An anxious-looking woman, whom Ivy presumed was the boy's mother, sitting on the bed next to Joey, smiled and said, 'Like Matteo? He's going to give you a new kidney, so he's very cool, too.'

'I do not think I'm all that cool. But maybe I should get a vest saying *Kidney Man!* on it? And a cape? Will that help me fly too? I quite like that idea.' Matteo examined one of the tubes, then grinned, his face boyish but wise. 'But first we have to make you better. And I'm going to do that this morning. We're going to go along and see my friend Mo who's got special medicine that helps you to go to sleep, and when you wake up you'll be feeling a bit sleepy, but much better. And you'll have a new kidney that means you can stop all the dialysis and a lot of the medicine and then we'll just have to see you sometimes and not every week. And soon you'll be able to go back to school and not be tired. How d'you feel about that?'

The boy nodded sagely. 'Good. Will it hurt?'

'We'll give you special medicine, and if you have any bits that hurt we'll make them all better for you.' As if he sensed Ivy's presence, he glanced over and raised his eyebrows, beckoning her over. 'Hey, this lady works at the hospital. She's new and she's learning how we do things. Is it okay with you all if she watches the operation?'

'Yes. Hello.' The boy stuck out his hand in such an old-fashioned, too grown-up gesture that tears pricked Ivy's eyes. He should be out playing, running around with his friends, getting into mischief, not here in a bed, waiting for the gift of life.

She blinked the tears away—because what use were they to him?—and took his sweaty little hand in hers. She'd never had a broody bone in her body but, heck, she felt everything soften at the faith the boy put in Matteo, and his acceptance of everything. Such trust. And the injustice that someone so little and innocent would even have to go through this. But Matteo was handling it so perfectly Joey didn't appear concerned. 'Hey, Joey. How are you?'

'Okay.'

His mum interrupted, 'He was a bit nervous earlier, but he's fine now Super-Matteo is here, aren't you, Joey?'

Ivy knew exactly how all that felt. The sick feeling in the pit of your stomach, the panic, the fear of the general anaesthetic. The fear of not knowing if she was going to wake up again. The fear of a pain that was uncontrollable. *Run*, she wanted to say, Run! But before she knew what she was doing she stepped forward, her voice low but as friendly and reassuring as she could make it.

'It does feel a bit scary at first, doesn't it? I know, I really do. It's perfectly normal to feel like that, but you'll be fine. Honestly.' She hoped to God he would be. 'Matteo and his friends are really great and you'll be all fixed up.' *And I'll be in there, making damned sure it'll happen.*

And if anything cemented the rightness of her taking this job it was this. Right here. That she was in the perfect place and that she would do her best to make sure everything went exactly to plan, for Joey and kids like him. She couldn't do it for the whole city, or the country, or right the wrongs of the world, but she could do this, make a difference here to these lives. Of course she recognised that Matteo, and his colleagues, were not at all like the surgeon who had operated on her—that these guys were capable and competent and fully aware of their expertise and limitations. And that this child's life and future was in their hands.

She also knew, without a shadow of a doubt, that Matteo would never take a needless risk. And that she would trust him wholeheartedly with her own child's life. And that recognition shuddered through her. She believed in him. Was swept up in the passion with which he attacked his job—and, to her chagrin, the humility too. He may have been the single most irritating man she'd ever met but she trusted him. To do his job properly, at least. Anything more than that was a step too far for her right now.

He was looking at her with a strange expression and she realised she'd given away more than she'd intended. 'Yes, thank you, Ivy. We'd better all get along now. You want to bring anything with you, Joey? A special bear? Teddy?'

'Can Spidey come?' The boy held up a plastic miniature of the superhero, which Matteo took and stuffed into the boy's pyjama pocket. 'Absolutely. Where would we be without him?'

And with that he gave them all a nod, his gaze lingering on her for just a little longer than she felt comfortable with.

Game on.

CHAPTER SIX

SEVEN HOURS AND two operations later Ivy was definitely feeling the effects of standing and tensing and standing and tensing. Trying to stop herself from swaying, she shifted from one foot to the other, ignoring the sharp pain that shivered up her leg, and was so very grateful that she hadn't fallen over or fainted or shown herself up in any way. In fact, she was feeling pretty proud of herself.

At the operating table Matteo was deep in conversation with the medical students, showing them the difference between a renal vein and an adrenal one. She knew that herself, having studied it ad infinitum on the internet—firstly through her fingers and with noise-cancelling headphones. Then, as her confidence had grown and she'd remained upright, with more and more ease. Still not exactly comfortable, but less at risk of falling over. The good thing was that she knew what to expect, what was going to happen, and so knew when to look away or sing a little song in her head to mask the commentary.

Watching him work, she had a full flush of something like nerves, which she knew was all part of the attraction she now admitted she felt for him. And it was rash and stupid and she just wanted it to go and leave her in peace. Because before she'd ever laid eyes on that spectacular pair of buttocks she'd been quite happy. Okay, so maybe she'd been feeling a little like she was missing out on something in her life. But not enough that she'd been bothered to care. Work had been too all-consuming and she'd liked it that way.

But now? Now she wanted to put her hands on him again. To feel that chest fall and rise under her fingertips. To feel his lips pressed against hers.

His voice floated over to her as she focused on the floor and controlled her breathing. 'Yes…thanks for the help, guys. Great job. Now we can go and talk to the boy's parents with an update. Then off to the Dragon for Friday night drinks,' he was saying. 'Not too late for me today as I have to prepare for tomorrow. It's going to be an incredible game. You just wait, we'll give your team a good thrashing.'

'Can't believe you got tickets for Twickenham,' someone answered him. 'How much did you pay for them?'

Matteo laughed. 'I sold my soul. But it will be worth it. This time tomorrow we'll be two tries up, three if we stick to the game plan. Go, Italia! Okay, everyone, let's go.'

So they were finished for the day. Just fine. The OR staff bustled around her as Matteo flicked his gloves into the bin. 'Congratulations, Ivy, you have mastered the art of watching an operation.'

She smiled—not wanting to admit that she'd spent the better part of the time not looking where everyone else had been looking. She knew the floor intimately. 'Well, it hardly warrants congratulations, but I'm feeling pretty elated for the patient and his family after such a long wait and worry. How long will it take Joey to feel better?'

'Almost immediately. He'll be a little groggy, but the cadaver kidney is working—clearly, we need to keep a very close eye on it—but the magic works straight away.' Taking her by the shoulders, he steered her out of the OR and pointed towards a door. 'I need to talk to the parents and my covering on-call staff… I'm not rostered on this weekend but I trust them completely,' he explained. 'Go sit down in there and wait for me. I'll be in shortly to debrief.'

'I should really get back to my desk. I've got an important case coming up next week that I really need to do some work on.'

His eyes darkened as he shook his head. 'And you can work all through the night and every hour of the weekend once you leave here. But, Ivy, it's been a long day. Just go in there and sit for a few minutes. You are allowed to rest. In fact, I insist and I'm the doctor. This is my domain and I call the shots. Go. I'll be in soon.'

'Okay. Okay.' To be honest, she was feeling just a little too exhausted to argue. God only knew how he felt after concentrating so hard for so long, and now he had to pull on a smiling face and meet anxious parents. It had been an emotional day, and a seemingly endless one. 'You can have two whole minutes, but then I do need to go. Cases don't get won by sitting around, doing nothing.' She started to walk towards the door and her heart lifted at the promise of a seat, but she couldn't resist adding, 'But...for the record...'

His eyes flashed with something as he turned back to her. 'Yes?'

'You did really well.'

'I know.' His shoulders relaxed and he laughed. 'Praise from you? Wow, what can I say?' He patted his heart and with a sarcastic grin said, 'It means so much.'

'It should. I don't give it lightly.'

She slipped into the staffroom, slumped onto the sofa and kicked her shoes off. *Wow.* That felt good. Rubbing her left foot with both hands, she massaged the gnarls and dips and scars and eventually managed to get the blood flowing properly, and gradually the numbness started to ease. What they'd achieved in there had been truly amazing. In Matteo's words, they'd given Joey a future. That was something to be proud of. But how could he do this, day in, day out? How could they all? It was exhilarating but so emotionally draining.

One thing she knew—he'd been right when he'd suggested she live a little in his world. Now she felt she understood that it was intense and necessary and so, so important.

But so was hers. Behind-the-scenes stuff that kept them all focused and kept everyone away from harm. They both had their roles to play.

But now…exhaustion dropped over her as she laid her head back and closed her eyes, just for a moment…

'Hey, Ivy.'

Was it a dream? A dark, soothing voice that worked magic over her skin. 'Ivy?'

Not a dream. Actually, here in person. Better than a dream. Or worse. She was here. He was here. Alone. And… hell, she was sleeping. That was so not the way she wanted people to see her, especially people like him.

Her eyelids shot open. He was close, kneeling on the floor next to her, an easy, teasing smile on his lips. 'Ivy? Are you okay?'

'Oh. Hello, Matteo. I…er…' She sat bolt upright, shoving her feet back into her shoes. Had he seen? 'Whoa, how long was I asleep for? I should be getting back to work.'

'No. Wait. Here.' He handed her a hospital-issue white porcelain cup with something that smelled like heaven in it. 'Drink this first. I smuggled it in from Enrico's so don't breathe a word to anyone.'

He'd brought her coffee? Staring at the cup, she grimaced. 'Did you put poison in?'

'Me? Poison the enemy? I wouldn't stoop so low. Besides, I get the feeling I've won this part of the battle.'

'I think I'm starting to see things a little from your point of view. But that doesn't mean I'm backing down or admitting a darned thing.' She took a sip and smiled, leaning her head back against the lumpy cushions. He'd brought her coffee? She didn't want to read anything into that. 'It's perfect. Thank you. How did you know what I liked? Guesswork?'

'When I described you to Enrico he said you always have the *caffe lungo. Americano… Grande…*whatever you all call it here. Strong and black.'

She didn't know what to say. 'Thank you. That's very nice of you.'

When he'd stormed into her office that first day she hadn't imagined he could be like this. She'd jumped to the conclusion that he was all mucho macho Italiano. And, yes, he was. But he was so much more than that. So much more that she was trying hard to resist. And he was making it harder by the minute.

'Ivy.' His eyes shot to her foot and back again, his voice softer. 'What happened?'

Oh, wow again. Straight to the point. 'That? Nothing much. It was all so long ago.'

'And yet still you try to hide it.' Slipping her shoe off, he examined her foot, holding it firmly when she tried to wriggle it away. 'An accident? A car? Crush injury or something?'

'A-ha. Or something.' What to say? She took a breath and thought, struggled for a moment. This was too personal, she never spoke of it, never referenced it—had tried to put that experience to the back of her mind—but even so, it fuelled her job every day. Would it matter if she told him? Was that opening up too much of herself?

Yes. 'Look, it's not important. Thanks for an awesome day. I'll get going now.'

His hand closed over her foot. It was warm. It was safe. The safest she'd felt for a long time. 'I'm not going to let you walk out of here until I know what caused this. I know that's hard for you. I know you don't understand the need to be open. But it will be fine to talk of it. It will help. Maybe. I want to know. For you.'

For you. God, what did that mean? But trying not to talk about it would make it seem like an even bigger issue—and, really, she wanted to downplay it.

'I…er…' She didn't know where to start, so she just started at the beginning. 'I was four. My stepdad was new to us, not married to my mum yet, in fact they'd not long met, and he was trying to show off—to *bond*. He had me by the feet and was swinging me round and round and at first I was enjoying it. But his grip was so, so tight and I was going too fast and too high and no matter what I said he just kept on doing it to impress my mum. I started to panic and wriggled out of his grip. Hit the floor. Broke my ankle.'

'Ouch.'

'Yep. Mum didn't believe it hurt as badly as it did so I tried to walk on it. A few days later it was just so swollen and painful I talked her into taking me to the hospital. Turned out it was broken in a couple of places and had started to heal badly. The orthopaedic surgeon was new and…well, let's say he wasn't in the right head space to be working. He attached an external metal frame to fix it—but he didn't do it properly. The upshot was I ended up with a badly deformed foot and twelve more surgeries to try to fix it.'

'When you say not in the right head space…?'

The all-too-familiar anger rippled through her. 'Drunk. On whisky and power.'

'Oh.' He started to stroke over the scars that snaked round her foot, her ankle, her calf, the knobbly, mottled skin more sensitive to his touch. And again she tried to pull away. How many men had flinched at the sight of it?

How many had laughed at her? How long had she endured the teasing at school and beyond? The revulsion? His eyes widened. 'That's a real shame. I'm so sorry.'

'Don't be. It's in the past.'

He let her foot down then settled himself on the other end of the couch. Lifted her foot again and continued to stroke it as if it was the most normal thing he'd ever done. He smelt of dark brown Betadine, that distinctive hospital smell, but over-laced with his own particular scent of spice and pure raw man. 'But you are still affected by it, Ivy, I can see.'

'Plenty of people have worse than this, you only have to spend a day in this hospital to see that. It doesn't hurt much.' Actually, it did. Not a day or an hour went by without pain, but talking about it made it worse. What had hurt much more had been the reaction from everyone else. *Cripple. Ugly. Time-waster.* Her own mother hadn't been bothered enough to listen, to care, to fight.

'But that's why you're here, doing this job.'

'Yes.' She twisted round and leant back on the arm of the sofa to get comfortable. As if having a man like Matteo touching her skin would ever be a comfortable experience. It was terrifying. It was lovely. 'Sure, that's my calling. Righting the wrongs. Capturing the evildoers and taking them to task. Saving the world. Maybe I should get a cape too. Super-Lawyer.'

'Sure, you'd look cute in Lycra. We could be a dynamic duo. But now I understand a lot more about you.' He paused, waited until the smile had faded. 'And he apologised, this man?'

'The surgeon? Never. But he was eventually struck off after he got caught doing a similar thing—maybe six years later. Turns out he was a serial drunk and had hurt a lot of people over the years.'

'And the man who was swinging you round and round?' His face darkened. 'You went through too much because of him.'

She thought about how much to say. Did it matter? Was she breaking any of her own cardinal rules by just talking to Matteo? It was only words. She could do words easily. She just didn't have such a great handle on emotions. Especially not these new ones—desire, lust, need.

'My mum married him. They all said it was my fault for wriggling while he was swinging me. Said he thought my screams were because I was having fun, not because I was frightened. And Mum was so bowled over by him she believed anything he said. She wasn't interested in my version of events, or in seeking any recompense from the surgeon, or to try make sure he didn't maim anyone else's kid.' It was all too much trouble.

'So that's why you distrust people too. Ah, you are textbook.' He raised his eyebrows and wagged a finger at her.

She grabbed it and twisted slightly. 'Glad I'm so transparent when I thought I was much more complex.'

'And twelve more surgeries?'

She shrugged, trying at the same time to shrug off the memory and the pain she'd endured time after time after time. And learning to walk. Over and over. 'Yep. Internal fixations, pins, plates. Infected wound debriding… You could say I was more of an in-patient than an out-patient for a lot of my growing up. It got to the point that I used to take myself to my out-patient appointments on the bus on my own.'

'As a child?'

'As a young girl. A teenager. Mum wasn't very good at the parenting details of being a mother. There were always too many other things for her to do…' Or, rather, men to pursue. Relationships to sort out. Dramas. Lots and lots of dramas. Unfortunately, not one of them had involved looking after the only child she'd ever had. 'It was just easier to do it on my own than try to rely on her. Although, obviously, she had to come to sign the consent forms for the surgeries, but she didn't tend to hang around much.'

It had always felt as if it had been just too much of a hassle for her. That her needs had been a hindrance to her mother's social life. Until, that was, every time her mother's life had imploded, and then she'd clung to Ivy the way she'd clung to her husbands—with the desperate, all-consuming need that they all learned to despise in the end. The need that Ivy had seen once too often in her friends—the need for a man that overwhelmed them.

So she'd vowed never to be like that. Ever. Never to let a man take over, to take so much of her that there was too little left. But she didn't feel in any danger of that happening with Dr Delicious here—she knew exactly the score with him. He was the kind of guy who didn't offer any promises, and that was just fine, because she didn't want any.

The stroking of his hands had become more intense, the sensation he instilled reaching more than just her leg. It was travelling through her, heating every part of her. He nodded. 'So this is why you're so independent and argumentative? Because you want justice. And because you need to be heard. Because your mum let you down.'

She thought about it, and, yes, he was probably right, but she didn't want him to know that. Like a lot of things, it was easier to shove them deep down than face them. 'I suppose you could say that my relationship with my mother is as broken as my foot.' In fact, the thought of even discussing anything other than the weather with her mum brought Ivy out in hives. As far as she was concerned, it was better to be on her own than risk her heart again. A girl could only take so much emotional fallout.

'Thanks for the psychology lecture. But I'm just who I am, Poison Ivy, who won't tolerate defective people thinking they're immune to the law or to recrimination. Or surgeons who think they're God. Or people who don't take me seriously. Okay, so I've learnt to be like this, but I'm not ashamed of it.'

'You are Ivy. Yes. And you are stronger for your experiences.'

'And do you know, I don't think I've ever really talked about them before.' Not in so much detail. So God only knew what the hell that meant. That she'd exposed her weakness, not only allowed him to see her scars but discussed them too.

Suddenly she felt a little vulnerable. She shrugged her foot from out of his hand and scuttled her feet under her bum as she sat up, inadvertently shuffling closer to him as she resettled herself. 'So, please, please, don't say anything to anyone, I don't really want this to be hospital gossip. Every surgeon's going to think I'm on some kind of witch hunt and I'm not at all. I just want to do my job to the best of my ability, and scuttling out dodgy surgeons is only a tiny part of it. The rest is to put systems in place to prevent these things happening again.'

He frowned. 'Of course. But the scarring and the injury are hardly something you should be ashamed of.'

'If you'd seen the cruel reaction of the kids I grew up with, and then the men I dated who wanted tabloid perfect, you wouldn't be saying that.'

'Then they are all idiots.'

Yes. Maybe they were. And so was she for being taken in by his words. By his touch. By the way he sounded so unlike every man she'd ever dated—his words like a salve to her wounds. By the little dimple in the cleft of his chin. And by that tiny frozen part of her that had started to thaw, just a little, leaving her open and vulnerable.

She did not want this. Did not have space in her life for this. And, really, she should have stood up and left, but she reached to him anyway, placed her hand over his. Because it seemed a perfectly natural thing to do. 'Thank you. That was a nice thing to say.'

'My pleasure.' His hand cupped her face and he looked at her with such intensity that her heart beat a wild staccato against her ribcage. 'So don't be so hard on yourself.'

He was just being kind in that Italian way of his. He was being gallant and it was so nice to actually be on the receiving end of something like that. Just for once in her life. And he was so close. Looking down with a heated gaze that stoked something deep inside her. Something that answered the question in his eyes.

Then, unable to stop herself, she lifted her face and pressed her lips to his.

What kind of madness was this? Matteo mused in a barely coherent thought process as his hands curled around her, dragging her onto his lap and returning the kiss like a starving man. He was jaded and cynical and not able to offer anything more than this.

Her fingers spiked his hair and she moaned his name, her voice tinged with that cute accent that was so different and refreshing and intriguing and haughty. She tasted delicious. Of risk and freedom and the melting of barriers. Of layers and depth and heat. And wetness.

Her tongue slipped into his mouth and meshed with his, dancing an age-old dance that fired an intense need within him. He pulled her against him, relishing her soft body against his, and then, unable to wait any longer, he slipped his hand underneath the scrub top to her bra. With one easy flick of his fingers he'd undone it and palmed a hand over warm silken flesh and the tight bud of a nipple.

At his touch she moaned again, wriggling her backside against his erection, slowly gyrating on his lap. She was driving him crazy. Wild with desire. That clever mouth that kissed as well as it shot out smart retorts. This achingly sexy body with the softest skin and the scars of a history that made his gut clench. And that drive deep within her that had elevated her from her experiences and made her so much more. He wanted to do anything to erase that hurt.

But wait.

Taking her in the staffroom? That was not his plan. She was worth more than that, deserved more. What kind of madness indeed. But he wasn't thinking straight. It had been a long, hard day and she was just so irresistible. Such a bundle of contrasts, and so damned hot. And he did not know what any of it meant, what this need that drove him was about, that he dreamt about her. But he knew it was intense. That it was something he should be afraid of, yet at the same time he was intrigued and, *mio Dio*, he just couldn't keep away.

A vibrating whirr and a tinny sound had her jumping off him, swiping a hand across her mouth and straightening her top. She reached into her pocket, pulled out a phone and frowned. 'Oh. Er…strange? I should probably get this.'

'Sure.' It would give him time to calm down a little and get things into perspective. Actually, to man up and put a stop to this fooling around in a public place. *Said the guy with his ass hanging out over the internet.* The more he thought about that, the more he realised what a stupid prank it had been. But he wasn't about to admit that to Ivy.

She turned away from him, her shoulders rising up to her ears as she talked. 'Oh. Okay. I see. When? Where?'

A silence stretched as she listened. The longer she stood there the more her body tensed, her hand slowly moving up to her mouth. And, as if in harmony with her, Matteo's heart clutched too. Clearly there was a problem and it went deeper than a work issue.

'Of course,' she said finally, her voice weak and wobbly. 'I'll be there as soon as I can. Please, tell her to… I don't know… Tell her to hold on.'

As she slung the phone back into her pocket she turned to him, her face pale now, all traces of their passion erased. 'I have to go back to York. My mum's sick. She's had a heart attack…they think, they're running tests as we speak. Er… she's asking for me.'

'Of course. You must go.' But there was something about her hesitation that gave him pause too. After all, it hadn't sounded like she had the best relationship with her mother. And he knew how being angry and disillusioned with family could affect someone. 'You think that's the right thing to do?'

She raised her head enough to hold his gaze, and in her darkened, hooded eyes he saw fear and sadness and determination. Her voice was calm. 'Just because she's a lousy mother, it doesn't mean I have to be a lousy daughter. If she needs me, I'll be there for her.'

'Of course, and you shall go. Do you need help organising things?'

'Oh. Well, I guess I need to either hire a car or get the train. Driving's crap on a Friday, but it means I'll be able to go see her straight away, and also pop home for things she might need. But I think the train might be quicker… but…I don't know…' She took a step forward, then back. Almost as if she didn't know how or where to start. For the first time since he'd met her she seemed totally out of her depth. Blindsided.

And he needed to step up.

Didn't want to—because that would make things infinitesimally more complicated. But it wasn't about him. Or this. It was about her and healing things with her *mamma*. 'I'll take you.'

'What? No. No. No, don't be silly. It's fine. I can drive. I just need…' she fished her phone out again '…to call a decent car hire place…or something.'

Wrapping his arms around her, he took the phone from her hands, gave her a hug that she clearly didn't know what to do with but accepted anyway. And he was probably doing this all wrong and sending the wrong message, but he couldn't stand here and watch her sink. She was too proud for that. 'You are upset. Look, you're shaking. You shouldn't drive. Let me take you?'

She shook her head vehemently. 'No, it's too much to ask anyone. This is my problem, not yours. Besides, it's a hell of a long way, a good four hours' drive on a Friday night—more, probably, the traffic's usually a nightmare. You can't do it there and back in one go, not after a long day. And don't you have plans for tomorrow? A rugby game you sold your soul to the devil for or something?'

He hugged her to him, as he would have any friend who was suffering, trying through his actions to say what he wasn't yet ready to say in words. Hell, he didn't know what he was trying to say.

'It's rugby. We will win. It will be over in eighty minutes. This is more important.' *You* are more important, was what he actually thought. The shock of that shuddered through him. He didn't know her. He didn't like her, goddamn. Okay. So he could probably admit to liking her when she wasn't being a prim lawyer chasing his ass. Literally.

She spun out of his arms, looking embarrassed and flustered and about as far from a prim lawyer as anyone could get. 'And what about Joey and your other patients? They need you here.'

'I told you, the on-call team is fabulous—the best in the city. In fact, Dave Marshall taught me everything I know about renal surgery. So they're all in the best hands. It is fine. Really. I'm not due at work until Monday as it is, and I'm only a phone call away.' And he should have heeded the warning bells again then, but he didn't. Should have remembered the last time he'd allowed a woman to invade his life and his heart—and then plundered it and smashed it into tiny pieces and thrown it into the trash. The betrayal. The double whammy of hurt.

But this was different. Ivy needed help and he could give it to her. What kind of a man did otherwise?

CHAPTER SEVEN

IT WAS LATE and dark when they arrived at the hospital, after a long journey where Ivy had felt herself withdraw into her worries. But Matteo had kept a constant stream of trivial conversation to dredge an occasional smile and for that she was grateful.

Now she knew he liked rugby more than football. That he preferred bottled beer to wine. That he'd had his wisdom teeth removed when he was twenty. Nothing deeper than that. But it had been enough. More than enough to keep her from going out of her mind with concern.

He pulled up outside the entrance, a hand on her knee as he spoke. 'I'll find a parking spot. You go in, I'll find you.'

'She'll be in the cardiac ward, I imagine. Or High Dependency or something…I'll ask at Reception. Perhaps I should text you?' She went for her phone in her bag. Did she have his number?

He put his hand on hers and gave her a smile that went bone deep. 'Ivy, I know my way around a hospital. I'll find you. Go.'

'Of course. Yes. Yes.' What was wrong with her? One stolen kiss and she'd been reduced to fluff. Her brain wasn't functioning. Maybe it was the worry about her mum…

After she watched him pull away she went to find her mother, feeling empty and bewildered, her own heart bruised and broken enough too. There was so much between them that needed to be said, that she wanted to fix but wanted to avoid at all costs.

The hospital corridors were silent as she walked to the reception desk, a grey-haired lady pointing her in the direction of Cardiac Care. Darkness outside the windows penetrated her heart. She'd been talking about her mum and then something bad had happened. What did that mean?

She didn't want to rail at her, to blame her for the crappy upbringing she'd had—it was too late for that. All Ivy had ever wanted was recognition that she was important in her mother's life. But, in the end, she supposed, it didn't matter a jot. Ivy's mother was important to her and if love only went one way, then so be it. It was too late for recriminations.

One of the nurses greeted her and showed her to her mother's bed with a stern warning to be quick and quiet.

'Ivy.' Her mum looked frail and old, lying on pale green sheets that leached colour from her cheeks. Tubes and wires stuck out from under the blanket, attached to a monitor that bleeped at reassuringly regular intervals. A tube piped oxygen into her nostrils, but she sucked in air too, pain etched across her features. 'Thank you for coming, I said not to bother you. I know you're busy—too busy to have to come all this way to see your old mum.'

'Mum, you've had a heart attack—since when was that not enough to bring me to see you?' Guilt ripped through Ivy, as she'd known it would. It was what happened every time she saw her mum—whatever Ivy had done it had never been enough to make her mother love her and she just didn't know how to make things better. She gave her a hug, which was always difficult, and this time it was hindered by the tubes. Movement made her mother's monitor beep, and consequently made Ivy's heart pound—loudly—and so she quickly let go. The space between them seemed to stretch.

'How are you feeling?'

'Lousy.' Breathless and wheezing, her mum settled back down and the beeping stopped. 'I had…an angioplasty. They've cleared the occlusion…put in a stent…so I just need a short stay in here…then do some rehab…as an outpatient.'

It was fixable. Just faulty plumbing. Relief flooded through her as she held her mum's hand. But once again she felt very much like their roles had been reversed, that she was the one taking the care, being the parent. 'That's great news. I was…I was worried about you.'

'Thanks, love. I'm glad you came. You're all I've got now. Can you stay…you know, a while?'

Responsibility tugged Ivy in every direction. Her job, everything, could be put on hold. Couldn't it? She'd only been there a few weeks—but they'd understand. Wouldn't they? She had a nagging sensation that things weren't going to be easy, that she'd have to fight to take time off—time she hadn't yet earned. And she had that upcoming sexual harassment case that was so important for everyone involved. She needed to be in London all clued up for that.

And she needed to be here with her mum. Someone who had never been there for *her*. Maybe she could trust the case to a junior? Maybe she could teleconference with them all. Maybe, *surely*, they'd understand? What would happen if they didn't? She didn't want to contemplate that. She'd finally got her dream job, and now… She looked at her mum, frail and anxious. 'I'll stay here with you as long as you need, Mum.'

'I'd appreciate it. I don't have anyone else.'

'You have me.' Even though it had never seemed enough. 'Is there anything you need? Once they have you settled…'

'I've been thinking, Ivy. About everything… We need to talk. *I* need to…' Her mum's eyes drifted to a spot just behind Ivy and as her skin prickled in response to an external stimulus, also known as Dr Delicious, she turned. Her mum's voice suddenly sounded a lot more healthy. 'Who's this?'

'Oh. Yes. Mum, this is Matteo, my…' What the hell was he? Other than a giant pain in the backside and a damned fine kisser? And, okay, so he was wearing her down a little with his huge generosity of spirit and the four hours' of driving on a soggy spring evening through interminable traffic on a motorway that had been as clogged as her mother's arteries. He was also messing with her head. 'He's my colleague at St Carmen's. He drove me here.'

'All the way from London? Lucky you.'

'Yes, well…' She'd never introduced a man friend to her mother before. 'He's just helping me out.'

Ivy shot Matteo a look that she hoped would silence any other kind of response. Because it was late and she was frazzled, her mum was sick and this wasn't the time or place for explanations. *I met his bottom first, the rest came later, and I have no idea what any of it means.*

And, truth be told, I'm scared. Right now, of everything. Of you dying. Of him becoming too much to me. Of losing myself in either grief or love.

Of not being able to let go.

The nurse bustled over and fiddled with an IV line attached to a large bag of fluid. 'Hello, there. Look, I know you've come a long way and I hope you don't mind me saying this, but visiting hours finished a long time ago. I let you sit with her for a while but, really, she needs to get her rest and so do my other patients…'

'It's okay, Ivy. You go.' Her mum's eyes were already closed, but she squeezed Ivy's hand. A gesture that was the simplest and yet most profound thing Ivy had received from her mum in a very long time. Tears pricked her eyes.

'Of course. Yes. Of course. I'm so sorry. I'll be back tomorrow, Mum.'

'Good. Bring me some toiletries, will you? A nightgown. Make-up.'

'Make-up? What for?'

'Standards, darling.' Typical Mum. But it did make Ivy smile—she couldn't be at the far end of danger if she wanted to put on mascara.

'Let's go, Ivy.' Matteo touched her arm and he drew her away from the ward and out into the silent corridor of eternal half-night. That was how hospitals felt to her—places where reality hovered in the background, and time ticked slowly in an ethereal way.

It was good to have him there, despite the strange unbidden feelings he provoked. Emotions washed through her—elation that her mum wasn't going to die, sadness about the gulf between them, and then, interlaced with all of this, the comfort of being with Matteo. A comfort that pulsed with excitement and sexual attraction. Which seemed really inappropriate and out of place right now. But there it was. Maybe she just needed another human being to metaphorically cling to. There was, after all, a first time for everything.

He waited until they were outside before he spoke. 'So it's good news, then? She's going to be okay?'

A long breath escaped her lungs. 'Yes, it would seem so. She's had an MI and angioplasty and the outlook's good.'

'So why the sad face?'

She tried to find him a smile, because it was good news. 'I don't know… I'm really pleased she's okay. I just feel terrible for saying those awful things about her, for thinking bad things when she was so sick. She could have died and I'd never have forgiven myself.'

He stopped short and looked at her. 'Ivy, her only job was to love you. If she didn't do that then you're right to be angry at her.'

She got the feeling that he was talking from personal experience, that there was something that had happened to him. That he understood what she felt because he'd felt it too. 'Matteo, do you have a good relationship with your family? Were things okay when you were growing up?' It was so not her way to ask direct questions like this—to go deeper than she ever wanted to go herself—but maybe learning how other people coped with things could help.

And she'd quite like to feel she wasn't the only one around here who'd got issues.

At a time like this, in the dark, late at night, with worry hovering around the edges, maybe it was the best time to talk about these things. The things that really mattered.

He shrugged, sucking in the cool fresh northern air. 'My mum could only be described as wanting to love us all to death. She's your typical Italian mother—overfeeding, over-smothering and over-loving us.'

'And your father?'

He shrugged. Opening the car door, his demeanour changed, his voice took on a forced jolly tone. 'Now, we need to eat something half-decent that isn't wrapped in plastic packaging and sold for a fortune in a motorway service station, and you need to get some serious sleep. It has been a long day.'

'Matteo…' She wanted him to continue talking about his family. This was the guy who believed in openness and honesty. But only, it seemed, when he felt like it.

'No, Ivy. It's too late for talking. Now, show me the way to your house.'

* * *

The emotions didn't wane as she shakily put the key in the lock of her mum's central York Georgian townhouse. It had been a long time since she'd been here—too long. And that last time they'd argued—but that was nothing new. Ivy couldn't even remember what it had been about. It didn't matter, it could have been one of a zillion things, as there'd always been an undercurrent of dissatisfaction between them. But she did remember that she'd left in a storm. And now she was back because her mum had nearly died.

They were immediately greeted by the smell of coffee—that was one thing she had inherited from her mum, a love of decent coffee. Then the warm press of Hugo, the fat ginger cat, who purred as he rubbed himself against her legs, preventing a step forward or backwards.

'Hey, cat.' Matteo took a sidestep through the front door, carrying Ivy's suitcase, a small overnight bag of his own and two large brown paper carriers. He walked through to the kitchen, knowing exactly where to go as if he had homing radar, and plonked them all on the floor. Looking around at the modern granite surfaces and white cupboards in a house that was over two hundred years old, he smiled. 'Very English. Nice. My mum would be green with envy if she saw this place. She's been talking about having a new kitchen since I was born.'

It felt strange, having him here in her space—her old space. It wasn't as if it felt like home any more and yet it was filled with so many familiar things and smells that gave her strange sensations of hurt and loss and loneliness. She'd always envied her friends who'd had happy chaos at home, whereas hers had been all bound up with suffering of one kind or another.

'So what's your home like, Matteo?'

'I guess you'd call it quaint. Old. Small. Traditional.

Stone walls, dark wooden cupboards, terracotta tiles, in a village where everyone knows everyone and everyone tries to outdo each other. That's why I like London, you don't have to live in each other's pockets.' He nodded to the bags. 'Okay, so I got what I could from the little supermarket next to the hospital after I parked. It wasn't great, but it had the basics. I have some chicken breasts, pesto sauce and mozzarella cheese. A plastic bag of something the label refers to as salad but which appears to be just leaves. Olives. Bread. And red wine.'

'I thought you said you preferred beer.'

Not hiding his smile, he started to unpack the carriers. 'So you were listening? I thought you were nodding your head in time to the music as you stared out of the window at something no one else could see.'

'I was listening.' It wasn't a lie. She'd been half occupied with dreary thoughts, and half enthralled by the thought of being with him for the next few hours. Alone. 'Well, thank you. I like red wine.'

'I know.' He rustled in the cupboards and fished out a frying pan, some bowls, a chopping board, two glasses and a knife. Then he opened the wine, filled two glasses and handed her one, gently pushing her to sit at the breakfast bar. 'Drink this while I cook.'

She did as she was told, enjoying having someone to look after her for a change but simultaneously feeling a little ill at ease. 'Why are you being like this? So kind and helpful?'

Slicing the chicken, he threw it into the pan and tossed it around in garlic-infused oil, then emptied the leaves into a bowl. 'Because you looked like you needed a helping hand.'

She thought about that. With his explanation it all seemed so obvious and easy. It wasn't. 'You once said, too, that I looked like I *needed* kissing. Do you always presume things, Matteo? Make up your own reality to suit yourself?'

He stopped chopping for a moment, the knife held in mid-air. 'As you appear not to be able to express your wants and needs, but to repress them and create barriers instead, in some sort of stiff-upper-lip thing, I have to go by gut instinct. Women! You should say what you want. Be honest. Ask and we'll help. Hinting and hiding stuff just confuses us. Pretending to be okay when you're not doesn't help anyone in the end. And definitely not men…' He pushed the olives towards her. 'We're easily confused.'

'Poor men.' She shot him a sympathetic grimace. 'How did you get so knowledgeable about women?'

'I have two sisters, remember? You learn a lot rubbing shoulders with them twenty-four hours a day.'

'And girlfriends?'

His forehead creased into a little frown and he paused, this time the hand in mid-air holding a bowl of olives. 'Of course. I'm a man. We have few desires, but some of them do involve having a woman around.'

Oh, yes, she could see that he was man, thank you very much. In dangerous proximity. And she had no idea why she was taking the conversation down this particular track. 'Anyone…serious…ever?'

'Not really…' He shook his head, eyes guarded. 'No. I'm an emotional Neanderthal, apparently. Selfish. Unfeeling. Because I like to put work first, because I devote myself to my patients.'

'Poor you.' She leaned forward and gave him a kiss. A gentle one, on the cheek.

He rubbed the spot her lips had touched. 'What was that for?'

Shrugging, she threw him a smile. 'You looked like you needed kissing.'

His eyebrows rose and he laughed, full and heartily. 'Round three to Miss Ivy.'

She hardly knew him—and yet there was something soul deep that attracted her to him, a peace and yet a disturbing excitement. It felt natural to talk to him, and the silences were comfortable. She couldn't remember having had that before with a man. She'd spent a lot of time in previous relationships trying to be perfect, to make up for her leg and her limp and her over-officious use of words, her weird sense of humour, trying to give a little of what she held so precious. In the end it had all been hugely disappointing and not worth the trouble.

But Matteo wasn't like that. He was fun to be around. Plus he was pretty damned useful in the kitchen. With a nice bum. Or maybe he was just Mr Too Good To Be True? She flashed him a smile. 'Round three? Are we battling again? Why, when you know you won't win?'

'I will win. Just wait and see.'

She took an olive and popped it into her mouth. Swallowed. Thought a little more about Matteo, who was stir-frying with gusto. 'I suspect this "not really" woman broke your heart?'

'No.'

'Come on.' She narrowed her eyes. 'I thought you were all about being honest and open.'

His frown stuck in place as he emptied the frying-pan contents onto a plate, which he pushed into the centre of the breakfast bar. With a swirl of salt and a crackle of black pepper he finished the presentation with flair. Then carved a few thick slices of fresh white bread and loaded them onto side plates with the mozzarella, handing one to Ivy. 'In truth, she broke my trust and that's worse.'

'Oh, yes. Indeed. I understand that.' So there had been someone significant. And why that knowledge made her heart beat a little faster she didn't want to know. The way the colour had drained from his face told her he'd been hurt badly. That deep down he kept some truths to himself.

He stuck his fork into a piece of chicken and nudged her to do the same. 'Come on. Eat. It's getting cold.'

She didn't miss the fact he'd changed the subject. Or that he hadn't said he was happily looking for The One. But, then again, neither was she.

For that matter, she wasn't looking for anything—fling or attachment, or the whole wedding catastrophe. She was looking for peace of mind and a lifetime doing her own bidding. Of reaching her full potential. Of being the person she was destined to be. Without a man in tow. Without giving anything up. Without losing any of herself.

But a little fun on the side might be nice.

That wine was going to her head. She pushed the bottle away from her. No more. 'I think I'll make a start on the washing up.'

'Let me. It's past midnight, you look exhausted. Go to bed.' He reached for her dirty plate and his hand brushed against hers. They both froze as the connection, the electricity between them, blazed again, bright. He frowned. 'Go. Go to bed, Ivy. I'll sleep down here on the sofa.'

'You don't need to, there's a spare room upstairs. I'll make it up for you—give me a couple of minutes. First door on the right.'

'Okay. If you want.'

What she wanted was for him to sleep in her bed.

My God. She didn't?

She did. And to wake up to that gorgeous smile tomorrow. Preferably with all her current worries wiped clean and her sense of self intact. She wanted to sleep with him and to have no ramifications. No angsty emotions. To be freed up enough to trust him. To trust herself to not be like her mother.

Like that was going to happen.

'Matteo…' She didn't know what she wanted to say. Well, actually, she did, but she didn't know *how* to say it. Or what saying it would mean for both of them. So she chickened out. 'Thank you. For everything. You've been very sweet.'

'My pleasure.' He ran his thumb down her cheek, his eyes kind and startling and misted. She caught his gaze and they stood for a few moments just looking at each other. So much was being unsaid, so many needs and wants. Eventually he dragged his gaze away. 'Now go.'

'But—'

'Please.' He must have known what she was going to ask, knew what she was thinking of offering him—it was written in her eyes, in her body language, in every word, in every gesture. But instead of reaching for her he shook his head. 'Ivy, it's late and it's been an emotional day. First the surgery, then your mum. Don't let's get things mixed up. Don't do something you'd regret.'

I wouldn't regret it.

But, then again, he was probably right. She had enough problems already without adding him to the list.

CHAPTER EIGHT

SOMETHING WARM AND heavy and very noisy pressed against Matteo's chest. Gingerly opening one eye, he came nose to nose with a fat cat that was purring so loudly it sounded like a dentist's drill. 'Hugo? *Ma, che sei grullo.* Eh? You *are* joking? A beautiful woman next door and this is the only offer of bedtime action that I get?'

Matteo wiggled and jiggled his torso but the cat didn't move. He just stretched a lazy leg, gave it a lick, then resumed the loud drill noise. 'Go, cat. Go.'

Purr. Purr. Another lazy lick.

'Okay. Stay there. See if I care. Because I don't.' It was six-thirteen in the morning. He was in bed with a cat. At Ivy's house. She, however, was sleeping elsewhere. That cross mouth and taut, hot body under covers in another room in a house that felt like it was the furthest thing from a home that he'd ever known. There were few pictures on the walls, nothing to say that a family lived here. Or a proud mother. Nothing like the chaos of his home, where you couldn't move for people and things. And the comparison made his heart ache for Ivy and what she hadn't had, growing up.

It had been a mistake to come here, that he knew with certainty.

He'd been so close last night to suggesting things that

would have taken them way beyond this strange relationship they had right now. But just because he'd kept silent didn't mean he was happy about it. Or that he wanted her any less. But he was stuck here for the next few hours at least—he'd promised to take her back to the hospital to see her mum, which meant he had a period of being here… alone with Ivy. He could manage a few hours. Just. Then he would get the hell out and back to the sanitised sanity of his chaotic but uncomplicated life.

In the meantime, he had to make the most of this unexpected downtime. Inching his way from underneath the soggy furball, crawling out of bed and shrugging on some running gear, he left the house in silence to explore what wonders York had to offer. A leafy path opposite the front door headed off next to a slow flowing river, towards what looked like the business centre. What better way to put a woman out of your mind than by sprinting through a new city?

The air was fresh and crisp and rich with something sweet—something delicious, like sugar candy. It made his gut curl with hunger. But again, as with thoughts of Ivy, he put everything aside and focused his effort into each footfall. Few people were out and about this early so he was able to up his pace and circumnavigate what appeared to be an old city surrounded by ancient, crumbling walls and lush greenery.

Weak sunshine fought its way through light grey clouds. It was quiet, the cobbled streets were deserted, and his mind began to settle a little with the rhythmic thud of each step.

An hour later, and much calmer, he found her in the lounge curled up on a window seat that overlooked a typical country garden filled with the fragrant blooms of spring flowers. Her laptop was open and files were scattered around her feet. She was wearing dark blue pyjamas and had wrapped a thick cream woollen cardigan around herself, and his heart clutched a little to see her working so early. Seemed the woman had so much to prove. Too much.

Even though she'd been out of his head briefly while he'd pondered some historical ruins likely put there by some old Roman ancestor of his, she settled firmly back into it the moment he set eyes on her again.

She jumped a little as she realised he was watching her, her eyes narrowing, breath quickening. 'Matteo! Gosh, you must have been up early.'

'*Buongiorno*. I had a strange companion with his own quirky alarm.' If he went to her he might just kiss her good morning. So he stayed exactly where he was, at the door.

'Ah. Yes. Hugo. Sorry about him. He's a freeloader and body heat is his catnip. You should have just kicked him off and turned over.'

'The cat wasn't for kicking.'

'No, you're probably right. He's like you. Stubborn and wilful. Now, there's coffee in the press. Just put a light under it. Actually…' She slapped the lid of her laptop down and swivelled to a stand. Her toes were painted a bright pink that matched her cheeks. And why he noticed such a small, innocuous detail he couldn't say. 'I can finish up for a few minutes if you like. Make you some breakfast. It's the least I can do for you. Where did you get to on your run?'

Sticking firmly to the wall, he tried to remember a route that he hadn't paid a great deal of attention to. 'I stuck to the river path into town, took a detour to see some of the old black and white buildings with the overhanging top storeys and the sagging middles, had a look at the ruined walls, and went down past the railway museum. Pretty place all in all.'

'Well, that at least means I don't have to worry about showing you round, apart from the Minster and a proper walk through the Shambles—you've got to go see them, everyone else does. You can't come here and not see all the most famous bits.' She smiled and it was like sunshine, warming and welcome. He cringed internally at that thought. He was getting too soft. All that work at hardening his heart and she had to start melting it.

No.

It wasn't going to happen. 'You don't have to worry about me. You're here for your mum. I've got calls to make as it is—I need to check up on Joey.'

Busily stacking her files into a pile, she looked up at him. 'Oh, yes. Let me know how he's doing. And you're going to miss your game. I feel very guilty.'

'Don't waste your energy. Stay where you are, you're working. I can fix myself something.'

'I feel guilty about that too. And about not getting enough work done. I'd planned to get through so much this weekend. I've just phoned the ward to see how Mum's doing and the nurse said she was comfortable and asking for some breakfast.' She walked through to the kitchen, flicked the heat under a stovetop coffeepot. Then turned to him, biting her bottom lip.

'Matteo, how am I going to manage to work while I'm here? I know this sounds really mean and very selfish, but I need to be in London. And I need to be here for my mum. I can't do both. How do people juggle these things?'

His eyebrows rose. 'It's very important, this sexual harassment case?'

'It is to the three women making it. And to the guy who could lose his job and reputation if it turns out he's been falsely accused—although I doubt it. It's a delicate issue and I need to be there.'

'Work, work, work. You have to learn to put yourself first. Put family first.' God forgive him for that. Because when it came to family he chose not to be there too. 'Is there anyone else who could fill in?'

The coffee fizzed and spluttered and she decanted it into two cups. 'I have a junior, but he's still very inexperienced. Becca's my assistant, but I don't really know her strengths as yet and this is too important to get wrong. I'd wanted to go through it all with her, have her watch how I do things. Besides, work is me. I am work. And that sounds really sad. But at least it's clear cut. There's nothing confusing about getting up every morning and heading in to the office. No room for anything else, like extraneous distractions.'

No room for a life. And that was the way he liked it too, although he was starting to wonder just what he was missing. He trotted out the line he gave his overworked junior staff. 'Life's all about the stuff that's not work, too. No wonder you end up so strung out. Ivy, there is so much more, you just have to give yourself a chance. Couldn't you postpone the case?' When she didn't answer he touched her arm. 'Ivy? Couldn't they put it off? How long do you think you need to be here?'

She shrugged. 'You're the doctor. How long does she need?'

'You're the daughter. Same question.' It was a challenge that seemed to hit home, but she didn't show that she understood his inference. It wasn't his place to tell her what was important in her life. *Mio Dio*, who was he to judge?

Her smile was genuine. 'Did anyone ever tell you that you're a giant insufferable pain in the backside?'

'All the time.'

'Does it make a difference?'

He fluttered his eyelashes at her. 'What do you think?'

'That you make me crazy.' She threw her hands in the air in an exasperated gesture that was more Italian than

English. He liked it. She made him laugh. She turned him on. Plain and simple.

None of this was simple, he was realising. 'I think you were crazy long before you met me.'

'You, Matteo, are everything I hate about men. You're bossy and…well, bossy. And, well, let's just say you annoy me. A lot.'

So funny, because she was very definitely not annoyed right now. She was hot and sweet and looking like she needed kissing again. He caught her chin between his thumb and forefinger and pulled her to look at him. 'Aha. But still you kissed me. And not just once.'

'I was trying you out. Sizing you up.' This close to that pouting mouth he was very tempted to do it again.

'And what?'

'And nothing. Absolutely nothing.' She flapped a hand at his chest and it struck ever so lightly against his skin. He caught her wrist and she turned full into him, so close he caught her scent mingling with the smell of her shampoo. Saw the dark green of her eyes, the honeyed flecks, all golden and melting. God, she was breathtaking. He wanted to kiss her. To have her, right now, here on the kitchen table. Wanted to be inside her. He wanted her with a passion he'd never had for anyone, ever.

A little dalliance would be fun, but then what? At what cost to both of them? Neither wanted…*anything* from anyone else. They were two islands of independence with a large ocean of complication between them.

So he tried to make it playful, dropped her hand, gave her a smile. 'Okay, so take me out for breakfast. And I want to see the Minster that everyone's so keen on showing me.'

She stepped back and held her wrist—not in pain, no, he hadn't hurt her—but she just held it close to her chest. Her voice was sultry and shaky, as if she'd just had the best sex of her life—or wanted to. 'Yes. Good idea, let's go outside. First, phone about Joey?'

Matteo looked down at his running gear. 'No. First a shower. I need to get out of these things.'

'A shower. Okay. Shower…water…over your body…' Her gaze scanned his face slowly from his eyes to his mouth, where it lingered. The memories of those kisses hovered in the silence. Heat rose within him. Need curled through the kitchen, thick and heavy and tangible.

He took a step back. 'I'll go now.'

'Yes. Do.'

This thing was getting more intense, like a flame that had suddenly erupted into life and was consuming everything in its path, blazing a trail between them. He needed to get away from her before he did something stupid. Like kiss her again. If he didn't douse himself in cold water he wouldn't be able to function around her.

'Wait!' She walked towards him, the cardigan slipping from her shoulders and falling to the floor. Without a word she walked up the stairs and he followed her, hungry to see what she was doing. Was she going to…? Did she want…? A shower? With him? Was this the beginning?

His heart began a strange thumping against his ribcage and for the first time in his life he felt less than sure of his next move.

She stopped short at a door, turned to look at him and gave him a smile, eyebrows cocked. Then she dragged the door open, reached in and pulled out… 'Towels, Matteo. I forgot to give them to you last night.'

Mio Dio. He'd thought he was going to have a heart attack. And now she was so close to him he wanted to touch her. To run his fingers through her hair. To feel that soft skin against his. He was hot and hard for her. Every part of him strained for her.

Holding the towels at hip level, he cursed the flimsy running shorts. 'Thanks. I'll go. Now…'

'Just so you know, the shower's a bit temperamental. Turn the cold water on first then adjust the hot to suit you. That is…' Glancing towards his nether regions, she gave him a wry but cheeky smile that was so not the buttoned-up Ivy he knew—but was a whole lot more of the Ivy he wanted to get to know. 'If you want hot at all.'

The cardiac care ward was locked. Ivy pressed the intercom button and waited. And waited some more. Inside she could see a blur of people running along the corridor. *Running.* To the blare of a siren. *Crap.* Her hand hit her mouth as her heart developed a fast, jerky rhythm. 'What's happening? What is it?'

She knew what it was.

Matteo's hand slipped into hers. 'It's an emergency. Crash call, I imagine. It's okay, Ivy. They're all experts.'

'Do you think…?' *It's my mum?* She couldn't get the words out. Pain crushed her chest as she held her breath.

'Try not to think at all.' With a gentle smile that shone through his eyes he cradled her head against his chest and she inhaled his now familiar scent, which steadied her nerves. He was solid and strong and she felt safe with him. Apart from the fact that there was an emergency in there. And she was out here. That pain intensified. 'Put your arms around me,' he said softly.

'No.' She didn't know whether she'd be able to let go. Whether holding on tight was giving him the wrong message. So, digging deep inside herself, she steadied her reactions. She'd managed this far in her life without needing anyone else. She could manage some more.

He shook his head and took her hand. 'Don't think about it, just do it. Hold on.'

'Oh.' Her defences worn down, her grip on her mum's bag lessened. The bag dropped to the floor. Ivy did as she was told, wriggling her arms round his waist, feeling the breadth of him, his warmth. 'I'm scared.'

'I know.' He didn't give her any pithy pep talks about how fine she would be, how everything would be okay, he just held her. And for that she was grateful. She just took strength from him. Leaning against him, she felt the regular beat of his heart, the unrushed intake of breath. The safety net that she knew would be willing to hold her up if she needed it.

And she wondered what it would be like to be part of something. To be a half of a whole. If that could even happen. All that *you complete me* stuff wasn't real, was it? It was something her mum had been looking for her whole life, and had never found. All those wasted years of chasing a ghost.

No, maybe it wasn't real. But it felt damned nice to be held like this in her worst moments. She'd never had that—not from anyone. Someone to be with her and focus just on her. Someone who seemed to know what she needed without her having to tell them, without her having to strive for their attention.

Eventually the alarm stopped. The rushing slowed and after a few minutes a smiling doctor came to the door. 'Oh, were you waiting? So sorry. Come on in.'

An air of calm pervaded the place. It was as if the running hadn't happened. Or as if the doctor took everything in his stride. Like Matteo. So Ivy tried to stop herself from running too. 'If something bad had happened they'd have stopped me from coming in, right? Surely? They'd take me to one side?'

Matteo nodded. 'Of course. You think too much, like you expect something bad to happen.'

'Well, I just want to be prepared if it does.' Her mum was standing, in an old faded hospital nightie and dressing gown, at the side of her bed, smiling and chatting to a man about her age. Ivy almost ran to her in relief. 'Hey, Mum. Thank God. You look a lot better today, up and about even.'

Her mum's face brightened as she gave a hesitant smile. 'Oh, yes, well, you always look better when they get rid of some of the tubes. This is Richard. He's visiting my neighbour in bed eight. Funnily enough, he lives on West Mews, just round the corner from us.'

From you. Ivy didn't live there any more. It wasn't home. Hadn't ever been, really. And what now? Her mum chatting someone up already—she really was getting back to normal. 'Hi, Richard. Mum, what was going on before? That alarm? All those doctors rushing around? That wasn't… that wasn't for you?'

'Oh, that. It was someone in the first bay. Poor chap. I'll be happy when they move me off here.'

So will I.

'Hello, Mrs Leigh.' Matteo stepped forward and Ivy realised she was still holding his hand and that her mum was looking at her strangely.

Her mum's eyebrows rose. 'Montgomery. Actually, it's Dr Montgomery. But that's okay, you can call me Angela. Everyone does. Has Ivy shown you around the town?'

'Yes. And he was impressed with the Minster, but it's not as beautiful as Siena Duomo, apparently. As if. It's a darned sight older. Or at least the foundations are.' Ivy felt the smile in her voice. She just couldn't help it. Cathedral wars, really? Seemed they had to differ on most things, or rather they both had opinions they liked to air. But it was a good challenge. Kept her on her toes. 'The man's a philistine.'

'I said it was impressive. It is,' he clarified. 'I liked

it, truly. It just doesn't have the romance of the Duomo's structure.'

Angela gave him an interested smile, her lips twitching. 'You're right, there. I did love all that marble.' Then she turned back to Ivy. 'Did you bring my things? I need to freshen up.'

'Sure.' Ivy proffered the bag while taking in the plethora of tubes attached to her mum. 'Do you need any help?'

'Okay. Yes.' Angela's eyes flitted between Ivy and Matteo, and Ivy sensed a mother-daughter talk or something was brewing. Which would be novel. 'Actually, that would be great.'

As her mum hobbled off towards the bathroom, IV stand in tow, Matteo squeezed Ivy's hand and she realised she didn't want to let it go. It was nice to have someone on her side. Which was a whole crock of crazy considering that a couple of weeks ago they'd been at loggerheads. But he gave her a gentle push. 'Off you go. Start now.'

'Start what?'

'Fixing things.'

'What if she doesn't want to?'

He rolled his eyes. 'Would you ever want to look back and regret that you didn't give it a go? Just be honest.'

'She might not want to hear it.'

'How else can you work things through, without honesty?'

'Okay. I s'pose.' He was right. He was often right, goddamn him. Not always...but enough to annoy her just a little bit more. She hid her smile.

As she followed her mum towards the ladies' bathroom she felt his gaze on her back, realising that for the first time in years she hadn't been conscious of her limp—that she was rarely self-conscious when she was with him.

Sensing him still watching her, she injected her gait

with a jaunty swing of her bottom. It felt good. Mischievous, and out of character. Or maybe she had a part of her that she'd repressed? Maybe there was a part of her psyche that did want the trappings, the sex, the man? A part that she'd chosen to deny?

Wow. That was an eye-opening thought. But not one she was going to pay any more attention to. She hadn't come this far in her life to give it all up for a life of compromise and dependency.

As if to remind her of that, her mum's bag handle dug into her palm. Ivy tried to ignore those feelings of regret and…well, fear. Fear of feeling things. Of hurting. Of being let down. Of rejection all over again. She'd spent a good deal of her life closing herself off to people. But if Matteo was right, she needed to stop being scared. At least where her mum was concerned.

Let her in.

Let her in.

Let her in.

And she wanted to. She did. She wanted a chance.

'How do I look?' Angela was looking in the mirror and patting her hair, which was matted and flattened at the back. In truth, she looked tired and washed out and old. Blue-red bruises bloomed on her papery skin and her eyes were clouded.

'Like I said, you look great, all things considered, and getting better every day. You've just had a life-saving operation, you're not meant to look like something out of a magazine.' Lifting her mum's arm, threading the IV bag up through her nightgown sleeve and then hanging the fluid bag on the stand, Ivy gave her a smile. 'I was so worried about you.'

'Don't be. I'm fine. Listen, Ivy, I need to talk to you.'

Ivy spoke to her mum's reflection in the mirror. 'Mum, you're healing, you have to take it easy.'

'There's something I need to say.'

'Save it for another time.' Matteo's big honest kick could wait until her mum was feeling better. 'This isn't the time or the place. You're not well.'

'But I need to talk about this.' Angela nodded, still breathless, still pale, but clearly trying to act normal. Whatever that was. 'I know I haven't been easy to live with, Ivy. Things have been hard over the years. Depression has clouded so much, it was so disabling at times. But this scare has made me take stock of things. I want to put things right.'

'Depression?' Ivy had considered that over the years, but her mum had always seemed so content with a man and so unhappy without one that Ivy had thought her mum's moods had been linked entirely with her relationship status at the time. Guilt shook through her again, but sadness too. 'I didn't realise. I should have, but I didn't.'

'You were too busy just being a girl, Ivy. I didn't want to bother you with my problems. But I suspect you lived them anyway?'

Her childhood had been no fairy-tale. She hadn't exactly been shielded from the dramas, especially when her step-family had been ripped away from her. She'd lost her normal, and had been plunged into her mum's darkest moments, borne the brunt of her insecurities.

Even though this conversation was the last thing Ivy wanted, she nodded. If Angela felt up to saying this—and she really did seem to want to talk—then Ivy needed to let her say it.

Angela looked genuinely sorry. 'I'm sorry. I wasn't very good at all that. I know you got caught in the cross-fire and I leaned on you a lot at times. But I was grateful to have you.'

It never felt like it.

Hurt surged through her. This truth gig wasn't pleasant. In fact, it was downright painful. Ivy didn't want to relive everything that had happened, she just wanted things to be different going forward. Why drag over the old pain? Why not just try to fix things from now? 'I'm sure you did your best.'

'I don't know… Now that I look back, I can see so many mistakes.' Holding onto the sink rim, Angela looked down at her thin hands, then back at Ivy. 'I don't know if we can make things better. Just a little? I don't know…'

'Me neither.' Was it too late for them? Ivy didn't know. What she did know was that she didn't want her mother to die—that had to mean something. Stepping forward, she stroked a hand on Angela's shoulder. 'We could try.' Whatever that meant. There was no blueprint for the next steps they were going to take. Did her mum really mean it? Or would she revert to her old ways once she'd regained some strength?

It was a risk Ivy was willing to take. She pushed away the dark cloud hovering at the back of her mind. Things would be better now. Surely?

Her mum's smile was a little wobbly. 'Yes, I think we should try, Ivy. I'd like to. I'm so glad you're here to stay for a while, we can do some nice mother-daughter things together.'

But, despite wanting to fix everything, Ivy's heart lurched. And, yes, she knew it was terribly self-absorbed to be thinking of herself, but if she stayed too long in York and lost her job then everything she'd worked for would be gone. She'd have no security.

And no seeing Matteo.

That thought bothered her more than she'd thought it would. Over the last couple of days he'd become more than a colleague. Despite his annoying ways. Despite every barrier she'd put up.

But, on the other hand, how could she leave her mum?

Would this time to heal be any different from the rest?

It was the first time they'd ever been so open with each other, that they'd acknowledged out loud that there had been problems. It felt scary. Strange, kind of wobbly, but hopeful. Angela looped her arm into Ivy's as they made their way slowly out of the bathroom, dragging the IV stand with them. 'Your man seems nice.'

'He's not my man.' Ivy lowered her voice—even though he was metres away. Healing the rift with her mother was one thing, but she hadn't envisaged diving straight into confidences about her personal life. 'He's just a friend.'

Angela threw her a sideways look. 'Yes, I hold hands with my male friends too. All the time. And the way you look at him—that's not the way a friend looks at another friend.'

'Oh, no. Really? *Eurgh.* Really?' Was it obvious to everyone? Somewhere along the line he'd wriggled his way under her skin. She cared for him. A fierce panic gripped her chest. 'Great. Brilliant. It's so not the right thing to do.'

Her mum looked at her as if she'd gone mad. 'Calm down. It's not a crime to have a bit of fun.'

'That's just it, Mum. I haven't really done this before and I don't know what to do.' Was she really asking relationship advice from the serial divorcee? Apparently so. 'I don't want anything from him, I don't want a relationship. I just want to do my job and to be left in peace.'

But I do want him. That's the damned problem.

'Hey, don't overthink it like I do—that's the kiss of death to any relationship. Just enjoy it. That's what I'm going to do with Richard, anyway.'

'Richard? Really? You've only just met him.' Ivy came

to a halt so the men couldn't hear her. What was her mum saying? She was unbelievable. She hadn't changed a bit, she was the same old lady saying the same old things, doing the same old routine. She'd spent the best part of her working life as a doctor fixing people, but in the end the only person she'd failed to fix was herself.

She's fragile, Ivy reminded herself. She's had a scare and is reaching out for comfort.

Or was she just up to her old tricks again? Her mum needed people around her, she couldn't function on her own, and regardless of anything Ivy did or said, she couldn't change that. Happiness was fleeting, she'd learnt. And if Richard made Angela happy, even for a short while, who was she to interfere?

But she needed to say how she felt, just to know that she'd tried to protect her mum from yet another relationship disaster. 'You're in hospital. You had a heart scare. A serious medical problem. You can't start flirting with someone's visitor.'

'Ah, there you go again, overthinking. To tell you the truth, Ivy, I'm lonely, I need a little companionship. It's not as if you're living next door, popping round for sugar every other day. You're miles away and I never get to see you.' Angela gave Ivy's hand a pat. 'And that's you through and through, always so independent, doing your own thing, forging your way in the world. You never accepted any help from being about four years old. I have no idea where you got that from.'

Necessity. 'My dream job is in London, Mum, I have to go where the work is. I'm sorry I can't be here all the time, but that doesn't mean you have to jump into a...friendship...with the first person you meet. You need to be careful. Remember what happened with the others...' The tears, the drama.

'Of course I'll be careful, dear. But I need to do what I need to do, too. I just want some company. It's not a lot to ask for after everything I've been through. Really, darling, I know we've never done the heart-to-heart thing, but when you're ready I can listen. Mind you, don't ask my advice. I'm useless with men.'

'Oh?' Ivy threw her a smile. There was only so much she could say or do to stop her mum following her well-trodden path. Angela seemed undeterred. 'I hadn't noticed.'

When they arrived back at the bed Matteo and Richard were discussing something to do with an article in an open newspaper on the table. Matteo looked up as she arrived, helped her settle her mum back in bed, all concern and interest and polite nodding.

He'd been so nice Ivy wanted to give something back, even if it meant sacrificing something for herself. Drawing him to one side, she whispered, 'Matteo, I know you're probably thinking about heading off back to London soon, but I wondered—when we've done here, could we go to the pub? Watch the game on TV? What do you think?'

Those dark stubborn eyes glinted. 'I was going to listen to it on the sports radio on the drive back.'

'Oh. Well, that's okay, then.' Disappointment rattled through her. She had an insane desire to spend just a few more minutes with him. 'I feel as if the last two days have been all about me. You've sacrificed your days off to be here, I just thought it would be a way of saying thank you. It's not… I don't want you to get the wrong impression. It's just a pub, maybe some food. The game. I'm not offering any more than that.'

Was it her imagination, or did he look just a little relieved? 'Well, I would prefer to watch it than listen to it. But what about your work? I thought you had too much to do already?'

She shrugged. 'So maybe I can take a little time off? Just a couple of hours.'

His eyebrows rose in surprise. 'Whoa. Watch out, Ivy Leigh, you might get into the habit of relaxing. Then what would happen?'

Staring into his eyes, his heated gaze focused on her, she felt relaxed and excited and scared and comfortable all at the same time. This man was too easy to fall for and she was tumbling deeper and deeper. But she could handle it. She'd laid out the parameters. 'I can't imagine, Matteo. I just can't imagine.'

CHAPTER NINE

'COME ON, ENGLAND! Yes! Yes! Yes! Go!'

So this was the unleashed version of Ivy Leigh? Matteo laughed as she stood, eyes glued to the huge wall-hung TV in the sports pub, body tensed and fists punching the air. 'God,' he groaned into his pint. 'This is terrible. Less than an hour ago you did not know a thing about rugby. Now look at you—England's most fervent fan.'

High-fiving the two open-mouthed English supporters at the next table, she beamed. 'This is fun. We're beating you, Matteo, that's all that matters.'

'There's time yet.' He shrugged, far more entertained by her reactions than the game.

'You think? In the history of the Six Nations championship there have been over twenty games between England and Italy, and England have won them all. Your chances are zero, Mr Hero.'

'Twenty games—how the hell…? Since when did you know that?'

'The wonders of the internet. You just have to know where to look.' She winked at him. 'I did my research. You didn't think I'd invite you to watch a game we had the remotest chance of losing, did you?' On-field action caught her attention again, she paused, breathing heavily as her eyes glued themselves to the game. 'Come on, mate. Pass it. Yes. Yes!'

Thank God for half-time. She sat down, all flushed and hot-cheeked, her chest heaving with excitement. 'This is brilliant. Why did no one ever tell me that watching sport was such fun?'

He drained his glass and put it back on the table. The fun was in watching her watching the game. 'It is when you're winning. And I have to say you are very entertaining.'

She patted his arm condescendingly. 'Poor pet, you're a very sore loser. But still glad you came?'

'To watch you beat us? No.' *Yes.* But he was confused as all hell now. He should have gone when he'd had a chance, instead of being drawn in by those large green eyes sparkling so coyly at him, offering *no more* than a game of rugby. And despite every brain cell screaming at him to climb into the car and head down the motorway, he'd grabbed the chance for a couple more hours with her, like a starving man thrown paltry crumbs.

Her tongue darted out to moisten her lips and he was mesmerised by the action, every part of him wanting to taste her. She gave him a smile. 'I mean, are you glad you came to York? I know it wasn't exactly for your benefit but I hope it hasn't been too bad.'

'What? Spending my non-hospital hours in a hospital, not sleeping with a ginger cat that purrs like a drill? Sure, it has been the best weekend ever.' He felt a laugh rumbling from his throat. Being here with her, on the other hand… 'And now we are losing. It is getting better all the time.'

'I hope it does, for your sake. Although I'm not sure I want to give up that win—so you'll have to find something else to make you smile.'

He let that thought hover for a while, not wanting to admit the way he was feeling so conflicted about how much she made him smile. 'It's too late, Ivy. The weekend is doomed.'

'Oh, poor sweetheart. Things can only get better. So, tell me, when did you come to live in England, and why?'

He did a quick mental calculation. 'It was about six years ago. I wanted to work with Dave Marshall, he has such a great international reputation—the very best and cutting-edge work in our field—so when we met at a conference in Milan and he invited me to join his team, I jumped at the chance. I haven't looked back.'

'And you already spoke English? I'm impressed.'

'I was pretty rusty. We had learnt it at school from a young age, but even so I was pretty terrible when I first got here. It has been a steep learning curve.'

'I'll bet. Where did you train to be a doctor?'

So she wanted his life history, which was fine by him. He could give her a short version and veer away from anything that might make her ask deeper questions. 'In Florence. Then I went to Milan to specialise, they have a great renal unit there.'

She took another drink of wine. 'You said you don't go home. Why not?'

Straight to the point. Now he wished he hadn't encouraged her to be like this. 'I see you have taken notice of your lawyer training, you have...how do you say it? Cut to the chase. You can do it to me but not for yourself.'

'That, my boy, is called self-preservation.' She twiddled with the stem of the glass then focused her gaze at him again, which made him hot under the collar. 'Now answer my question. Why don't you go home?'

'I'm too busy. Work takes up my time. And there's not a lot there for me.'

'What, a whole load of siblings and parents? That's a lot of reasons to go home.'

Not enough. 'Some of them come here. I see them. Liliana, my little sister with the renal problems, lived with me for a year in London. You can imagine how much fun that was. She is years younger and about five times the trouble of all the others put together.'

'But you love her, I can tell.' Ivy smiled again. It was sweet and soft and real and for a moment he wanted to do nothing but stare at that mouth.

'Of course I love her.' And now he had time to think about it, he did miss the closeness they'd all had, growing up. But betrayal had blown a hole into that that could never be healed. He'd purposely left them all to their lives and chosen disconnectedness. That way he would remain intact, heart and soul. To go home would be to have a constant reminder of what had happened.

But, of course, Ivy did not need to know any of this. Why go deep when this was not that sort of relationship?

This was a weekend for her to be with her family, not for him to get intense about his. Or intense about anything, for that matter, or to lose himself at the whim of emotions that he knew never lasted.

Ivy ran a hand across her blonde hair and fluffed it up nonchalantly. She didn't seem to care that it stuck up in tufts. She had stopped hiding her limp. She was cheering like a madwoman. He was seeing a very different Ivy from the one at work. She was letting her guard down; was that a good sign, or a dangerous one? He had a bad feeling it was the latter. And all he knew was that she was in his head and he couldn't get her out of it.

'Don't you miss it all, though, Matteo? Your family. The sunshine. Decent food. Blue sky. All that wine. Amazing architecture. Art…? Nah, there's nothing there at all for you, is there? God, I'd love to live in Italy.'

'You have a very touristy image of my home.' Which

was indeed all the things she'd mentioned but with a large dose of reality. And feuding families. And hurt. 'But now you come to mention it, I guess it does have a few things going for it. Decent coffee, for a start. Although you do have some pretty amazing architecture here too. The Minster is stunning, with its stained glass, and the intricate carving and the history.'

'Yeah, right. Just not marble enough?' After she'd signalled to a glass collector and given a repeat order for beer and wine she turned back to him. 'What do your parents do?'

He shrugged. 'So clichéd. A small taverna. My mum's the…I suppose you'd call it the maitre d'. She makes it work, ruling with a fist of iron. My dad is the chef. We all did our time there, growing up, in the kitchen, waiting tables.'

She eyed him suspiciously, eyes narrowing. 'What's the problem with your dad?'

'What do you mean?' But he was aware that he had become tense and tried to loosen his shoulders.

'Your voice changed, you paused. Your eyes narrowed. Your shoulders are trying to break for freedom. You're not the only one who can ace elementary psychology. You have father issues.'

No, he'd solved them years ago and never looked back. 'He's not worth wasting your time over. None of it is. Live in the now, Ivy. Oh, look, the game's beginning again.'

Her eyes flicked to the TV screen and back to him again. 'Sod the game.'

Forcing a smile he shook his head. 'Ivy, Ivy, you are too…what is the word?…fickle. I thought you were the world's biggest rugby convert?'

'Not when there are more interesting things to talk about.'

Thankfully the waiter brought their drinks, buying Matteo some time. He took a long drink and tried to watch the game. But he'd underestimated her. She nudged him. 'Your dad?'

'Trust me, my past is not interesting.'

'It is to me.'

That was an admission. Her eyes clashed with his and he saw the moment she also realised the enormity of what she had just said.

What the hell was happening here he didn't know. Because he was as shocked as she was. Right when part of him was keeping that door slammed closed there was a part of him that wanted to talk. That wanted out-and-out openness. It wasn't that he had made a solemn vow never to talk about it, he just hadn't ever wanted to expose so much of his damaged past.

This was neither the right time nor the right place. 'You need to focus on yourself. On healing things with your mum, on how you're going to do your job next week. And the fact we just scored a try while you weren't paying attention. Now we are drawing. England are on the run.'

She looked at him for a long time. Long enough for Italy to miss the conversion. For them to stay just behind their opponents.

Nothing was said. She didn't push. She didn't nag him, she let him off. Which was the sweetest thing she could do right then, when he didn't want his past interfering with this moment. It seemed she knew when to ask, when to stop. She knew every damned button he had and pressed them all. Too much.

Something shifted in his chest, something momentous. Something real. Something he hadn't been looking for and didn't know if he wanted. In fact, something that scared the hell out of him because he'd felt similar things before and it had ended horribly. He didn't want anything close to that happening again. He needed to get away from here. From her.

He sat back in his seat, putting distance between himself and the woman who he knew was taking up more of his heart and his head than she should. But Ivy didn't seem to notice, fixed her eyes on the game.

She wasn't quiet for long.

'Come on, boys. Come on. That's it. Pass it out. To the left. Yes! *Yes!* We won! You beauty!' She jumped up, turned, squeezed his cheeks between her thumb and forefinger and kissed him on the lips, hard and fast. And another. 'Beat that, Matteo.'

For a second he stilled. He didn't want to touch her.

Could not. Would not.

Who was he kidding? No matter what he thought, his body was hell-bent on betraying him at every turn. He wanted her.

It was a normal, natural attraction. It didn't have to mean more than that. It didn't have to be dangerous. He was worrying over nothing. He'd had sex many times with many women and he'd made sure he'd got out with his heart unscathed. He could do that with Ivy, couldn't he?

He was through thinking about it, he was getting as bad as she was.

'Oh, no, you don't get away that easily.' Yanking her towards him amongst the cheering supporters who had all left their seats, he gripped her waist. Planted another kiss on her lips. Then another. My God, she tasted divine. Heat shimmied through him, heat and need. Hot and hungry.

She wrapped her arms around his neck and deepened the kiss with equal hunger. Her body pressed against his, curling into him. When she wriggled her hips against his erection he felt her sigh. With a dirty smile she pulled away but kept a grip on his arm, her words forced out. 'Sod the game. Sod everything. Matteo, do you have to go home tonight?'

'Typical northern weather.' For an early evening the sky was dark. Heavy clouds loomed overhead, threatening a downpour. Ivy's hands were shaking as she stepped out into the thick raindrops that began to fall. This was so out of her comfort zone. She didn't do this. She didn't straight up ask a man to come back to her place. She didn't have wanton sex. She never made a move, first or otherwise. Her heart jittered as she quickened her pace, more out of a desire not to lose her nerve than anything else. 'Come on, we'll have to hurry or we'll get soaked.'

Matteo was uncharacteristically quiet as they headed down the river path to her mum's house. Slipping his hand into hers, he pulled her against him. Rain fell in relentless waves feeding the swollen river, water dripping in gullies between their layers of clothes.

'Ivy.' His eyes were dark and intense and misted. And she knew from one look that he wanted her, wanted this as much as she did. There was a promise between them, silent and yet overt. Dangerous. Dark. So very sexy. One step over an invisible line. Her tummy danced and curled and tightened as the sexy look in his eyes seemed to reach into her gut and tease.

He ran his thumb down her cheek, traced a path over her bottom lip.

She bit down.

His eyes grew darker, hotter. His body tensed. '*Mi fai impazzire*.'

She groaned. 'What are you saying? Please, tell me that means come to bed.'

'Almost. It means you make me crazy.'

'It could mean *two tickets to Leeds, please,* and I swear I wouldn't care, I just love how you sound. Say more…'

'*Sei cosa bella. Due biglietti per Leeds, per favore.*'

'Yes. Yes. Anything you want.' Without thinking further than this moment, she pulled him towards her, fixed her mouth on his and tasted him again. Maybe it was the wine that had relaxed her reserve but she felt tipsy with desire, filled with a need that seemed to become more intense, more breathtaking every time she looked at him.

As she heard a moan coming from her throat she was shocked by the spiralling need at her core. She wanted this man. So much. Too much. Her hands circled his waist, palm flattening against that famous backside. With a sudden rush of excitement she pressed herself against him. She wanted to feel every inch of him against her. Naked. Wet.

She began to explore the taut ridges of his back, hands running over wet linen that stuck to a body she'd dreamt about, that she'd seen butt naked on a screen. Until now out of reach, but still stalking her thoughts. Now it was real. It was real and she wasn't going to think too deeply about it. She was going to do what her mother said…she was going to enjoy it. She was going to not overthink it.

Her mother…good God. Ivy felt her body shut down.

No way in hell.

Her heart pounding fast and hard, Ivy turned away from him, away from the path, and strode towards the road. It was slippery and cold and she tried to concentrate on putting her weight onto her right foot but her head was filled with Matteo and his kisses and the wrongness and the rightness. And she was so torn and muddled. The only thing she knew with any clarity was that she wanted to kiss him. To hold him. And that, for so many reasons, seemed the worst course of action.

'Ivy?' His voice was behind her.

'I'm sorry, Matteo. I just need to go home.' She knew she was being a jerk. But she couldn't do this. Not with him. Not if it meant she was following in her mother's footsteps. She had to take some time out to think about what the hell she was doing at all. If she was going to do anything, she'd do it on her own terms.

'Wait. Ivy. Stop! Sto—!'

She kept her head down and eyes fixed forward.

'Ivy!'

It was fear, not anger she could hear in his voice. Fear? What the—? 'What's wrong?'

As she turned she felt a thump against her body, and at the same time she heard a screech and a scream. Then pain seared through her leg. Someone flew across her path. A whirr of wheels filled the air and a crash. A bicycle? A man on a bicycle?

Off now. On the ground. Shouting at her. Her leg hurt.

Blood was starting to drip from his knee. His face was scrunched up. There was blood. Uh-oh. What did she have to do? Breathe? Tense? Relax? She couldn't remember.

Breathe.

Matteo? Where was Matteo?

Strong, warm arms circled her, lifting her off the road as her knees buckled and her vision began to swim.

'Ivy. What the hell? Are you crazy?' Matteo was sitting her down on the kerbside, his hands on her leg, on her foot, ripping her shoe off. She didn't have the energy to stop him. 'Are you okay? Ivy?'

She swallowed the pain and didn't look at the man with the bike. It was her fault.

All her fault. She'd spent her whole life being cautious and this one time…this was her fault. She should have been more careful. Right from the get-go. Right from the second she'd downloaded that picture. She should have been more careful.

She did a mental body scan. Her leg hurt, more than usual, but she wasn't badly injured. 'Yes. Yes, I'm fine. You'd better go and see the man. I didn't see him. He came out of nowhere. He wasn't there and then he was.'

'He didn't have any lights on. In this weather.' Matteo glanced towards the guy on the ground. The whirring of the wheels were slower now. The man groaned. 'Please. Help me.'

Within an instant Matteo was gone from her side, giving her time to take stock. Every time she let herself go just a little, something happened to remind her of the folly of her actions.

'Ivy.' Matteo's voice was the one he used in the operating theatre. 'Ivy. I need you to focus.'

'Y-yes?'

'Call an ambulance. *Now.* Then come here and give me help.'

'Okay.' As rain teemed down and soaked through to her skin she did as she was asked, telling the ambulance receiver their location. Her hands wouldn't stop shaking and her body felt as if it had gone into shock. She tried to take a few breaths to steady herself, her voice, mirroring Matteo's demeanour when in medical scenarios. She would not think about the blood dripping from the man's head. 'What is the injury?' she called over to Matteo. 'Head injury? Broken arm?'

His voice was too casual as he undid his trouser belt and fashioned a sling around the man's wrist and neck. 'Tell them it looks like a…' He slowed down his speaking so she could understand and repeat his words. 'A displaced clavicle fracture. A bump to his head, a laceration. No loss of consciousness. Tell them it would be really great if they got here pretty soon.' Then he turned to the man. 'Okay, mate. Sit up and take a few deep breaths. The ambulance will be here soon. You'll be fine.'

'It hurts like hell,' the man groaned, as he sat on the opposite kerb to Ivy, Matteo's hands guiding him into place but supporting the elbow and taking it very slowly so as not to jolt his collarbone.

Ivy limped across the road, her left foot bruised and becoming more sore as she put weight on it. The man's collarbone looked misshapen at its mid-point. But it wasn't sticking out, as she'd assumed it might. It looked as if it had buckled in on itself. 'I'm so sorry.'

'Yeah. You should…watch where…you're going.' Their patient heaved out between breaths. 'But I should have… had lights on…I know. I know…'

'Save your energy, both of you.' Matteo interceded. 'What is done is done. We now have to get this fixed. And quickly.'

Something about his tone had Ivy looking over at Matteo. His eyes were darkened and his jaw taut. There was something more here that she didn't understand. But he clearly couldn't discuss it in front of…

'What's your name?' she asked, trying to keep the conversation light, and to keep the man focused on something other than his injury. He grimaced, his eyes fluttering closed as he spoke. 'Pete. Pete O'Donnell.'

'Well, Pete.' She smiled at him, digging as deep as she could into her failing reserves. 'I don't suppose you caught the rugby game today?'

He shook his head. 'No. I was…going home…to watch… it. Win? Or lose?'

'A great seventeen-fifteen win.'

Matteo gave a hollow laugh. 'Depends who you support.'

'He's Italian,' she explained, hoping to keep Pete interested enough to forget a little of his pain and shock. 'And not particularly happy. But, really, they played well. It was touch and go at one point.'

In the distance a siren blared shrill and welcome. It came closer and closer and louder and louder and Ivy could see Pete starting to become agitated. Mixed with her relief was a little bit of panic. 'If you can just hang on a bit longer, they'll have something to help with the pain.'

Pete tried to push her away with his elbow. 'I think I'm going to be sick.'

'Okay.' She rubbed her palm gently up and down his back. 'It's shock setting in. Take some deep breaths. In. That's it…' She watched as he followed her lead. 'Great. Now out. In again…'

Within seconds the paramedics were out of the ambulance and giving him some gas and air to help with the pain. Within minutes they'd stabilised his injury, stemmed the bleeding from his grazed head and loaded him into the ambulance. Within half an hour she was alone again with Matteo, facing the real reason this whole sorry scenario had played out. She'd wanted to kiss him so badly it had frightened her.

Her heart hammered. 'God, that was awful.' Now her hands began to shake again as the images of broken bones and blood flitted back into her brain. 'I wish I'd seen him.'

'It is dark and raining and he had no lights. How can he expect to ride on a cobbled street in those conditions and not get hurt? But…' Matteo took her arm and prised her gently from her seated position to standing. 'He's gone and is going to be fine. But you? Not so much? Tell me what the hell was going on.'

'I was in a hurry to get back.'

'Yes? But because you wanted to get away from me.' His hands clenched and he shook his head. 'One minute you were willing, the next you were running away. I don't understand.'

'Mixed messages. I'm so sorry. That wasn't my intention. I just got a little spooked.'

He shook his head. 'You should have told me what you were feeling. Talked to me, Ivy. Not run out into the road. Especially with your leg being so damaged. It could have been serious for you too.'

'I did not run. I was walking. And I looked before I crossed.' She took his arm and tried not to wince as they turned the corner towards her mum's place. 'I don't care about my leg and neither should you.'

'I don't care about your leg. No, I do care. I mean I don't care about how it looks. But now it hurts and I don't want to see you in pain because of me.' He stopped and took her by the shoulders to face him. 'What is the matter?'

How honest could she be with him without making herself vulnerable? 'I don't know. I panicked, suddenly. I didn't know what I was doing.'

'You were kissing me. And it was good. And now you're shivering and we're both soaked and a man has a potentially life-threatening injury.' His thumb ran across her cheek, and his eyes were concerned as he gazed at her. He wasn't cross, as she'd thought he might be.

Even so, her stomach felt as if it had dropped to her toes. 'Was it really bad? I thought you were worried, I could tell by your voice. But you stayed so calm.'

'And you managed to distract him while I stemmed the bleeding and stabilised the break. We were a great team. And you didn't flinch at the blood—too much. A major step forward.' His eyebrows rose and did she see just a little pride there simmering in his pupils? 'His collarbone broke inwards—it could have punctured a blood vessel or his sternum. He may have—we don't know. But it was an emergency in any case.'

'Thank God you were there. I feel so bad.' She bit her lip as she thought. How honest should she be? It felt as if the inside of her head was about to explode. How she wanted to be free and open and honest with him, to relax into something good. To tell him all her thoughts and feelings, to lay herself bare metaphorically. Because that was when true and mutual trust happened, she imagined. But she was conflicted, fighting, knowing that by opening her heart she would be gifting him a part of herself—and she didn't know if she could do that. If she dared. Because what else would she be tempted to give him? What else would he take from her? But he did deserve some kind of coherent explanation. 'I was thinking about my mum.'

Confusion flared, mixed with a little humour. 'That is not a good sign. You were thinking about other things when you were kissing me. Is my kissing that bad?'

'No, your kissing is wonderful. But I was thinking about how she does things and how I don't want to end up like her. She's so dependent. So needy. I don't want to be like that.' *I don't want to lose myself.*

He peeled his jacket off and hooked it over her shoulders, rubbing his hands up and down her arms. 'And you aren't. You could never be like her. You shouldn't have been thinking about anything except the kiss. You want to try again?'

Yes! At just seeing the look in his eyes, feeling his heat, despite the cold and the rain, she knew without a shadow of a doubt that most of her wanted to do it again. This was so unfair. She was holding onto a very fragile line of sensibility here. Torn between her heart and her head. Between doing the right thing and doing the very wrong one. Although she knew which one would be the most fun. 'I don't know.'

'You need convincing? You are a woman and I am a man and there are things we could do that will make us feel amazing.' Scudding his fingers through his chestnut-coloured hair, he shook his head. '*Mio Dio*, this is the hardest I have ever had to work to get a woman to kiss me. Ever.'

A surge of pride swelled in her chest now. 'Good.'

'Good? How can it be good if we are losing valuable time? We could have been kissing for the last hour. Instead, you want to dissect everything into tiny pieces. It is like you're at a trial and everything's under examination. You want to pick. Pick. Pick.' His fingers tickled her ribs with every pointed word.

Squirming away from him, she giggled. This was supposed to be serious, and he was making her laugh? 'I don't want to pick. I'm just being careful. I'm—' *I'm a coward.*

'Stop talking. You and your words drive me insane. Sometimes you just have to go with your gut feeling. Yes?' The pale light of a streetlamp illuminated him. He was glorious. Tall. Strong. Dark. His head tipped back with a smile that would light up a million rugby stadiums. Just being under his heated gaze made every part of her light up too. Anticipation of his kiss, of his touch, skittered across her skin, then penetrated her body, heating her inside.

She thought about what he was saying. What he was asking of her. Her gut feeling was that he would be a very good lover. That he would look amazing with no clothes on. That she wanted to kiss him, to lose herself in the pleasure he was promising. He was asking, sure, but she had to answer. Everything from this moment rested with her next decision. If she said no then she would live to regret it. The same could be said if she said yes. But she could allow herself one small regret in her life, couldn't she? She remembered a phrase she'd heard once before… Always regret something you've done, not something you haven't. She made herself say the word. 'Yes.'

'*Buono.*' Sliding his arm underneath her knees, he stooped and picked her up. 'Now stop the talking. Let's get some action happening.'

'Hey, what the hell do you think you're doing?' Although she didn't try to too hard to stop him.

He shrugged as he walked up the path to her house, carrying her as if she was no weight at all. 'You are cold and wet and shivering. You have an injured foot…'

'It's not that bad…'

'Humour me. Perhaps if I take the lead and make you want me so bad you won't think so much?'

'So bad? No, Matteo, the word is bad*ly*.'

With that he stopped short and grimaced. 'Yes, it's official, you will drive me completely insane.'

Then he plastered her mouth with his, whipping her breath away, along with any further thought process. His kiss was greedy. Hard. Long. Everything she imagined a perfect kiss would be. When he pulled away he was grinning, and breathing heavily. 'But I'm quite happy to go mad if it means I can make you moan again.'

CHAPTER TEN

'ER...MATTEO...' SHE was laughing so hard now she could hardly draw breath. 'That's not the bedroom.'

Opening the bathroom door with a single push of his hips, he tipped her onto the tiles, where she landed feet first. He steadied her. 'A shower first? I'm freezing, and it's one way to heat up. And I thought maybe we just need to start again—with a clean slate.'

'Ooh. Are your jokes as bad in Italian as they are in English?' Her heart was pounding, every nerve-ending was on fire. She didn't need heating up—she was already very, very hot.

Flicking on the tap in the walk-in shower area, he grinned. 'Very bad indeed. Come here.' He pulled her closer, one hand covering hers, the other palming the back of her head as he kissed her again. She gasped as heat and need curled inside her. As he dragged the coat and then her soggy cardigan from her arms his eyes never left her face. 'Yesterday I was in here, praying you would join me. Yesterday I thought you might but I was disappointed. Today I am so glad you are here.'

'Me too. If it's any consolation, I almost did come in here. I was trying to do the right thing. It almost killed me,' she admitted. Her hands fisted his T-shirt, running over dips and curves of muscle, across his chest, down his biceps. She stepped into the shower and pulled him in with her, feeling the most liberated she'd ever felt. Warm water sluiced over them, running in rivulets over their shoulders. And she laughed. It sounded brave, new, echoing across the tiles. Wow. She blinked. So that was what freedom sounded like.

Dragging his T-shirt over his head, she sighed at the sight of his naked torso. My God, he was gorgeous—a heady combination of rippled muscle and tanned skin. She followed the contracting muscles down his chest to his belly. Then her fingers made contact with his jeans waistband. His excitement was evident, and it stoked hers. He wanted her and, *God*, she wanted him. She played a little, running feather finger strokes over his zipper. 'Ah, shucks, now everything's wet. You're just going to have to take these off.'

'Of course. But only if you take these off.' Before she could argue about who should go first, he undid the button on her trousers palmed the fabric and pulled them down. When he reached her feet she lifted one foot then the other and he threw the trousers to one side. On his way back up he stopped briefly to kiss her belly button, the underside of her ribs, her throat. 'My God, Ivy. *Sei cosi bella.*'

So beautiful. And she felt it. For the first time in her life she felt like a goddess. But she was distracted by what she could see. He was every bit as amazing as the picture she'd seen that first morning when her life had been about to fundamentally change. When she'd had no idea what was going to happen; never in her wildest dreams had she thought she would be in such achingly close proximity to that body. Lathering some body wash between her hands, she worked up a decent amount of citrus-scented bubbles.

Running them over his chest in slow circles, her hands

kneaded down his abdomen. There were dips there too, a groove she hadn't noticed until now. 'What's this?'

He took her hand and kissed it. 'Nothing. Just an operation scar.'

'Funny place to have an operation.' Looking closer, she found another groove. Across his belly but further down, another. 'They look like bullet holes.'

His laugh reverberated around the room. 'Didn't I teach you anything in my OR? They're laparascope scars. You see? Nothing important.' He took her hand on a journey to each dip then kissed the tips of her fingers. 'You aren't the only one who has lived an interesting life.'

'Mine wasn't interesting. It was just…unusual.' His scars looked pretty. Did he hate them like she hated hers? Did hers look this pretty to him? She doubted that very much. 'From what? What operation?'

'Kiss me again and I'll tell you.' His fingers played over her breasts and for a moment she almost forgot the question. Heat pulsated through her. She wanted to kiss him again. To feel his mouth on hers, to taste him. But she wanted to play too.

'Tell me or I won't kiss you again.'

'Madness. You and your words.' He didn't give her a chance to argue but pushed her against the glass wall and crushed his mouth on hers until she couldn't think straight, until all she wanted to do was touch him. This thing that had been building between them for the last few weeks was so acute, so overpowering. 'I want you, Ivy. I want you too much. You drive me crazy.'

She wasn't going to argue about that. Talking was wasting time. She ran her hands round his waist, grabbed a handful of his bum, making a mental note to ask him later about his scars. Right now she wanted more, she wanted everything he had to offer. With a sharp slap she whacked him on the backside. 'This is the cause of all the trouble. I want to see it. I want to see it right now. I want to see you naked.'

He laughed. 'You already have. The whole world has.'

'Don't I know it.' She pressed herself against him, the water still sluicing over them, the last of the bubbles draining down the plug. 'I want a private audience with your bottom, Mr Finelli. Make it happen.'

'Ah, okay. If you insist.' He turned and began to hum a sexy striptease song as he started to peel his jeans down, a wiggle of the hips, a coy wink, the teasingly slow lowering of his zip. Her mouth watered—every part of her hot. The best private show of her life. *The only one.*

He was the only one.

For a second she hesitated, her heart pounding loud and hard. What did that mean?

She pushed that thought away—no more dissecting things.

Then, her attention firmly back on Matteo's now naked back and…ass…assets, she swallowed. Hard. Her body was simmering. Her core hot. There it was, in all its glory. Peachy indeed. And ripe. God, yes. Extraordinary.

With a quick wiggle he looked over his shoulder, faking the pose from the picture, arms raised against the shower wall. 'Impressive, yes?'

'Hmm, I've seen better.' Oh, holy cow. *If Becca could see me now.* 'Maybe I need a closer look.'

'Feel, I think. Examination is always important. But first…' He turned, fully naked. And she gasped again. He was beautiful. Big. Hard. So damned confident. So dazzling.

Then he, in turn, reached for the shampoo. With slow sensual strokes and in a silence split only by sighs and moans he began to wash her hair, sensually releasing all fear of being here with him, doing this, all shock of the bicycle incident washed away. The shaking that remained came purely from her desire. The quickened breaths only from his touch, from the anticipation of more.

She tried to reach for him through the steam but he shook his head, concentrating on rinsing the shampoo away. Then he started to massage her shoulders, her neck, tantalisingly close to her breasts...nuzzled against her throat, kissing a trail to her collarbone, down to her bra. Which he undid with supreme ease. The man was clearly used to seducing women.

His fingers went lower, caressing her abdomen, her bottom...and he removed her panties... Every part of her strained for his touch. Heat spiralled through her.

Every part of her thrummed with desire. She felt dizzy. To steady herself she grabbed onto his shoulders, reaching, on tiptoe, to give him another kiss. But he had other ideas for his mouth.

When his lips closed around her nipple she thought she had died and gone to heaven. When his fingers slid between her thighs she knew she was definitely there. *Floating.* 'Oh, Matteo. That is...amazing.' She wrapped a leg round his as his stroking became more intense. She wanted him inside her. Wanted him now. Desperation and urgency began to claw through her gut. She was losing...losing all control to his expert touch.

Losing herself...

She could feel his erection against her thigh. Hard and hot. Her fingers closed around it. Now it was his turn to gasp. *'Mio Dio.'*

'Matteo. I need you.' He was so tantalisingly close. 'I need you inside me.'

His forehead rested against hers as his fingers slowed. 'Not yet. Not yet.'

'Now, Matteo. Please. I want you.' She found his mouth again, kissed him hard in a flurry of wet hunger. She bucked against his hand, faster.

'Oh, God.' His eyes shifted from the shower to the door, and back to her. 'Condom…we need…'

Nooooooooo. Don't stop. 'I don't have any.' For a moment she almost didn't care.

The water came to an abrupt stop. He was already out of the shower area. 'In my bag. In the bedroom.'

Shoving past him, she grabbed his hand. 'What are we waiting for?'

'We are all wet.'

'I don't care, Matteo. I just need you.'

That was a thought.

She pushed that away too.

The journey to the bedroom was too long. The faffing with the condom was really too long. But then he was lowering her onto the bed that already smelt of him, and she wanted to sink deep into it and never re-emerge.

'Yeeeogh!'

'What the hell…?' She followed Matteo's jump from the bed as a ginger furball streaked across the room, yowling.

'Your damned cat. My damned butt.' He was peering over his shoulder and rubbing a cheek.

'Oh. No! Not picture perfect any more? It's his bed, I'm afraid. You're just trespassing as far as he's concerned.' Looking at the claw marks indenting those perfect cheeks, she bit back a smile. 'Oh. Goodness. But thank God it was the backside and not the front. Come here and let me kiss it better.'

Eyeing an unrepentant Hugo sitting smugly in the corner, washing one leg with no care in the world, Matteo hissed. 'I do not like making love with an audience.'

Making love. It was too soon, too immense a thing to

imagine that that was some place they'd reached. 'I think he wants to show you who is the alpha male.'

'No contest. Hands down. I win. Every time.'

Yes, he did. No argument there. She opened the door and shooed the cat out, then came back to Matteo, spiralling fingers through his hair. 'But I think you have to prove it. I might need some convincing, because up until now Hugo's been the only significant male in my life. Show me how alpha you are.'

'Pah. I have nothing to prove. I'm not fluffy. I'm not fat. And I would never, ever hurt you.' Matteo pulled her to him and smothered her mouth with his and she let herself believe him. Let his fingers work magic, let the doubt fairies creep back into the dark place they'd come from. This time the kiss was slow and deeply sensual. His eyes fixed on hers, so dark and misted and full of something…something deep and honest and true. She couldn't look away. Needed to watch him, to see in his eyes what she knew was mirrored in hers. This was pure. Real. Profound.

The stroke of his tongue against hers sent shockwaves through her, stoking the heat again. Bringing her to fever pitch. 'Matteo.' She didn't know what to say, couldn't find enough words to describe the emotions rippling through her. Enough that everything she thought, everything she felt came down to one word. 'Matteo.'

'Ivy. Ivy...' He wanted her. He called her name. He was losing control. This amazing, accomplished, sexy man was here. With her. For her.

He laid her down on to the bed. Then he was sliding inside her in one deep thrust. And she felt the initial stretch and an intense sharp sting that melted into need. But she still kept watching him, watching that beautiful face showing every nuance of emotion. The intensity of pleasure. The pain of ecstasy. The wonder of such honesty. And she felt every bit as he did. She was raw. Open.

As he increased the pace she went with him. As he began to shake she went with him. Then as he moaned her name over and over again into her mouth she was crashing and flying and soaring with him. And her heart felt as if it had cracked wide open, shifting, making space, letting him in. That last piece of her that wanted to hold back shook loose—tumbling over and over and away until it was barely there, out of reach, so far away, then nothing at all. For a moment panic gripped her. And so she forced herself to look deeper into his eyes, because there, surely, she'd find an answer.

Then she couldn't think at all. She just went with him, giving herself up to this feeling. Losing herself in him.

It was a few minutes before Matteo really had himself under control.

Pah! He wasn't in any kind of control at all. Never had he had such an intense experience. Never had he been so wholly under the spell of a woman. He didn't know what to make of it all, what this feeling in his heart was. It was like a long slow fall into something exciting yet comfortable. To familiarity, and yet a whole new experience of learning. It was exquisite and unique. It was beautiful.

And it scared the hell out of him.

He gave her a soft gentle kiss, his heart lighter when she responded. Cupping her cheek to look at her, he finally managed some words. 'Okay, good, you're still breathing.'

'Only just.'

'That was intense.'

She hesitated before she spoke again. Gathering her breath and, he imagined, her thoughts. What was going through her head? He wondered whether it was messed-up crazy thoughts like his. The pull of intimacy and the push of fear.

Wriggling out from underneath him, she snuggled into the crook of his arm, her head on his chest, blonde hair tickling his nose. 'Yes. That was…just amazing, Matteo. Just amazing.'

'Yes. It was…amazing.' His heart was too full to find any more words to describe what had just happened.

Normally he'd start his leaving routine about now. Faking tiredness, faking a reason to go. Because staying the night, actually sleeping with a woman was a commitment too far that gave too many messages, meant too many things that he did not or could not feel. And, with his head swimming in and out of rationality, distance would have probably been a good thing right now.

Should he leave? How could he leave? A better man would leave when there was no possible future for them. No long-term promises doomed to fail. She was warm, so beautiful. Anchoring him in a place he wanted to stay a while.

An insane man would leave.

Her fingers tiptoed down his chest. 'Oh. I just remembered, you were going to tell me about the scars.'

'Not this again. They are nothing.' His heart began to thud. Not from the memory of the operation—that had been like child's play in comparison—but because of the associations, the ramifications of his time in hospital. But he never talked about this. Especially not after something so intimate that had made him off balance. 'It is time to sleep.'

'Matteo, it's still early. I'm wired…' She shifted over him and he could feel her heart beating against his stomach. Tender kisses across his abdomen.

He gave her backside a gentle tap and tried to play, to distract her from what felt like her only conversation choice. 'You know, you have a peachy bum too, Miss Leigh. Maybe we could do his and hers calendars. That would raise a bit of money for the hospital.'

'Matteo! That's hysterical. It would raise a lot of eyebrows, and knowing the board it would probably lose me my job. If I don't lose it anyway when I don't turn up for work on Monday.'

A tremor of irritation rippled through him. It was supposed to have been a joke. 'Always your job…it's like it's the only thing that matters.' He got it. It was what he'd always prided himself on too. But now…?

No. Now it was still the same. Nothing had changed. He was still the same Matteo, she was still the hospital lawyer who he happened to be in bed with. Nothing more.

At least, that was what he was trying to convince himself.

She gave him a confused look. 'It's not the only thing that's important. Surely you know that about me now? I'm here, aren't I? I mean…here, for my mum, of course.' Her eyes had flitted away from his face and he had no idea what she was thinking—perhaps, like him, she was surprised at how quickly things had moved from the pub to the bed. The intensity of emotions.

She ran fingertips across the top of his pubic bone. Her voice had been serious for a moment, but now it was lighter. 'So, you have four laparoscopy scars and a longer one here, stretching across your abdomen. That looks…' Levering herself up onto one elbow, she looked straight at him. 'Wait a minute…am I right? Did you…no? Matteo? Did you donate one of your kidneys?'

That was so obvious he couldn't lie. 'Elementary, Miss Leigh. You can be my number-one student. So don't ever ask me to give you a kidney, because now I don't have any to spare.'

'But why?' Her eyes darkened. A stormy sea. 'Who did

you give it to? Wait...let me guess. Oh, my God. It was you. You gave the kidney to your sister?'

'Very good.'

She jerked upright, grasping the sheet and wrapping it round her breasts. It looked like she was settling in for a long talk. 'You donated your kidney. My God, when? How old were you?'

He didn't need to lay his life out to her. But he knew she would not stop asking. And this one act he had done he was proud of. 'Eighteen. It was one of the first laparoscopic transplants in Milan.'

'You saved her life.'

Not wanting to see any more questions in Ivy's eyes, he laid his head on her lap and looked up at the ceiling. 'I gave her more time. Transplants can last for ten, twenty years. Sometimes up to forty—after that we just don't know.'

'Wow. You must have been such a hero to your family.'

'It was the easiest decision I've ever had to make. Ever. No one else was such a close match.' That time...those memories. Without being able to control it, the tension rose through him.

She must have sensed it too because her voice lowered, a hand went to his shoulder. 'What? What happened?'

'It is too long ago.'

'Let me see...' Drumming her fingers on his ribcage, she thought for a few minutes. 'Your sister...and... It's something to do with your father. Let's examine the evidence.'

Per l'amor di Dio. It was so long ago and yet the pain still lingered—not overtly but under the surface. A stark reminder of why he never trusted his heart to anyone. Why he never could.

Ivy needed to know that, especially now. 'Okay. Okay. I was engaged to be married. Elizabetta. She lived in the same village as me. Her family were like our family too.

We grew up together. We fell in love at eight years old. Our lives were planned in the cradle.'

'What has this got to do with these?' She popped a finger into the dip of each of the faded round scars. 'I don't understand.'

'We...we were always "we" from as far back as I can remember. We had plans—big plans—fuelled by my father, who saw the village as a tie and the restaurant as a failing burden with no future. He filled our heads with dreams, to go to Florence to study medicine, to conquer the world. So that was my life. Study. Working in the restaurant. Elizabetta. It was all leading up to us escaping the small closed-in village and exploring the world.'

Ivy looked at him as if she'd never had those kinds of dreams. Then he realised that escape for her had meant just getting out of hospital. Escape had meant being able to put one foot in front of the other. Escape was knowing there was someone who cared about her enough to help her fight the injustices she'd faced.

Maybe if he'd narrowed his world down to such singular things then he wouldn't have run the risk he had. But he'd had no choice in the end.

'Then my sister got sick. It was sudden and irreversible and she was going to die without a transplant. Dialysis could only help her for so long. We were all tested and I was the lucky one who went off to Milan with her and we had more tests and were away for a few weeks with sporadic contact with our families.' He gave a hollow laugh. 'Who knows, if we'd had your fabulous social media back then, things might have been different.'

He felt Ivy's quiet laugh against his chest.

If things had been different he wouldn't be here, doing this. He wouldn't have found her. A twist of fate that meant his life was more now, richer.

'When we eventually came home Elizabetta had changed. She was quiet and distant—one minute she was loving, the next she couldn't bear to look at me. Eventually she told me she was pregnant. That she had to stay in the village, that we had to change our plans. So I…what do you say?…*sucked* it up. I put my plans aside. I stopped studying. I missed the start of the medical school course. I started to build a life there, working for my father—who berated me every day for giving up on my dream so easily. For not escaping as he'd wanted to do. He laughed at me. Said I should go far away and take Elizabetta with me.'

'Easy for him to say.'

But hard to watch his son throw his life away, Matteo guessed. Hindsight was a wonderful thing. How would he have reacted if he'd watched his son give up his dreams? 'I had made the same mistake he had—got a girl pregnant—and he could see the same pattern happening. He was angry and disappointed. And so, deep down, was I. Everything started to crowd into my head. It was a dark time. I had no future that I wanted and a fiancée who hardly spoke to me. But I tried to make the best of it and grew to love the child inside the woman I wasn't sure loved me any more. This was my problem and I was dealing with it.'

She had started to stroke his hair. It was comforting. Sweet. 'Big decisions at such a young age.'

And he'd thought himself such a man. How wrong he'd been. 'One day I was out walking, trying to piece my life together, when I caught her and Rafaele together in the fields. Something they'd apparently been doing since I'd gone to Milan. And probably before.'

'Rafaele?'

'A friend.' He could barely even say the word because it did not describe how Matteo felt about Rafaele. Not at all.

'When I confronted them Elizabetta admitted she loved us both, that she was torn between us. And that she hadn't known how to tell me. That the baby I'd given my future up for wasn't even mine. Rafaele just stood there. Silent. He had nothing to say.'

'What did you do?'

Matteo shrugged. 'She'd lied to me. He'd lied to me, too, and there he was, not defending himself. Not saying anything. He had insulted me and any honour or pride I had. So I hit him. Then I told Elizabetta that I would make the decision easy for her and went to pack my things. Back at the house my father laughed in my face. Told me I'd been taken for a ride, that I'd given up my future for nothing. That I was worth nothing. Thank God I didn't hit him too. But I wanted to. I so very nearly did. In the end I just walked away.'

It was the first time he'd ever spoken about this. It was at once cathartic and yet disturbing to relive it again. But the anger wasn't as intense as it had been. It felt like the dark stain on his heart had finally begun to fade. Ivy's soothing voice encouraged him to go on. 'I don't blame you. It sounds very messed up.'

'They have four children now. They have the life I had been prepared to have, in the village where we all grew up.'

Ivy's fingers massaged the tops of his shoulders now. 'Which explains why you don't want to go back. I understand now. And why you insist on honesty. Because you had your trust broken completely. I get that. But you have an amazing life now. Look at all the good you do.'

It was, he realised, an empty life that he filled with work. A life like Ivy's. They were the same, the two of them. Trying to convince themselves that they were okay. That they were living just fine. Because that way they didn't have to risk any part of themselves. They were scared, underneath it all. Scared.

'But it stays with you. Even just a little bit, no matter how much you try to let it all go. Lies can ruin lives. But not as much as love does.'

CHAPTER ELEVEN

Scratch. Scratch. Scratch.

Ivy opened her eyes and tried to work out where the noise was coming from. For that matter, what the noise was. And where the hell *she* was.

Scratch. Meow.

Hugo. Of course. The spare room. With… Wriggling a foot to the other side of the bed, she tested the temperature. Cold. He was long gone. She was in the spare room and *not* with Matteo.

But his scent remained, and, with it the memories of a wonderful night of lovemaking. Of intense emotion. Of discovering that part of him that he held back. The reason he had his famous reputation of non-commitment. It wasn't hard to see why. His history was punctuated with hurt and betrayal and she knew how that felt.

Like right now. When she wanted so much to believe in the fairy-tale ending, and yet he had already disappeared into the night like a guilty gigolo. It would have been nice if he'd had the decency to at least say goodbye. It wasn't as if she hadn't known this would happen, especially after his words last night, but what surprised her was how much it hurt.

Getting out of bed, she pushed the negativity away. It had been a wonderful weekend, and she had begun to feel things she'd never thought possible. She'd laughed and worried and held onto him, exposed her inner fears and experienced such intense joy. He'd made her feel important and special and worthy.

And that, she realised, was the problem.

Downstairs in the kitchen Hugo wound around her feet as if she was the last person alive on earth. In danger of being knocked off balance between her dodgy foot and a starving, needy cat, she picked him up. 'At least someone's pleased to see me.'

Snuggling her face into his fur, she got some comfort from a warm, beating heart under her fingers and the purr that sounded, indeed, like a drill. So what if it was all cupboard love? She was under absolutely no pretences with the cat. Shame she couldn't say the same about her own love life.

And there it was again. That feeling of panic. It wasn't love. It had been one night, the only thing they could ever share. She knew that, they both did. It would be ludicrous to want otherwise.

Plopping Hugo back on the floor, she turned to the fridge. 'Hold on, buster. Here's some food—'

Whoa. A magnet with a pretty terrible amateurish painting of Scarborough beach held a handwritten note on the fridge door:

Ivy

Joey is sick. I have gone back to London in a hurry. I will phone you.

Matteo x

She was disappointed at how much her heart soared at those few words. At the hope she imbued into the one tiny letter at the end of the note. What was wrong with her? Instead of worrying about that poor boy, she'd been buoyed by the thought that Matteo had not run away but had left because of an emergency. She'd never been like this before—living in hope of a word, a caress. Been desperate for a man's touch, a kiss. It was infusing everything she did. Infecting her thoughts. Making her feel anxious and excitable.

So being here helping her mum to recuperate had come at the right time. It meant she didn't have to face Matteo right now, she could hunker down and get on top of her wayward emotions, work out a way of avoiding him when she got back, and then she'd back to her normal self.

Talking of which… Ivy glanced at the oven clock. Damn. She was late.

Two hours later she bundled her mum—and Richard, which was a strange turn of events, but, really, not so surprising after all—out of the taxi and back into the house. 'Okay, sit down, Mum, and…er…Richard.'

'Thank you, Ivy. Shoo. Shoo.' Richard pushed Hugo roughly from the sofa, sat down and got a hiss in return. 'Oh, and, please, you can call me—'

'Right. Okay…so…' *Please, don't do that* you can call me dad *routine.* She'd been through too many dads all in all. And they had all turned out like her real one—absent. Picking up Hugo, she gave him a conciliatory stroke. 'I'll pop the kettle on, make a pot of tea and start on lunch.'

Angela gave her a weary smile that was irritated or exasperated or something that Ivy couldn't put her finger on. But was all too familiar. 'That's very kind of you, darling, especially when I know how much you need to be getting back to your important job. Are you packed yet? What time's the train? Should we call you a taxi?'

What? Train? Taxi? 'I was going to stay a few days,

make sure you're okay. You know, like we agreed.' *Mum and daughter time*. 'I want to make sure you're okay.' *That we're okay.*

'Oh, don't worry about that. Richard said he'd cook me dinner tonight, and he's going to pop in every day to check up on me.' Her mother reached out and gave Richard's hand a squeeze, and then left her hand there, tight in his fist, and they looked comfortable and settled—how had they done that in such a short space of time? How had they given themselves up to this, whatever it was. For as long as it lasted. 'Every day, he says. So I'll be fine. Don't feel like you have to stay on my account. We'll be just fine.'

'Oh. Of course, yes, I see.' Ivy didn't know what else to say as she turned away. But she could see very clearly that she wasn't any use now. Richard was going to fill the hole in her mother's life, Ivy could go back to her job, to her other life in London with no need to worry. Except she'd so wanted to fix things with her mum now she was here.

But she didn't want to do it with an audience, and she knew it would need a lot more than the few precious minutes they had right now—and with a mother who had a focus on that and not on another potential husband.

It was yet another example of her mum's erratic behaviour. Her short attention span where Ivy was concerned. And, yes, it hurt.

Damn it, don't cry. She squeezed her eyelids shut and forced back any sign of distress. Maybe leaving was for the best.

She looked back over at her mum and had to admit she did look happy and relaxed, and the best she'd been since her heart scare. Ivy caught a smattering of her conversation with Richard. 'Stay right there,' he was saying in a quietly calm voice. 'I'll get a cushion for you. Wait...wait... I want to make sure you're comfortable.'

The man was certainly attentive, even if he didn't appear to like cats. And who was she to deprive her mum of some happiness? If she'd been suffering from depression for all those years and now she wasn't—if this man made her happy and this was what Angela wanted, then she had to let it go. Regardless of her own misgivings.

'I don't know,' her mother replied, looking up at her new man with a sort of adoration as he plumped a cushion and fussed around her. 'You and your fussing ways, you'll drive me crazy.'

'You'll get used to it. See that my way is best.' Richard gave her mum a smile and Ivy's heart lurched.

You drive me crazy.

They were only words. But she'd used them to Matteo and he'd used them right back. And it was the sentiment, it was the same—you drive me crazy, but that's okay. What's a bit of madness between friends? Losing sanity. It was two people becoming a little less of who they were for the sake of someone else. It was Ivy becoming Angela.

Her hand went to her mouth. Oh, my goodness. Of all the things she'd dreaded. She couldn't let that happen.

But it was too late, Ivy *was* different. He had made her different, he'd made her yearn for more. For more in her life than just work. Which was impossible. Just downright impossible, if she was going to be true to her herself and her years of promises and grit.

If she went back to London tonight she would have to face Matteo again too soon and she didn't know what she would say, or how to act, or how to be the same person she'd been before. Before she'd ever met him.

Truth was, she wasn't sure of anything any more. Of where she fitted in her own life, or in other people's. Fighting back the sting of more tears, she walked into the kitchen. At that same moment her phone rang. She pulled it out of her pocket, unable to see the number for the teary blur, which she scrubbed away as quickly as it arrived.

There was absolutely no point in getting emotional about any of this. She just needed to compartmentalise her feelings and move on, like she always did. 'Hello?'

'Ivy?'

Matteo. She swallowed back the lump in her throat and disregarded the accompanying jittery heart rate at the sound of his voice. She would not show him any reason to feel sorry for her, she would not let him know her feelings. She infused her voice with cheeriness. 'Hello! How's Joey?'

'Good, you saw the note. He's a lot better now. He had a ureteral obstruction, which didn't resolve with a nephrostomy. I operated early this morning.'

'Er...English, Matteo?' Cradling the phone between her ear and her shoulder, she filled the kettle, plonked two teabags into a teapot and tried very hard to act normally.

'I had to take him back to Theatre to unblock a blockage. What is wrong?'

'Nothing. Nothing at all.'

'But your voice isn't right. You are upset?' He knew the timbre of her voice? He knew her so well he could tell when she was upset, without words? He knew her too well. She'd let him in too—she'd let him in and she was going to get hurt. Because that's what happened if she let her guard down. There was a pause she didn't know how to fill. Then he was back again.

'Are you cross because I left? I'm sorry I had to leave so quickly and so early. I didn't want to wake you.' Another pause, then his voice was more serious. 'I need to talk to you.'

Uh-huh. She knew exactly what was coming, but she couldn't do a heart-to-heart, not without understanding what the heck was going on in her head and why her body had become a quivering mess. Why she desperately needed to feel his arms around her when it was the opposite of what she should be needing.

But something had to be said, surely? They'd moved further into something last night. Something tangible and deep and frighteningly wonderful. And so very, very dangerous. A line had been crossed and it couldn't be ignored.

But it could be delayed. Until she'd got a better grip on herself. 'Another time, Matteo. I'm busy… I have too much to do.'

'That is what I mean.'

'Sorry? You're not making sense.'

'I saw the boss today at the hospital. Pinkney. I told him your dilemma and he agreed to a week of compassionate leave. You can stay with your mum and work can wait. I fixed it for you.' He had a smile in his voice and she imagined that wonderful mouth curving upwards, the light in his eyes. And felt a stab of pain in her solar plexus.

You drive me crazy.

And he did. And that was the problem. He drove her wild with desire, he drove her to the edge, he drove her to want things she couldn't have. To dream impossible things. And now he was trying to fix her messed-up life. And it would be so easy to let him do it—so easy, and yet the hardest thing in the world. Because she could not let go of her grip on her life.

'But, you see…I don't want you to do that. I don't need you to fix things for me, I can manage quite well on my own. I don't need you. I don't need anyone.' It was harsh. And it was everything she needed to believe and feel again but didn't, but if she kept on saying it he'd get the message and she wouldn't have to face him. Or this. Or herself.

'I thought that was what you wanted. I was trying to

help.' She could hear the building anger in his voice. And, yes, he'd been kind, as always, and thought he was doing the right thing. But, as it turned out, she hadn't needed him to. Once again she was surplus to Angela's requirements.

'Thank you. But I won't be needing it. Please, don't interfere in things like that again. Not my work. Thank you.'

'Hey! Stop right there. Do not talk to me as if I am just a colleague, as if there is nothing between us. Ivy, we need to talk.'

'I'm not sure there's anything to say.'

His voice was louder, harsher. 'And I think there is. I think that what happened last night meant something. Did it mean nothing to you?'

She could lie, but he'd know. He *knew* her. He knew what had passed between them last night, the startling honesty and the wonder—that wasn't something she could deny. It had been too profound, too…too *much*—and it had shocked them both. She lowered her voice, the truth of her words like glass shards in her gut. 'Yes. Yes. It meant something.'

'So explain to me what is happening here, because I'm confused. You're distant and different from the woman I know. Damn it, Ivy, tell me the truth.'

I'm saying that you mean too much to me. That I have to let you go. 'I'm sorry, really. I do have to go.' Her heart twisted keenly, making her inhale. But her lungs wouldn't work. She forced the words through a closed throat. 'Goodbye, Matteo.'

It was for the best. It was. And one day she'd thank herself for it.

Without waiting another moment, she flicked the phone off and went up to her room to pack. It was time to go home.

Wherever the hell that was. But it wasn't here. And it wasn't in Matteo's arms.

* * *

Round three. Part one.

Matteo circumvented the tasteless coffee table and surreptitiously drank out of his clandestine cup as he mingled with the waiting group. The only saving grace was that Ivy wouldn't be here to tempt him, to confuse him. To drive him mad all over again.

In fact, it was very useful that he'd had to leave in the night to come and see Joey, before he'd had a chance to do anything even more foolish than make love to a woman who was destined to trample all over his heart. She'd proved that enough when she'd answered his attempts at intimacy with silence. Refuted his well-intentioned intervention into her work life—which, for the record, he'd thought was the right thing to do.

But that would never happen again, not if it generated such a response. He could feel his blood pressure rising at the memory of her sharp words and the swiftly ended phone call. The reminder that relationships brought about all kinds of problems that he was better not having.

He took a seat in the front row, glared at the clock. Willed the day to be over so he could get the big fat tick on his attendance sheet and eventually put this whole exercise behind him. Then he wouldn't have any more unreturned calls to Ivy Leigh. Along with the whole bunch of questions and no answers.

The door swung open and her assistant walked in, handed out the day's schedule. And—

In walked Ivy.

Matteo's head pounded. That blood pressure was rising at an alarming rate. Why was she not in York?

'Good morning, everyone.' She was all business and no eye contact. Well, no eye contact with him at any rate. 'Welcome to the third day in our social media course. Today we are going to expand on branding and why it is important in this technological age to capitalise on it. I'm going to give a few pointers about how we do this as a company, and how you can help...'

He didn't want to help. He wanted it to be over. He wanted to be alone with her. He wanted her. That was the startling, raw, naked truth of it. And at the same time he knew that wanting a woman who did not want him back was the first step to madness.

Two hours later they were split into more infuriating groups to discuss brand statements. Ivy walked over, her limp undiminished—in fact, worse than usual. He put it down to the bicycle accident. She looked tired and frazzled and distant. To stop himself from spending too much time just looking at her, at the proud, straight back, the curve of a breast he knew was lush and sweet, the unintentionally honest green eyes, he started to give his ideas to the group. 'Brand statements... Okay. We help children. We save lives. I know...we save children's lives...er... Children first? Kids first...? *Aargh.* This is pointless. I'm a doctor, not a marketing person. I instinctively know what the brand is, I live the damned thing every day—why do I have to come up with a statement?'

She stopped at his shoulder. 'So that we are all on the same page, Mr Finelli. If we have a mission statement and a brand statement that are symbiotic then we all have a pathway for our work.'

Mr Finelli now, was it? 'I already have one and, I imagine, so does everyone here. It's about doing our best...for everyone. And about being *open* and *honest* about intention.'

Judging by the two hot spots on her cheeks, she took the veiled meaning for what it was. He didn't like playing guessing games. He didn't like hot and cold. He liked to know exactly where he stood. On all things. He didn't like having the phone put down on him when he was trying hard to work things through.

'I…I…understand…' She looked away. 'So—'

'I am not sure you do, Miss Leigh. This hospital is about children, we all know that. Children are not a brand, they are people. Living, breathing, vulnerable and sick people. Show me how branding can really, actually, honestly change a single life more than what we do here every day then I'll be impressed. Until then, well, I just want to do my job in peace. Like you, I presume, with no needless distractions.'

For a moment she stared at him open-mouthed, the two hot-spots spreading across her neck like a rash. And he immediately regretted allowing his frustration to overspill into this public domain.

She gave a quick clap of her hands. 'Okay, everyone, let's break for morning tea.' Then she turned to him and whispered, 'Outside. Now.'

A cruel wind whipped at the side of the red-brick hospital building as they huddled in a disused doorway. She'd made sure they were well away from prying ears and eyes. So typical. Anything to keep the work-life divide real. He cut through the tension. 'Ivy. How come you are here? Your mum?'

'Is fine, it appears. I came back on Sunday. The train…' Her tone was dismissive, not allowing for any more discussion on that subject. 'It's not important.'

'I see.' This was a surprise, especially given the compassionate leave she'd been granted and her stated intention that she wanted to fix things. She clearly wasn't going to expand on this, she was closed off and wound as tight as that first day he'd met her. Was this really the warm-hearted woman who had held him so tightly outside the cardiac care unit? Who had screamed loudly in a pub? Who had laughed heartily at his jokes? Who had gripped him and exposed her fears? Who had lain breathless and spent on his bed after the best lovemaking of his life?

She looked at him now with a taut line of a mouth. With eyes that she clearly hoped were cold and distant but which gave away a traitorous flicker of heat. She would not like to know that, he supposed. 'So work won out in the end? I'm surprised, Ivy. I thought you had changed your priorities a little. What do you want to say to me?'

'Work did not win. My mother simply didn't need me.' That flicker of heat gave way to sadness. Something had happened between her and her mum and she was dealing with it badly. 'Now, I'd be grateful if you could keep our personal life out of the work environment.'

'Since when did I bring it in?'

Her eyes fired up again. 'When you spoke to Pinkney. And with the between-the-lines comments in there. I'm at work. We both are. Please, remember that.'

Leaning against the wall, he looked at her, barely trying to disguise his surprise and growing anger. 'No one knows anything. And since you have refused to speak to me in private I'm stuck with having to put things between the lines. I told you about my life, I told you how much I value honesty. What the hell is going on, Ivy?'

'I...' She shook her head, the tautness of her mouth softening, wobbling slightly, and for a moment he thought she might cry. 'I don't know what to say. Just that I'm sorry, but...'

And it was all well and good being angry with her, but he knew deep down that she was not a hurtful kind of woman. That she was facing challenges that were testing her, pushing her to the limits. That she was warm and funny and with a lot to give and usually had too many words but now had none.

Matteo stepped closer but ignored the need to pull her to him. She was so proud she would never allow that. He kept his voice low. 'Okay. Talk to me. Please, that's all I ask. I will start. This all took me by surprise. Things went from slow to fast in a heartbe—'

'Yes. Yes.' She held her hand up and stopped him from saying more. 'Thank goodness you feel the same. Too fast, Matteo. Too deep. Too quick. I never wanted this. I like being on my own. I like not having to make decisions for someone else. I'm too independent for all this. Last weekend was…nice. And thank you. But we can't… I can't—'

'Nice? Nice? All the words in the world and that's the one you choose. Oh, Ivy. What kind of game are you playing? Because I don't understand your rules. One day you were happy to be with me, and now…this coldness.'

'I'm not playing a game. I'm being serious. I don't want a relationship. I can't…do it. I can't give myself… I don't want to.' She looked down at her watch. 'Damn. Look, I have to go back in and start.'

'Just like that, it is over?'

'Yes. Yes, it is.'

He waited for relief to flood in, but it didn't. Only bitter sadness, a hole in his chest. Which was surprising and startling and bleak. The thought that he'd see her over and over again in the hospital and never get to kiss those lips. To hold her close and stroke her cheek. To be at the end of a smart quip. This was not how he'd envisioned he would feel and he didn't know what to do or say. He was out of his depth here, with feelings swirling inside him. He didn't want them but he couldn't seem to let them go. What did it mean?

Did he love her? Surely he could not have done such a

thing? He had always protected himself from that. Because of the pain. Because of Elizabetta, because he had been so wary to give his heart to a woman and watch her toss it aside. Was Ivy any different from that? He'd hoped so, but now he wasn't so sure.

'No more talking about it? I have no choice?'

'No. Please. Don't make me say anything else. Because I don't know what more to say.' She gave a swift shrug of her shoulder and blinked away what he thought might be tears. 'I really do have to go and finish this workshop.'

'Always your job.'

'Oh, yes, well, you know me. No hard feelings?'

'I thought I did know you, but I was wrong.' He watched as she swivelled on the hard gravel and began to walk back towards the conference room. 'And, no, Ivy, I have no hard feelings. I have no feelings about this at all.'

And that was when he knew that he'd fallen completely for her. That he had given her much, much more than he'd ever intended; he'd given her his heart on a platter and all but invited her to chop it into pieces. Yes, he knew he'd fallen in too deep, because saying he had no feelings was the first real lie he'd ever told.

CHAPTER TWELVE

'BACK FOR MORE, I see? You're a glutton for punishment.' Nancy gave Ivy a little smile as she gave her wet hands a shake and scanned the OR prep-room sinks, looking for the paper towels. 'You've done so well, considering what you were like that first time.'

'Thanks.' It was all Ivy could muster. She was feeling much worse than that first day—she may well have mastered the sight of blood, but mastering the sight of Matteo Finelli was something she would probably never be able to do. She could see him through the glass door in the OR, talking and laughing with the anaesthetist. Her stomach clenched into a tight ball.

She didn't want to face him today, because yesterday she'd felt as if her heart was shattering. She'd summoned every single ounce of strength she'd had to tell him it was over, when it felt like the words had been stuck in her throat, refusing to come out. She'd had no sleep, curled up with Hugo, who she'd rescued from the clutches of *daddy Richard*. And, unsurprisingly, Hugo had been about as helpful with relationship advice as her mother.

And now...well, now she had to stand with Matteo all day and watch him save another life. Watch him laugh and joke and be lovely and warm to all those people and feel her heart beating to the rhythm of his voice, feel the pull of her body towards him, and know that it made no sense to take those steps, no matter how much she was compelled to.

The door swung open and he strode in.

Looking around, she realised Nancy had gone and they were alone. She took a deep breath. 'Matteo, hello.'

'I thought it was Mr Finelli these days.' He wasn't wearing a surgical mask so she felt the full effect of his indifference. No, actually, it was a simmering deep anger that he'd dressed up as indifference. She'd hurt him and that had not been her intention.

'Matteo, please—'

He shook his head. 'Miss Leigh, I can honestly say that I have no problem whatsoever about bowing out of our petty little war. I'm even happy to admit you to be the winner—in truth, it makes no difference to me. So you have no need to be here.' He came a little closer, not close enough that she could touch him but enough that she felt the magnetic pull towards him, and feel, too, the venom in his words. 'In fact, I'm asking you leave.'

'To leave? But—why?'

His eyes bored into her, stern, angry, righteous. 'Because having you here distracts me. I need to be fully focused on my work. It is better if you're not here, particularly for the patient. And that, after all, is the full focus of *your* job, right?'

'Matteo, please—'

This time he held up his hand and she shut up immediately. 'Did you really think I would let you in? What an idea! When you don't let anyone in yourself? When you don't even know how?'

'I can't. I tried, but I can't.' Because the second she'd let him in she'd started to be someone else. She hadn't been Ivy Leigh any more…and she didn't want that. She wanted to keep herself intact.

'Things might have worked if we'd both wanted to try.'

'But…' She finally found the words to admit how she was feeling. 'I don't want to lose myself.'

'I know. I understand that. Who does? Have you ever thought that perhaps, just perhaps, we could have had a… what did you call it?…symbiotic pathway? Walk it together? Be ourselves and yet part of something?'

She thought of her mum and her flatmate and of the weekend and of how desperately she'd ached for Matteo when he hadn't been there. How he had become the focus of her thoughts. 'Everything I've ever seen has shown me that independence becomes interdependence and then dependence. I don't want to depend on anyone. That wouldn't be me. I don't want to be like that.'

He huffed out an exasperated breath. 'It doesn't have to be like that. I know plenty of people who have managed to have happy relationships. You don't even want to take the risk.'

Please, don't ask again. Because I might just say yes. 'No, Matteo. I don't. For both of our sakes. It wouldn't be fair.' She turned away from him, unable to keep looking at those dark eyes that drew her in so deep. 'Okay. I'll go, if you insist. But I won't say I've won. I don't even want to think about that.' This was no victory at all. 'I think we've both won. And lost. And now I'm talking in circles. I'll just go.'

'Yes. Please.'

She went to leave, biting back the shout, *I want you. Please, don't do this.* Fighting back tears, knowing that stopping this before it became too intense, too hard to handle, too overpowering was the very right thing to do, even though her heart told her otherwise. But she hadn't achieved all those amazing things in her life by listening to her heart. So it had no right to interfere now.

Her head bobbed a little as she leaned towards the door. She was going.

'Ivy. Stop.' Matteo felt the blood boiling through his veins. This was not the best way to start a difficult day in the OR. This was not how he had planned this conversation to go. He had been going to ban her from the theatre, yes, but he hadn't wanted to see her look so accepting of his rejection. So vulnerable. 'This…this is… Just listen, you're making me say things I don't mean. You're making me crazy.'

She turned a little, her eyes brighter. Her mouth made a tentative attempt at a smile, but it just looked sad. 'I know, and that's the biggest problem of all. Apparently it doesn't get any better with age. So my mum says, and she should know.'

'She is better now?'

'She's exactly the same as always. With a slightly damaged heart. But haven't we all?'

He laughed. He actually laughed. Right in the middle of this…break-up of something that wasn't even a whole of anything. He laughed. Because she was impressive, this woman. She was more than impressive. She had shown up today knowing that it would be the hardest thing to face him, but she had done it anyway. She had kept her sorrows to herself. She had hidden her emotions and kept on working. It was either admirable or downright destructive. Or both.

And no matter what words came out of his mouth the feelings remained the same. He was awash with anger at her decision, with joy at knowing the real woman underneath the hard veneer, with a frustration that she was so damned private. With pride that she'd chosen him to take to bed, to tell her secrets to when she'd been ready. With a yearning for more and more and more, and he didn't know what any of that meant.

And then he did. The pieces began to slip into place.

He had fallen in love with her. Of all the women in the damned hospital, in the damned city, in the whole damned world to fall in love with, he had chosen the most complicated, stubborn, uptight one of all. And now she was walking away and there was nothing he could do or say to make her stop because she didn't believe she could do it. She didn't believe that love could happen for her.

And so this was what he was left with: he loved her and he didn't know what to do with it. He didn't want to love her. He didn't want to like her even. Because, *oh, mio Dio,* she could be very difficult and all she cared about was her work.

Like him. Like he used to be.

He turned away and tried to steady himself. Panic swirled in his gut. He had protected himself for years against this. But, it seemed, it was something you could not fight in the end.

'*Ciao*, Matteo. And thank you for everything. It was a hell of a lot better than nice.' She was going. Leaving, because he had made her go. His mind began to swirl too. Why this? Why now? Why, in hell, *her*? But the only answers were right in front of his eyes.

'Wait.'

Taking too many steps closer to her, he touched her cheek. Pulled her to him. And he felt hesitation. For a moment he thought she might push him away, but instead she dragged him to her, clamped her mouth hard against his.

'Matteo…'

She was in his arms and the emotions filled his chest thick and heavy and yet weightless, and he tried to hold them back but they just kept coming, rising and filling him with this urgent need. 'Ivy, *ti amo*.'

And he hoped she did not understand or hear him, because the moment he'd said those words he'd known it was the wrong thing to say. The last thing he should do was open his heart to her.

Then he was kissing her again. A rough, hard kiss filled with every damned ounce of emotion he had in him, and she was kissing him back with just as much. With anger. With joy and frustration that they just wouldn't work, because she didn't want them to.

And because that had been the one startlingly honest thing she had said, he kissed her some more.

'Okay, people, let's get going. Oh. God. Sorry. Oops. Bad timing.'

It was Nancy. Matteo winced. Now, to add humiliation to Ivy's list of worries, their privately public display would definitely be hospital gossip.

Ivy jerked away, the space where she'd been in his arms now just a heavy emptiness. She was swiping her hand across her mouth. Then she was gone. Along with his hope.

He looked around for something to kick, to hit, to assuage these feelings of hurt and anger and…this new feeling of love. But there was a surge of people into the adjoining room. A child who needed an operation. A family waiting for his skills. A team needing to be led. So he just balled his hands into fists and took a minute to let the emotions wash through him.

His heart was as empty as his arms. Because he knew, with certainty, that she would never come back. That he had lost her. Because she had never known such a thing as love and she was so desperately in need of it but, oh, so afraid. And now he had lost it too.

* * *

'Well done. You were great in there! Scary, but great.' Becca gave Ivy a high five as they walked away from the sexual harassment tribunal. The wind had dropped and the afternoon was promising to be unseasonably warm. They took the shortcut through Regent's Park back towards the hospital, dodging what appeared to be some kind of kiddie fun run event as they walked. 'You knew exactly what you were doing, and you wiped the floor with his defence.'

Ivy smiled. Ah, the naivety of the inexperienced. 'I just let the evidence speak for itself. There really wasn't anything he could say in the face of three witnesses.' But Becca was right. She had felt like a fight this morning. In fact, she had felt like a fight quite a lot recently. She put it down to lack of sleep. Which in turn was a result of… She wouldn't think about it. She wouldn't think about him any more. It was too exhausting. Too damaging to ache and want and dream, and need someone so badly. She just needed to focus on work some more and he'd be gone from her brain soon. He would.

The trouble was, almost a week on and he was still there, looming large inside her head.

'But you just kept on. You were epic. I started to feel a bit sorry for him by the end. You needled and needled until he admitted everything.' Becca put her hand on Ivy's arm. 'Girl crush alert. I think I'd like to be you when I grow up.'

'Oh, no, you wouldn't. Believe me. I do everything wrong.'

Becca shook her head. 'What? You just won a case, you did that right. You want to celebrate?' They'd stopped outside a café, the smell of strong dark coffee irresistible. And, for some reason, Ivy felt like staying a while, not rushing back. The thought of her stuffy office was nothing compared to the fresh air, the kids' squeals and cheers as they crossed the finishing line. Ivy envied them their innocence.

'Okay. A quick one.'

Ivy placed the order and found Becca sitting at an outside table, swatting a large bee away. 'I asked them to be quick. Shouldn't be too long.'

'Doesn't matter if it is. To be honest, with the hours you've put in this week you're owed a small break and… Oh, don't they look pretty? So fresh and gorgeous.' Becca was pointing towards a carpet of red and white flowers. 'Tulips? I never know the names of flowers.'

Ivy pulled out her notepad. 'So, about tomorrow's course. Are you sure you can handle it? You know the schedule?'

Becca rolled her eyes. 'We've been over and over this. Yes, I can handle it. It's only the wrap-up, question time and feedback. It won't be hard. But, you know, I did just point out that absolutely stunning tulip bed over there, and can you smell that divine smell? There are some seriously beautiful plants here but you don't appear to notice them. Or anything out of the confines of your office.'

Becca inhaled and looked a little apprehensive. 'I wasn't going to say anything, but I can't let you go on like this. I know you're not running tomorrow's social media course because Dr Peachy Bum will be there…but I don't know why. What on earth happened?'

'Becca. Please.' Ivy didn't need this. She was coping just fine, and would continue to do so as long as she didn't have to speak about it. Or think about him. 'I have an unavoidable meeting with the board tomorrow, you know that.'

'You could have rearranged it. Said you had an important previous appointment. And, yes, I'm overstepping again, but I'm worried about you. Seriously. You've been head down all week, locked in your office until all hours—and

I know you think we all believe you're working, but I can see straight through you. There's not much more done than this time last week.'

'There is. I would never let anything interfere with my work.' Had she? Had she spent time staring out the window? Yes. But that had been critical thinking time. Had she thought about Matteo at all?

Okay, yes. She'd thought about little else. She missed him. Missed having his arms wrapped around her, missed feeling able to tell him anything. Missed his smile and his laugh and...okay, yes. She missed his bum too.

Becca tapped her finger on the tabletop. 'Besides, there are doodles...incriminating doodles...'

'What?'

'In your bin. Words, doodles, hearts. Tearstained hearts...'

And Ivy had thought she'd managed to hide them away at the bottom of the rubbish bin. Hearts. Yeah, right. It was all fluff and nonsense and wishful thinking. 'You are seriously deranged. Either that or you'll go far in this profession—observation and attention to detail are key.' For a moment Ivy thought Becca might explode with such an admission of excited suspicion. 'But sorry to disappoint you, there weren't any tears, I just spilled my water—'

Becca's voice dropped and softened. 'Something happened, something momentous, and you think you can hide it all. But you can't. Guess what? You're human, Ivy, and you're allowed to bleed.'

Sure, but what if it never stops? 'It wasn't...I didn't...'

'What happened?'

'Nothing.'

The coffee came and it was satisfactory, but not as nice as the one Matteo had bought for her that day he'd kissed her in the staffroom. Seemed she couldn't do the most mundane of things without thinking about him. *Fade, please, memory. Fade.* But it didn't fade, it just sent shooting pains to her chest instead. 'I can't talk about it.'

Replacing her cup in its saucer, Becca shook her head. 'Okay. Fine. Spend all your days solving everyone else's problems just so you don't have to think about your own.'

Like her mother? 'That's not why I do this job.'

Her assistant's eyebrows rose. 'Really?'

'No. I do it because I want everyone to get a fair go. I love this job.' Although recently it hadn't held her attention quite as much as it always had. And she knew the reason. She just wasn't ready to admit it. She wanted more in her life than files and injunctions and other people's messes. She wanted a chance at her own happy mess. Hugo had filled a little space, but she ached for more.

For Matteo.

Becca ran her finger round the froth in her cup and licked. 'You love being needed here. Does it…does it stop you from needing something else? Love? A peachy—?'

'Stop it. I should fire you for insubordination.'

'Well, you could, but that would mean you'd have to do tomorrow's course on your own.'

Panic twisted in her stomach. 'I can't see him, Becca. I just can't.'

Becca breathed out and smiled reassuringly. 'Sure you can.'

'I can?' Yes, of course she could. He was just a man. She was fine. 'I don't think I can.'

'So you had a thing?'

Oh, what was the point in denying it? She knew any secrets shared would stay with Becca. She shrugged. 'A small one.'

'Wait, though, you look crushed. You've been so hyped up recently. Oh, Ivy…it wasn't small at all. Was it? Not for you.' Her hand slid across the table to Ivy's shaking one. 'You've fallen in love with him?'

Do not cry. Do not cry. Do not cry. 'I haven't got time to do anything like that. I have a busy job—'

'You do. You love him.'

'And there are a lot of long hours involved. I have to review all the employment contracts starting from next Monday—'

Becca patted her hand. 'It's okay, you know. It's okay to be frightened. It's okay to meet someone halfway. You don't have to give all this up. You can do both. People do both.'

'And then…' Ivy stopped talking. Simply because there was a rock in her throat that she couldn't squeeze words past. But she thought about her life. How she'd been forging forward her whole life because she so wanted people to take her seriously. Wanted people to notice her for the right reasons, and not because she couldn't walk properly. And he had. Matteo had plucked her from the three billion women on the planet and had made her feel important. He'd given her the one thing she'd craved all her life. And it scared her so much. That responsibility, just taking what he was offering, it was overwhelming… Man, she was so scared. 'Yes.'

'Yes, what?'

And she thought about her sleepless nights, and about how much she missed him. How she had never wanted to believe all that *you complete me* guff, but she could see how it could be possible that one person could make you more whole, better, stronger than before. That plenty of people weren't like her mum, plenty of people had happy stable lives that they shared very successfully. It was a question of finding the right person for you.

That person was Matteo. Her heart softened a little at the thought of him. And then filled with panic at the thought that she'd lost him already. 'Yes. I think I love him. I don't know for sure, but I think I could. I'd like to try.' And that scared her the most.

'Hallelujah. Great. Finally, we have a breakthrough.' Becca raised her hands to the sky and cheered. 'But does he love you back?'

'I sincerely doubt it after everything I've said and done to stop that happening. He thinks I'm selfish and self-centred and only think about my work.'

'Hmm, clearly the man's a good judge of character.' Becca flashed a smile. 'Seriously, though, did he ever do anything that might make you think he felt the same?'

Ivy thought about the kisses and the night of lovemaking, and driving her all that way home in the rain, and just the simple, sweet look in his eyes when he talked to her. The kisses, though—they couldn't lie about the way he felt. No one could kiss like that and not mean it. 'Yes. Lots and lots.'

'So show him that you're all of those things and so much more. You're driven and dedicated and passionate. Italians like that.'

'He does.' And for the first time in for ever Ivy began to feel a little glimmer of hope blooming in her chest. She breathed deeply, the gorgeous scent of some exotic plant catching in her throat. He was right, there was so much more to life than work. There was him, Matteo Finelli. And her, Poison Ivy. Maybe they could try to be part of something. Something together. 'But I really messed up. I just need to find a way to convince him.'

Becca punched the air. 'Yes! If anyone can, you can. Why don't you just march right up to him and tell him?'

Because she wasn't that brave. 'Because he's the kind of man who judges by actions. I know him, Becca, he's tired of all my words. He was hurt badly once by a girl who said she loved him but acted otherwise. She broke his heart and he's waited all this time to take a chance on someone else. And when he did it backfired and he's retreated to lick his wounds. It's enough for me to accept that I love him, but I need to work out a way to prove it to him.'

CHAPTER THIRTEEN

It was late. The transplant he'd just finished on a thirteen-year-old girl had been very difficult but she was recovering well. He had pre-op blood results to go through for the list tomorrow and an informal ward round to complete. He had a headache. And heartache. And he wanted to go to bed.

But to top off the day from hell, someone had organised a night walk through Regent's Park to raise money for the department. Tonight. For a dialysis machine. So he was duty bound to attend.

'Wow, what's happening?' Regent's Park was one of his usual running spots but as he approached it he was surprised at the size of the crowd. Everywhere he looked he saw people; adults, kids, baby strollers, all dressed up in green, a surging emerald sea. Getting closer, he heard clapping start. Quietly at first, but with every step he took it got louder and louder. And then he began to recognise faces. Joey's mum and dad. Portia, who he'd operated on last year, and her family. Mathilde. Ahmed. Benjamin. All these familiar faces greeting him with cheers and smiles. What the hell? Why were they clapping?

Confused and a little humbled, he stopped at the first marquee with a banner reading *'KIDney Kidz—Give a little, save a life.'* He spoke to a nurse from the intensive care unit. 'Hi. I'm Matteo. I need to pay for my ticket. I think I'm a little late. Where's the start?'

She beamed at him. 'Hi, yes, I know who you are. I think everyone does.'

That damned picture again. 'But—'

'Thanks for everything you've done.' She gave a quick nod. 'We're five minutes away from starting—the line's over there.' She pointed down the crowd of people to the right. 'And it's okay, VIPs don't have to pay.'

VIPs? Now he was really confused. Was this another unfunny Ged joke? 'It's for a good cause. I'd like to give something—'

'I think you've given enough, Matteo.'

He froze. That voice. The northern accent. *Ivy*. His heart thumped. Would it ever stop its Pavlovian response to her? Four weeks and he'd managed to keep out of her way. Four long weeks of hell wondering how to fix something that appeared irrevocably broken.

Sucking in a deep breath, he turned. She was dressed in a green T-shirt and shorts, her hair covered by a green baseball cap. She wore a tentative smile. In her hands she had a clipboard and a large net bag stuffed with green fabric. It was good to see her. Good and bad as his gut tumbled over and over. 'Ivy. What are you doing here?'

Her pretty smile faded. 'A fun run, obviously.'

His gaze flitted from that beautiful, heart-breaking mouth to her leg. 'But your foot?'

'Will be fine, I'm sure. It's only ten kilometres.' Although she looked more defiant than convinced. He had no doubt that if anyone would do it, she would. 'Good turnout.'

'I've never seen so many people at one of our events before. It's miraculous.'

Her head dipped a little as she replied, 'No, Matteo. It's called using the internet for what it's good at.'

'You? You did this?' *What the hell is going on?*

'Yes.'

'How?' *Why?* For some reason his voice was croaky, his throat blocked.

Hers clearly wasn't. She was determined and forthright. Vibrant in her passion for what she'd done. 'I sent out a call. I contacted Joey's mum and dad, who are part of the kidney kids support network, who in turn contacted your previous patients, who promoted the idea on all their social network sites. Within twenty-four hours the buzz got picked up by a radio station. That got covered by the local newspaper. That was online and got clicked on by hundreds of people. Like your bottom, my call went viral. It doesn't happen every time, but this seems to have captured people's imaginations. Your patients and their families wanted to do this, for you. Because of what you'd done for them.'

Whoa. That was humbling and affirming at the same time. 'What was your message?'

'I said...and please don't be angry because only you and I really know what happened...' From her clipboard she peeled off a leaflet with his photo on it. His work profile one, not the one in the locker room. Thank goodness for small mercies. 'Dr Matteo gave the gift of life, now you can too. One step at a time. Join us on a night walk. Wear green to be seen. KIDney Kidz: We won't fail them.'

'You make me sound too perfect.'

She grinned and her green eyes shone with a fire he'd only seen once before. When he'd been in bed with her. *Mio Dio*, she was beautiful. She'd broken what had been left of his heart—he understood that now. 'Nah—you're just the pretty face poster-boy. Amazing what you can do, even with clothes on. I thought that there must be a lot of people out there who want to show their thanks, and who want to help others in the same situation. It's amazing how many people said yes as soon as your name was mentioned. You have quite a fan club.'

But the one person he wanted wasn't a member. 'I don't know what to say.'

'"Thank you" will suffice. Oh, and at three thousand people, ten quid a head, you've pretty much got your dialysis machine.' He followed her, walking slowly towards the start line, and they became engulfed with people on all sides, chatting, cheering, patting him on the back.

He still couldn't believe it. 'And you organised this in four weeks?'

'I pulled a few strings. Someone I was at university with knows someone who could make it happen. Becca helped too. We were stuffing the goody bags at three this morning.' Her face lit up as she looked at all the smiling faces around them. And he could see the tired edges of her face and he longed to touch her, but he wouldn't. 'It was worth every second.'

'But why? Why did you do this?'

She turned to look at him, her eyes misting. 'Because you got to me in the end. I believe you need this equipment. I believe you, Matteo, when you say children are vulnerable and not a brand. I believe in you. And I wanted to show you how using the internet for the right things can really pay off.' A loud crack split the sky. 'Oh. Looks like we're starting. Come on.'

She stuffed a T-shirt—green, of course—into his hand and started to walk along the path. If her ankle was hurting she certainly had no intention of showing it. She'd done all this for him? Using her skills and knowledge and pure raw grit.

'No. Stop a minute.' He pulled her off the path for a moment onto lush, warm grass. 'I was wrong about you. Well, kind of wrong and right at the same time. I suppose I can concede that the internet has its advantages. Look at how many people *you* have helped.'

She shook her head. 'I started to do this for you, Matteo. It would be wrong of me to say otherwise. I wanted to make you happy. But, actually, as the whole thing began to gain traction I got so completely invested in it that I had to make it work. Look at Joey there—you've made such a difference. To all of them.'

What was she saying? That this grand gesture was for him? Why? 'I don't understand you, Ivy. You said it was over. You said you didn't want me. And that's okay. Sad, but okay. We have our own lives.' He didn't want to have this conversation. Enough that it was all over between them, without this prolonged attachment. He watched as people streamed by, green balloons bobbing above their heads in the fading daylight, and felt overwhelming emotion. For them. For this. For him and Ivy. Between them they could have made an excellent team.

But that was useless. She'd been trying to prove a point that she could use social media for a good cause. This wasn't about them. Or about piecing together a broken heart. 'Thank you for doing this—the department will be grateful. I am grateful. We should be going.'

This was not how Ivy had envisaged things going. She'd thought he would be pleased, thrilled enough that she wouldn't have to completely open herself up to him. That he'd accept this whole night run as a sign of how she felt. Which was…overwhelmed. Just being with him again left her breathless and aching for more. To touch him. To kiss him.

Say it.

Bleed if you have to.

She watched him moving quickly in the crowd. 'Matteo.

Stop.' Damn. This had not been such a great idea after all. How to declare yourself in front of three thousand runners? *Really?* She doubled her pace, her leg jarring with every footfall, but, damn it, she was going to get through to him, all ten kilometres if she had to—shouting his name all the damned way. 'Matteo! Stop.' He did, finally. 'What I'm trying to say…badly…is that I'm sorry for how I reacted to everything. I didn't want it to end. Not really.'

He began to walk back to her, frowning. 'But you made it very obvious you didn't want me. Are you saying that you do now? You've changed your mind?'

His words were like tiny daggers stabbing at her heart. 'I always wanted you, you idiot. But I was scared. It went from a game, a battle of wills and a point to prove, to very serious, very quickly.' How else could she show him how she felt? Was this not enough?

'Matteo, I've been trying to prove that I'm worth something my whole life—it was hard, bloody hard, and there were times even I didn't believe it. But I learnt to fight for myself, I learnt not to rely on anyone, not to let anyone in because I just knew I'd get hurt in the end. And then you came along and I didn't need to try too hard with you because you seemed to accept me as I was—which was new and weird and exciting. And then I didn't know what to do. You took me by surprise—I needed to make space for you and I didn't want to let go of the safety blanket I'd shrouded myself in. My life was fine before you and your magnificent bottom came along, thank you very much, I wasn't expecting to fall in love with you…'

'You love…?' His eyes widened at her admission.

She placed a finger over his mouth. If she didn't say it all now, she might never say it. 'I felt frightened by the intensity of how I was feeling. My mum…she never wanted me around. Even now I'm of no use to her and I guess I got used to being on my own. But the thing is, I'm lost without you. I'm lost with you too, but that's okay…I'd kind of like us to be lost with each other. If you'll give me a second chance?'

He looked at her for a while. Took her finger from his lips and pressed a kiss onto the tip. 'I'm not lost at all, Ivy. I found you and you are worth more to me than everything else.'

'Oh, so good…'

But he still didn't look convinced. He wasn't. 'How do I know you mean it this time? How do I know you will not throw it all back in my face?'

Oh, so bad. Was he for real? Could he not see the love she knew was in her eyes? Could he not hear it in her voice? 'You want *more* than thirty thousand pounds, a massive show of support and a new dialysis machine? Really? That's not enough? This isn't enough? I'm not enough? I love you, Matteo. I don't know how else to show you. Please, believe me. I'm not Elizabetta. I'm not your father. I won't throw your love back at you. I don't know what else would prove to you how I feel.'

The crowds had all moved along, balloons bobbing in the distance, the park now silent except for the whistle of wind through the trees and a dull buzz from a hovering bee. And she was left standing with Matteo, alone, in a garden that smelt of sunshine and roses. Then she smiled to herself. She'd noticed them. Becca would be proud.

He looked away, at the balloons and the children and the banners. At the posters and the marquee. A slow smile flitted onto his lips as his gaze went from her eyes to her mouth. 'A kiss maybe?'

'Oh. Yes. Of course. Good idea.' She took a step closer, hardly daring to believe that this could be happening. Maybe he did believe her. His arms snaked round her waist and he dragged her to him. She bunched his work shirt into her fists, choking back the tears that were threatening. 'But how do you feel? About me? Us?'

'I love you more than anything. I told you already.'

She blinked, trying to remember. She would have remembered. 'When? When did you say that?'

'Our last kiss. I whispered it to you.'

'I wish I'd heard it.'

His mouth was close to her ear. 'I said, *Ti amo.*'

She tried it, to see how it felt. '*Ti amo,* Matteo. I love you.' Goddamn, it felt great, however she said it. Then she couldn't say anything else because the lump in her throat had got jammed there so tightly she could barely breathe. What little breath she did have left was whipped away by his kiss. A slow, gentle, heart-warming kiss that told her exactly how he felt.

He pulled away, a huge grin on his face. 'No more wars? No more games.'

'None.'

'Good.' His finger stroked the side of her cheek. 'So we have some catching up to do.'

'Oh, yes, the run… We'd better hurry up, we're going to be last.'

He shook his head, those dark eyes blazing with desire, a smile that was at once innocent and dirty. 'I wasn't thinking about that. I want you so bad…'

'*Badly.*' She saw the flicker of a frown then the smile. Then the grimace. 'Oh, whatever, I don't care how you say it. Just keep on saying it… I want you right back.'

'You know, you will drive me crazy.' He held out his hand.

She took it, held on tight, promising to never let go. 'That sounds like a very good plan.'

* * * * *

THE DOCTOR'S REDEMPTION

SUSAN CARLISLE

To Kathy Cooksey and Jeanie Brantley.
Thanks for sharing Mardi Gras with me.

CHAPTER ONE

THE PARADES WERE what Laura Jo Akins enjoyed most about the Mardi Gras season in Mobile, Alabama. This year was no different. She placed a hand on the thin shoulder of her eight-year-old daughter, Allie.

Her daughter smiled up at her. "When does the parade start?"

"It should already be moving our way. Listen. You can hear the band."

The faint sound of a ragtime tune floated from the distance.

Allie looked up at Laura Jo. "Can we stay for the next one too?"

The sure thing about Mardi Gras was that the parades kept coming. The closer the calendar got to Fat Tuesday the more heavily the days were filled with parades. Sometimes as many as four a day on the weekends.

"No, honey. They're expecting me at the hospital. We'll watch this one and then we have to go."

"Okay, but we get to see one another day, don't we?"

"Maybe on Wednesday. Next Monday and Tuesday you'll be out of school for a long weekend. We'll be sure to watch more then."

"Why can't I be in one?" Allie asked, turning to look at Laura Jo.

It had been a constant question during last year's Mardi Gras season and had become more demanding during this one. "Maybe when you get older. For now we'll just have to watch."

As the banner holders at the head of the parade came into sight the crowd pushed forward, forcing her and Allie against the metal barriers. A bicycling medical first responder or mobile EMT circled in front of them then rode up the street. He looked familiar for some reason but, then, most of the medical help during the carnival season were employed at the hospital where she worked. Dressed in red biking shorts and wearing a pack on his back, he turned again and pedaled back in their direction. Laura Jo squinted, trying to make out his features, but his helmet obscured her view.

Members of the medical community volunteered to work during Mardi Gras to help out with the crowds. Most of the nurses and doctors gave up their days off during the season to work the parades. It wasn't required but many enjoyed being a part of the celebration. Laura Jo knew most of the employees at Mobile General, at least by face. Although she couldn't place the rider, he looked just fine in his form-fitting pants. He must bike regularly.

"Look, Mommy." Allie pointed to a group of people who had come through the barriers and were entertaining the crowd standing on both sides of the street. They were dressed in clown-type outfits and were riding three-wheeled bikes with bright-colored fish attached to the side.

Laura Jo smiled down at her daughter. "That's the Mystic Fish."

They made a circle or two in the open parade area and then disappeared into the crowd across the street from her and Allie. Laura Jo knew from years of watching parades that they would appear somewhere else along the parade route.

"What's a mystic fish?" Allie asked.

"You know what a fish is. In this case it's a club or group of people. It's also called a krewe. Because they meet in secret they are mystic or mysterious. It's all just fun."

"Are you in a queue?'

"It's krewe. Like a crew member. And, no, I'm not." She placed a hand on her daughter's head. "I have you to take care of, work at the shelter and at the hospital. No time."

Laura Jo understood being a member of a krewe. Her family had been participants all her life. In fact, they had been a part of the largest and most prestigious krewe in Mobile. She'd been one of the Mobile society that had celebrated her coming of age at carnival time. But no more.

The noise level increased as the first high-school band approached. She positioned Allie between her and the barrier so Allie could see. As the first ostentatiously decorated float rolled by the spectators pressed closer to them. The float was designed in a dragon motif and painted green, purple and gold with piles of beads hanging off pegs. Members of the krewe were dressed in costumes and wore masks.

She and Allie joined those around them in yelling, "Throw me something, mister."

Raising their hands along with everyone else, she and Allie tried to catch the beads, plastic cups with the krewe name printed on them or stuffed animals that were being thrown from the float. Bands playing and music blaring from large speakers mounted on the floats made it difficult to hear.

One krewe member made eye contact with Laura Jo and pointed at Allie. He threw a small stuffed gorilla to

Laura Jo, which she handed to Allie, who hugged it to her and smiled up at the grinning man. The float moved on.

When a strand of brightly colored beads flew through the air in Allie's direction from the next float, Laura Jo reached to catch them. She couldn't and they were snatched by the man standing behind her. He handed them to Allie. She smiled brightly at him. That was one of the special things about Mardi Gras in Mobile. It was a family affair. Any age was welcome and everyone saw that the children had a good time. Twenty minutes later a fire truck that signaled the end of the parade rolled by.

The man standing next to them shifted the barrier, creating an opening. A few people rushed through in an effort to snatch up any of the goodies that had fallen on the pavement.

"Mama, can I get those?" Allie pointed out into the street, now virtually empty except for a few children.

Laura Jo searched for what Allie was asking about. On the road lay a couple of plastic doubloons. "Sure, honey. There won't be another parade for an hour."

Allie ran through the opening and ran in the direction of the strand of gold and silver disks. In her exuberance to reach her target she stumbled and fell, stopping herself with her hands. Laura Jo gasped and rushed to her. Allie had already pushed herself up to a sitting position. Tears welled in her eyes but she'd not burst into sobs yet. There was an L-shaped hole in the thin material of her pants and a trickle of blood ran off the side of her knee.

"Oh, honey," Laura Jo said.

"My hands hurt." Allie showed Laura Jo her palms. The meaty part looked much like her knee.

"Friction burns." Laura Jo took one of Allie's wrists and raised her hand, blowing across it. Here she was a registered nurse with not a bandage to her name. Allie's injuries were going to require far more than what Laura Jo was doing.

"Can I help here?" a deep male voice said from above them.

Laura Jo glanced up to see the bike medic she'd admired earlier. She'd been so adsorbed with Allie she'd not noticed him ride up.

"Do you have any four-by-fours? Some antibiotic cream?" Laura Jo asked.

The man gave her a curious look then stepped off the bike. He slung the red pack off his back and crouched down on his haunches. "Let me see what I can do."

Laura Jo looked at him through moisture in her eyes. She knew him. Or more accurately knew who he was. Mark Clayborn. She'd had no idea he was back in town. But, then, why would she? "If you'll just share your supplies I can handle it. I'm her mother and a nurse."

"I appreciate that but I need to treat your daughter since it happened at the parade. I'll have to make a report anyway."

She gave him room. Years ago she'd been very enamored of Mark Clayborn. Just young enough to hero worship him, she'd often dreamed of "what if" when he'd glanced her way. Which he never had, unless it had been to smile at the gaggle of young maids in his queen's court. He'd had it all. Good looks, social status, education and a bright future. And to top it off he'd been Mardi Gras King that year. Every girl had dreamed of being on his arm and she'd been no different. She had watched him so closely back then no wonder he seemed familiar.

Allie winced when he touched the angry skin of her knee.

Laura Jo's hands shook. As an emergency room nurse she'd seen much worse, but when it came to her own child it was difficult to remain emotionally detached. Still, she should be the one caring for Allie. She'd been her sole caretaker and provider since her daughter's father had left Laura Jo when she was three months pregnant. Having been pushed aside before, she didn't like it any better now than she had then. No matter how irrational the reaction.

"So what's your name, young lady?" Mark asked Allie.

She told him.

"So, Allie, what have you liked best about Mardi Gras this year?"

Allie didn't hesitate to answer. "King Cake."

He nodded like a sage monk giving thought to the answer. "I like King Cake, too. What's your favorite? Cinnamon or cream cheese?"

"Cinnamon."

"I'm a fan of cream cheese. So have you ever found the baby?"

"Yeah, once. I had to take a cake to school the next week."

"So you baked one?"

"No, my mother did." She pointed at Laura Jo.

Mark glanced at her with a look of respect but there was no sign of recognition. Even though their families had known each other for years he didn't remember her. The last she'd really heard, he'd been in a bad car accident and had later left for medical school.

"You mom didn't get it from a bakery?"

"No. She likes to make them." Allie smiled up at Laura Jo. "She lets me put the baby inside."

Allie continued, telling him how she liked to stand beside Laura Jo as she rolled the pastry out. She would wait patiently until it was time to put the miniature plastic baby into one of the rolls before Laura Jo braided them into a cake. When it came out of the oven Allie begged to be the one to shake the green, purple and gold sugar on top.

"Well, that sounds like fun. Are you ready to stand?"

Laura Jo couldn't help but be impressed. Mark had cleaned up Allie with little more than a wince from her.

He placed a hand below Allie's elbow and helped her to stand then said to Laura Jo, "Keep the area clean. If you see any infection, call a doctor right away or take her to the ER."

Laura Jo rolled her eyes. "I'm a nurse, remember?"

"I remember, but sometimes when it's someone we love our emotions get in the way."

That was something close to what her father had said when she'd announced that she was marrying Phil. "He's only interested in your last name and money." Her father had gone on to say that Phil certainly wasn't worth giving up her education for. When she'd asked how her father knew so much about Phil he admitted to having had someone check into his background. That Phil had already been married once and couldn't seem to hold down a job. "He's not good enough for you. Not welcome in our home," had been her father's parting words.

She'd chosen Phil. Even though she'd soon learned that her father had been right, the situation had created a rift between Laura Jo and her parents that was just as wide today as it had been nine years earlier. She had sworn then never to ask her parents for help. She had her pride.

Taking Allie's hand, Laura Jo said, "Let's go, honey. I'm sure we have taken enough of the medic's time."

"Bye," Allie said.

Mark bent and picked up the doubloons off the pavement and placed them carefully in Allie's hand. "I hope you find a baby in your next cake. Maybe it'll bring you luck."

Allie grinned back at him with obvious hero worship.

"Thank you." She led Allie through the barrier. "Bye."

That would be it for the reappearing Mark Clayborn. He had been a part of her life that was now long gone. She wouldn't be seeing him again.

Mark had never planned to return to Mobile to live permanently, but that had changed. He'd worked hard to make LA home. Even the few times he'd come back to Alabama he'd only stayed a few days and then gone again. When his father's houseman had phoned to say Mark Clayborn, Sr. had suffered a stroke, Mark could no longer refuse not to make southern Alabama his home again. His mother was gone and his brother was in the military with no control over where he was stationed. Mark was left no choice. Someone needed to live close enough to take care of his father.

Pulling up the circular drive framed by a well-manicured yard in the center of the oldest section of homes in Mobile, Mark stopped in front of the antebellum mansion. This house had been his home for the twenty-five years before he had moved to LA. Now just his father lived here. Mark had chosen to take up residence forty-five minutes across the bay in the Clayborn summer house in Fairhope, Alabama. He had joined a general practice group made up of five doctors. The clinic was located in the town of Spanish Fort, which was halfway between Mobile and Fairhope. He lived and worked close enough to take care of his father and far enough away that memories of the past would remain murky instead of vivid.

It had been carnival season when he'd left for LA. He'd been riding high on being the king. His queen had been his girlfriend for the last two years and one of the most beautiful girls in Mobile society. He'd gotten his pick of medical fellowships that had allowed him to only be a few hours away in Birmingham. Gossips had it that he and his queen would ride off into the happily-ever-after as soon as he finished his fellowship. Mark had not planned to disappoint them. That was until he and Mike had decided they needed to drive to the beach after the krewe dance on Fat Tuesday night.

How many times since he'd been back had he picked up the phone to call and see how Mike was doing? How many times had he not followed through? He'd seen Mike a few times over the years. Those had been brief and uncomfortable meetings. Mark had always left with another wheelbarrow of guilt piled on top of the mountain that was already there.

He and Mike had made big plans. They had both been on their way to Birmingham, Mark to complete his fellowship and Mike to earn his Master's in Business. They would return to town to set up a clinic practice, Mark handling the medical end and Mike overseeing the business side. They'd even talked about their families building homes next door to each other. But after the accident Mike's longtime girlfriend had left him. Those dreams vanished. Because of Mark.

As time had gone by it had become easier to satisfy his need to know how Mike was doing by asking others about him. Often when Mark had spoken to his father he'd ask about Mike. His father had always encouraged him to call and talk to Mike if he wanted to know how he was doing. Mark hadn't. That way the guilt didn't become a throbbing, breathing thing.

Mark pushed the front doorbell of his father's house then opened the door. He was met in the high-ceilinged hall by John, the man who had worked for Mark, Sr. since Mark, Jr. had been a boy.

"Hi. How's he doing today?"

"Your dad has had a good day. He's out by the pool."

Mark headed down the all-too-familiar hall that led

through the middle of the house and out onto the brick patio with the pool beyond. His father sat in a wheelchair in the sun, with his nurse nearby, reading a book. Mark winced at the sight. It hurt his heart to see the strong, commanding man brought to this by a stroke. Only with time and patience and massive amounts of physical therapy would he regain enough strength to walk again. At least his father had a chance of getting out of the chair, unlike Mike, who had no choice.

Mark circled his father so he faced him. "Hi, Dad."

His white-haired father gave him a lopsided smile. "Hello, son."

Fortunately his mind was still strong. His nurse closed her book and after a nod to Mark made her way toward the house.

Mark pulled a metal pool chair close so he could sit where his father could see him. "How are you doing today?"

"Fine. Emmett has been by to tell me what went on at the board meeting. He said you didn't make it."

"No, I had patients to see. We've talked about this already. You've put good people in place to handle the company. Let them do it."

"It's not the same. We need a Clayborn there."

"I know, Dad."

His father continued. "I'm glad you stopped by. I wanted to talk to you about attending the krewe dance next week. I can't go and our family needs to be represented. You're the only one to do it."

Mark had always enjoyed the fanfare and glamour of The Mystical Order of Orion dance, the visit from the king and queen and their court. But after what had happened twelve years ago he was hesitant to attend. He took a deep breath. "It's not really my thing anymore but I know it's important to you to keep up appearances."

"You were king. That is and was a high honor. You owe it to the krewe, to the Clayborn name to attend."

"I know, Dad. I'll do my duty."

"This used to be your favorite time of the year. You need to let yourself off the hook, son. It wasn't your fault."

Maybe everyone thought that but Mark sure didn't. He carried the horror of what had happened to Mike with him daily. Now that he was back in Mobile it was more alive than it had ever been. Time hadn't healed the wound, only covered it over.

Mark had dinner with his father then headed across the bay to Fairhope, a small township where the family summer home was located. When he'd arrived in Alabama he'd needed a place to live. Staying in Fairhope gave him a house of his own, a safe haven. Since he was working at a clinic in Spanish Fort, a city just north of Fairhope, living there was convenient.

Entering the large dark room with hardwood paneling, Mark walked through to the family-style kitchen. There he pulled a drink out of the refrigerator and went out to the deck. Mobile Bay stretched far and wide before him. He could see the tall buildings of the city in the distance. The wind had picked up, rustling the shrubbery around the deck. A seagull swooped down and plucked a fish out of the water near the end of the pier. No, this wasn't LA anymore.

Mark had agreed to pitch in and work the parades as a first responder when one of his new partners had said that they did that as a public service during Mardi Gras season. He'd agreed to do his part but had expected that it would be in some of the surrounding smaller towns. When he'd been assigned the parade in downtown Mobile he hadn't felt like he could say no. He needed to be a team player since he'd only joined the medical group a few months earlier. Despite the parade location, Mark had enjoyed the assignment. Especially helping the young girl. Her mother had been attractive. More than once since then he'd wondered where she worked.

He'd spent the rest of the parade scanning the crowd. His chest still contracted at the thought he might see Mike. He'd spent years making a point of not thinking about the automobile accident. Now that he was back it seemed the only thing on his mind.

His cell phone rang. He pulled it out of his pocket. "This is Dr. Clayborn."

"Hey, Mark, it's Ralph. We need you again the day after tomorrow if you can help us out. Afternoon parade in Dauphine."

He didn't mind working a parade in Dauphine. It was on his side of the bay. As long as it wasn't in Mobile. There the chance of facing his past became greater. "Yeah, I'm only seeing patients in the morning. Will I be on a bike again?"

"Not this time. I just need you at the med tent. It'll be set up in the First Baptist Church parking lot."

"I'll be there."

"Marsha?" Laura Jo called as she and Allie opened the door of her best friend's apartment Wednesday afternoon.

"Hey, we're back here," a voice came from the direction of the kitchen area located in the back of the apartment.

She followed Allie down the short hallway to find Marsha and her son, Jeremy, decorating a wagon with purple, green and gold ribbons.

Marsha looked up as they entered. "You know Mardi Gras almost kills me every year. I say I'm not going to do anything next year then here I am, doing even more."

Allie had already joined in to help Jeremy with the decorations.

"I know what you mean. It makes working in the ER

interesting. I've enjoyed my day off but I'll pay for it, no doubt, by being on the night shift. I appreciate you letting Allie spend the night."

"It's not a problem. I love her like my own." She ruffled Allie's hair.

Laura Jo had met Marsha at the Mothers Without Partners clinic. Phil had lived up to all her father's predictions and more when he'd left her pregnant and cleaned out their bank account to never be seen again. Even after all these years he hadn't even checked to see if he had a son or daughter. Marsha's husband had died in a fishing accident. She and Marsha had hit it off right away. Circumstances had brought them together but friendship had seen to it that they still depended on each other.

They'd shared an apartment for a few months and had traded off their time watching the kids while the other had worked or gone to school. They had their own apartments now but in the same complex and Marsha was more like family than the one Laura Jo had left behind.

They had joined forces to help other mothers who didn't have anyone to fall back on. They had convinced the city to sell them an old home so these women would have a place to live and receive help while they were getting their lives in order. The deadline to pay for the house was looming. Finding the funding had become more difficult than Laura Jo had anticipated.

Marsha announced, "I heard from the city contact. He said we had to move soon on the house or the city will have to announce it's for sale. They can't hold it forever."

Laura Jo groaned. That wasn't what she wanted to hear. "How much time do we have?"

"Week or two. At least until things settle down after Mardi Gras. We've got to come up with a good way to raise a lot of money. Fast. I know you don't want to do it but you do have the contacts. Maybe you could put on a party dress and go pick the pockets of all those society friends you used to hang around with."

Laura Jo shook her head. "That's not going to happen. We'll have to find another way."

What if she had to face her mother and father? Worse, have them see her asking for money. That's what they had thought she'd be doing if she married Phil. That's what he'd wanted her to do, but she'd refused. After her fight with her parents she and Phil had gone to Las Vegas that night to get married.

When they'd returned Phil had left to work on an oil rig. Three weeks later he'd come home. A week later all his pay had gone and he'd admitted he'd been fired. He'd made noises about looking for a job but in hindsight she didn't think he'd ever really tried. Things had got worse between them. The issue that finally snapped them had been Laura Jo telling him she was pregnant. Phil's snarling parting words were, "I didn't sign on for no kid. You can't put that on me. Having you is bad enough."

Marsha gave her questioning look. "You know I'm kidding but…"

"I'll come up with something." She checked her watch. "Now, I have to get to the hospital." Stepping toward Allie, Laura Jo said to Marsha, "I'll meet you at the parade tomorrow evening."

"Sounds like a plan."

Laura Jo leaned down and kissed Allie on the head. "See ya. Be good for Marsha."

"I will," Allie replied, then returned to what she was doing.

"Thanks, Marsha." Laura Jo called as she went up the hall.

Six hours later, Laura Jo was longing for her dinner and a moment to put her feet up. She wasn't going to get either anytime soon. Working in a trauma one level hospital meant a constant influx of patients, not only the regular cases but Mardi Gras's as well, which brought out the revelers and daredevils. Weekend nights were the worst and the place resembled a circus with not enough clowns to go around. Everyone had their hands full. The doors were swishing open regularly with people coming in. The constant ringing of the phone filled the area, blending with the piercing scream of ambulance sirens.

As she stepped back into the nursing station the phone rang again. Seconds later the clerk called out, "Incoming. Sixty-seven-year-old male. Heart attack. Resuscitating in transit. Child with head trauma behind that. ETA ten."

"I'll take the heart. Trauma six." Laura Jo hurried to set up what was needed before the patient arrived.

Minutes later the high-pitched sound of the ambulance arriving filled the air and Laura Jo rushed outside. The double rear doors of the vehicle stood wide open. Usually by this time the EMTs would be unloading the patient.

Looking inside, she immediately recognized the EMT working over the patient but not the other man. Then she did. *Mark Clayborn.* Again he was wearing red biking shorts and a yellow shirt of a first responder.

Mark held the portable oxygen bubble away from the patient as the EMT placed the defibrillator paddles on the patient's chest. The body jerked. The beep of the machine monitoring the heart rate started and grew steadier. Putting the earpieces of the stethoscope that had been around his neck into place, Mark listened to the man's heart. "Let's get him inside," he said with a sharp tone of authority. He then made an agile jump to the ground, turned toward the interior of the ambulance and helped bring out the patient on the stretcher.

Although confused by why he had been allowed in the

emergency vehicle, she still followed his lead. It was against policy to ride in the back unless you were part of the EMT staff. But now wasn't the time for questions. She stood aside while the two men lifted out the stretcher. The wheels dropped to the pavement and Laura Jo wrapped her hand around the yellow metal frame and pulled. Mark kept his fingers on the pulse point of the patient's wrist while the EMT pushed.

They had reached the doors when Mark said, "We're losing him again."

Tall enough to lean over and push on the patient's chest, he began compressions. Another nurse met them and gave oxygen. Laura Jo kept moving ahead, her arm burning. To her relief, they got the patient into the trauma room. There Mark and the EMT used the defibrillator once again. Seconds later the monitor made a beep and the line went from straight to having peaks and valleys. After they gained a steady pulse, she worked to place leads to the monitors on the patient. The ER doctor rushed in.

Mark and the EMT backed away with exhausted sighs, giving the ER doctor, Laura Jo and the other staff members space to work. For the next twenty intensive minutes, Laura Jo followed the ER doctor's instructions to the letter. Finally they managed to stabilize the patient enough to send him to surgery.

Laura Jo had to talk to the family. They must be scared. When she asked the admission clerk where they were she was told exam room five.

"Why are they in an exam room?"

"The man's granddaughter is being evaluated."

Laura Jo headed for the exam room. It shouldn't have surprised her that Mark was there, too. He came out as she was preparing to go in.

"Well, fancy meeting you here," he drawled in a deep voice that made her think of a dark velvet night.

"It's not that amazing really. I work here."

"I figured that out. So how's your daughter? Healing nicely?"

"She's fine. A little tender but fine."

"Good. By the way, I'm Dr. Mark Clayborn."

"Yes, I know who you are. As in the Clayborn Building, Clayborn Bank, Clayborn Shipping.

He gave her a studying look. "Do I know you?"

"I'm Laura Jo Akins. Used to be Laura Jo Herron."

"Herron? My parents used to talk about the Herrons. Robert Herron. Real estate."

She looked away. "Yes, that's my father."

He had pursed his lips. "Well, that's a surprise. Isn't it a small world?"

Too small for Laura Jo's comfort. It was time to change the subject. "Thanks for helping out. Now I need to talk to the family." She gave the door to the exam room a quick knock and pushed it open.

It turned out that she was wasting her time. "The nice Dr. Clayborn" had updated them and also seen to Lucy, their little girl, but they appreciated Laura Jo coming in. By the time she'd returned to the nursing station things seemed to be under control in the ER. All the exam and trauma rooms were full. The critical cases were being cared for. Those waiting were not serious.

"Why don't you take your supper break while you can?" the lead nurse said.

"Are you sure?"

"It's now or never. You know the closer we get to Fat Tuesday the merrier it gets around here."

Laura Jo laughed. "If merry is what you want to call it. Okay, I'll go."

"I'd rather call it merry otherwise I think I might cry," the lead nurse said with a grin.

Laura Jo grabbed her lunch box. It had become a habit to pack a lunch when money had been so tight even before Phil had left. Reaching the cafeteria, she scanned the room for an empty table. The busy ER translated to a full room. As soon as a table opened up she headed for it. Before she could get to it Mark slid into one of the two seats available. Disappointed, she stopped and looked around for another spot.

He waved her toward him. "You can join me, if you like."

Laura Jo looked at him. Did she really have a choice? She was expected back in the ER soon. "Thank you."

He grinned at her. "You don't sound too excited about it."

What was he expecting her to say? *You're right, I'm not?* "I have to eat. The ER won't stay calm for long."

"It did look a little wild in there. I've certainly had more than my share this evening. I haven't done this much emergency work since I was on my med school rotation. Don't see many head trauma and heart attacks in family practice."

Laura Jo pulled her sandwich out of the plastic bag. "I understand that the girl was sitting on top of her father's shoulders and toppled off. When the grandfather saw what had happened he had a heart attack."

"Yeah. Thank goodness it all happened within running distance of the med tent. For a few minutes there wasn't enough of us medical personal around to handle all that was going on. I'm just glad the girl has regained consciousness and the grandfather is stable."

"The girl will be here for observation for at least one night and the grandfather for much longer, I'm afraid."

He took a large bite of his hamburger and they ate in silence for a while before he asked, "So you knew who I was the other day. Why didn't you say something?"

"There just didn't seem a right moment."

"So you've seen a lot of Mardi Gras."

She straightened her back and looked directly at him. "I'm not that old."

He grinned. "I'm sorry, I didn't mean to imply that."

Laura Jo had to admit he had a nice smile. She grinned. "That's not what it sounded like to me."

"I was just trying to make pleasant conversation and didn't mean—"

"I know you didn't." Still, it would have been nice if he'd at least thought she looked familiar. She'd been invisible to her parents, unimportant to her husband and just this once it would have been nice to have been memorable. But, then, it had been a long time ago.

"So do you attend any of the krewe festivities?" He chewed slowly, as if waiting patiently for her answer.

"No. I don't travel in that social circle anymore." She took a bite of her sandwich.

"Why not? As I remember, the Herrons were a member of the same krewe as my family."

"I'm an Akins now."

"So Mr. Akins isn't a member either, I gather."

"No, and Mr. Akins, as you put it, isn't around to be a member."

"I'm sorry."

"I'm not. He left years ago."

"Oh, I thought…"

"I know. For all I know, he's alive and well somewhere."

Having finished his meal, Mark leaned back in his chair and crossed his arms over his chest. "Well, it has been a pleasure running into you, Ms. Atkins."

Laura Jo stood to leave. "You, too, Dr. Clayborn. We do seem to keep running into each other."

"Why, Ms. Akins, you don't believe in serendipity?"

"If I ever did believe in serendipity, that would've been a long time ago. Now, if you'll excuse me, I need to get back to work."

CHAPTER TWO

ON SATURDAY AFTERNOON Mark made his way through the side streets of Mobile, working around the parade route, which was already blocked off. It was one more week before Mardi Gras weekend and there would be a large parade that afternoon and another that night in downtown Mobile.

Throughout the week in the surrounding towns parades were planned, culminating in three or four per day until the final one on Fat Tuesday. Then Ash Wednesday would arrive and end all the revelry.

He'd been assigned to work in the med tent set up just off Government Street at a fire station. He'd wanted to say no, had even suggested that he work one or two of the parades in a nearby town, but he'd been told that he was needed there. His gut clenched each time he crossed the bay but his partners wouldn't like him not being a team player during this time of the year. Plus, Mark had no desire to admit why going into Mobile bothered him.

All he hoped for now was a slow day, but he didn't expect it. He wanted less drama than the last time he'd worked a med tent a few days earlier. Still, there had been some interesting points.

Dinner with Laura Jo Akins had been the highlight. He had at least found out she wasn't married. And she seemed to be anti-krewe for some reason. He had no doubt that she'd grown up on the social club festivities of a krewe, just like him. Why would she have such a negative view now? Or was her pessimistic attitude directed toward him? Did she know about the accident? His part in it?

Laura Jo Akins also appeared to be one of those women who knew her mind and stood her ground, but it also seemed there was a venerable spot to her, too. As if she hid something from the world. What was that all about?

Mark looked over the crowd again. At least she took his thoughts off worrying that he might see Mike at a parade. He looked forward to seeing her pixie face if they ever met again. People were creatures of habit and usually showed up in the same places to watch the parades. He wasn't sure why she interested him so, but she'd popped into his head a number of times over the past few days.

He had been at the med tent long enough to introduce himself to some of the other volunteers when he looked up to see none other than Laura Jo walking toward the tent. She caught sight of him about the same time. He didn't miss her moment of hesitation before she continued in his direction. He smiled and nodded at her. She returned his smile.

A few minutes later he was asked to help with a woman who was having an asthma attack in the unseasonably warm weather. It was some time later before he had a chance to speak to Laura Jo.

"I believe we might be caught in some Mardi Gras mystical mojo," he said, low enough that the others around them couldn't hear.

"I don't believe any sort of thing. I'm more of the dumb luck kind of person," she responded, as she continued to sort supplies.

He chuckled. "Didn't expect to see me again so soon, did you?"

She spun around, her hands going to her hips. "Did you plan this?"

"I did not," he said with complete innocence. "I was told when and where to be."

"I thought maybe with the Clayborn name…"

What did she have against the Clayborns? Did she know what he'd done? If she did, he couldn't blame her for not wanting to have anything to do with him. "Excuse me?"

"Nothing."

"Dr. Clayborn, we need you," one of the other volunteers called.

Mark had no choice but to go to work.

Half an hour later, the sound of a jazz band rolled down the street. Because the med tent was set up at the fire station, no one could park or stand in front of it. Mark and the others had an unobstructed view of the parade. Thankfully there was no one requiring help so they all stepped out toward the street curb to watch. Laura Jo seemed to appreciate the parade. She even swayed to the music of "Let the good times roll."

He wandered over to stand just behind her. "You enjoy a good parade as much as your daughter does, I see." Mark couldn't help but needle her. She reacted so prettily to it.

"Yes, I love a good parade. You make it sound like it should be a crime."

"And you make it sound like it's a crime that I noticed," he shot back.

"No crime. Just not used to someone taking that much notice."

"That's hard to believe. You mean there's no man who pays attention to you?"

"Getting a little personal, aren't you, Doctor?" She glanced back at him.

"No, just making conversation."

"Hey, Mom."

They both turned at the sound of Laura Jo's daughter's voice. She was with another woman about Laura Jo's age and there was a boy with them about the same height as the daughter.

Before her mother could respond the girl said to Mark, "I know you. You're that man who helped me the other day. Look, my hands are all better." She put out her hands palms up. "My knee still hurts a little." She lifted her denim-covered knee.

"And I know you." He smiled down at her. "But forgive me, I've forgotten your name."

"Allie."

He squatted down to her level. "I'm glad you're feeling better, Allie." Standing again, he glanced in the direction of the woman he didn't know. Laura Jo must have gotten the hint because she said, "This is Marsha Gilstrap. A friend of mine." She looked toward the boy. "And Jeremy, her son. I thought ya'll were going to watch the parade over on Washington."

"We wanted to come by and say hi to you," Allie said.

Laura Jo gave her daughter a hug then looked down at her with what Mark recognized as unbounded love. He liked it when he saw parents who really cared about their children. Her actions hadn't just been for show when her daughter had been hurt at the parade. She truly cared about her child. He recognized that love because his parents had had the same for him. That's why his father had insisted Mark not get involved with Mike's case after the accident. His father had feared what it might do to Mark's future. He been young enough and scared enough that he'd agreed, despite the guilt he'd felt over leaving the way he had. Now he didn't trust himself to get close enough to care about someone. If he did, he might fail them, just as he had Mike. He hadn't stood beside Mike, whom he'd loved like a brother, so why would he have what it took to stand by a wife and family?

A float coming by drew Allie's attention. Mark put a hand on her shoulder. "Come on. This is a great spot to watch a parade."

Allie looked at her mother in question. Laura Jo took a second before she gave an agreeable nod but he got the sense that she didn't want to.

Allie glanced at the boy. "Can Jeremy come, too?"

"Sure."

Jeremy's mother, in contrast to Laura Jo, was all smiles about the boy joining them.

"We'll just be right up here if you need us." Mark made an effort to give Laura Jo his most charming smile.

He nudged one of the volunteers out of the way so that the children had a front-row place to stand. A couple of times he had to remind them not to step out beyond the curve. Because they were standing in front of the fire station, there were no barriers in place. After a few minutes Laura Jo and her friend joined them.

"Thanks, we'll take these two off your hands," Laura Jo said, as if she was helping him out. What she was really doing was trying to get rid of him.

"Look at the dog. How funny." Allie squealed. The dog was wearing a vest and a hat. "I wish I had a dog to dress up. Then we could be in a parade."

Laura Jo placed her hand on top of Allie's shoulder. "Maybe one day, honey."

There was something in the wispy tone in the girl's voice that got to him. It reminded him of how he'd sounded the first time he'd asked if he could be in a dog parade. When he and his brother had participated in a parade it had been one of the greatest pleasures of his childhood. He could surely give that to Allie without becoming too involved in her and her mother's lives. "You could borrow my dog. Gus would be glad to let you dress him up," Mark offered.

"Could I, Mom?" Allie looked at Laura Jo as if her life depended on a positive answer.

"I don't know."

"I think Allie and Gus would make a great pair." He had no doubt Laura Jo hated to say no to something her daughter so obviously wanted to do. But why was he making it his job to see that Allie had a chance to be in a parade? Was it because Laura Jo was a hard-working mother who couldn't do this for her daughter and it was easy enough for him to do? It would be a great memory for Allie, just as it had been for him.

"Please, Mom."

"Fairhope has a parade on Sunday evening that I believe dogs are allowed in. Why don't you and Allie come and meet Gus that afternoon? You could bring some clothes for him and see how he likes them."

Laura Jo gave him a piercing look that said she wasn't pleased with the turn of events.

In a perverse way he liked the idea he was able to nettle her.

"Allie, I don't think we should take advantage of Dr. Clayborn's time."

"Please, call me Mark. And I don't mind." He really didn't. Since he'd been back in town he had kept to himself. It would be nice to spend the afternoon with someone. "I'm sure Gus will be glad to have the company. I've not been around much the past few days. Marsha, you and Jeremy are welcome, too."

"Thanks. It sounds like fun but I can't. Jeremy can if Laura Jo doesn't mind," Marsha said, smiling.

Laura Jo shot Marsha a look as if there would be more to say about this when they were alone.

"Mom, please," Allie pleaded. "Please."

"Won't your wife mind us barging in? Won't your children be dressing him up?"

"No wife. No children. So there's no reason you can't."

"Then I guess we could come by for a little while but I'm not making any promises about the parade." Laura Jo looked down at Allie.

"Great. I'll expect you about two. Here's my address." He pulled out a calling card, turned it over and, removing a pen from his pocket, wrote on it. "I'll have Gus all bathed and waiting on you."

Allie giggled. "Okay."

Mark looked at Laura Jo. "See you tomorrow."

She gave him a weak smile and he grinned. He was already looking forward to the afternoon.

Laura Jo wasn't sure how she'd managed to be coerced into agreeing to go to Mark's. Maybe it was because of the look of anticipation on Allie's face or the maternal guilt she felt whenever Allie asked to do something and she had to say no because she had to go to work or school. Now that she was in a position to give her child some fun in her life, she couldn't bring herself to say no. But going to Mark Clayborn's house had to be one for the record. She didn't really know the man. She'd admired him with a young girl's hero worship. But she knew little about the man he had become. He'd been nice enough so far but she hadn't always been the best judge of character.

She'd searched for a sound reason why they couldn't do it. Marsha certainly hadn't been any help. It was as if she had pushed her into going. For once Laura Jo wished she had to work on Sunday. But no such luck.

Allie was up earlier than usual in her excitement over the possibility of being in the dog parade. Jeremy had been almost as bad, Marsha said, when he ran to meet them at the car later that day.

"So are you looking forward to an afternoon with the handsome, debonair and rich Dr. Mark Clayborn?" Marsha asked with a grin.

They'd had a lively and heated discussion over a cup of coffee late the night before about Mark. Marsha seemed to think she should develop him as an ally in funding the single mothers' house. Laura Jo wasn't so sure. That was a road she'd promised herself she'd never go down again. She wasn't ever going to ask her parents or her society friends for anything ever again. That certainly included Mark Clayborn.

After today she didn't plan to see him again. This afternoon was about Allie and seeing a smile on her face. That only. Allie had been begging for a dog for the past year but they didn't have a lifestyle that was good for taking care of a dog.

Laura Jo pulled her aging compact car off the winding, tree-shaded road into the well-groomed, riverbed-pebbled drive of the address she'd been given. The crunch made a familiar sound. Her own family's place just a few miles down the road had the same type of drive, or at least it had the last time she'd been there.

The foliage of the large trees with moss hanging from them gave the area a cozy feel. Soon she entered an open space where a sweeping, single-story beach house sat with a wide expanse of yard between it and the bay beyond.

"Do you see Gus?" Allie strained at her seat belt as she peered out the window.

"Now, honey, I don't want you to get your hopes up too

high. Gus may not like being dressed up." Laura Jo didn't want to say "or you." Some owners thought their dogs loved everyone when they often didn't.

"He'll like it, I know he will."

"I think he will, too," Jeremy said from the backseat.

Laura Jo looked at him in the rearview mirror and smiled. "We'll see."

She pulled to a stop behind a navy blue high-end European car. To Mark's credit, it wasn't a sports car but it was finer than Laura Jo had ever ridden in, even when she'd still been living with her parents.

Her door had hardly opened before Allie ran toward a basset hound, whose ears dragged along the ground. Not far behind him strolled Mark. For a second her breath caught. He had all the markers of an eye-catching man. Tall, blond wavy hair and an air about him that said he could take care of himself and anyone else he cared about. It was a dazzling combination.

She'd been asked out a number of times by one of the men at the hospital, but she'd never had a man both irritate her and draw her to him at the same time. That was exactly what Mark Clayborn did.

He looked down with a smile at Allie, with her arms wrapped around Gus, and Jeremy, patting him, then at Laura Jo.

Her middle fluttered. If it wasn't for all the baggage she carried, her inability to trust her judgment of men, maybe she might be interested. She'd let Allie have her day and make a concerted effort not to see Mark again.

"Hey. Did you have any trouble finding it?"

"No trouble. I knew which one it was when you told me you lived in Fairhope."

"Really?"

"I remember passing it when I was a kid." She'd been aware all her life where the Clayborn summer home was located.

He glanced back to where the children played with the dog. "I think they're hitting it off."

Laura Jo couldn't help but agree.

"Allie, did you bring some clothes for Gus? I got a few things just in case you didn't," Mark said, strolling toward the kids and dog.

"They're in the car."

"I'll get them, honey," Laura Jo called, as the kids headed toward the large open yard between the house and bay. "Don't go near the water and stay where I can see you."

She walked to the car and Mark followed her. "You're a good mother."

Laura Jo glanced at him. "I try to be."

"So when did Allie's father leave?"

Laura Jo opened the passenger door then looked at him. "When I was three months pregnant."

Mark whistled. "That explains some of your standoffishness."

She pulled a large brown sack out of the car and closed the door with more force than necessary. "I'm not."

"Yeah, you are. For some reason, you don't want to like me, even when you do."

She was afraid he might be right. Thankfully, squealing in the front yard drew their attention to the two children running around as a dog almost as wide as he was tall chased them.

Mark checked his watch and called, "Allie and Jeremy, we need to get started on what Gus will wear because the parade starts in a couple of hours."

The kids ran toward them and Gus followed.

"Why don't we go around to the deck where it's cooler? We can dress Gus there," Mark said to the kids.

Mark led the way with the kids and Gus circled them. Laura Jo hung back behind them. Mark was good with children. Why didn't he have a wife and kids of his own? She imagined she was the only one of many who didn't fall at his charming feet.

The deck was amazing. It was open at one end. Chairs and a lounge group were arranged into comfortable conversation areas. At the other end was an arbor with a brown vine that must be wisteria on it. Laura Jo could only envision what it would look like in the spring and summer, with its green leaves creating a roof of protection from the sun. She'd love to sit in a comfortable chair under it but that wasn't going to happen.

"Allie, why don't you and Jeremy pull the things you brought out of the bag while I go get what I bought? Then you can decide how to dress Gus."

Allie took the bag from Laura Jo. With the children busy pulling feather boas, old hair bows, purple, green and gold ribbon from the bag, Laura Jo took a seat on the end of a lounge chair and watched.

Mark quickly returned with an armload of stuff.

"I thought you only got a few things," Laura Jo said.

He grinned. Her heart skipped a beat.

"I might have gotten a little carried away." He looked directly at her. "I do that occasionally."

For some reason, she had the impression he might be talking about sex. She hadn't had a thought like that in forever. Not since Phil had left. He'd made it clear that she hadn't been wanted and neither had their child.

Mark added his armload to the growing pile on the deck.

"Okay, Allie, I want you and Jeremy to pick out a winning combination. They give prizes for the funniest dog, best dressed, most spirited and some more I don't remember. Let's try to win a prize," Mark said, as he joined them on the planks of the wooden deck and held Gus. "I'll hold him while you dress him."

Laura Jo scooted back in the lounge to watch. It was a February day but the sun was shining. It wasn't long until her eyes closed.

She didn't know how long she'd been out before Mark's voice above her said, "You'd better be careful or you'll get burned. Even the winter sun in the south can get you."

"Thanks. I'm well aware of that. Remember, I've lived here all my life."

"That's right, a Herron."

"Who is a Herron, Mommy?"

"They're a family I used to know."

Mark's brows rose.

"Now, let me see what ya'll have done to Gus while I was napping," Laura Jo said quickly, before he could ask any more questions in front of Allie.

Mark didn't question further, seeing that Laura Jo didn't want to talk about her family in front of Allie. But he would be asking later. Allie didn't even know who her grandparents were? There was a deep, dark secret there that he was very interested in finding out about. Why hadn't he recognized Laura Jo? Probably because she had been too young to take his notice. His mouth drew into a line. More likely, he had been so focused on his world he hadn't looked outside it.

"My, doesn't Gus look, uh…festive?"

Mark couldn't help but grin at Laura Jo's description. Festive was a good word for it, along with silly. His dog wore a purple, gold and green feather boa wrapped around his neck. A dog vest of the same colors was on his body, bands on his ankles and a bow on the end of his tail. This being the one thing Allie had insisted he needed. Mark was amazed the Gus was as agreeable as he was about that.

Allie pronounced him "Perfect."

"I think we should be going if we want to make the start time."

"Start time?" Laura Jo asked.

"For the Mystic Mutts parade."

"I don't think—"

"We can't miss it. Isn't that right, Allie and Jeremy?"

"Right," both children said in unison.

Great. Now she was being ganged up on.

"Come on, Mommy. We have to take Gus," Allie pleaded.

Laura Jo glared at Mark. "I guess I don't have much of a choice."

Allie and Jeremy danced around her. "Yay."

"Let me get Gus's leash and we'll be all set." Mark went inside and returned with a lead.

As they rounded the house and headed toward the cars he looked at Laura Jo's. It was too small for all of them.

"I don't think we can all get in my car," Laura Jo said from beside him.

Mark stopped and looked at hers again. "I guess I should drive."

"You don't sound like you really want to do that. We could take two cars but I'm sure parking will be tight."

Mark's lips drew into a tight line. The thought of being responsible for Laura Jo and the kids gave him a sick feeling. Children had never ridden in his car. Since the accident he'd made it a practice not to drive with others in the car if he could help it. Often he hired a driver when he went out on a date. Unable to come up with another plan, he said,

"Then we'll go in my car. Please make sure the children are securely buckled in."

Laura Jo gave him an odd look before she secured Allie and Jeremy in the backseat. Gus found a spot between them and Allie placed an arm around him. Laura Jo joined him in the front. Mark looked back to check if the children were buckled in.

"Is there a problem?" Laura Jo asked.

If he kept this up he would make them all think he was crazy. He eased his grip on the steering wheel and let the blood flow back into his knuckles. "No. I was just double-checking they were okay."

Laura Jo shook her head as she ran a hand across the leather of the seat. "Worried about having kids in your fancy car?"

"No."

"Nice," she murmured.

"Like my car?"

"Yes," she said, more primly than the situation warranted, as she placed her hand in her lap.

He grinned. At least this subject took his mind off having a carload of passengers. "It's okay to say what you think."

"I wouldn't think it's very practical. The cost of a car like this could help a lot of people in need."

"I help people in need all the time. I also give to charities so I don't feel guilty about owning this car." Taking a fortify breath, he started it and pulled away from the house. At the end of the drive, he turned onto the road leading into town.

"I'm just not impressed by fancy cars and houses. People with those think they can tell you what to do, how you need to live. Even look down on others."

He glanced at her. "That's an interesting statement. Care to give me some background?"

"No, not really."

"Well, you just insulted me and my family and yours as well, and you won't even do me the courtesy of telling me why?"

"I'm sorry I insulted you. Sometimes my mouth gets ahead of my brain." She looked out the side window.

Yes, he was definitely going to find out what gave her such a sour view of people with money. He'd always prided himself on the amount he gave to charities. He had nothing to be ashamed of where that was concerned. Standing beside someone he loved when there was a disaster was where he failed.

A few minutes later he pulled the car into a tight space a couple of blocks from the parade route. It was the only spot he could find after circling the area. How had he gotten through the short drive without breaking into a sweat? Amazingly, talking to Laura Jo had made him forget his anxiety over driving. "This is the best I can do. We'll have to walk some."

Laura Jo saw to getting the children out. He leashed Gus and then gave him over to Allie. The girl beamed.

"I checked the paper this morning and the start of the parade is at the corner of Section and Third Street."

They weaved their way through the already growing crowd. As the number of people increased, Mark took Gus's leash from Allie and made sure that space was made for the dog, children and Laura Jo. A few times he touched her waist to direct her through a gap in the crowd. At the first occurrence she stiffened and glanced back at him. When he did it again she seemed to take it in her stride.

Mark was pleased when his little party arrived at the starting line without a loss of personnel. He looked at Laura Jo. "Why don't you wait here with the kids while I check in?"

"We'll be right over here near the brick wall." She took Gus's lead and led Allie and Jeremy to the spot she'd indicated.

"I'll be right back."

"You hope." She smiled.

It was the first genuine one he'd seen her give. It caught him off guard. It took him a second to respond. "Yeah."

Fifteen minutes later he had Gus, Allie and Jeremy signed in for the parade. He found Laura Jo and the kids waiting right where she'd said they would be. She had her head down, listening to something that Jeremy was saying. The angle of her head indicated she was keeping an eye on her daughter at the same time. Once again he was impressed by her mothering skills. The women he'd gone out with had never shown any interest in being mothers. He'd always thought he'd like to be a father, but he wouldn't let that happen. What if he ran out on them, like he had Mike, when the going got tough? He couldn't take that chance.

There was nothing flashy or pretentious about Laura Jo. More like what you saw was what you got. He'd grown up within the finely drawn lines of what was expected by the tight-knit Mobile society. He hadn't met many women who'd seemed to live life on their own terms. Even in California the women he'd dated had always worn a false front, literally and physically.

Laura Jo's face was devoid of makeup and she wore a simple blouse and jeans with flats. She reminded him of a girl just out of high school. That was until she opened her mouth, then she left no doubt she was a grown woman who could defend herself and her child. Nothing about her indicated she had been raised in one of local society's finest families.

Allie said something and Laura Jo turned her head. Both

mother and child had similar coloring. Pretty in an early-spring-leaves-unfolding sort of way. Easy on the eye. Why would any man leave the two of them?

If he ever had a chance to have something as good in his life as they were, he'd hold on to them and never let them out of his sight. He sighed. What he saw between Laura Jo and Allie wasn't meant for him. It wasn't his to have. He'd taken that chance from Mike and he had no right to have it himself. What they had he couldn't be trusted with.

"Hey, there's Dr. Clayborn," Allie called.

Mark grinned as he joined them. He ruffled Allie's hair. "That's Mark to you. Dr. Clayborn sounds like a mouthful for such a little girl."

Allie drew herself up straight. "I'm a big girl."

Mark went down on one knee, bringing himself to eye level with Allie. "I apologize. Yes, you are a big girl. Big enough to walk with Gus in the parade?"

"Really, you're going to let me take Gus in the parade?"

"Yes, and Jeremy, too. But I have to come along with you."

She turned to Laura Jo. "Mommy, I'm going to get to be in the parade."

"I heard, honey, but I don't know."

"I'll be right there with them the entire time." Mark reassured Laura Jo.

The look of hesitation on her face gave him the idea that she didn't often trust Allie's care to anyone but her friend Marsha.

He reached for Gus's leash and she handed it to him. The nylon was warm from her clasp. "She'll be perfectly safe. We'll meet you and Jeremy at the car when it's over. The parade route isn't long."

"I guess it'll be okay." She looked at Allie. "You and Jeremy do just what Mark tells you to do." Laura Jo pinned

Mark with a look. "And you turn up with my daughter and Jeremy at the end of the parade."

"Yes, ma'am." He gave her a smile and a little salute. "I'll take good care of them, I promise. Let's go, kids. We need to get in line."

Laura Jo watched as Mark took her daughter's much smaller hand in his larger one and Jeremy's in his other one. Gus walked at Allie's heels as they were swallowed up by the crowd.

What was it about Mark that made her trust him with the most precious person in her life? She'd never allowed anyone but Marsha that privilege. Maybe it was the way he'd care for Allie's knee, or his devotion to the grandfather and later the girl he'd cared for. Somehow Mark had convinced her in a few short meetings that he could be trusted. Now that she was a mother she better understood how her parents had felt when she had insisted on going off with someone they hadn't trusted.

Alone, she made her way through the crowd to the curb of a street about halfway along the parade route. Taking a seat on the curb, she waited until the parade approached. For this parade there would be no bands involved. All the music would come from music boxes pulled in carts by children. The floats would be decorated wagons and dogs of all shapes and sizes.

Twenty minutes later the first of the parade members came into view. Not far behind them were Allie, Jeremy and Mark. Laura Jo stood as they approached. She'd never seen a larger smile on Allie's face. Mark and Jeremy were grinning also. Gus was lumbering behind them, looking bored but festive. Allie held his leash proudly.

She screamed and waved as they came by. Allie and Jeremy waved enthusiastically back at her. Mark acknowledged her also. As they came closer he stepped over to Laura Jo and said, "The kids are having a blast."

Laura Jo smiled.

An hour later Laura Jo stood waiting outside Mark's car. Anxiousness was building with every minute that passed. Something had to have gone wrong. Mark and the children should have been there by now. Had something happened to one of the kids? She shouldn't have let them out of her sight. Was this how her parents had felt when she'd run off with Phil?

He had been a master of manipulation. Before they'd got married he'd made her believe he had a good job and he would take care of her. "Don't worry about what your parents think, I'll take care of you," he would say. The worst thing was that he'd made her believe he'd loved her.

Had she let Mark do the same thing? Persuade her to let the kids be in the parade. Had she made a poor character judgment call again? This time with her daughter? Her palms dampened. She'd promised herself to be careful. Now look what was happening. She headed in the direction of where the parade had ended, and soon recognized Mark's tall figure coming in her way. He pulled a wagon on which Gus, Allie and Jeremy rode. With relief filling her chest, she ran toward them.

Mark was red-faced. Jeremy wore a smile. Allie looked pleased with herself as she held Gus's head in her lap. The dog was wearing a crown.

"Where have ya'll been? I was getting worried." Laura Jo stopped beside them.

"Mommy, we won first place for the slowest dog in the parade." Allie beamed.

Laura Jo gave her a hug. "That's wonderful, honey."

"Sorry we made you worry. I should have given you my

cell number. Gus also got slower after the parade. I carried him halfway here until I saw a kid with a wagon. I had to give him fifty dollars for it so I could haul Gus back."

At the sound of disgust in Mark's voice Laura Jo couldn't help but laugh. His look of complete exasperation and her sense of relief made the situation even more humorous.

"I'm glad someone thinks it's funny." Mark chuckled.

Laura Jo had to admit he was a good sport and he'd certainly made her daughter happy. Every time she tried to stop laughing she'd think of Mark begging a boy for his wagon and she'd burst out in laughter again. It had been a long time since she'd laughed hard enough to bring tears to her eyes.

"If you think you can stop laughing at me for a few minutes, we can load up this freeloader..." he gave the dog a revolted look "...and get him home."

"Had a workout, did you?" Laura Jo asked, trying to suppress the giggles that kept bubbling up.

"Yeah. No good deed goes unpunished."

"Whose idea was it to be in the parade?"

"Okay, it was mine."

Laura Jo burst into another round of snickers.

"Mommy, are you all right?" Allie looked at her in wonder.

"Oh, honey. I'm fine. I'm just glad you had a good time." She looked over the top of her head and grinned at Mark. Had it really been that long since Allie had seen her laugh?

Mark scooped Gus up in his arms. "If you'll get the door, I'll get this prima donna in the car."

Laura Jo's snort escaped as she opened the door. Allie climbed in next to the dog then Jeremy clambered in. Laura Jo saw they were buckled in. Mark put the wagon in the trunk and slapped the lid down harder than necessary.

"So you plan on being in another parade anytime soon?" she asked him, as she took her place in the front seat.

Mark sneered at her as he started the car. Laura Jo's smile grew. Before they left the parking spot, he twisted to study the children. As he turned the first corner, she looked back to find both of the children asleep. Most of the people at their end of the parade had left already, which made it easy for him to maneuver out of town and back to his home.

As they drove down the drive, Laura Jo said, "Thanks for going to so much trouble for Allie. She had the time of her life."

"You're welcome. Despite Gus being in slow motion, I enjoyed it. I've been a part of a number of parades in my time but never one like today's."

Laura Jo grinned. Something she seemed to have been doing more of lately. "Well, I appreciate it. I'll get the kids loaded up and we'll get out of your hair."

"Mommy, I'm hungry."

Laura Jo sighed and looked back at her daughter. "I thought you were asleep."

"I bet they are hungry. They've had a busy day. I've got some hot dogs I could put on the grill," Mark suggested, as he pulled the car to a stop.

"You've already done enough. I think we had better go." Laura Jo didn't want to like him any more than she already did, and she was afraid she might if she stayed around Mark much longer. The picture of him pulling the dog and Allie and Jeremy put a warm spot in her heart. He wasn't the self-centered man she'd believed he might be.

"Can't I play with Gus a little while longer?" Allie pleaded.

"Face it, you're not going to win this one." Mark grinned.

"You're sure about this?" Laura Jo realized she'd lost again.

"Yeah. It'll be nice to have company for a meal."

"Okay," she said to Mark, then turned and looked at Allie. "We'll stay for a little while longer but when I say it's time to go, we go without any argument, understood?"

"Yes, ma'am," Allie said, and Jeremy, who had awoken, nodded in agreement.

Laura Jo opened the door for Allie while Mark did the same for Jeremy and Gus.

"If you both give your mom and me just a few minutes, we'll have the hot dogs ready. Why don't you guys watch the parade on TV? Look for us."

"Do you think they'll have it running already?" Laura Jo asked.

"They should. When I told friends on the West Coast that we had Mardi Gras parades on TV they were amazed." Mark turned to the kids again. "I'll turn the TV on and we'll give it a look."

They all followed Mark through the front door of the house. Laura Jo studied the interior. The foyer had an easy, casual feel to it but every piece of furniture was placed so that it reminded her of a home decorating magazine. From the entrance, it opened into a large space with an exterior glass wall that gave the room a one-hundred-and-eighty-degree view of the deck area and the bay. Full ceiling-to-floor green-checked curtains were pushed back to either side of the windowed area. The late-afternoon sunlight streamed into the room, giving it an inviting glow.

Overstuffed cream-colored couches faced each other. A table with a chess set on it sat to one side of the room. Opposite it there was a large-screen TV built into the wall, with bookshelves surrounding it. Comfortable-looking armchairs were placed throughout the room. The house gave her the feeling that a family had lived and loved here.

"What a wonderful room," Laura Jo whispered.

"Thanks. It's my favorite space."

She turned, startled, to find Mark standing close. She had been so caught up in the room she hadn't noticed him approach.

"I'll turn the TV on for the kids then get started on those dogs. You don't need to help. You're welcome to stay with them."

"No, I said I would help and I will. After all, I haven't carried a dog around town all afternoon," she said with a grin.

"You're not going to let that go, are you?" He gave her a pained look.

She shook her head. "The visual is just too good to let go of."

He picked up a remote and pushed a button. The TV came on. The kids had already found themselves a place on a sofa. After a few changes of channels he stopped. "I do believe this is ours."

"You guys stay right here. Don't go outside," Laura Jo said.

Mark headed toward the open kitchen Laura Jo could see off to the left. She followed. It was a modern and up-to-date space that was almost as large as her entire apartment. She ran a hand across the granite of the large counter in the middle of the room with a sigh of pleasure. "I wish I had a place like this to cook. I bet you could make a perfect king cake on this top," she murmured, more to herself than Mark.

"You're welcome to come over anytime and use it. I get nowhere near the use out of it that I should." Mark put his head in the refrigerator and came out with a package of hot dogs.

"Thanks for the offer. But I don't really have time to do a lot of cooking." She wished she did have. Even if she did, she wouldn't be coming here to do it.

"That's not what Allie led me to believe." He picked through a drawer and found some tongs.

"I'd like to but I don't think we'll be getting that friendly."

He came to stand across the counter from her. "Why not? You might find you like me if you'd give me a chance."

"We're from two different worlds now and I don't see us going any further than we did today."

"What do you mean by two different worlds? Our parents have been acquaintances for years. I don't see that we are that different."

Had she hurt his feelings? No, she couldn't imagine that what she thought or felt mattered that much to him. But he had been nice to Allie and he deserved the truth. "I have nothing to do with that society stuff anymore."

"I had no idea you were such a snob, or is it narrow-mindedness?"

"I'm not a snob and it has nothing to do with being narrow-minded and everything to do with knowing who the Clayborn family is and what they represent. I want no part of that world again."

"Once again, I think I have been insulted. Do you know me or my family well enough to have that opinion? What have we done to you?" His tone had roughened with each sentence. "I think I deserve to hear you expound on that statement."

"Well, you're going to be disappointed."

Mark's brows came together over his nose.

"Instead, why don't you tell me what has you living on this side of the bay when I know the other side is thought to be the correct one?"

He placed some hot dog buns on the counter. "I needed a place to stay when I moved back and no one was staying in the summer house. It's no big mystery."

"That's right. I remember hearing talk that you were in a bad accident and left town afterwards."

He winced. "Yeah, I left to do my fellowship in California."

"Well, do tell. I am surprised. I would have never thought a Clayborn would live anywhere but Mobile."

"And for your information, my brother and I both moved away. I came back because my father had a stroke and needs someone close."

"I'm sorry to hear about your father." And she was. It was tough to see someone suffer that way. She remembered Mr. Clayborn, Sr. being a larger-than-life man whom everyone noticed when he came into the room. Much like Mark. She admired Mark for giving up his life in California to return home to care for his father. In comparison, she lived in the same town and didn't even speak to her parents.

"He had a bad stroke but he is recovering. Working every day is over for him but at least he's alive."

"Mommy," Allie called. "I'm hungry."

Mark shrugged. "I guess we'd better save this conversation for later. If you really want to help, why don't you get the plates and things together while I get these hot dogs on the grill? The plates are in that cabinet—" he pointed to one to the right of the stove "—and the silverware is in that drawer." He indicated the one right in front of her. "Condiments in the refrigerator. What few there are." He went out the side door of the kitchen without another word.

What Mark didn't realize was that she was through having any type of conversation about her past. Why she'd told him so much she had no idea.

CHAPTER THREE

MARK STARTED THE gas grill and adjusted the flame, before placing the hot dogs on the wire rack above it. He glanced back into the house through the window of the door. He could just see Laura Jo moving around.

She had a real chip on her shoulder about the world in which they had been raised. For a moment there he'd thought she might open up and tell him why but then she'd shut down. Why did it matter to him anyway?

Maybe it was because for some reason he liked the brash, independent and absolutely beautiful woman, especially when she laughed. He couldn't get enough of that uninhibited embracing of life. Would she act that way in bed?

Whoa, that was not where he was headed. He didn't really know her and what he did know about her was that she'd sooner sink her teeth into him than allow him to kiss her.

Just what was going on between her and her family? He knew of the Herrons. They were good people but Laura Jo had certainly had a falling out with them. She hadn't even told Allie she had grandparents living in town. Who did that? It just didn't make sense.

He'd enjoyed his afternoon with the children. It had been tough to drive with them in the car but he'd done it. He'd had a taste of what it would be like to have a child in his life and he rather liked it. In fact, he liked it too much.

Laura Jo made another trip by the door. He jerked around when she called from the doorway, "Hey, do you need a platter for those?"

"Yeah." Why did he feel like he'd just been caught in someone else's business? What was going on between her and her family wasn't his problem.

"Where do I find it? I'll bring it to you."

She looked so appealing, framed by the door with the afternoon sun highlighting one side of her face. The urge to kiss her almost overwhelmed him. He'd like to prove that they weren't different in the areas that mattered. He had to say something to get rid of her until he regained his equilibrium. "Cabinet below the plates."

Laura Jo disappeared into the house again. A few minutes later she came out and stood beside him. Her head reached his shoulders. She was close enough that he smelled a hint of her floral shampoo but not near enough that they touched. He was aware of the fact that all he had to do was take a half step and her body would be next to his.

"You might want to turn those. They look like they're burning."

Great. He had been so focussed on her that he wasn't thinking about what he was doing. "So now you're going to come out here and start telling me how to cook my hot dogs. Do you like to be bossed?"

She took a step back. Her eyes turned serious. "No. I don't. I'm sorry." She moved to leave.

He caught her wrist. "Hey, I was just kidding. They're just hot dogs."

Laura Jo pulled her arm out of his grip. "I know. But I need to get us some drinks. I saw the glasses when I was looking for a bowl." With that she was gone.

This was a woman better left alone. She had more hang-ups than he did and, heaven knew, he had plenty.

Twenty minutes later, Allie and Jeremy were picnicking, as they called it, in front of the TV so they could watch another parade. Mark had persuaded Laura Jo to join him on the deck. This was what he remembered it being like when he'd been a kid. He liked having people around. Being part of a family. Could he ever have that again?

He and Laura Jo ate in silence for a while, but not a comfortable one. Mark worked to come up with a subject they could discuss. Finally, he asked, "So you remembered me from years ago, so why don't I remember you?"

She grinned. "Oh, I don't know. Maybe because the only person you saw was Ann Maria Clark."

He had the good grace to turn red. "Yeah, we were a hot item back then."

"That you were. There was no reason you'd see a simple lady-in-waiting."

His gaze met hers. Something about her tone made him think she might have liked him to notice her. "You were in her court?"

She nodded. "I was."

"I can't believe it."

"Well, it's true."

"We were that close all those years ago and it took a skinned knee at a parade for us to get to know each other."

She fingered the hot dog. "Life can be strange like that."

"That it can."

"I thought you two would get married," Laura Jo said, more as a statement of fact than someone fishing for information.

"That had been the plan but things changed."

"That happens. Especially where people are concerned."

She sounded as if she was speaking about herself more than him.

It was time to change the subject. "Have you and Jeremy's mom been friends for a long time?"

"No. We only met a few years ago."

Well, at least he was getting more than a one-word answer.

"She works at the hospital?"

Laura Jo gave him a speculative look. "Are you interested in her?"

"I'm just trying to make conversation. Maybe learn a little more about you."

Laura Jo placed her half-eaten hot dog on the plate in front of her. She looked at him from across the table for a second before saying, "We met at a group for mothers without partners. Her husband had died. We became friends, at first because we needed each other, then we found we liked each other."

"So she was there when you needed someone." He knew well what it was like to be alone and need someone to talk to. There had been no one when he'd arrived in LA. He had been lonely then and, come to think of it, he'd been lonely in Mobile at least up until the last week.

"Your parents weren't around?"

"No. Hers had died. Mine…well, that's another story. That's why Marsha and I are trying to open a house for mothers who are on their own."

"So how's that going?"

"The city has agreed to sell us a house at a good price that would be perfect but we're running out of time to raise the money."

"Maybe I could be of some help. Atone for my car."

"A check for three hundred thousand would be great."

She grinned at him as if she was making a joke but he could see hope in her eyes.

He winced. "That would be my car and at least one or two more."

"I've seen you ride a bike." She grinned.

He threw back his head and laughed. "You'd make me resort to that to get your house?'

"I'd do almost anything. This chance might not come again."

She took a swallow of her drink as if her mouth had suddenly gone dry.

Why did that thought of her in bed, beneath him, pop into his head? He raised a brow.

Her eyes widened. A stricken look covered her face. "You know what I mean."

"I have an idea. We could go to the Krewe of Orion dance together. See some of our old friends. There should be plenty of people there willing to donate. All you'd have to do is get one to agree to support you and then the others would line up to help out."

"I don't think so."

"To going with me or that others would help?"

"To going."

"Do you mind if I ask why?" He caught her gaze.

"That's not my idea of a good time anymore."

What had brought on that remark? He pushed his plate away. "Well, this is a first. A woman who doesn't want to get dressed up and go to a party."

"Not all women like that sort of stuff."

"It's just one night. Attending with me isn't like going to the gallows." He chuckled. "I promise."

"It's still no, thank you." She pushed half of her leftover hot dog bun across the plate.

"Well, I guess you have other plans for the way you're

going to get the money for the house. I'm sorry, I need my car. However, I'll make a donation to the cause."

As if she was all of a sudden concerned about sounding rude, she said, "I do appreciate you trying to help. I'll take you up on that." She stood with plate in hand. "I guess I better get the kids home to bed. They have school tomorrow."

Mark also gathered his plate and joined her as she walked into the house. They found Allie and Jeremy on the couch, Gus snoring between them.

"I'll write that check and help you get them loaded," Mark said as he took her plate and walked into the kitchen. While there he wrote a check. When he returned, Laura Jo already had Allie in her arms. He scooped Jeremy up and followed her out of the house. They worked together to get each child in and secured.

Digging in his front pocket, he pulled out the check and handed it to Laura Jo.

Laura Jo read it. Her eyes widened. She looked at him. "Thank you. This is very generous."

"You're welcome."

"Also thanks for giving Allie today. I don't have much of a chance to do things like this for her."

"I didn't just do it for Allie." They walked around to the driver's door and Laura Jo opened it.

"I know Jeremy also had a good time."

"What about you?"

"Me?'

"Yeah. I was hoping you had a nice day, too."

"I did."

She acted as if it was a foreign idea that he might be interested in her having a good time. "Good. Maybe we could do it again sometime. Just you and me."

"I've already told you. We have nothing in common."

"Nonsense. We have a lot in common. Our childhoods,

medicine, parades and laughter. That's more than most people have." When she'd been teasing him about Gus there had been an easiness between them. He wanted to see if she was putting up the front he believed she was. To make her act on her attraction to him. He was tired of being dismissed by her. "I bet if you tried, you could find something you like about me. Maybe this could help."

He wrapped an arm around her waist and pulled her to him. She only had time to gasp before his lips found hers. She didn't react at first, which gave him time to taste her lips. Soft, warm and slightly parted. Then for the briefest of seconds she returned his kiss. His heart thumped against his ribs at the possibilities before her hands spread wide against his chest. She shoved him away, hard.

His hands fell to his sides.

"You had no right to do that," she hissed.

"I can't say that I'm sorry."

She slid behind the steering wheel and before she could close the door he said, "Goodnight, Laura Jo."

"It's more like goodbye." She slammed the door.

Not a chance. Mark watched her taillights disappear up his drive. They'd be seeing each other again if he had anything to say about it. She was the first woman he'd met who had him thinking about the possibilities of tomorrow, even when he shouldn't.

It intrigued him that she put up such a fight not to have anything to do with him. That was except for the moments she'd melted in his arms. Could he get her to linger there long enough to forget whatever stood between them? Long enough to make her appreciate something they might both enjoy?

Laura Jo couldn't remember the last time a man had kissed her, but it sure hadn't been anything near as powerful as the brief one Mark had just given her. Her hands shook on the steering wheel. Why had he done it? Hadn't she made it clear to him that she didn't want to become involved with him? Had she been giving off a different signal?

It didn't matter why. It couldn't, wouldn't happen again. There couldn't be anything real between them anyway. When she did open up again to a man she would know him well. She wanted someone settled, who wouldn't leave town at any moment. Someone who cared nothing for being involved in Mobile society. From what she knew about Mark so far, he had none of those qualities.

The lights of the cars flickered across the water as she traveled over the low bay causeway back to Mobile.

Thinking about and fretting over Mark was a waste of time. Laura Jo fingered the check he had given her. It was literally a raindrop in a pond to what she needed. She had to find some way to raise the money needed to buy the house. There was also Allie to see about and her job to keep. Mark Clayborn hadn't been hers years ago and he wasn't hers now.

Mark, she'd already learned, was a man with a strong sense of who he was. If she let him into her life he might try to control it, like her father and Phil had. She needed a partner, a father for Allie, someone sturdy and dependable. Until that happened it was her job to make decisions about her life and Allie's. She would never again depend on a man or let him dictate to her.

Marsha was there to greet her when she pulled into the parking area of the apartment complex. She had to have been watching for them. Knowing Marsha, she'd want details of the afternoon and evening. When Laura Jo had called her earlier to inform her that they would be staying a little longer at Mark's for supper, her speculative tone had made Laura Jo feel like she needed to justify her decision.

She'd told Marsha, "Don't get any ideas. There's nothing going on here."

"Okay, if you say so." Marsha hadn't sounded convinced before she'd hung up.

Allie and Jeremy woke when she parked. They got out of the car, talking a mile a minute about the parade and Gus. Marsha grinned over their heads at Laura Jo. "Come in and tell me all about your visit to Dr. Clayborn's," Marsha said, as if to the children but Laura Jo had no doubt she meant her.

"There's not much to tell and the kids have school tomorrow." Laura Jo locked her car.

"I know they have school tomorrow but you can come in for a few minutes."

Laura Jo straightened. Marsha wouldn't let it go until she'd heard every detail but Laura Jo wouldn't be telling her about the kiss. The one that had shaken something awake in her. It wouldn't happen again, even if there was an occasion, which there wouldn't be. She doubted that her path and Mark's would cross again. They didn't even live on the same side of the bay.

Allie and Jeremy ran ahead on the way to Marsha's apartment. She and Marsha followed more slowly.

A few minutes later, Marsha set a glass of iced tea in front of Laura Jo and said, "Okay, spill."

"Mark let the kids dress up Gus, his dog."

"So you're on a first-name basis with the good doc now?"

Laura Jo rolled her eyes. It was starting. "He asked me to call him Mark and it seemed foolish not to."

Marsha nodded in a thoughtful way, as if she didn't believe her friend's reasoning. "So what else did you do?"

"We went to the parade. Mark walked with the kids while I watched." She chuckled.

"What's that laugh for?"

"I was just thinking of the look on Mark's face when he showed up pulling a wagon with the kids and the dog in it he'd bought off a boy."

Marsha gave her a long look. "That sounds interesting."

"It was." Laura Jo launched into the story, her smile growing as she told it.

She ended up laughing and Marsha joined her.

"So you went back to his place?"

"I wish you'd stop saying 'so' like that and acting as if it was a date. The only reason I agreed to go was because Allie wanted to dress up the dog and be in the parade so badly."

"So..."

Laura Jo glared at her.

"You didn't enjoy yourself at all?" Marsha continued without paying Laura Jo any attention.

"I don't even like the guy."

"This is the most you've had to do with a man since I've known you. I think you might be a little more interested in him than you want to admit."

"I think you're wrong." Laura Jo was going to see to it that it was the truth. "There's one more thing and I probably shouldn't tell you this, but he did ask me to the krewe dance."

"And you said no." Marsha said the words as a statement of a fact.

"I did. For more than one reason."

Marsha turned serious. "We could use his contacts."

"I've already told you that I'm not going to do that. What if I saw my parents and they found out I was there, asking for money. I couldn't face them like that."

"Even at the cost of losing the house? Laura Jo, you've

been gone so long I can't imagine that your parents would see it as crawling back."

"You don't know my father. It would be his chance to tell me 'I told you so.' I lived though that once. Not again."

Marsha didn't know that Laura Jo hadn't spoken to her parents since before Allie's birth.

"So I guess we'll put all our hope in that grant coming through."

Laura Jo took a sip of her tea then said, "Yes, that and a moneybags willing to help us out."

"You've got a moneybag in Mark Clayborn."

"Oh, I forgot to show you this." Laura Jo pulled the check Mark had given her out of her pocket."

Marsha whistled. "Very generous. He must really like you."

"No. It was more like I made him feel guilty."

"Whatever you did, at least this will help. We just need to get others to be so kind."

"Now I'm not only indebted to him for giving Allie a wonderful afternoon but for helping with the shelter."

"You don't like that, do you, Ms. I-Can-Do-It-Myself?"

"No, I don't. We have nothing in common. He and I don't want the same things out of life anymore."

"Oh, and you know that by spending one afternoon with him?" Marsha picked up both of their glasses and placed them in the sink. "You do know that people with money also care about their families, love them, want the best for them?"

All of what Laura's Jo's father had said to her just before he'd told her that Phil was no good. Had her father felt the same way about her as she did about Allie? Worry that something bad might happen to her? Worry over her happiness?

"Well, it's time for me to get Allie home."

As Laura Jo and Allie made their way to the front door Marsha said, "We've got to find that money for the shelter. There are worse things in life to have to do than dress up and go out with a handsome man to a dance."

"What handsome man, Mama?"

"No one, honey. Aunt Marsha is just trying to be funny."

Mark was handsome. But what Laura Jo was more concerned about was the way his kiss had made her feel. Had made her wish for more.

Mark came out of a deep sleep at the ringing of his cell phone.

What time was it? He checked his bedside clock. 3:00 a.m. This was never good news. Had something happened to his father?

Mark snatched up the phone. "Hello."

"Mark, its Laura Jo."

The relief that he felt that the call wasn't about his father was immediately replaced with concern for her.

"I'm sorry to call…"

He was wide awake now, heart throbbing. "Are you all right? Allie?"

"Yes. Yes. We're fine. It's a child staying at the shelter. The mother has no insurance and is afraid of doctors. I think the child needs to be seen. Fever, sweating, not eating and lethargic. The mother won't agree to go to the hospital. Will you come?"

"Sure, but will she let me examine the child if I do?"

"I'll convince her that it's necessary before you get here. If she wants to stay at the shelter then she'll have to let you."

"Give me directions."

Laura Jo gave him an address in a less-than-desirable area of the city.

"I'll be there in about thirty minutes."

"Thanks, Mark. I really appreciate this."

The longest part of the trip was traveling the two-lane road between his house and the interstate. Even at this early hour it took him more time than he would have liked. Finally, he reached the four-lane, where he could speed across the two-mile causeway that bisected the bay.

The child must really be worrying Laura Jo or she would never have called him. She'd made it clear she didn't plan to see him again when she'd left his house. He'd thought of nothing but their kiss for the rest of the evening. To hear her voice on the other end of the phone had been a surprise. The child's symptoms didn't sound all that unusual but with a small person it wasn't always straightforward.

He drove through the tunnel that went under Mobile River and came up on Governor Street. There were no crowds now, only large oaks and barriers lining the main street. A number of miles down the street he made a left and not long after that he pulled up in front of what looked like a building that had been a business at one time. The glass windows were painted black and there were dark curtains over the door window. One lone light burned above it. It looked nothing like a place for pregnant woman or children. He could clearly see why they needed a house to move to.

Laura Jo's car was parked near the door and he took the slot next to hers. Picking up his cell phone, he pressed Return. Seconds later, Laura Jo's voice came on the line. "I'm outside."

"I'll be right there."

Mark stood at the door for only seconds before the dead bolt clicked back and Laura Jo's face came into view.

After making sure it was him, she opened the door wider. "I appreciate you coming."

He entered and she locked the door behind him. The room he was in resembled a living room with its couches and chairs spread out. There was one small TV in the corner. At least it looked more welcoming from the inside than it did from the outside.

"Anna's family's room is down this way." Laura Jo, dressed in jeans, T-shirt and tennis shoes, led him down a hall toward the back of the building, passing what he guessed had once been offices. Were families living in nothing more than ten-by-ten rooms?

"Has anything changed?" Mark asked.

"No, but I'm really worried. Anna has been so distraught about the loss of her husband I'm not sure she's been as attentive to her children as she should have been."

"I'll have a look and see what we come up with. Don't worry."

They stopped at the last door.

"Anna isn't a fan of doctors."

"I'll be on my best behavior." He gave her a reassuring smile.

Laura Jo nodded and knocked quietly on the door before she opened it. "Anna, someone is here to check on little Marcy."

Laura Jo entered and he followed close behind. A lone light shone, barely giving off enough light for him to see the room. There was a twin bed shoved into the corner and another at a right angle to that one where two children slept feet to feet. There was also a baby bed but it was empty because the child was in her mother's arms. The woman was reed thin, wide-eyed and had wavy hair. She couldn't have been more than twenty-five.

"Hi, Anna, I'm Mark, and I've come to see if I can help little Marcy. Why don't you sit on the bed and hold her while I have a look? I promise not to hurt her."

Anna hesitated then looked a Laura Jo.

"I'll sit beside you." Laura Jo led her over to the bed.

Mark went down on one knee and placed his bag beside him. He pulled out his stethoscope. The heat he felt as he put his hand close to the child's chest indicated she was still running a fever.

"I'm only going to listen to her heart and lungs now. Check her pulse." He gave the mother a reassuring smile and went to work. Done, he asked, "How long has she had this fever?"

"Since yesterday," the mother said in a meek voice.

He looked a Laura Jo.

"I had no idea." She sounded defensive and he hadn't intended to make her feel that.

To Anna he said, "I'm going to need to check Marcy's abdomen."

"Let's lay Marcy on the bed. That way she'll be more comfortable," Laura Jo suggested.

Mark moved his hand over the child's stomach area. It was distended and hard. Something serious was, without a doubt, going on. He glanced at Laura Jo. Their gazes met. The worry in her eyes was obvious.

"Anna, thank you for letting me see Marcy." He looked at Laura Jo again and tilted his head toward the door. As he stood he picked up his bag and walked across the room. Laura joined him. He let her precede him into the hall and closed the door behind him.

Laura Jo looked at him.

"Marcy has to go to the hospital."

"I was afraid of that. What do you think the problem is?"

"The symptoms make me think it might be an obstructive bowel problem. This isn't something that can wait. Marcy must been seen at the hospital."

"I'll talk to her." Laura Jo went back into the room.

Mark pulled out his phone and called the ER. He gave the information about Marcy and they assured him they would be ready when he arrived. Finished, he leaned against the wall to wait.

Soon Laura Jo came out, with Anna holding Marcy in her arms.

"Anna has agreed to go to the hospital as long as you and I stay with her," Laura Jo said. "I need a few minutes to let someone know to see about her other children. Will you drive?"

His stomach tightened. He didn't want to but what was he supposed to say, "No, I might injure you for life"?

"If it's necessary," Mark answered.

Laura Jo looked at him with a question in her eyes before he turned to walk down the hallway to the front.

"The car seat is by the front door," Anna said in a subdued voice.

"I'll get it."

He was still working to latch the child seat into his car when Laura Jo arrived.

"I'll get that."

With efficiency that he envied she had the seat secured and Marcy in it in no time. Laura Jo didn't comment on his ineptness but he was sure she'd made a note of it. She would probably call him on it later.

Anna took the backseat next to Marcy, and Laura Jo joined him in front. Before pulling out of the parking space, he looked back to see that the baby was secure and that Anna was wearing her seat belt. "Are you buckled in, Laura Jo?"

"Yes. You sure are safety conscious."

Yes, he was, and he had a good reason to be. Mark nodded and wasted no time driving to the hospital. He pulled under the emergency awning and stopped.

As they entered the building Laura Jo said to Anna,

"We'll be right here with you until you feel comfortable. They'll take good care of Marcy here."

Anna nodded, her eyes not meeting Laura Jo's.

They were met by a woman dressed in scrubs.

"Lynn, this child needs to be seen," Laura said.

"Is this the girl Dr. Clayborn called in about?"

"Yes," he said. "I'm Dr. Clayborn." Because he wasn't on the staff at the hospital he couldn't give orders. They would have to wait until the ER physician showed up.

"Exam room five is open. Dr. Lawrence will be right in."

Two hours later Marcy was in surgery. Mark's diagnosis had been correct. Thankfully, Laura Jo had called him or the child might have died. They were now sitting in the surgery waiting room with Anna. With Laura Jo's support, Anna had accepted that Marcy needed the surgery. Mark was impressed with the tender understanding Laura Jo had given the terrified mother. He liked this sensitive side of her personally. What would it take for her to turn some of that on him?

Mark approached the two women and handed each one a cup of coffee from the machine. He slipped into the chair beside Laura Jo. Waiting in hospitals wasn't his usual activity. He'd always been on the working end of an emergency.

While Anna was in the restroom Laura Jo said, "I think you can go. She seems to be handling this better than I thought she would."

"No, I said I'd stay and I will."

"You make a good friend."

Mark's chest tightened. No, he didn't. He'd already proved that. Mike certainly wouldn't say that about him. Mark hadn't even gone to the hospital to see Mike before he'd left town. Laura Jo shouldn't start depending on him.

"You might be surprised."

Laura Jo gave him a speculative look but he was saved

from any questions by Anna returning. Soon after that the surgeon came out to speak to them.

The sun was shining when he and Laura Jo stepped outside the hospital. Marcy was doing well in PICU and Anna had insisted that she was fine and no longer needed them there. They left her in the waiting room, dozing. Laura Jo had promised to check on her other children and that she would see to it they were cared for properly.

As he and Laura Jo walked to his car, which he had moved to a parking place earlier, Mark asked, "Where do you get all the energy for all you do?"

"I just do what has to be done."

"You sure have a lot on your plate."

"Maybe so, but some things I can't say no to."

What was it like to feel that type of bond with people? He understood the practical side of doing what needed to be done medically to save a life but it was a completely different concept to support another person emotionally without reservation. Mark understood that well. He hadn't been able to stand beside his best friend when he'd needed him most. He had even ignored his conscience when it had screamed for him to do better. It hadn't gotten quieter when he'd moved back to town but he still couldn't muster the guts to go visit Mike.

"I wish I had your backbone."

"How's that?"

"You face life head-on."

"You don't?"

"What little I have falls short of the amount you have."

"Thank you. That's a nice compliment."

They had reached his car. "How about I buy us some breakfast then take you home? I'm guessing Marsha has Allie."

"Yes. I really need to check on her and Anna's kids. I

need sleep. I'm sure you do also. I have to work this afternoon. Don't you have to be at work this morning?"

"I don't go in until two and you need to eat. I'm hungry so why don't you let me get us some breakfast without disagreeing for once?"

She walked to the passenger door. "I'm already too far in debt to you."

"I don't mind that."

She sighed. "I pick the place."

"Ladies choice, then."

A smile spread across her lips. "I like the sound of that."

Had no one ever let her make a choice of where they went? He liked seeing Laura Jo smile. She didn't do it often enough. She was far too serious.

"Where're we going?"

"I'll show you."

She got in the car and put her seat belt on. When he was ready to pull out he looked over at her.

Laura Jo said, "Yes, I have buckled up."

He had to sound crazy to her, or over-the-top controlling, but he just couldn't face hurting someone with his driving ever again. Somehow it seemed easier when he had her in the car with him; she accepted him for who he was. As he drove she gave him directions into an older and seedier part of downtown Mobile. He had last been to the area when he'd been a teen and trying to live on the wild side some.

"It's just down the street on the right. The Silver Spoon."

Mark pulled into the small parking area in front of a nineteen-fifties-style café that had seen better days.

"You want to eat here?"

"Sure. They have the best pecan waffles in town." Laura Jo was already getting out of the car. She looked back in at him. "You coming?"

Mark had been questioning it. He wasn't sure the place could pass a health inspection.

"Yes, I am." He climbed out of the car. "I wouldn't miss it."

She was already moving up the few steps to the front door.

Because all the booths were full, Laura Jo took an empty stool at the bar. She didn't miss Mark's dubious look at the duct-taped stool next to her before he took a seat.

"You don't frequent places like this, do you?"

"I can say that this is a first."

She grinned. "I thought it might be."

Mark picked up a plastic-covered menu. "So I need to have the pecan waffles."

"They're my favorite." She was going to enjoy watching Mark out of his element.

"Then waffles it is. You do the ordering."

"Charlie," she said to the heavy man wearing what once must have been a white apron, "we'll have pecan waffles, link sausage and iced tea."

"Coming right up, Laura Jo," Charlie said, and turned to give the cook her order.

"I see you're a regular," Mark said.

"I come when I can, which isn't often enough."

Charlie put their glasses of iced tea on the counter with a thump.

"I don't normally have iced tea for breakfast." Mark picked up his glass.

"If you'd rather have coffee..." Laura Jo made it sound like a dare on purpose.

"I said I wanted the same as you and that's what I'm having. So how did you find this place?"

"Charlie gave one of the mothers that came through the shelter a job here after her baby was born."

"That was nice. I'm impressed with what you're doing at the shelter."

"Thanks. But it never seems like enough. You know, I really appreciate you helping me out with Anna and Marcy. I hated to call you but I knew I couldn't get her to the hospital and I was uncomfortable with how Marcy looked."

Mark really had been great with Anna and Marcy. He'd stayed to give moral support even when he hadn't had to. Maybe she had better character radar than she believed.

"I'm glad you thought you could call."

She'd been surprised too that she hadn't hesitated a second before picking up the phone to call him. Somehow she'd just known he would come. "Were you always going to be a doctor?"

"I believe that's the first personal question you have ever asked me. You do want to get to know me better."

Laura Jo opened her mouth to refute that statement but he continued, not giving her a chance to do so.

"Yes, I had always planned to go into medicine. My parents liked the idea and I found I did, too. I've always liked helping people. How about you? Did you always dream of being a nurse?"

"No, I kind of came to that later in life."

"So what was your dream?"

"I don't know. I guess like all the other girls I knew we dreamed of marrying the Mardi Gras king, having two kids and living in a big house."

He looked in her direction but she refused to meet his gaze. "Marrying the Mardi Gras king, was it? So did you dream of marrying me?"

"I don't think your ego needs to be fed by my teenage

dreams. But I'll admit to having a crush on you if that will end this conversation."

"I thought so."

"Now we won't be able to get your head out of the door."

Charlie placed a plateful of food in front of each of them with a clunk on the counter.

"Thanks, Charlie." She picked up her fork and looked at Mark. "You need to eat your waffle while it's hot to get the full effect." She took a bite dripping with syrup.

"Trying to get me to quit asking questions?"

"That and the waffles are better hot."

They ate in silence for a few minutes.

"So I remember something about an accident and then I didn't hear much about you after that. I later heard you'd left town. Did you get hurt?"

Mark's fork halted in midair then he lowered it to the plate.

Had she asked the wrong thing? She looked back at her meal. "You don't have to tell me if you'd rather not."

"I wasn't really hurt. But my friend was. I had to leave a few days later to start my fellowship."

"What happened?"

"It's a long story. Too much of one for this morning."

So the man with all the questions was hiding something. Minutes later she finished her last mouthful. Mark said something. She turned to look at him. "What?"

He touched her face. His gaze caught and held hers as he put his finger between his lips. Her stomach fluttered. She swallowed. Heaven help her, the man held her spellbound.

"You had syrup on your chin."

"Uh?"

"Syrup on your chin." Mark said each word slowly, as if speaking to someone who didn't understand the language.

"Oh." She dabbed at the spot with her napkin. Mark was starting to shatter her protective barriers. "We'd better go."

She climbed off the stool and called, "Thanks, Charlie." She was going out the door as Mark pulled a couple of bills out of his wallet.

Her hand was already on the door handle of his car as Mark pulled into a parking place at the shelter. She needed to get away from him. Find her equilibrium. That look in his eye as he'd licked the syrup on his finger had her thinking of things better left unthought. She stepped out of the car. "Thanks for helping out last night. I don't know how I'll repay you."

"No problem."

"Bye, Mark."

Why did a simple gesture from Mark, of all men, make her run? She had to be attracted to him for that to happen. Surely that wasn't the case.

CHAPTER FOUR

FOUR DAYS LATER, as Laura Jo was busy setting up the med tent on North Broad Street, she was still pondering how to raise the money needed for the single mothers' shelter. The grant they were hoping for had come through, but with a condition that the board match the amount. There were only five more days of Mardi Gras season, then things would settle down. After that the city would place the house on the market. She couldn't let that happen. They had to move out of the too-small building they were in now.

She didn't want anyone to get hurt at the parade but if she was busy tonight it would keep her mind off the issue of money…along with the thoughts of how agreeing to go to the dance with Mark just might solve her problem.

Think of the devil and he shows up. Mark rode over the curb of the street and up onto the grassy lot where the med tent was stationed. His tight bike shorts left little to the imagination and there was nothing small about the man. He unclipped his helmet and set it on the handlebars, before heading in her direction. For a second her heart rate picked up with the thought that he'd come to see her. She wasn't sure if it was relief or disappointment that filled her when he stopped to talk in depth to one of the ER doctors working with her. Mark should mean nothing to her. She shouldn't be feeling anything, one way or another.

Laura Jo returned to unpacking boxes, turning her back to him.

A few minutes later a tenor voice she recognized said, "Hello, Laura Jo."

She twisted, making an effort to act as if she hadn't been aware of where he'd been and what he'd been doing during the past ten minutes. "Hi, Mark. I didn't expect to see you today."

"It would be my guess that if you had you'd have seen to it you were reassigned to another med tent."

"You know me so well," she quipped, returning to what she'd been doing.

"I wish I did know you better. Then maybe I'd understand why I find you so fascinating."

A ripple of pleasure went through her at his statement. She resisted placing a hand on her stomach when it quivered. "It might be that I don't fall at your feet like other women do."

"I don't know about that."

"They used to. I figured now wasn't any different. In fact, I saw and heard the ER nurses swoon when you came in the other day."

"Swoon. That's an old-fashioned word." He leaned in close so that only she could hear. "Did you swoon over me, too, Laura Jo?"

She had but she wasn't going to let him know that. Straightening and squaring her shoulders, she said with authority, "I did not."

He grinned, his voice dropping seductively. "Something about that quick denial makes me think you did."

Her heart skipped a beat. "Would you please go? I have work to do."

He chuckled. "I'm flattered. I had no idea girls swooned over me."

I bet. Laura Jo glared at him.

"I'm going. I wouldn't want to keep you from your work. See you later."

She glanced up to see him disappear through the crowd. Their conversations had been the most thought-provoking, irritating and stimulating ones she'd ever experienced. And that didn't count how he'd made her feel when he'd kissed her. She had to think fast to stay ahead of him. Somehow that made her life more exciting and interesting.

Mark made one more circle around his patrol area along the parade route. He'd not worked patrol in three days and his muscles were telling him they had noticed. Busy at his practice, getting his patient load up, it required late hours to accommodate people coming in after work hours. As the newest man in the six-doctor general practice, it was his duty to cover the clinic for the hours that were least desirable.

He was pulled out of his thoughts by a boy of three or four standing in the middle of the street. The child looked lost. Mark parked his bike and scanned the crowd for some anxious parent. Finding none, he went down on his haunches in front of the boy. "Hello, there, are you looking for someone?"

"My mommy."

"Can I help you find her?"

The boy nodded.

Mark offered his hand and he took it. They started walking along the edge of the crowd, Mark looking for anyone who might claim the boy.

A woman clutching her cell phone stepped out from behind the barriers just ahead of them and hurried toward them. "Lucas, you shouldn't have walked off."

The woman looked at Mark. "I was talking on my phone and then he was gone," she said with a nervous little laugh.

Mark nodded. "I understand. Little ones can get away from you when you aren't paying attention."

The woman's lips tightened. She took her son's hand and left.

He went back to patrolling. Returning to Mobile so close to Mardi Gras season, he had social obligations to consider. He'd been king the year he'd left and now that he was back in town he was expected to attend certain events. He'd once lived for all the fanfare of the season but now it held no real thrill for him. Still, certain things were expected of him. He just wished doing so didn't bring on such heavy guilt.

Mark hadn't expected to find Laura Jo working the same parade as he was but he wasn't disappointed either. He'd missed their sparring. It was always fun to see how she'd react to something he said or did. Especially his kiss. He'd kissed enough women to know when one was enjoying it.

He wasn't disappointed with her reaction today, either. When he'd asked her about swooning over him he'd have to admit her pretty blush had raised his self-esteem. She had been one of those teens who'd wanted to be noticed by him. The sad thing was that he would've crushed her admiration with the self-centered attitude he'd wore like his royal cloak if he'd even noticed her.

Clearly he had noted the woman she'd become. There hadn't been another female who kept him on his toes or stepped on them more than she did. There were so many facets to her. He still didn't understand what made her tick. He couldn't count the number of times she'd been on his mind over the past few days despite his efforts not to let her intervene in his thoughts.

He compared the mother who'd been too busy talking on her phone to show any real concern for her child with

Laura Jo's motherly concern over a skinned knee. She won. Laura Jo had seen the humor when he'd had to carry Gus. He could still hear her boisterous laughter. Under all that anti-society, I-can-do-it-on-my-own attitude, she hid a power to love and enjoy life.

From what he'd heard and read between the lines, she hadn't had much opportunity to take pleasure in life in a number of years. She been busy scrapping and fighting to keep Allie cared for. To go to school, then work and start a shelter. It had to have been hard, doing it all without family support. What was the deal with her family anyway?

No wonder she was so involved with the single mothers' house. She identified with the women, had been one of them. As if she didn't have enough going on in her life now, she was trying to raise funds to buy the house. Was there anything Laura Jo couldn't do?

Mark made another loop through his section of the parade route. He wasn't far from the med tent when he pulled over out of the way to let the parade go by. One girl in a group of dancers he recognized from other parades. She was limping badly. Seconds later, the girl left the line and collapsed to the curb.

To help her, he had to cross the parade route. He raised his hand and the driver of the next float stopped. Mark pushed his bike over to where the teenage girl sat. She was busy removing her tap shoe. Mark noticed that her foot was covered in blood.

He parked his bike and crouched beside her. The girl looked at him with tears in her eyes. "I just couldn't go any further."

It wasn't unusual to see members of the dance groups abusing their feet. Some of the dancers did up to four parades a day when it got closer to Fat Tuesday. More than once Mark had wondered how they kept it up. Almost everyone in the parades rode while these girls danced for miles.

"I don't blame you. That looks painful. How about we get you cleaned up and ease that pain?"

The girl nodded then started to stand. Mark picked up her discarded shoe and placed his hand on her shoulder. "The med tent isn't too far. Do you mind if I carry you? That foot looks too painful to walk on."

The girl nodded. Mark handed her the shoe and scooped her into his arms. The crowd parted so he could get through. "Would someone please follow us with my bike?"

A middle-aged man called, "I'll bring it."

Mark headed for the med tent a block away. As he walked people turned to watch. He was within sight of the tent when he saw Laura Jo look in his direction. It was as if she had radar where he was concerned. She seemed to sense when he was near. He would have to give that more thought later. He hefted the girl closer in his arms. This was turning into a workout.

Laura Jo moved away and when he saw her again she was pushing a wheelchair across the dirt and grass area between them. Mark faltered. The girl's arms tightened around his neck. The blood drained from his face as Mike crossed his mind.

When Laura Jo reached him, he lowered the dancer into the chair.

Laura Jo mouthed over the girl's head, "Are you okay?"

He nodded. But the look on her face had him doubting he'd convinced her.

"What happened?"

"Blisters."

"I'll get things ready." Laura Jo turned and hurried back toward the tent.

Mark let his hands rest on the handles of the chair for

a moment before he started pushing. He wished he could have let Laura Jo do it. Bringing the wheelchair up on its two back wheels, he maneuvered it across the rough ground. When he arrived at the tent Laura Jo was waiting with a square plastic pan filled with what must be saline. He lifted the footrest off the chair. Going on one knee, he removed the girl's other tap shoe. Laura Jo then slipped the pan into position and the girl lowered her feet into the water with a small yelp of pain.

"Do it slowly and it will be less painful. It'll hurt at first but as soon as they are clean we'll bandage them and you'll feel a lot better. Are you allergic to anything?"

"No," the girl said.

Laura Jo then offered her a white pill and a small glass of water that had been waiting on the table beside them. "That should ease the pain." She looked at him. "I'll take care of her from here, Dr. Clayborn."

Had he just been dismissed? He had. Grinning at Laura Jo and then the girl, he said, "I'll leave you in the capable hands of Nurse Akins."

"Thank you," the girl said.

"You're welcome. I hope you get to feeling better. I'll miss seeing you in the parades."

The girl blushed a bright pink then looked away.

Laura Jo gave a dramatic roll of her eyes.

Mark smiled. He looked around to find his bike leaning against a nearby tree. He climbed on and prepared to ride off. He glanced back at Laura Jo. She looked away from caring for the girl's feet to meet his gaze.

He grinned. Maybe he could still make her swoon.

Two hours later, after the last parade of the day, he pulled up beside the med tent. He would leave his reports of the minor injuries he'd handled with them. The city officials liked to keep a record of anything that happened during Mardi Gras season in order to plan for the next year.

Allie came running toward him. "Hey, did you bring Gus with you?"

"No, not today. I couldn't get him to ride the bike."

Allie giggled.

"Had any king cake this week?"

Allie nodded. "I even found the baby."

"Then I guess you're planning to take a cake to school."

"We're out of school today. It's our Mardi Gras break."

"Well, then, how about bringing me one? I haven't even had the chance to find the baby this year."

Laura Jo walked over "I don't think—"

Mark looked at her. "It just so happens that your mother owes me a favor."

"I do?"

"Anna."

Laura Jo's heart fell. She did.

"So how about you and your mother come over to my house tomorrow night and I'll fix sausage gumbo and you bring the king cake. Better yet, your mother can make it at my house." He looked at Laura Jo when he said, "She did say my kitchen was the perfect place to make a cake."

"Can we, Mommy? I want to see Gus. You don't have to work tomorrow."

"Great. Then it's all settled. I'll expect you at four o'clock."

"Do you two think I could say something since you're making plans that involve me?"

Mark looked at her and grinned. "Talk away."

"Allie, I think we need to take it easy while we have a day off. The next few days are going to be busy."

Mark leaned forward, making eye contact. “And I think that you owe me a favor that you are trying to welch on.”

Laura Jo shifted from one foot to the other. She did owe him big for helping her with Anna, and the check, and Allie being in the parade. Even so, going to Mark’s house again wasn’t a good idea. “I thought you might be enough of a gentleman that you wouldn’t stoop to calling in a favor.”

He gave her a pointed look. “Sometimes you want something badly enough that the social graces don’t matter.”

She swallowed. The implication was that she might be that “something.” When had been the last time she’d felt wanted by a man? It had been so long ago she couldn’t remember.

Mark looked at Allie and grinned. “Manners don’t matter when you’re talking about king cake.”

Allie returned the smile and nodded.

Why was she letting Mark talk her into it? Because the least she owed him was a king cake for all that he’d done for her. And she had to admit that deep down inside she’d enjoy cooking in his kitchen and spending time with him.

Mark couldn’t remember the last time he’d looked forward to a king cake with such anticipation. He suspected that it had nothing to do with the cake and everything to do with seeing Laura Jo. She and Allie were due any minute. He gave the gumbo a stir. He’d missed the stew-type consistency of the dish while he’d been in California. As hard as he’d tried, he hadn’t been able to get the ingredients to make good gumbo. What he had used had never tasted like what he was used to having when he was in Mobile.

He slurped a spoonful of gumbo off the tip of the ladle. It was good.

The doorbell rang. Should a man be so eager to spend time with a woman? For his own self-preservation he’d say no. With a smile on his face, Mark opened the door. To his amazement, Laura Jo smiled in return. He hadn't expected that when he'd given her no choice about coming to his home today. Allie brushed passed his legs.

"Where's Gus?" she asked as she went.

"He was in his bed, sleeping, the last time I saw him."

He liked Allie. He'd never spent much time around children but he found Allie a pleasure. She seemed to like him as much as he did her. What would it be like to be a father to a child like her? Maybe if he had Allie as a daughter he'd have a chance of being a good father.

"I hope Gus is prepared for this," Laura Jo said.

"I wouldn't worry about Gus. Can I take those?" He reached for the grocery bags she carried in either hand.

"Thanks." She handed him one of them. "I guess I'd better get started. It's a long process."

It occurred to him that she'd be anxious to get away as soon as she had met her obligation. He didn't plan to let that happen. "We have plenty of time. I have nowhere to be tonight—do you?"

"Uh, no, but I'd still like to get started."

"Okay, if that's the way you want it." To his astonishment, he said, "I'm going to take Gus and Allie outside to play. Gus needs some exercise." When had he started to think that he was capable of overseeing Allie?

"All right. Just don't let Allie get too close to the water."

"I'll take good care of her." He was confident he would. He headed in the direction of the living room.

Laura Jo watched as Mark left the kitchen after he'd placed the bag on the kitchen counter. He headed out as if he'd given her no more thought. For some reason, she was disappointed he'd not worked harder at encouraging her to join him and Allie. She was even more surprised that she trusted him without question to take care of Allie. Was it because she'd seen him caring for others or that she just innately knew he would see to Allie like she was his own?

Running a hand over the granite counter, she looked around the kitchen. It was truly amazing. If she had this kitchen to cook in every day, she might never leave it. But she didn't. What she had was a small corner one and it was plenty for her and Allie. Mark's kitchen reminded her of her childhood when she'd stood beside Elsie Mae, their cook, and helped prepared meals.

It was time to get busy. She planned to make the most of Mark's kitchen while she had it. Shaking off the nostalgia, Laura Jo pulled the bread flour and eggs out of the bag she'd brought. Over the next twenty minutes she prepared the dough and set it aside to rise.

Going to one of the living-room windows, she looked out. Allie was running with Gus as Mark threw a ball. Laura Jo laughed. Gus showed no interest in going after the ball. Seconds later Mark opened his arms wide and Allie ran into them. He lifted her over his head. Laura Jo could hear her daughter's giggles from where she stood. Her chest tightened.

Allie wrapped her arms around Mark's neck as he brought her back down. They both had huge smiles on their faces. Laura Jo swallowed the lump in her throat. The man had obviously won her daughter over and Laura Jo was worried he was fast doing the same with her.

She pulled open the door and walked out to join them. Allie and Mark were so absorbed in playing that they didn't see her until she had almost reached them. Seeing Allie with Mark brought home how much Allie needed a male figure in her life. Had she done Allie a disservice by not looking for a husband or keeping her away from her grandfather? Had she been so wrapped up in surviving and trying to take care of other mothers that she'd neglected Allie's needs?

"Is something wrong?" Mark asked.

"No, everything is fine."

"You had a funny look on your face. Was there a problem in the kitchen?"

"No, I found what I needed. Now I have to wait for the dough to rise before I do anything more."

"Then why don't we walk down to the dock?" Mark suggested.

"Okay."

"Come on, Allie," Mark called.

"So, do you boat or water-ski?" Laura Jo asked.

Mark stopped and looked at her. "You know, I like you being interested in me."

"Please, don't make more of a friendly question than there is. I was just trying to make conversation. You live on the water, were raised on the water so I just thought..."

"Yes, I have a small sailboat and the family also has a ski boat."

She and Mark walked to the end of the pier and took a seat in the Adirondack chairs stationed there.

"How about you?" he asked.

"I don't sail but I do love to ski." She watched the small waves coming in as the wind picked up.

"Maybe you and Allie can come and spend the day on the water with me when it gets warmer."

Allie ran past them to the edge of the pier.

"Be careful," Mark called. "The water is cold. I don't want you to fall in."

"You sure do sound like a parent."

Mark took on a stricken look that soon turned thoughtful. "I did, didn't I?"

"I don't know why you should act so surprised. You're great with kids."

A few minutes went by before he asked, "I know who your parents are but I can't remember if you have any brothers or sisters."

"Only child." Laura Jo wasn't pleased he'd turned the conversation to her and even less so to her parents. She didn't want to talk about them. The people who had been more interested in their social events than spending time with her. Who hadn't understood the teen who'd believed so strongly in helping the less fortunate. Who had always made her feel like she didn't quite measure up.

"Really? That wouldn't have been my guess."

"Why not?"

"Because you're so strong and self-sufficient. You don't seem spoiled to me."

"You do have a stereotypical view of an only child."

He shrugged. "You could be right."

Laura Jo kept an eye on Allie, who had left the pier and was now playing along the edge of the water as Gus lumbered along nearby.

"So tell me about growing up as a Clayborn with a big silver spoon in your mouth."

"I had no silver spoon that I can remember."

She gave him a sideways look. "I remember enough to know you were the golden boy."

"Well, I do have blond locks." Mark ran his hand through his hair with an attitude.

"And an ego."

They watched the water for a while before she stood and called to Allie, "Do you want to help braid the dough?"

"I want to do the colors," Allie said.

"Okay, I'll save that job for you."

Laura Jo headed back along the pier and Mark followed

a number of paces behind her. As she stepped on the lawn her phone rang. Fishing it out of her jeans pocket, she saw it was Marsha calling and answered.

"Hey, I've just been given tickets to see that new kids' movie. Jeremy wants Allie to go with him. Would you mind if I come and get her?"

"I don't know, Marsha…" If she agreed, it would leave her alone with Mark.

"You mean you'd keep your child from seeing a movie she's been wanting to see because you're too afraid to stay by yourself with Mark Clayborn."

Put that way, it did sound kind of childish. But it was true.

After a sigh Laura Jo said, "Let me speak to Allie. She may rather stay here with the dog."

Laura Jo called to her daughter. Hearing the idea, Allie jumped up and down, squealing that she wanted to go to the movie.

"Okay, Marsha, but you'll have to come and get her. I'm in the middle of making king cakes."

"I'll be there in thirty minutes."

While they waited for Marsha to arrive, Laura Jo punched the dough down and placed it in the refrigerator to rest. She then cleaned Allie up so she'd be ready to go when Marsha arrived.

"Who's going to hide the baby if you leave?" Mark teased Allie.

"I bet Mommy will let you."

He looked over at Laura Jo. "Will you?"

"Yes, you can hide the baby." She made it sound like she was talking to a mischievous boy.

"Mark, will you do the colors for me too?" Allie asked, as she pulled on one of Gus's ears.

"I don't know if I know how to do those." Mark was

sitting in a large chair in the living area with one foot on the ottoman.

"Mommy will show you. She knows how to do it all."

Mark met Laura Jo's gaze over Allie's head. "She knows how to do it all, does she?"

A tingle went down her spine. Leave it to Mark to make baking a king cake sound sexier than it really was.

Five minutes later there was a knock at the door. Allie skipped to it while Laura Jo and Mark followed behind her. Laura Jo stepped around Allie and opened the door.

"Come on, Allie," Marsha said. "We need to hurry if we're going to be there on time." Marsha looked at Laura Jo. "Just let her spend the night since she was coming to me early in the morning anyway. Enjoy your evening. Hi, Mark. Bye, Mark." With that, Marsha whisked Allie away.

"Does she always blow in and blow out with such force?" Mark asked.

Laura Jo closed the door with a heavy awareness of being alone with Mark. "Sometimes. I need to finish the cake and get out of your way."

"I invited you to dinner and I expect you to stay. Are you scared to be here with me, knowing Allie isn't here to protect you?"

"She wasn't protecting me!" Had she been using Allie as a barrier between her and men? No, her first priority was Allie and taking care of her. It had nothing to do with fear.

"Then quit acting as if you're scared I might jump you."

Laura Jo ignored his comment and headed toward the kitchen. She pulled the large bowl of dough out of the refrigerator.

"So what has to be done to it now?" Mark asked.

"Roll it out." She placed the bowl on the corner. "Will you hand me that bag of flour?"

He reached across the wide counter and pulled the bag to him. He then pushed it toward her. Leaning a hip against the cabinet as if he had no place he'd rather be, he asked, "So what happens now?"

"Are you asking for a play-by-play?" She spread flour across the counter.

"Maybe."

"I have to divide the dough." She pulled it apart and set what she wasn't going to use right away back into the bowl.

"Why're you doing that?"

"This recipe makes two cakes. Are you sure there isn't a basketball game on that you want to watch?"

"Nope, I like watching you."

Focusing her attention on her baking again, she dumped the dough onto the granite corner top. She reached into one of the bags and pulled out a rolling pin.

"You didn't think I'd have one of those, did you?" Mark asked from his position beside her.

"Do you?"

"I'm sure I do around here somewhere. I'd have to hunt for it."

"That's why I brought my own." She punched the dough flat with her palms then picked up the pin and started rolling.

"While I roll this out, would you find the cinnamon? It's in one of these bags."

"Sure." He walked to the other side of the room and pulled a bowl out of the cabinet. They each did their jobs in silence."

Heat washed over her. She was far too aware of him being near. All her disquiet went into making the dough thin and wide. "Would you also open the cream cheese? I set it out to soften earlier."

"Will do."

Laura Jo had never had a man help her in the kitchen. Her father had no interest in cooking, not even grilling. Phil had seen it as woman's work and never helped. It was nice to have someone interested in the same thing that she was. To work with her.

"I'm going to need the sugar. I forgot to bring any." Maybe if she kept him busy, he wouldn't stand so close.

"That I do have. Coming right up." Mark reached under the counter and pulled out a plastic container. "Here you go."

"Thanks." Laura Jo brushed her hair away with the back of her hand, sending flour dust into the air.

"Turn around," Mark said.

"Why?"

"Just turn around. For once just trust me."

Behind her there was the sound of a drawer being pulled open then pushed back.

"What are—?"

Mark stepped close enough that she felt his heat from her shoulders to her hips. Strong fingers glided over her scalp and fanned out, gathering her hair.

Her lungs began to hurt and she released the breath she held. Every part of her was aware of how close Mark stood. His body brushed hers as he moved to a different angle. One hand drifted over her temple to capture a stray strand. His warm breath fluttered across the nap of her neck. She quivered.

There was a tug then a pull before he said, "There, that should help."

He moved and the warmth that had had her heart racing disappeared, leaving her with a void that she feared only Mark could fill.

She touched the back of her head. He had tied her hair up with a rag. "Thanks."

"Now you can work without getting flour all in your hair."

He'd been doing something practical and she had been wound up about him being so close. She needed to finish these cakes and go home as soon as possible.

"Would you mind melting a stick of butter?"

"Not at all," Mark said in an all-too-cheerful manner.

Laura Jo continued to roll the dough into a rectangle, while keeping an eye on Mark as he moved around on the other side of the counter. "One more thing."

He raised a brow.

"Would you mix the cinnamon and sugar together?"

"Yeah. How much?" Mark headed again to where the bowls were.

"Like you are making cinnamon toast."

"How do you know I know how to make cinnamon toast?"

"Everyone knows how to do that," she said, as she finished rolling the first half of the dough. "While I roll out the other dough, will you spread butter on this one then put the sugar cinnamon mixture over that?"

"I don't know. All that might be out of my territory."

She chuckled. "I think you can handle it."

Over the next few minutes they each worked at their own projects. Laura Jo was used to making the cakes by herself but found she liked having a partner even in something as simple as a cake. She glanced at Mark. His full attention was on what he was doing. He approached his assignment much as he did giving medical care, with an effort to do the very best, not miss any detail.

She looked over to where he was meticulously shaking

the sugar mixture on the dough from a spoon. "You know you really can't do that wrong."

"Uh?"

He must have been so involved in what he was doing he hadn't heard her. "Enjoy what you're doing a little. It doesn't have to be perfect."

Mark straightened. "This comes from the person who only laughs when my dog gets the best of me."

"I laugh at other times."

"Really?"

Was she truly that uptight? Maybe she was but she could tell that lately she'd been starting to ease up. Ever since she'd started spending time with Mark.

"Speaking of uptight, what's your issue with a wheelchair?"

CHAPTER FIVE

DAMN, SHE'D NOTICED. Mark had thought, hoped, Laura Jo had missed or he'd covered his feelings well enough when he'd seen a wheelchair, but apparently not.

Maybe he could bluff his way out of answering. "I don't know what you mean."

Laura Jo was looking at him. His skin tingled. He glanced at her. She had stopped what she was doing.

"Please, don't insult my intelligence," she said quietly.

He sighed before answering. "My friend who was in the accident is now in a wheelchair."

"I'm sorry to hear that."

"Me, too." He put the empty bowl in the sink.

"What happened?"

"He was thrown from the car."

"Oh, how awful."

"It was." He needed to change the subject. "So what do I need to do now?"

"Roll it into a log, like this." Laura Jo moved close and started working with the dough.

He looked at the honey nape of her neck exposed and waiting for him. Mike went out of his mind and all he could think about was the soft woman so close, the smell of cinnamon and sugar and the need to touch her, kiss her.

The wisps of hair at her neck fluttered as he leaned

closer. He touched the tip of his tongue to her warm skin. He felt a tremor run through her and his manhood responded. His lips found the valley and he pressed. Sweet, so sweet.

She shifted away. “Mark, I don’t have time in my life to play games.”

“Who said I was playing a game?”

“I have Allie to think about.”

He spoke from behind her. “So you’re going to put how you feel and your life on hold for Allie? For how long?” He kissed her behind the ear.

Her hands stopped rolling the dough. She stepped to the side so that she could turn to look at him. “What I’m not going to do is get involved with a man I have no intention of marrying.”

Mark put some space between them. “Whoa, we’re not talking about marriage here. More like harmless fun. A few kisses. Some mutually satisfying petting.” He stepped back and studied her. “Are you always this uptight around a man?”

“I’m not uptight.”

“The best I can tell is the only time you’re not is when I’m kissing you or you’re laughing at my dog.”

“I wasn’t laughing at Gus. I was laughing at you.”

He took a step closer, pinning her against the counter. “No one likes to be laughed at. But what I’m really interested in is you showing me how you’re not uptight. I want to kiss you, Laura Jo. Just kiss you.”

She didn’t resist as his lips came down to meet hers. His mouth was firm but undemanding as if he was waiting to see if she would accept him. When had been the last time she had taken a moment’s pleasure with a man? What would it hurt if she did? Just to have something that was simple and easy between two adults.

Laura Jo wrapped her hands around his neck, weaved her fingers through his hair and pressed herself against his lean, hard body. With a sigh, she returned his kiss.

Mark encircled her waist and lifted her against him. His mouth took further possession, sending wave after wave of heat through her. He ran the tip of his tongue along the seam of her mouth until she opened for him. The parry and thrust of his tongue had her joining him. He pressed her against the counter, shifted her until his desire stood ridged between them.

Something poked at her bottom just before there was a loud thump on the floor. She broke away. Mark's hand remained at her waist. Her breath was shallow and rapid. She was no longer a maiden but she sure was acting like one. Her heart was thudding against her rib cage. She couldn't look at Mark.

When she did glance at him through lowered lashes, to her great satisfaction he looked rattled, too. He leaned toward her again and she broke the embrace before stepping away. "I need to get these cakes ready to put in the oven." She was relieved that her voice sounded steadier than she felt.

Mark looked for a second as if he might disagree but he didn't move any closer.

"I think I like the sugar you just gave me better than what is on a king cake."

She had to regain her equilibrium. The only way she knew how to do that was to go on the defensive. She placed her hands on her hips. "You haven't tasted one of my cakes."

"No, but I have tasted you," he said in a soft and sultry voice.

Pleasure filled her. Mark had a way of making her feel special.

"Why don't you spread the cream cheese on this cake while I finish braiding the other one?"

"Yes, ma'am."

Minutes later Mark dropped the spatula he had been using in the sink. Laura Jo placed the cake she was working with on a baking pan. She had been aware of every movement he'd made as he'd spread the creamy cheese across the thin pastry.

"While you finish up on this one I'm going to get us each a bowl of gumbo." Mark went to a cabinet and pulled down two bowls.

Laura Jo was both relieved and disappointed when he moved to the other side of the center counter. If Mark was close he made her feel nervous and if he wasn't she missed his nearness.

"We forgot to put the babies in." Laura Jo reached into a bag and brought out a snack-size bag with tiny hard plastic babies in it. Their hands and feet were up in the air as if they were lying in a crib, laughing.

"I'll put those in. I promised Allie I would. I keep my promises."

Mark joined her again and she handed the babies to him. They looked extra-small in his large palm.

"Turn around. And don't peek."

Laura Jo did as he instructed.

"Okay. Done."

Laura Jo started cleaning up the area. "You know, it doesn't have to be such a secret. Mardi Gras will be over in four days and we won't be having another cake until next year."

He met her gaze. "Well, maybe I'll ask for something besides cake if I find the baby inside my piece."

"That's not how it works."

"Then we could just change the rules between us."

Laura Jo wasn't sure she wanted to play that game.

"Are you ready for gumbo?"

"I can eat while these rise." She looked over at the cakes.

"I had no idea this much work went into making a king cake."

"They are labor intensive but I enjoy it. Especially when I can make them in a kitchen like this one."

Mark filled the two bowls he'd gotten out earlier. "Do you mind carrying your own bowl to the table?"

"Of course not. I don't expect you to wait on me."

They sat across from each other in the small breakfast nook adjoining the kitchen. From there they had a view of the bay.

"This is delicious." Laura Jo lifted a spoonful of gumbo. "I'm impressed with your culinary skills."

"I think culinary skills is a little strong. It's not hard really."

"Either way, it tastes good." She was glad that they were back to their old banter. She'd been afraid that after their hot kiss, which had her nerves on high alert, they wouldn't be able to have an easy conversation. She rather enjoyed their discussions, even if they didn't always agree.

"How's Marcy doing?"

She looked at him. "Very well, thanks to you. She'll be coming home tomorrow."

"I didn't do anything but provide encouragement. I meant to go by to see them again but I had to work late on the days I wasn't patrolling parades."

"Ann really appreciated the one day you did check in on them. That was nice of you."

"I'm a nice guy."

He really was. She'd done him a disservice when she'd first met him. He'd proven more than once that he was a good person.

"So have you found the funding for the shelter yet?" Mark asked as he pushed his empty bowl away.

"We qualified for the grant I was hoping for but it requires we find matching funds."

"Well, at least you do have some good news." He stood, gathering his bowl. "Do you want any more gumbo while I'm getting some?"

"No, I'm still working on this." Laura Jo watched him walk away. He wore a lightweight long-sleeved sweater and worn jeans. He really had a fine-looking butt.

For a second she'd been afraid he'd ask her about going to the dance. A hint of disappointment touched her when he didn't. He probably had a date with someone else by now. She didn't like that thought any better.

They finished their dinner with small talk about the weather, parades and the coming weekend. Together they carried their bowls to the dishwasher. Mark placed them in it while Laura Jo checked on the rising cake.

"How much longer on those?" Mark asked.

"They need to rise to double their size. Then I'll bake them and be on my way. I can finish the topping when I get home."

"Oh, no, you won't. I want to eat some as soon as you get them done. Besides, I want to do the topping."

"You're acting like Allie."

"Did you think I was kidding when I told you that I liked king cake as much as she did? I haven't had any in a long time and I'm not letting you out of the house without a piece today. While we're waiting, why don't we go out on the deck and have a cup of coffee and watch the sunset?"

She wasn't sure if watching the sunset with Mark was a good idea but she didn't know how to get out of it gracefully. Those darned cakes were taking too long to rise for her comfort. "Make that another glass of tea and I'll agree."

"Done. Why don't you go on out and take your pick of chairs and I'll bring the drinks."

Laura Jo walked through the living area and out one of the glass doors. Gus got up from his bed and ambled out with her. She took one of the lounges, making sure it wasn't near any others. Having Mark so close all the time was making her think of touching him, worse, kissing him again. She needed to put whatever distance she could between them.

Gus lay at the end of the lounge.

"Here you go," Mark said, placing her glass and his mug on the wire mesh table beside her. He then pulled one of the other lounges up on the opposite side of the table. He stretched his long body out and settled in.

"You mind handing me my mug?"

With shaking hands, Laura Jo passed him his drink.

"This is the best part of the day. I miss this when I have to work late."

She had to agree. It was nice to just slow down and be for a few minutes. "Is working here a lot different from your clinic in California?"

"The patients' backgrounds are different but sick people are sick people."

"Do you regret leaving California?"

"I have to admit I like the slower pace here." Mark crossed his ankles and settled more comfortably into the lounge.

"I couldn't leave Mobile and move all the way across the country."

"Sometimes you do things because you don't think you have a choice."

She watched a bird dipping into the water after its evening meal. "I know about not having choices." Maybe in some ways they weren't so different after all.

They both lapsed into silence as the sun slowly sank in the sky.

Laura Jo took a sip of her tea at the same time a breeze came in off the water. She shivered.

Mark put his mug down on the decking and stood. "I'll be back in a sec."

He returned with a jacket in his hand and handed it to her. "Here, you can put this on."

She slipped her arm into one sleeve and Mark held the jacket for her to put the other in. He sat beside her again. She trembled again and pulled the jacket closer around her.

As the wind blew, a scent of spice and musk that could only be Mark tickled her nostrils. She inhaled. For some reason it was a smell she wanted to remember.

Again they lapsed into a relaxed silence.

As the daylight was taken over by the night, Mark reached over and took her hand, weaving his fingers between hers. It was strong, secure and soothing. Laura Jo didn't pull away. Didn't want to.

When the stars came out Mark said, "We need to go and put those cakes in."

Laura Jo started. She'd been so content she'd forgotten about having anything to do. Her hand being surrounded by Mark's added to that feeling. For some reason it made her feel protected, as if she weren't facing the world alone. She hadn't had that in her life for so long it had taken her time to recognize it.

Mark not only made her feel protected but she had seen his security in tangible terms. He was great with Allie. More than once he'd seen to it that she was safe and cared for and that made her happy. She'd also seen him showing that protection to others. He'd been there when she'd called for help with Anna and Marcy. There hadn't been a moment's hesitation on his part about coming. Not once had he acted like her having a daughter was an issue. In fact, he embraced Allie, included her.

Why was Mark the one man who made her feel that way? His background said he wasn't the man for her. She wanted someone who was more interested in her than what her last name had been. But hadn't he proved her background didn't matter? He'd shown his interest well before she had told him her maiden name was Herron.

She might have questioned whether or not he had become a doctor for the money and prestige but the Clayborns already had that. After she'd viewed him seeing to a patient she'd seen his concern was sincere. He was a man interested in caring for people. He had offered to help with the shelter and had proved it with his donation and medical care. How different could he be from Phil, who was the most self-centered man she'd ever known?

She slipped her hand out of his. "I'll bake the cakes. You should stay here. It's a beautiful night."

"I'll help you."

"It won't take me long."

"Do you promise to come back? Not disappear out the front door?"

Laura Jo smiled. "Yes, I'll come back."

"I'll be waiting."

She liked the sound of that. People didn't wait for her, they left her. Mark was starting to mean too much to her. Laura Jo put the cakes in the ovens. Thankfully, Mark had double ovens and she could bake them at the same time.

Still wearing his jacket, she went back outside to join him. If he hadn't stated his fear that she might leave she might have considered going home without telling him. Her attraction to him was growing beyond her control. She didn't trust herself around him.

As she passed him on the way to her lounge he sat up

and snagged her wrist. “Come and sit with me.” He pulled her toward him.

She put a hand down next to his thigh to stop herself from falling.

“Mark...” she cautioned.

“I’m not going to jump you. I’d just like to have you close.”

“Why?”

The light from inside the house let her see well enough his incredulous look. “Why? Because I’m a man and you’re a woman. I like you and I think you like me more than you want to admit. You’re as aware of the attraction as I am. You just won’t admit it.

She looked down at him for a moment.

“All I want is to sit here with a beautiful woman and watch the stars. Nothing more. But if you don’t want to, I’ll live with that.”

He made it sound like she was acting childishly. “Scoot over.”

“If you’re going to get bossy then maybe I need to reconsider my invitation.”

She snickered and lay on her side next to him. He wrapped an arm around her shoulders and her head naturally went to his chest.

“Now, is this so bad?”

“No. I’m much warmer.”

“Good. I’m glad I can be of service.” Mark’s breath brushed her temple.

“I can’t get too comfortable. I don’t want to burn the cakes.”

“How much longer do they need to cook?” His hand moved up and down her arm.

“Another forty minutes.”

He checked his watch. “Then I’ll help you remember.”

It took her a few minutes to relax and settle into her warm and cozy spot alongside Mark. The lights of Mobile glowed in the distance and the horn of an occasional seagoing freighter sounded. It was a lonesome noise, one that up until this minute she could identify with. Somehow she no longer felt lonely. As they sat in silence her eyelids drooped and closed.

The next thing she knew Mark was shaking her awake. "We need to get the cakes out."

She jerked to a sitting position. "I'm sorry. I went to sleep on you."

"I'm not. It would be my guess you needed to rest after the week you've had."

Laura Jo couldn't argue with that. She struggled to get up.

"Let me climb out first then I'll pull you up," Mark suggested.

As he moved, his big body towered over her. She was tempted to touch him. Before she could stop herself she placed a hand on his chest.

"I'm squishing you?"

"No. I just wanted to touch you," she murmured.

He gave her a predatory glare. "Great. You decide to touch me when the king cakes might be burning. You need to work on your timing."

She nudged him back. "Let me up."

He hesitated a second before he took her hand and pulled her to her feet. "Let's go."

In the kitchen Mark peeked into an oven. He inhaled dramatically. "Smells wonderful."

"If you'll get your nose out of it, I can take it out." Laura Jo handed him a hot pad. "I'll get this one and you can get the other." Laura Jo pulled the golden-brown mound out of the oven and set it on the counter. Mark did the same and placed his beside hers.

Again he leaned over and inhaled deeply. “Perfect.”

“I need to mix the icing and then we can put the colors on.” Laura Jo found a bowl and added powdered sugar then water. She stirred them into a creamy white mixture. Using a spoon, she drizzled the icing back and forth over the top of the cakes.

Mark dipped a finger through the bowl and put it in his mouth. “Mmm.”

She tapped the top of his hand when he started after the cake.

“Ouch.”

“I believe you have a sweet tooth.”

“I think you are sweet.”

“I think you might flatter the cook in order to get your way. It’s time for the colored sugar.” Laura Jo picked up the food coloring she’d left on the other end of the counter. “We’ll need three bowls.”

Mark went to a cabinet and brought those to her. Laura Jo put granulated sugar in each of the bowls and added yellow coloring to one, purple to another and green to the last one. She mixed until each granule had turned the color. She sprinkled one color over a third of one cake. In the middle section another and on the last third another.

“Do you know what the colors stand for?” Mark asked.

“No self-respecting citizen of Mobile wouldn’t know. Purple is for justice, green is for faith and gold for power.”

“You are correct. Can we have a slice now?” Mark asked, sounding much like a child begging at his mother’s side.

“You want to eat it while it’s hot?”

“Why not?”

“I’ve just never had it that way. I’ve always waited until it’s cooled.”

"Well, there's a first time for everything." Mark pulled a knife out of a drawer and sliced a hunk off the end of one cake. Picking it up, he bit into it. "This is delicious. Allie is right, you do make the best cakes. I've never had one better from a bakery."

His praise made her feel warm inside. She cut a small section and placed it in her mouth. It was good.

"Hey, look what I found." He held up a baby.

"You knew where that was."

"I did not," he said in an indignant tone. "Just good luck."

Laura smiled and placed the items she had brought into bags. She needed to leave before she was tempted to stay longer. Being with Mark had been far more enjoyable than she'd found comfortable. What if he tried to kiss her again? Could she handle that?

"What're you doing?" Mark asked.

"I'm packing up."

"You don't have to go."

"Yes, I do. Do you have something I can wrap one of these cakes in? Allie will be expecting to eat some tomorrow."

Mark opened a drawer and handed her a box of plastic wrap.

She pulled out a length of wrap and started covering the cake. "Do you mind if I take your baking pan? I'll return it."

"I don't mind," he said in an aggravated tone, as if he knew she was dodging the issue.

"Are you running out on me, Laura Jo?"

She refused to look at him. "No, I've been here for hours and I was more worried about wearing out my welcome."

Mark took the wrap from her and put it on the counter. "I don't think that's possible. I believe you're running scared."

"I'm not."

"Then why don't you go to the dance with me on Tuesday night?"

"I've already said I can't." She reached for a bag and put the rest of the items she'd brought in it.

"I think it's 'I won't.'"

"Please, Mark, just leave it alone. I'm not going to change my mind. It's not because of you but for other reasons."

"Care to tell me what those are."

"I'd rather not. I need to be going." She pulled the bags to her.

"I'm a good listener."

"That's not the problem. I just don't want to talk about it. Now, I need to go."

Mark took them from her. "I'll get these. You can get the cake. I'll walk you to your car."

Laura Jo was a little disappointed that he hadn't put up more of an argument to her leaving. Had her refusal to open up about why she didn't want to go to the krewe dance put him off? Wasn't that what she wanted?

"I need to wrap your cake up before I go and clean up this mess."

"Don't worry about doing that. I'll take care of it. Theresa will be in tomorrow."

"Theresa?"

"My housekeeper."

Just another shining example of the fact they lived in two different worlds. "Well, I'm not going to leave anyone, including a housekeeper, this mess."

"I'm not surprised. It's in your nature to see to other people, make it better for them. Who makes things better for you?"

She hadn't ever thought of herself in that context but he might be right. She wouldn't let him know it, though. "I don't need anyone taking care of me."

"We might be perfect for each other because I'm no good at doing so," he said in a dry tone.

What had made him say that? He was always taking care of people.

She went to the sink, picked up the cleaning cloth and started wiping off the counter.

"Leave it." Mark said, taking the cloth and placing it in the sink. "I'll take care of it."

Laura Jo then picked up the cake and headed for the front door. Mark wasn't far behind. When they reached the car, he opened the front passenger-side door and placed the bags on the floor. He then took the cake from her and did the same.

She went to the driver's door and he joined her there. "Thanks for helping me with the cakes."

"Not a problem." Mark reached into his pocket and pulled something out.

Laura Jo could just make out with the help of the light from the porch that he was rotating the baby between his index and thumb.

"We had a deal."

Laura Jo had an uneasy feeling. Where was he going with this? "We did."

"I would like to collect now."

Every nerve in her hummed. Something told her that she might not like his request. "Just what do you want?"

Mark's lips lifted, giving him a wolfish appearance. He took a step closer, coming into her personal space.

Heat washed over her. She looked at him. In the dim light she couldn't see his eyes clearly but she felt their intensity.

"I want you to kiss me."

"What?"

"I want you put your hands on my shoulders, lean up and place your lips on mine."

He said the words in a form of a challenge, as if she would refuse. She'd show him. Placing her hands on his chest, she slowly slid them up and over his shoulders.

His hands went to her waist, tightening around her.

"Remember this is my kiss," she admonished him.

He eased his hold but didn't release her.

Going up on her toes, she took her time, bringing her lips to his. The tension across his shoulders told her Mark was working to restrain himself.

Taking his lower lip between her teeth, she gently tugged.

He groaned.

She let go and smoothed it over with the tip of her tongue. Slowly she moved her lips over his until she almost ended the contact.

At Mark's sound of resistance she grinned and moved her mouth back to press it firmly against his. She didn't have to ask for entrance, he was already offering it. Her tongue met his and danced but he soon took the lead. She'd been caught at her own game. It felt wonderful to have a man touch her. It had been so long. For Mark to be the one made it even more amazing. Wrapping her arms around his neck, she gave herself over to the moment. She wanted more, so much more.

Mark gripped Laura Jo's waist and pulled her closer. He pressed her back against the car. His hand slid under the hem of her shirt and grazed her smooth skin until his fingers rested near the prize. Wanting to touch, taste, tease, he had to remove the barrier. Using the tip of his index finger, he followed the line of her bra around to the clasp. When he hesitated Laura Jo squirmed against him. She wanted this as much as he did. Flicking the clasp open, he moved his hand to the side curve of her breast.

He released her lips and gave a small sound of complaint. Placing small kisses along her neck to reassure her, he skimmed his hand upward to cup her breast. His sigh of pleasure mingled with hers. He tested the weight. Perfect. Using a finger, he circled her nipple then tugged.

Her hips shifted and came into more intimate contact with his ridged manhood. He'd been aware of his desire for Laura Jo for a number of days but it had never been this overwhelming.

He pushed her bra up and off her other breast. Her nipple stood tall, waiting for his attention. That knowledge only fueled his desire.

Laura Jo cupped his face and brought his lips back to hers. She gave him the hottest kiss he'd ever received. Heaven help him, if she could turn him on with just kisses, what could she do to him in bed?

She ran her hands under his shirt and across his back.

When her mouth left his to kiss his cheek, he pushed up her shirt, exposing her breasts. He backed away just far enough to look at her. "Beautiful."

He didn't give her time to speak before his lips found hers again and his fingers caressed her breast. Thankful for her small car, he leaned her back over the hood. Her fingers flexed and released against the muscles of his back as she met him kiss for kiss. Standing between her legs, the heat of her center pressed against his. He pulled his mouth from hers. It went to the top of her right breast, where he placed his lips. Laura Jo shivered.

"Cold?"

"No."

His chest swelled with desire. What he was doing to her had caused the reaction, not the metal of the car. He lowered his mouth to her nipple and took it. Using his tongue, he spun and tugged. Laura Jo bucked beneath him.

Her hand went to the line of his pants and glided just beneath. She ran her hand one way and then the other before it returned to stroking his back.

She wasn't the cold fish she wanted him to believe she was. She was hot and all sensual woman. He smiled as he gave the other nipple the same devotion.

He wanted her here and now. In his driveway. On her car. But that wasn't what Laura Jo deserved. He wasn't that kind of man. She certainly wasn't that type of woman.

"Sweetheart, we need to go inside."

Mark saw her blink once, twice, as if she were coming out of a deep dream. She looked around as if trying to figure out where she was. He saw the moment she came back to reality and his heart dropped.

"Oh, God." She sat up and gave him a shove.

He stepped back and let her slide off the car.

She jerked her shirt down, not bothering to close her bra. "I have to go."

"No, you don't."

He stepped toward her and she stopped him with a hand. "I can't do this."

"Why not?"

"Because it is wrong for me on so many levels." She climbed behind the wheel of the car. "I'm sorry, Mark."

She couldn't have been any more sorry than he was. He stood there with his body as tight as a bike spoke, wanting to reach out to her. Laura Jo didn't even look at him as she started the car and headed out the drive.

It wasn't until the car stopped about halfway down that he knew she hadn't been as unaffected by what had passed between them as she'd acted. She had wanted him, too.

Guilt filled him. He had no business pursuing Laura Jo if he had no intention of the relationship going beyond what they had just experienced. He couldn't let it be more. He'd already proved he would run when the going got tough. Could he trust himself not to let them down, like he had Mike?

As her taillights disappeared, he turned and walked toward the house. All he had waiting for him tonight was a long, cold shower. He needed to stay well out of Laura Jo's life.

Laura Jo opened the door early the next morning to let Allie, Marsha and Jeremy in. Before Laura Jo could say hello, Marsha announced, "We've got a problem."

"Bigger than the one we already have?"

"Yep."

"Come on into the kitchen and tell me what's happened."

Marsha followed her while Jeremy rushed ahead and took the chair next to Allie.

Marsha sat in the other chair while Laura Jo got a bowl from the cabinet and placed it in front of Jeremy. She then sat down. "Okay, let me have it."

"I got an email from the city rep, saying that if we don't get half the asking price in cash to them by the end of next week then there's no deal,"

This was worse than Laura Jo had expected. "That only gives us five days, and three of those are holidays," she groaned.

"I know. That's why I'm here. Do you have any ideas?"

Laura Jo propped her elbows on the table and put her head in her hands. "No," she said in a mournful voice.

"I do," Marsha announced emphatically.

Laura Jo looked at her. "You do?"

"You have to go to the knewe dance. It's our only chance."

Laura Jo stood and walked to the sink. After last night, going to the dance had become less about her past and more about her reaction to Mark. She had been so tempted to throw all her responsibilities and concerns into the bay and find paradise in his arms. She'd been lying half-naked on the hood of a car, for heaven's sake. The man made her lose her mind. She'd had to stop at the end of his drive in order to get herself together enough to drive. Her hands had still been shaking when she'd started across the bay.

She couldn't stand the thought of losing the best chance they'd had in years to have a new house. But if she went to the dance she'd have to resist Mark, which she wasn't sure she could do, and face her parents and the social circle she'd left behind. The one she spoke so negatively about. She would be going back with her tail between her legs and begging them to help her. No, she would be asking for help for the shelter. It had nothing to do with her personally.

"I'll call Mark. If he hasn't asked someone else to go, I'll tell him I'll go."

Marsha joined her at the sink. "I wouldn't ask you to do it if I thought there was another way." She put an arm around Laura Jo's shoulders. "The house is too perfect for us not to give it our best shot. I'd go but I don't have the same influence as you or Dr. Clayborn have."

"I know. I just hope it works." Maybe going would not only benefit the house but give her a chance to lay some ghosts to rest.

"Me, too." Marsha squeezed her shoulder.

What if Mark had already found another date? That thought gave Laura Jo a sick feeling. Then she guessed she'd be going to the dance by herself. Not only to face her past alone but to see Mark holding another woman. Neither experience appealed to her.

CHAPTER SIX

IT WAS MIDMORNING and Mark was at his office desk when the woman he'd been planning to ask to the dance informed him that he had a call.

Picking up the phone, he said, "Dr. Clayborn here."

"Mark, its Laura Jo."

Like he wouldn't recognize her voice.

"If you don't already have a date for the dance, I'd like to go after all," she finished on a breathless note.

He'd thought of little else but her since those minutes outside his home. She'd kissed him so thoroughly, leaving him in need of not only one cold shower but two. Laura Jo had completely turned the tables on him with those hot, sexy kisses. He'd only hoped to kiss her one more time but instead he'd been left wanting all of her.

"No, I haven't asked anyone else yet."

After the way she'd left last night, something bad must have happened regarding the shelter for her to agree to go to the dance with him. He didn't care, he wasn't going to question the gift.

"So I'm still invited?"

"If you would like to go."

"I would."

"So what changed your mind?"

"They've moved up the timetable on the shelter house and I've been left no choice."

"Well, it's nice to know it isn't because you might enjoy an evening out with me," he said in his best serious tone.

He had to admit it stung to know that she had no interest in being seen at the most prestigious event of the year with him. The only reason she had agreed to go was because she needed help finding funds for the shelter. She had made it clear on more than one occasion that she didn't want to go, so he could only imagine how desperate she must be to pick up the phone and call him. She wanted that shelter enough to take this bold step. What impressed him most was that it wasn't for her but for someone else.

"I'll pick you up at seven."

"Make it eight. I have to work the parade."

That figured. When did she ever take time for herself? He was going to see to it that she enjoyed the evening out with him if it killed him.

"I'll be there at eight, then. We'll make a grand entrance."

"That's what I'm afraid of. Bye, Mark." With that she rang off.

"Laura Jo, stop fussing, you look beautiful," Marsha nagged as Laura Jo pulled up on the dress that showed far too much cleavage for her comfort.

She'd found the evening dress at the upscale consignment shop downtown. Ironically, it was the same one her mother had taken all the family's outdated clothes to when Laura Jo had been a child. Her mother would say, "Maybe someone less fortunate can use these." Like people who were less fortunate cared whether or not they wore couture clothing.

"I'm only going to this thing to try to drum up funds

for the shelter, not to have men staring at me. I'll have to wear the green dress. Would you get it? It's in my closet."

Laura Jo hadn't had time to look any further for a more appropriate dress. She'd taken the first one that was her size and looked suitable. She hadn't even tried it on and had had no idea this one would be so revealing.

"Isn't the dress formal?" Marsha said, as if she were reassuring a child having a temper tantrum.

"Yes, but I guess I don't have a choice." Laura Jo looked into the full-length mirror one more time. The plunging neckline left the top of her breasts exposed. Each time she breathed she feared more than that might be visible. For a brief second the memory of Mark's lips pressed against her flesh made her sizzle all over. She inhaled sharply.

"Is something wrong?" Marsha asked.

She circled around and faced Marsha. "Don't you have a pink shawl? I could put it around my shoulders and tie it in front. That would fix the problem."

Marsha sighed. "I don't see a problem but I'll go get it. I think you're overreacting. The dress is perfect the way it is."

Laura Jo looked at herself again. Was she overreacting? If so, why? Because she was going to the dance with Mark or because she was afraid she couldn't control herself around him?

She studied the dress. It was midnight blue with the slightest shimmer to it. The material hugged her in all the correct places. Twisting, she turned so that she could see the back. It closed close to her neck so that it formed a diamond-shaped peephole in the middle. It was the loveliest detail of the dress.

"Mommy, you look pretty," Allie said from behind Laura Jo.

"Thank you, honey." She leaned down and kissed the top of Allie's head.

The doorbell rang.

"I'll get it," Allie said, running out of the room.

Laura Jo followed. Surely it was Marsha, returning with the wrap.

Allie opened the door and Mark stood on the other side. Their eyes met and held. Everything that had happened between them the night before flashed through her mind. His gaze slid downward and paused at her breasts.

They tingled and her nipples grew hard. Heat pooled in her middle. What was happening to her? Something as simple as a look from Mark could make her feel alive like no one else could.

Was he remembering, too?

"Doesn't Mommy look pretty?" Allie asked, looking back and forth between them.

Mark's gaze didn't leave her. Seconds later, as if coming out of a stupor, he said, "Uh, yes, she looks wonderful."

Laura Jo swallowed hard. She'd never felt more beautiful than she did right now as Mark admired her. The man was starting to get under her skin and everything about his idea of life was so wrong for her. Or was it? She'd better guard her heart tonight or he might take it.

Allie looked up at Mark. "You look pretty, too."

He did, in the most handsome, debonair and charming way. His blond waves were in place and his eyes shone. Dressed in his formal wear of starched white shirt, black studs and tailcoat, he took her breath away. She'd seen many men wearing their finest but none compared to the man standing before her.

"Thank you, Allie." He was still looking at her when he said, "Do you mind if I come in?"

"Oh, no, do." Laura Jo gave Allie a little nudge back into the hall. She stepped out of the way and let Mark enter.

"Come in and have a seat. I'm waiting for Marsha to bring me a cover-up."

"From where I stand, you look perfect just the way you are." His voice had a grainy sound to it that wasn't normal.

"Thank you." When had she become such a blusher? When Mark had come into her life.

"Have a seat while I get my purse. Marsha should be back by then." Laura Jo indicated a chair in their small living area.

There was a knock on the door and Allie ran to open it. Laura Jo trailed behind her. Her friend breezed in, breathless. "I couldn't find it. I must have given it away at our last clothes drive. Hi, Dr. Clayborn. You look nice." Marsha let the last few words spin out.

"Thank you. I was telling Laura Jo she looks great just as she is."

"I think so, too." Marsha said. She offered a hand to Allie. "Come on. It's time to go. Jeremy will be home in a few minutes."

Laura Jo picked up a small bag and handed it to her daughter. "I'll see you tomorrow afternoon. I'll be picking you and Jeremy up from school." Laura Jo kissed her on the head.

"Okay. Bye, Mark." Allie happily went out the door.

"Have a good time and don't do anything I wouldn't do," Marsha quipped with a wink.

"Marsha!"

Mark's low chuckle didn't help to lessen Laura Jo's mortification.

She turned to him. "You do understand I'm only going to the krewe dance because I need funds for the shelter. Nothing else can happen."

"You more than made it clear that the evening has nothing to do with my company. Are you ready?"

Had she hurt his feelings?

"Mark, I'm sorry. I didn't mean to sound so rude." She looked down. "After the other night I just didn't want you to get the wrong idea. I do appreciate you taking me to the dance. It's just that I have a difficult time with the idea and I seem to be taking it out on you."

"Maybe if you explained, I would understand."

She looked at him again. "It's because…I shunned that world years ago."

"Why?"

"I fell in love, or at least what I thought was love, with a guy who my parents didn't approve of. 'Not of our social status,' my father said. My parents were adamantly against the marriage. They told me Phil was after my name and money, not me. That he was no good. My father was particularly vocal about Phil being the wrong guy. He forced me to make a choice between them or my ex.

"I always felt like I was an afterthought to them. I never quite fit the mold they had imagined for their child. They spent little time with me when I was young and now they wanted to start making parental demands, showing real interest. I had always been more headstrong than they liked, so my father's ultimatum backfired.

"I told my parents if the man I loved wasn't good enough for them then I didn't need them. I chose Phil. Turned out they were right about him. He was everything they said he was and more. I said some ugly things to my parents that I now regret but I couldn't go running back. My pride wouldn't allow that. I had to prove to them and myself I could take care of myself. Live with my mistakes."

Laura Jo would never let Mark know what it took for her to admit her mistakes. No matter how many times or how sweetly Marsha had asked Laura Jo, she had never told her as much as she had just told Mark.

"You haven't spoken to your parents in all that time?"

"I tried to contact them after Phil and I got back from Vegas but the housekeeper told me Mother wouldn't take my call. I phoned a few more times and got the same response. I finally gave up."

"They really hurt you."

Laura Jo fingered a fold in her dress. "Yes. After I had Allie I had a better sense of what it was to have a child's best interests at heart. But after they'd acted the way they did when I called I couldn't take the chance that they would treat Allie the same way as they had me. I'll never let her feel unwanted."

"Maybe they've changed. They might be better grandparents than they were parents. You could try again. At least let them meet Allie."

She shook her head. "I think the hurt is too deep and has gone on for too long."

"You'll never know until you try. I could go with you, if you want."

"I don't know. I'll have to think about that. Let's just get through tonight, then I'll see."

"I'll be there beside you all night. We'll both put in the appearance to get what you need and to also satisfy my father. Then we're out of there."

To her surprise, he didn't sound like he'd been that excited about going to the dance to begin with. Had she made some judgment calls about him that just weren't true? He'd never once looked down on her, her friends or where she lived. Did his status in the area truly not matter to him?

She made a chuckling sound that had nothing to do with humor and more about being resigned. "We sound nothing like two people expecting to enjoy an evening out."

At the car, he opened the door, took her elbow and helped her in. At least if she had to go to the dance she would arrive in a fine car and on the arm of the most handsome man in town.

Mark settled behind the wheel and closed the door but didn't start the engine. Instead, he placed his hand over hers. Squeezing it gently, he said, "I can see by the look on your face that you have no hope of this evening ending well. Why don't you think positive? You might be surprised."

"I'll try."

"Plus you're starting to damage my ego by making me think I no longer know how to show a woman a good time." Mark started the car then checked to see if she was buckled in. She patted her seat belt and he backed out of the parking space.

"This doesn't have anything to do with you personally." She studied his strong profile in the dim light.

"Well, I'm glad to know that. I was starting to think you thought being seen with me was comparable to going to the gallows."

She smiled.

"That's better. At least you haven't lost your sense of humor completely." He pulled out into the street.

They rode down now crowd-free Government Street toward the port. The building where the dance was being held was located on the bay. Mark circled to the elegant glass doors of the historic building.

Mark stopped the car. He handed the keys to the valet then came around to open the door for her. Taking a deep fortifying breath, she placed her hand into Mark's offered one. It was large and steady.

"You're an outstanding nurse, mother of a wonderful daughter and an advocate for mothers, Laura Jo. You're more accomplished than the majority of the people here."

She met his look. His eyes didn't waver. He'd said what he believed. She drew confidence from that. "Thank you."

He pulled her hand into the crook of his arm as they walked toward the door of the building held open by another young man in evening dress. Slowly they ascended one side of the U-shaped staircase to the large room above. Mark paused at the door just long enough for her to survey the space.

People were standing in groups, talking. The room was narrow and long with a black-and-white-tiled floor. Round dining tables were arranged to the right and left, creating an aisle down the middle. The white tablecloths brushed the floor. The Mardi Gras colored decorations centered on each table were elaborate and striking.

The area looked much as it had the last time she'd attended a ball when she'd been nineteen years old and a lady-in-waiting. A month later she'd met Phil and her world had taken a one-eighty-degree turn. Back then she'd been a child of wealthy parents with her life planned out for her. When she'd broken away from her parents, she would never have guessed her life would become what it was now. Still, had she made a mistake by keeping Allie away from them? Her parents had faults but didn't she, too?

Just as eye-catching was the dress of the active men of the krewe. They were all clad in their Louis XVI brocade knee-length satin coats trimmed in gold or silver braid. On their heads were large hats that had one side of the brim pinned up with a plumed feather attached and matched the men's coats. Their pantaloons, white stockings and black buckle shoes added to the mystique. The women who were married to the members of the board wore equally ostentatious dresses, some of them matching their husband's. Otherwise, men and women were dressed in formal wear.

Were her parents here in all their finery?

Mark must have felt her stiffen because he placed his

hand over hers, which was resting on his arm. "Let's go see and be seen."

They hadn't walked far when they were stopped by a man's voice calling, "Mark Clayborn, I heard you were back in town."

Mark brought her around with him. "Mr. Washington, how in the world are you?" Mark shook the man's hand and Laura Jo released his arm but remained beside him.

"I'm doing well."

"I heard about your father. He's recovering, I understand," the older man said.

"Slowly, but retirement is a must," Mark told Mr. Washington with ease.

"I imagine that's difficult for him. I'll make plans to get out to see him."

"I know he would like that."

When she started to move away Mark rested a hand at her waist. It warmed her skin. She was no longer worried about the people they might see. Her focus was on his touch.

Mr. Washington turned his gaze to her. Laura Jo knew who he was but had never met him.

Mark followed his look. "Mr. Washington, I'd like to introduce you to Laura Jo Akins."

Would he recognize her name? No, probably not. There were a number of girls in the south with double first names. Laura Jo wasn't that uncommon.

"Nice to meet you, Ms. Akins."

She forced a smile. "Nice to meet you, too." At least with her married name it wasn't obvious who she was.

"Laura Jo is a nurse at Mobile General and has started a shelter for abandoned mothers." Mark jumped right into helping her look for supporters.

"That sounds like a worthy cause," Mr. Washington said,

as if he was really interested. "What made you decide to do that?"

Laura Jo wasn't going to lie. "I was an abandoned mother. My husband left me when I was pregnant. I have a daughter."

"So you know the need firsthand." He nodded his head thoughtfully.

"I do." Laura Jo lapsed into her planned appeal. Mark offered a few comments and the fact he had made a donation to what he thought was a worthy cause.

"Contact my office tomorrow and I'll have a donation for you," Mr. Washington assured her.

"Thank you. The women I'm helping thank you also."

Mark looked across the room. "Mr. Washington, I think it's time for us to find a place at a table for dinner."

"It does look that way. Good to see you, son. Nice to meet you, young lady."

As Mark led her away she whispered to him, "I never imagined it would be that easy."

"I don't think it will always happen that way. But Mardi Gras season is when people are having fun so they're a little more generous." He took her hand and led her farther into the room.

"You're right about coming tonight. As much as I didn't want to, it was the right thing to do for the shelter."

After they were stopped a couple of times by people Mark knew, he found them a table with two seats left near the front of the room. She still hadn't seen her parents.

Mark remained a gentleman and pulled her chair out for her before he took his own. She could get used to this. As ugly as she had been about coming to the ball, he'd still helped her get a promise of funds from Mr. Washington and was treating her like a lady. She owed him an apology.

He knew a few people sharing their table and introduced her. She recognized a number of other couples by their names but they didn't act as if they knew her. Still, she might run into some of her parents' friends. She looked around.

Mark whispered in her ear, "They might not be here."

Laura Jo knew better. They didn't miss a Mardi Gras ball. One more pass over the crowd and she saw them. They had aged well. There was more gray hair at her father's temples but her mother had a stylish cut and kept it colored. They both looked as elegant as they ever had for one of these events.

"What's wrong?"

"My parents."

Mark looked in the direction she indicated. "Why don't we go and say hello?"

"They won't want to speak to me. I said some horrible things to them."

"I bet that doesn't matter anymore. At least you could give them a chance. They may regret what happened, just like you do. You'll feel better if you do. At least you will know you made the effort. Come on, I'll be right there with you." He stood and offered his hand.

Laura Jo hesitated then placed her hand in Mark's. It was large, warm and strong. A new resolve filled her. No longer the same person she had been nine years ago, she could do this. Mark held her hand tight as they crossed the room. The closer they came to her parents' table the more her gut tightened. The sudden need to run splashed over her. She hesitated.

"You can do this." The small squeeze of her hand told her she wasn't alone.

Her parents looked up at them. Shock registered on their faces.

Mark let go of her hand and cupped her elbow.

"Hello, Mother and Daddy."

"We're surprised to see you here. We had no idea you were coming," her father said in a blunt, boardroom voice.

Well, he was certainly all open arms about seeing her again.

"Hello, I'm Mark Clayborn. Nice to meet you, Mr. and Mrs. Herron."

Her parents looked at Mark as if they weren't sure they had heard correctly. She was just relieved he'd taken the attention off her for a moment.

"Mark Clayborn, junior?" her father asked.

"Yes, sir."

Her father stood and offered his hand. "Pleasure to meet you."

Leaving her seat, her mother came to stand beside her father. "How have you been, Laura Jo?"

She sounded as if she truly cared. "Fine."

"I'm glad to hear that. I understand you've started some type of shelter."

How did they know about that? Was she really interested? "I have."

Mark put an arm around her shoulders. "Laura Jo has helped a lot of women who needed it."

It was nice to have someone sound proud of her. Not till this moment had she realized she'd been missing that in her life.

"Are they unwed mothers?"

At least her mother had asked with what sounded like sincere curiosity. "Some are but most have been abandoned. Those that have no family they can or want to go home to."

Laura Jo didn't miss her mother's flinch.

"That sounds like a worthwhile project," her mother finally said.

"It is," Mark agreed. "She's now trying to buy a larger place for the shelter to move to."

Laura Jo placed her hand on Mark's arm. She didn't want to go into all that with her parents. "I don't think they want to hear all about that."

When Mark started to argue she added, "How have you both been?"

"We've been well," her father said.

They were talking to each other like strangers, which in reality they were.

"I understand you live over in the Calen area."

"I do." Laura Jo was astonished that he knew that. Had they been keeping up with her when she'd had no idea? Did her parents care more than she'd thought or shown?

Her mother stepped toward Laura Jo with an imploring look on her face. "Will you tell us about our granddaughter?"

"You knew?" Laura Jo was thankful for Mark's steady hand steady on her elbow.

"Yes, we've known for a long time." Her mother's look didn't waver.

They had known and they still hadn't helped? Or they'd known that Laura Jo would throw their help back at them if they offered?

"Please, tell us about her," her father pleaded.

Laura Jo spent the next few minutes telling her parents about Allie. They seemed to hang on every word. Had they changed?

"Thank you for telling us," her mother said with a soft sigh when Laura Jo finished.

They were interrupted by the krewe captain getting the attention of the people in the room. He announced the buffet dinner was being served and gave directions about which tables would go first.

"We should return to our table," Laura Jo said.

It was her mother's turn to give her an entreating look. "Laura Jo, may we see Allie sometime?"

Laura Jo stiffened but she forced her voice to remain even. "I'll have to think about that. She knows nothing about you."

Moisture spring to her mother's eyes.

The table next to her parents' rose to get in line for their meal.

"I think it's time that we returned to our table, Laura Jo. It was nice to meet you both, Mr. and Mrs. Herron."

Mr. Herron blinked as if he had forgotten Mark was standing there.

"Thank you for coming over, Laura Jo. It's wonderful to see you."

Her mother sounded like she truly meant it.

"It's nice to see you, too." Laura Jo turned and headed back to their table on shaky knees.

Mark leaned in and asked, "You okay?"

"I'm good." She smiled. "Really good, actually. Thanks for encouraging me to speak to them."

He grinned. "Hey, that's what a good date does. So are you going to introduce Allie to them?"

"I don't know if I'm ready for that but at least I'll think about it."

"Sounds like a plan. Hungry?"

"Much more than I was a few minutes ago."

"Good."

They returned to their table and had to wait until a few tables on the other side of the room lined up and then it was their turn. Mark placed his hand at the small of her back again. As disconcerting as it was to have him touch her, he'd done it enough over the past couple of weeks that she'd grown to not only expect it but to appreciate the simple gesture.

They were almost to the buffet tables in the middle of the room when Mark jerked to a stop. She turned to question him about what was wrong. He stood looking in the direction of a group of people who were obviously together. His face had darkened. All pleasantness of a few minutes ago had washed away. One of the group was in a wheelchair. Did he know the man?

Mark quickly regained his composure and closed the gap between him and her.

"Are you okay?" she whispered when he came to stand next to her.

"I'm fine." He added a smile that for once didn't reach his eyes.

They stood in line for a few minutes, working their way to where the plates were stacked. A large floral arrangement was positioned where the tables intersected. On the four tables were shrimp cocktail, gumbo, salads of all types and prime rib, with a man serving that and desserts.

As they slowly filled their plates, Laura Jo saw Mark glancing toward the end of the line. She noticed the man in the wheelchair. This time Mark seemed even more uncomfortable about the situation.

As they went through the line Mark spoke to people. Thankfully everyone accepted her as his date and nothing more. Maybe she could get through this evening after all. She'd been a teenager when she'd last been at this kind of function. She had matured and changed since then.

During the meal, Mark spoke to the woman to the right of him. Laura Jo had a light conversation with the man in full regalia to her left. Once during the meal Mark gave her knee a reassuring squeeze. That little gesture said, We're in this together. She appreciated it. Except for Marsha, it had been her and Allie against the world.

She had finished her dinner when Mark got her attention and asked her to tell the woman he'd been talking to about the shelter. The woman told Laura Jo that she would like to help and how to contact her.

The conversation was interrupted by the captain announcing that it was time to introduce the krewe directors.

Laura Jo smiled at Mark and mouthed, "Thank you."

He put his arm around her shoulder and gave her a gentle hug and whispered in her ear, "You're welcome. See, it's not as bad as you thought."

"No, it hasn't been. Thanks to you."

He kissed her temple. "You can really thank me later."

Before she could react to that statement the captain started calling names and people were lining up on the dance floor that was acting as a stage.

It was her turn to feel Mark stiffen. She saw the man in the wheelchair Mark had looked at earlier propelling himself across the stage, while an attractive woman walked beside him.

She glanced at Mark. His focus was fixed on the man. "Do you know him?"

"Yes."

"He's your friend from the accident, isn't he?"

"Yes." The word had a remorseful note to it.

The next man was being introduced and she didn't ask Mark any more. With everyone having been presented, the crowd clapped in appreciation for the work the board had done on the dance.

The captain then asked for everyone's attention again. "The king and queen and their court have arrived."

There was a hush over the room as the first lady-in-waiting and her escort were introduced.

The young lady wore an all-white dress made out of satin and adorned with pearls and sparkling stones. Her white train trailed across the floor. It was heavy, Laura Jo knew from experience.

When she had designed her train so many years ago it had had the family crest in the center with a large, pale pink flamingo rising from it. The bird's eye had been an onyx from her grandmother's train when she had been queen. Each pearl and precious stone were sewn on by hand. It had been edged in real white fox fur. She'd worn long white gloves that had reached above her elbows. She'd been told she'd never looked more beautiful.

And this happened every year. The pomp and circumstance of it all still astounded her.

She and her mother had designed and planned her dress and train for months. They had even taken a trip to New York to look for material. A designer there had made the dress then it had been sent back to Mobile, where a seamstress that specialized in embellishments had added them. What she would wear consumed their family life for the entire year before Mardi Gras.

She had no idea what her dress and train had cost but she was sure it would have been enough to run the shelter for two or three months.

"I bet you were a beautiful lady-in-waiting. I'm sorry I didn't pay more attention," Mark whispered close to her ear.

She smiled.

The couple walked to the captain and his wife on the stage and curtsied and bowed, before circling back to the rear of the room. By that time another couple had moved forward. The entire court was dressed in white, with the females having different dress and trains that had their personal design. The escorts wore identical outfits. Each couple paid their respects and this happened eighteen more times.

From the court would come next year's king and queen of Mardi Gras. Since her grandmother had been queen, Laura Jo had been on track to be the queen the year she turned twenty-one. The king would reign the year he turned twenty-five.

She glanced at Mark, who was watching the stage more than the couples parading up the aisle. "I did notice you and you were a handsome king," Laura Jo whispered.

"Thank you, fair maiden."

Laura Jo giggled. She knew well that there was a private and public side to Mardi Gras. It all started around Thanksgiving, with all the coming-out balls for the girls. The society families held the balls and she'd been a part of the process. She'd loved it at the time. Now she looked back on it and saw how spoiled she been and how ignorant of the world. Not until she had gotten away from her parents' house had she realized how many people could have been helped with the money that had gone into just her dresses for Mardi Gras.

As the royalty came into sight, Laura Jo couldn't help but be amazed at the beauty of the couple's attire. No matter how many times she had seen this type of event, she was still left in awe. They wore matching gold outfits trimmed in gold. The king's clothing was adorned as much as the queen's. She had gold beads that came to a peak halfway up the center of her skirt. The bodice had swirls and curls covering it. They carried crowns on their heads that glittered in the lights. The king carried a diamond-headed walking stick while the queen held a scepter that matched her crown.

Laura Jo had forgotten the artistry and how regal their trains were. They were both at least twenty feet long. Theirs, like those of the ladies-in-waiting, told a story of their life. The king's had his family crest with a hunting motif around it, which included an appliqué of a deer head.

The queen's train was also appliquéd but with large magnolias in detail. Around the edge was a five-inch border of crystals that made it shimmer. The neckline had a collar that went from one shoulder to the other in the back. It stood up eight inches high. It bounced gently as the queen walked. It was made from a mass of light and airy bangle beads formed into magnolias and leaves, the centers being made out of pearls.

Their trains alone could buy a room in the house they were looking at for the shelter.

"How did it feel to be the man of the hour?" Laura Jo asked Mark.

"At the time, amazing," he answered in a dry tone.

CHAPTER SEVEN

WITH THE INTRODUCTIONS COMPLETED, everyone returned to their meals and the band struck up a dance tune. Couples moved toward the dance floor.

"Why don't we have a dance before we go and talk to a few more people about the shelter? I think we could both use a few minutes of fun." Mark stood and offered her his hand.

"One dance."

As they entered the dance floor he brought Laura Jo close. She fit perfectly. Wearing high heels, her head came to his shoulder. The band was just beginning the first notes of a slow waltz. Laura Jo put her hand in his and the other on his shoulder. His hand rested on the warm, creamy skin visible on her back.

"You know, I think I like this dress more now than I did when I first saw you in it." The words were for her alone.

She glanced up, giving him a shy smile. Seeing her parents again seemed to have taken some fight out of her. She had to have missed them more than she'd admitted. Leaning in, she put her head into the curve of his shoulder. Mark tightened his hold and slowly moved them around the dance floor.

Other couples surrounded them but for him there was only he and Laura Jo. For once he wished he could hold one woman forever. He'd never allowed himself to dream further but with Laura Jo anything seemed possible.

They were returning to their table when Mr. Washington approached. "I was telling a buddy of mine about the work your young lady is doing. He would like to pledge fifty thousand."

Laura Jo gasped.

"Baba McClure has had a little too much to drink already and he has pledged another fifty."

Laura Jo squeezed his arm.

"The thing is," Mr. Washington went on, "you'd better go over there and get something in writing or they may not remember in the morning."

"Do you have a paper and pen in your purse?" Mark asked Laura Jo.

She picked up the tiny purse she had brought. "I have a small pen. I'll ask at the registration table if they have something we can write on."

Mark watched Laura Jo go. She was soon back. Mr. Washington showed them across the room and introduced them to the two men and let Laura Jo take it from there. Despite wanting to distance herself from her background, she had a way of charming people that had been instilled in her. She soon had a makeshift agreement from both men and had promised she would see them the next day.

Both men groaned and asked her to make it the day after. Before they left the table she gave Mr. Washington a kiss on the cheek. "Thank you."

The eighty-year-old man beamed. "You're welcome, honey."

"Come on, I believe this deserves a victory dance." She pulled Mark to the dance floor. A fast tune was being played.

"I don't fast-dance." Mark pulled to a stop.

"What was it you told me? Uh…let go a little." Laura Jo started moving to the music. She held her hands out, encouraging him to take them.

He wasn't going to turn that invitation down. After a few dances, both fast and slow, he said, "I'm ready to go if you are."

"You're really not any more into this stuff than I am, are you?"

"No, I guess being in California for so long got it out of my system." And what had happened to Mike.

He had glimpsed Mike a couple of times across the room. They had never been near each other and for that Mark was grateful. Once he had thought his onetime friend might have recognized him. Dodging Mike didn't make Mark feel any better. He still couldn't face him. He used having Laura Jo with him as an excuse not to.

"Let's go," Laura Jo agreed. "But I need to stop by the restroom on our way out."

Mark was waiting at the exit when Mike rolled up.

"So was the plan to leave without speaking to me?" he asked, looking directly at Mark. "Running out again?"

He stood dumbstruck. His gut churned. If Laura Jo showed up, would she recognize what a coward he was?

"No," Mark lied boldly. If he could figure out how to leave without having this conversation, he would. "I hadn't realized you were here." Another lie. "It's good to see you." At least that had a small margin of truth.

"I'm not sure that's true." Mike's gaze hadn't wavered.

The ache in Mark's chest increased.

"I hear you're back in town and practicing medicine."

"Yes, I'm in a clinic in Spanish Fort and living in Fairhope." If he could just make it through some small talk, Laura Jo would show up and they could go.

"You always did like it at the summer house," Mike said.

Mark glanced toward the other side of the room. "How have you been? I'm sorry I haven't—"

A blonde woman with twinkling green eyes and a cheery smile approached. "I'd like you to meet my wife." He reached behind him and took the hand of the woman. "This is Tammy."

Mike married? "It's nice to meet you."

"And you, too. Mike has told me a lot about you." Tammy continued to smile but it no longer reached her eyes.

Like how he'd been the cause of Mike being in a wheelchair for life, or the fact he had run out on him when he'd needed him most, or maybe the part where he hadn't bothered to stay in touch, like he should have. Yeah, there was a lot to say about him, but none of it good. Or to be proud of.

Laura Jo walked up beside him. Could she see how uncomfortable he was? He took her hand and drew her forward. "Uh, this is my friend Laura Jo. Laura Jo, Mike and Tammy Egan."

"Hey, I remember a Laura Jo. She was a friend of my kid sister's. I haven't seen her in years." Mike gave her a searching look.

"You're Megan's brother?" Laura Jo studied Mike for a moment.

Great. Mike remembered Laura Jo when he himself hadn't. He truly had been a self-absorbed person in his twenties. Maybe in many ways he still was.

"Yes, and you're Laura Jo Herron."

She smiled at Mike. "Was Herron. Now it's Akins."

"No matter the name, it's good to see you again."

It was time to get out of there. Mark said, "Mike, I'm sorry, we're expected at another dance." Great. He was still running from Mike and lying to do so.

Laura Jo glanced at him but said nothing.

Mike rolled back and forth in his chair with the ease

and agility of someone who had mastered the wheelchair. "I understand."

Somehow Mark was sure he did. All he wanted was to get away, forget, and find some fresh air. "Nice to see you again, Mike." Mark headed for the door. It wasn't until Laura Jo put her hand in his that he realized he had forgotten about her. He was running blind.

Mark didn't say anything on the way to his house. Laura Jo didn't either. They had both had an emotional evening. She let him remain in his thoughts, not even interrupting him to mention that he wasn't going toward her apartment. He didn't even register that he'd driven to his house until he'd pulled to a stop in his drive. "Why didn't you tell me to take you home?"

"Because I thought you needed someone to talk to."

How like her to recognize when someone was having trouble. He was in need, but of all the people he didn't want to look weak in front of it was Laura Jo.

"Let's go in. I'll fix us a cup of coffee." She was already in the process of opening the car door. Inside the house, she dropped her purse on the table beside the door, kicked off her shoes then headed straight for the kitchen. When he started to follow she said, "Why don't you go out to the deck? I'll bring it to you."

"Thanks. I appreciate it." He sounded weary even to his own ears.

"I'm just repaying all the times you've been there for me."

On the deck he sat in one of the chairs, spread his knees wide and braced his elbows on them. Putting his head in his hands, he closed his eyes.

Seeing Mike tonight had been as tough as it had ever been. Mark had prepared himself that he might see him at the dance but that didn't make it any easier. It only added another bag of guilt to the ten thousand he already carried on his shoulders.

Now, with Laura Jo having seen his shame, it made the situation worse.

"Here you go," she said from beside him.

He raised his head to find her holding a mug and looking at him with concern. At least it wasn't pity. He took the cup.

She put the mug she still held on the table nearby and said, "I'll be right back."

Laura Jo returned wearing the jacket he'd offered her the night they'd made the king cakes. Picking up the mug she'd left behind, she took the lounge next to him. They sat in silence for a long time.

Finally Laura Jo said, "Do you want to talk about it?"

"No."

She made no comment, as if she accepted it was a part of him that he wouldn't share. Something about her being willing to do that endeared her even more to him and made him want to have her understand. "You asked me a few days ago about Mike being in an accident, remember?"

He didn't see her nod but somehow he knew she had.

"It was a night like tonight. Clear and warm for the time of the year. I had this great idea that we'd drive to the beach after the dance was over. After all, I'd be leaving in a few days for Birmingham to do my fellowship. My girlfriend, who was the queen that year, was having her last hoorah with her friends, so why not? Mike was going to ride with me and some of the other guys were going to meet us down there."

He swiped his fingers through his hair.

"I'd had a few drinks but I'd been so busy being king I'd had little time to eat, let alone drink. Mike, on the other hand, had had too much. I told him more than once to buckle his seat belt. But he wouldn't listen. I was feeling wild and free that night. I knew I was going too fast for the road… Long story short, I ran off the road, pulled the car back on and went off the other shoulder. And the car rolled. I was hardly injured. Mike was thrown out. It broke his back."

"Oh, Mark."

He jumped up and started pacing. "I don't want your pity. I don't deserve it." Thankfully, Laura Jo said nothing more. "That's not the worst of it." He spun and said the words that he was sure would turn her against him. "I left. The next day I packed my bags, gave up my residency in Birmingham and accepted one in California. I've only seen him a few times since I watched him being put into an ambulance." He all but spat the last sentence.

Mark stopped pacing and placed his back to Laura Jo, not wanting to see the disgust he feared was in her eyes. She made a small sound of anguish. He flinched. His spine stiffened and his hands formed balls at his side. He hung his head.

Laura Jo felt Mark's guilt and pain ripple through her like the sting of a whip. How quickly and effortlessly Mark had worked himself past her emotional barriers. She cared for him. Wanted to help him past the hurt.

No wonder he was so hypervigilant about people buckling up in his car. Now that she thought about it, he'd even hesitated when he'd had to drive someone in his car. He found the responsibility too weighty.

She went to him. Taking one of his fists, she kissed the top of his hand and began gently pulling his fingers open until she could thread her own between his. She leaned her head against his arm. "It wasn't your fault, even if you don't believe it."

Mark snorted. "And it wasn't my fault that I was such a lousy friend that I ran out on him when he needed me most. That was unforgivable. But that wasn't enough, I've compounded it by years of not really having anything to do with him. I was closer to Mike than I was to my own brother. How could I have done that to him? Even tonight I was a coward."

"You know, it's not too late," she said quietly. "You're the one who has been telling me that."

"It's way past too late. How do I tell him I'm sorry I put him in a wheelchair while I still walk around?"

Laura Jo heard his disgust for himself in his voice.

"The same way I have to forgive my parents for the way they treated me. We have to believe people can change and grow."

He took her in his arms and looked down at her. "It's easy for someone with a heart as big as yours to forgive. Not everyone can or will do that."

His lips found hers.

Mark didn't ask for entrance. She greeted him. Welcomed his need. Her hands went to his shoulders. She massaged the tension from them before her fingers moved up his neck into his hair.

His desperation to lose himself in her goodness made him kiss her more deeply. She took all he gave with no complaint. There was a restlessness to his need, as if he was looking for solace. He pulled her closer, gathering her dress as he did so.

For tonight she could be that peaceful place if that was what he needed. Laura Jo tightened her arms around his neck and returned his kiss.

"I need you," he groaned. His lips made a trail down her neck.

Brushing her dress away, he dropped a kiss on the ridge

of her shoulder. His tongue tasted her. The warm dampness he left behind made her quake. His other hand slipped under the edge of the back of her dress and roamed, leaving a hot path of awareness.

"And I need you," she whispered against his ear.

Mark pushed her dress farther down her arm. His lips followed the route of the material, leaving hot points along her skin. Laura Jo furrowed her fingers through his hair, enjoying the feel of the curl between her fingers.

He released the hook at the back of her neck and her dress hung at her elbows. Her breasts tingled with anticipation. His head lowered to kiss the top of one breast. He pushed the edge of her dress away from her nipple and took it into his mouth and tugged lightly. She shivered from the sensation. His tongue circled and teased her nipple until she moaned into the evening air.

When his mouth moved to the other breast he cupped the first one. The pad of his thumb found the tip of her nipple and caressed it. He circled her nipple with the end of his index finger until it stood at attention. He lifted the mound and placed a kiss on it.

Her heated blood rushed to her center and pooled there. She wanted to see and feel as much of Mark as he was of her. Her hands found his lapels and slid beneath them to his hard chest. There she worked his coat off. She wanted to touch him. Feel his skin. This had gone beyond giving comfort to a desire that was building into a powerful animal. It had been feeding and waiting since the first time Mark had touched her. The more she knew about him, saw him, felt his kindness, that longing had grown. Now there was no denying it or fighting it.

Mark's lips came back to hers as he shook himself out of his tux jacket and let it fall down his arms. Laura Jo's fingers went to the bow tie and released it, pulling it away and dropping it beside his jacket. His lips returned to her neck as Laura Jo removed first one stud and then another until she found his skin beneath his shirt.

The tip of her fingers lightly grazed the small patch of hair covering his warm skin. Yes, she'd found what she was looking for.

As Mark's mouth moved to hers for a hot, sinuous kiss, she yanked at his shirt, removing it from his pants. She wrapped her arms around his waist then she ran her hands over his back. She enjoyed the ripple of his muscles as they reacted to her touch. Would she ever get enough of touching him?

Mark gathered her dress, bringing it up until he could put his hand on her thigh. His fingers made circular motions along her bare skin. Slowly, his hand slid higher and higher until he ran his finger over the barrier of her panties at her core.

Laura Jo involuntarily flexed toward him. She'd never wanted a man to touch her more than she did at that moment.

With a growl of frustration, he set her on her feet. "I hope I don't live to regret this." He kissed her on the forehead. "Promise me you'll stay right here."

With heart pounding and body tight with need, Mark hurried into the house and scooped up the bedding in the extra bedroom. He grabbed two pillows, as well. With long strides, he walked back through the house. When he exited he was relieved to find Laura Jo waiting for him right where he'd left her. She had pulled her dress straps up over her shoulders. That was fine. He'd soon be removing her dress completely.

"What?" she murmured, as he came out of the house with his load.

"I want to see you under the stars."

He flipped the heavy spread out, not taking the time to make it neat. He lay down on his side and stretched out a hand in invitation for her to join him. His heart went to drumroll pace when she put her hand in his. This amazing woman was accepting him, even with all she'd learned about him.

She lifted her dress, giving him a tantalizing glimpse of her leg as she came to her knees before him.

Letting go of her hand, he used his finger to run a caressing line down her arm from her shoulder to her elbow. There he circled, then went to her wrist. He was encouraged by the slight tremble of her hand when he took it and eased her closer.

"Kiss me."

She leaned into him, pressing her lips against his. His hand pulled at her dress, bringing it up her leg. Gliding his hand underneath, he ran it along her thigh, moving to the inside then out again.

Laura Jo deepened their kiss.

His finger found the bottom of her panty line and followed it around to the back of her leg then forward again. She placed small kisses across his forehead and then nipped at his ear. He captured her gaze and watched her eyes widen as he slid a finger beneath her underwear at her hip. She gasped as his finger brushed her curls. He moved his finger farther toward her center and found wet, hot heat. His length strained to find release. She moaned against his mouth and bucked against his finger as he entered her.

"Mark." She drew his name out like a sound of adoration as she put her head back and closed her eyes.

When her hand grazed his straining length behind his zipper he jerked. The woman had him aroused to a painful point. The raw need that had built in him sought release.

He feared he might lose his control and be like a teen in the backseat of a car as he fumbled to have all he dreamed of. Laura Jo ran her life with a tight rein and here she was exposing herself completely to him. That knowledge only increased his wish to give her pleasure.

"If you continue that I'm not going to be responsible for what I do," he growled. When had he been more turned on?

Laura Jo felt the same way. It had been a long time for her but she couldn't remember this gnawing hunger for another person that begged for freedom. She wanted to crawl inside Mark, be surrounded by him and find the safety and security she'd been missing for so many years.

He removed his finger.

She made a sound of protest.

"You have too many clothes on."

Could she be so bold as to remove her dress in front of him? She was thankful for the dim light. She was no longer a maiden. She'd had a child, gained a few mature pounds and things on her body had moved around. Would Mark be disappointed?

"Sit up on your knees, Laura Jo," he coached, as he moved to a sitting position.

Laura Jo did as he asked. As he gathered the fabric of her dress she shifted, releasing the long length of material from behind her knees. With it in rolls at her waist, he said, "Raise your arms."

She did so and he slipped the dress off over her head. Braless, she was exposed to Mark and the elements, except for her tiny panties. The cool air of the night licked her body, making her shudder. She was thankful for it because it covered her nervousness. She crossed her arms over her breasts.

"Please, don't hide from me," Mark said in a guttural

tone filled with emotion. "You're beautiful. I want to admire you in the moonlight."

She'd been so absorbed in him she hadn't noticed there was a full moon. Slowly, very slowly, she let her hands fall to her sides. Mark's look started at the apex of her legs and traveled upward. He paused at her breasts. They were already prickly with awareness and had grown heavy. She looked down to see her nipples standing ridged from the cool air and Mark's hot gaze.

He cupped both breasts and she quivered.

"So responsive," he murmured, more to himself than to her. "Lie down. I want to touch all of you."

"But you still have all your clothes on," she protested.

He chuckled dryly. "If I don't remain dressed I might not be able to control myself."

"But I want to—"

"Later. Now I want to give you pleasure."

He nudged her shoulder then supported her until she lay on her back.

Laura Jo felt exposed, a wanton. She shuddered.

"I'm sorry, you must be cold." He leaned behind him and brought a blanket over them. "I hate to cover up all this beauty but maybe next time..."

Would there be a next time? Did she want more?

He rested his hand on the center of her stomach. Her breathing was erratic and shallow. He kissed the hollow of her shoulder. She pushed his open shirt off his shoulders. He finished removing it and threw it over his shoulder to the deck.

Her hand went to the nape of his neck. "I want to feel your skin touching mine."

"Ah, sweetheart..." Mark kissed her gently and brought her against his warm, inviting chest.

Laura Jo went from shivering to feeling warm and sheltered in the harbor of Mark's arms.

Mark lay down, bringing her with him. His mouth found hers. One of his hands went to her waist and shimmered over the curve of her hip and down her thigh and back up to cup her breast.

Her hands found his chest. She took her time discovering the rises and falls as she appreciated the breadth of his muscles as her hand traveled across his skin. Her palm hovered over the meadow of hair, enjoying the springiness of it.

He sucked in a breath.

She let her hand glide downward along his ribs and lower. He groaned when she brushed the tip of his manhood. With that he flipped the blanket off, letting it fall over her. In one smooth, agile movement he stood. He sat in the closest chair and proceeded to remove his socks and shoes. Seconds later his pants found the deck. He looked like a warrior of old as he stood with his feet apart, his shaft straight, with the moonlight gleaming off the water behind him.

Laura Jo bit her lower lip. This piece of masculine beauty was all hers for tonight.

She pushed away the blanket and opened her arms. Mark opened a package and covered his manhood then came down to her. She pulled the cover over them.

His fingers looped into the lace band of her panties and tugged them off. She kicked her feet to finish the process.

"Perfect," Mark murmured, as he kissed the shell of her ear and his fingers traveled over the curve of her hip. "I want you so much."

Desire carried every word. She was wanted. Mark showed her in every way that she was desired by him. It fed her confidence. She arched her neck as his mouth traveled downward to the hollow beneath her chin, to the curve of a breast and out to her nipple. His hand went lower, where it tested and teased until she flexed.

Her core throbbed, waiting, waiting…

He slid a finger inside her, found that spot of pleasure and she bucked.

"So hot for me," he ground out, before placing a kiss on her stomach.

Mark said it as if he didn't think she could want him. Was the guilt he carried that heavy?

Laura Jo pushed him to his back. He made a sound of complaint. She slid on top of him and poured all she felt into making him feel desired. Positioning herself so that his tip was at her entrance, she looked into his eyes. Did he know how special he was to her? She pushed back and slowly took him inside her. His hands ran up and down her sides as his gaze bored into hers. She lifted and went down again.

Before she knew what had happened, Mark rolled her to her back and entered her with one bold thrust. His hold eased. "Did I hurt you?" His question carried an anxiousness that went soul deep.

"No, you would never hurt me."

He wrapped his arms around her as if he never wanted to let her go. When he did let her go he rose on his hands and pulled out of her to push in again.

She moaned with pleasure and his movements became more hurried. Her core tightened, twisted until it sprang her into the heavens.

A couple of thrusts later, Mark groaned his release to the starry night and lay on her.

Just before his weight became too much he rolled to his side and gathered her to him, twining his legs with hers. He adjusted the blanket around them.

"Perfect," he said, worshipful praise, before brushing a kiss over her temple.

* * *

Mark woke to the sound of thunder rolling in the distance. Laura Jo was warm and soft next to him. He shifted. Hard boards weren't his normal sleeping choice but with Laura Jo beside him it wasn't so difficult. He would have some aches in the morning but it would be more than worth it.

He moved to lie on his back. As if she couldn't be parted from him, she rolled in his direction and rested her head on his shoulder. She snuggled close. What would it be like to have Laura Jo in his life all the time?

Lightning flashed in the clouds. Thunder rumbled.

A hand moved over his chest. His body reacted far too quickly for his comfort. Could he ever get enough of her?

"What're you thinking?'

He tightened his hold and then released it. "That if we don't go inside we're going to get wet." The first large drops of rain hit the porch.

"I'll get the pillows. You get the blankets," she said, jumping up. He followed.

They scooped up the bedding and ran to the door, making it inside just before the downpour started. They laughed at their luck. They stood watching the storm for a few seconds.

"Oh, we didn't get our clothes." Laura Jo moved to open the door.

Mark grabbed her hand. "Forget them.

He dropped the blankets on the floor. "Leave the pillows here."

"Where're we going?" Laura Jo asked.

He gave her a meaningful look. "Like you don't know?"

When she only dropped one pillow he raised a questioning brow.

"I'm not used to walking around the house in the nude and certainly not with a man."

Mark chuckled. "I'm glad to hear that. But you have a beautiful body. You shouldn't be so self-conscious."

"Not everyone has thought that."

Her tone told him that she wasn't fishing for a compliment. Had her ex said differently? "Trust me, you're the sexiest woman I've ever seen. Come with me and I'll show you just how much."

She hesitated.

"You can bring the pillow."

Taking her hand, he led her to his bedroom. He was glad that he'd pulled the covers off his guest-room bed instead of his own. Something told him that if he gave Laura Jo more than a couple of seconds to think she'd be dressing and asking to go home.

Mark didn't want that. He made a point not to spend all night with the women he dated because he didn't want them to get any idea that there would ever be anything permanent between them. But he wanted Laura Jo beside him when he woke in the morning. He wanted her close until he had to let her go. For her own good, he would have to let her go.

He clicked on the lamp that was on the table beside his bed. Pulling the covers back, he climbed in, and turned to look at Laura Jo. "You have to let go of that pillow sometime."

There was a moment or two of panic that she wouldn't, before she slowly dropped it.

His breath caught. She'd looked amazing in the moonlight, but in the brighter light she was magnificent. Her husband had really done a number on her to make her believe she wasn't wanted. Mark sure wanted her more than ever.

"Move over."

He grinned. Laura Jo had gained some confidence. She found her place beside him. Where she belonged. But his feeling of ultimate pleasure quickly moved to the deepest depths of despair. He couldn't keep her.

Laura Jo gave him a look of concern that soon turned to one of insecurity. She slid her legs to the side of the bed.

"Oh, no, you don't. I'm not done with you." *Ever.* He rolled her to her back and kissed her.

Over the next minutes he teased, touched and tasted her body until he had her shaking beneath him. When he paused at her entrance she made a noise of disapproval. She wrapped her legs around his waist and urged him closer. He entered her and was lost forever.

Laura Jo woke up snuggled against Mark's hard body. She'd once thought he had none of the qualities in the man that she was looking for. She'd been so wrong. He had them all and more.

He was the opposite of Phil. When she had needed Mark to come help her at the shelter, he hadn't questioned it, just asked directions. He was good with Allie and she loved him. There had never been a question that he supported her cause with the shelter. He'd even been understanding about her relationship with her parents. He had been the support she hadn't had since she'd left her parents' home. Mark had become a person she could depend on, trust.

Her experiences with lovemaking had been about the other person doing all the receiving but Mark's loving had been all about giving, making sure she felt cherished. And she had.

She shifted until she could look at his face. His golden lashes tipped in brown lay unmoving against his skin. She resisted running her finger along the ridge of his nose. His strong, square jaw had a reddish tint of stubble covering it. She'd never seen a more handsome male in her life.

Her breath jerked to a stop. Oh, she couldn't be. But she was in love with Mark Clayborn!

"You're staring at me."

Her gaze jerked to his twinkling eyes. Could he see how she felt? Could she take a chance on trusting another man? She had Allie to consider. Had to act as if nothing had changed between them when everything had. In her best teasing tone she said, "You're so vain."

He moved to face her, propping his head on his hand. "That may be so but I did see you looking at me."

"So what if I was?" she asked in a challenging tone.

"Then…" he leaned into her "…I like it."

Putting an arm around her waist, he pulled her to him. His intention stood rock-hard ready between them. While he kissed her deeply, he positioned her above him and they became one.

CHAPTER EIGHT

AN HOUR LATER they were in the kitchen, working together to make breakfast. Laura Jo wore one of Mark's shirts while her dress hung on a deck chair, dripping, with Mark's jacket on another.

"I can't go home dressed in my evening gown," she mused, more to herself than to Mark.

"I'll find something around here that you can wear. Actually, I kind of like you in my shirt." He gave her a wolfish grin.

Warmth like the beach on a sunny day went through her. It was nice to be desired. It had been so long.

Wearing Mark's clothes and turning up in the morning instead of late at night in her evening gown was more than she wanted to explain to any of her neighbors. Allie deserved a mother who set a good example. More than that, she owed it to her not to become too involved with a man who wasn't planning to stay for the long haul. Mark had once said that marriage wasn't part of their relationship. Had that changed after last night? He'd said he wanted nothing serious. She had major responsibilities, which always meant some level of permanency. Either way, she had other issues to handle in the next few days. She would face that later.

"Butter on your toast?" Mark asked, as he pulled two slices out of the toaster.

"Yes, please." Waking up with Mark, and spending the morning doing something as domestic as making a meal, felt comfortable, right. Did he sense it, too? She liked it that he didn't expect her to prepare their breakfast. Instead, it was a partnership.

A few minutes later they sat across from each other at the table, eating. Mark wore a pair of sport shorts and nothing else. He hadn't shaved yet and the stubble covering his jaw was so sexy she was having trouble concentrating on her food.

"Do you have to work today?" Mark asked.

"No. I work tomorrow morning. But I have to go to the shelter, see Mr. Washington." She couldn't keep from grinning. "And pick up Allie and Jeremy from school."

"I have to work from noon to eight. Could we maybe have a late dinner?"

"Eight is Allie's bedtime. And it's a school night."

He hesitated, stopping his fork halfway to his mouth. Was he thinking about all that was involved in seeing her? She and Allie were a package and she wanted to remind him of that.

"What's your schedule for Thursday night?"

"Work morning then I have to see Mr. Washington's friend then Mr. McClure about their donations."

"That's right. You're supposed to get the house on Friday. We'll make it a celebration. Take Allie to someplace fun."

"That sounds doable. By the way, I don't think I said thank you for all your help with the shelter. We couldn't have done it without you. You're a good man, Mark Clayborn."

A flicker of denial came to his eyes before it changed to

something she couldn't name. He smiled. "Thank you for that, Laura Jo Akins. I think you believe it."

"And I think you should, too."

Mark had picked up his phone to call Laura Jo at least ten times over the course of the day. After returning her home, wearing a beach dress his sister-in-law had left there and one of his sweatshirts that had swallowed her whole, he had headed to work. He couldn't remember a more enjoyable morning. Laura Jo had just looked right in his kitchen. She was right for his life. The simple task of getting ready to leave for work, which turned out to include a very long shared shower, had been nicer when done with Laura Jo. He had it bad for her.

He picked up his phone. This time he texted her: How did it go with Mr. Washington?

Seconds later she returned, Good. Leaving now.

How like Laura Jo to say no more than necessary.

Unable to help himself, he typed, Looking forward to tomorrow evening.

She sent back a smiley face. He grinned. They had come a long way from the snarl that she had given him when they'd first met.

The next day, when he came out of one of the clinic examination rooms, he was told by the receptionist that there was a call for him. Was it Laura Jo? Was something wrong? His heart sank. Had she changed her mind about tonight? Mercy, he was starting to act lovesick.

"This is Dr. Clayborn."

"Hi, this is Marsha Gilstrap. Laura Jo's friend."

"Yes, I know who you are. Jeremy's mother."

"I'm calling because Laura Jo and I are getting ready to meet with the city about the shelter house. They have notified us at the last minute that they expect us to bring in the names of our board members. It has been only Laura Jo and I. Long story short, would you be willing to serve on our board? It would be for two years, with bi-monthly meetings. Would you be willing to serve?" Once again Marsha was talking like a whirlwind.

"Sure. Just let me know when and where I need to be." The shelter was a good cause and he would help Laura Jo in any way he could.

"Thanks, Dr. Clayborn."

"I thought we agreed to Mark."

"Thanks, Mark." With that she hung up.

That evening Mark drove straight from work to Laura Jo's apartment. He was looking forward to the evening far more than he should have been. Getting in too deep with Laura Jo could be disastrous. He wouldn't stay around forever and Laura Jo would expect that. But he couldn't help himself. He was drawn to her like no other woman he'd ever met.

Allie opened the door after he knocked.

"Hi, there." He went in and closed the door behind him. "Now that Mardi Gras is over, what do we need to look forward to next?"

"The Easter bunny bringing a large chocolate egg."

Mark nodded in thought. "Well, that does sound like something worth waiting for. Will you share yours with me?"

"Sure."

Laura Jo came up the hall. She wore nothing but a simple collared shirt that buttoned down the front and slacks but he still couldn't take his eyes off her. "Hello."

"Hi," she said, shyly for her.

He had gotten to her. She must be feeling unsure about them after the amount of time that had passed since they'd been together.

"Allie, would you do me a favor?"

She nodded.

"I'm thirsty. Would you get me a glass of water?"

As soon as she was out of sight Mark pulled Laura Jo to him. "What I'm really thirsty for is you." His mouth found hers.

Laura Jo had to admit that Mark had done well in choosing a place that would suit for a celebration and one Allie would enjoy. The pizza place was perfect. He'd even provided Allie with a handful of tokens so she could play games. Laura Jo was reasonably sure that this wasn't his usual choice of restaurant for a date.

"Thanks for bringing us here. Allie is having a blast." Laura Jo tried to speak loud enough to be heard over the cling and clang of the games being played and the overhead music.

"I love pizza, too," Mark said, as he brought a large slice of pepperoni to his mouth.

She liked his mouth, especially when it was on hers. His kiss at her door had her thinking of calling Marsha to see if Allie could spend the night then pulling Mark into her bedroom.

"So tell me what happened today about the shelter," Mark said, after chewing and swallowing his bite.

"I collected all the donor money." She grinned. "They didn't remember but when I showed them each the promissory note with their signature on it, both men called their accounting departments and told them to cut a check."

Mark chuckled. "Mr. Washington knows his buddies well."

"The only glitch is that the bank keeps throwing these roadblocks in our way. Today's was that we had to show we have a full board. It couldn't just be Marsha and I."

"Did you know she called me?"

"She told me afterward that she had. I would have told her not to if she had asked."

"Why?"

"I didn't want to put you on the spot." After the other night she didn't want him to feel obligated because of their one night of passion.

"It's not a problem. Besides being extremely attracted to one of the board members, I do think the shelter is a worthy cause. I'm more than happy to serve on the board."

Allie came running up. "I need one more token to play a game."

Mark handed her a token. "After you play your game, I want you to play one with me."

"Okay," Allie said, all smiles.

"Stay where you can see me," Laura Jo reminded her, before Allie ran back to a nearby game.

Mark leaned in close so that he was speaking right into Laura Jo's ear. "Is there any chance for you and me to have some alone time?"

"You'll have to wait and see," Laura Jo said with a smile. "There's one more thing about the shelter I wanted to tell you. Just before you picked us up, Marsha called. The city has decided to take bids for the house. They know of no one else who's interested but they want everything to look aboveboard so they have to offer it out for bids."

"Sounds reasonable."

"Yeah, but what if someone comes in and outbids us?"

He looked at her and said in a serious tone, "Then you'll just have to raise the money or find somewhere else. You now have new board members you can depend on to help you make a decision. You and Marsha won't be all on your own anymore."

She smiled at him just as Allie returned. "I'm ready to play."

"Are you ready to lose because I'm the best whack-a-moler you've ever seen," Mark announced as he puffed out his chest.

Laura Jo and Allie laughed.

He really was fun to be around. "Famous last words, the saying goes, I think," Laura Jo remarked. It had just been Allie and herself for so long. Was she ready to share their life with Mark? She smiled. Maybe she was.

"Come on, young lady," Mark said, taking Allie's hand. "Let me show you."

They arrived back at Laura Jo's apartment, laughing at something Mark had done while trying to best Allie at the arcade game. When they had gotten into the car to leave the pizza place, he'd looked back at Allie and then turned to her. Laura Jo had placed her hand on the seat belt and said, "Thank you for seeing to our safety."

He gave her a wry smile before he started the car but he seemed less anxious.

"It's bath- and bedtime," Laura Jo told Allie as they entered her apartment. "Why don't you get your PJs and the water started? I'm going to fix some coffee for Mark and I'll be right in."

Allie left in the direction of her room and she and Mark went to the kitchen. She took the pot out of the coffee-maker and went to the sink.

Mark came up behind her and took the pot from her, setting it on the counter. "I'll fix the coffee while you see to Allie. Right now, I want a kiss." He turned her round and gathered her close, giving her a gentle but passionate kiss.

Laura Jo's knees went weak. Her arms went around him and she pulled him tight.

"Mama, I'm ready," Allie called.

Slowly Mark broke their connection. He brushed his hips against hers and grinned. "I am, too."

Laura Jo snickered and gave him a playful push. "I'll be back in a few minutes. Behave yourself while I'm gone."

Ten minutes later, Mark walked down the hall in the direction of Laura Jo's voice. He stopped and stood in the doorway of the room where the sound was coming from. The lights were off except for one small lamp with a fairy of some sort perched on top. Allie lay in bed and Laura Jo sat on the side, reading a book out loud. He leaned against the wall facing them and continued to listen. Allie's eyes were closed when Laura Jo shut the book and kissed her daughter on the forehead.

His heart constricted. What would it feel like to be a part of their inner circle?

Laura Jo looked at him and gave him a soft smile. She raised her hand and beckoned him to join her.

His heart beat faster. This was his invitation to find out. But if he took that step he'd be lost forever. He couldn't take on the responsibility of protecting them. What if he failed them, like he had Mike? No, as much as it would kill him to do so, he couldn't tangle their lives up in his. He'd let them down. Hurt them, disappoint them at best. They'd both had enough of that in their lives.

Laura Jo's smile faded. He backed out of the door, walked to the kitchen and sat at the small table.

What had just happened? Didn't Mark recognize that she'd just offered her life and heart to him? He'd turned it down. Flat.

Laura Jo could no longer pretend this was a casual thing between them. She couldn't afford to invest any of her life or Allie's in someone who was afraid of their ability to share a relationship. She needed a confident man during the good as well as the tough times. Mark didn't believe he was capable of being that man.

Even if she believed in him and convinced him they could make it, Mark had to believe in himself. She couldn't take the chance of Allie experiencing that loss and devastation, the almost physical pain of believing no one wanted her, if Mark decided he couldn't do it. Allie wouldn't be made to feel as if she were a piece of trash being tossed out the window of a car. No, she wouldn't let it happen. Wouldn't go through that again.

She had to break it off before they became any more involved. Her heartache she would deal with, but her daughter's heart she would protect. Maybe with time, and many tears during the night, she would get over Mark.

Laura Jo found him a few minutes later, looking at his coffee cup as he ran a finger around the edge. She poured herself a cup of coffee she had no intention of drinking and took the chair across the table from him.

"This isn't going to work, Mark."

"Why?"

"Because I need someone who'll be committed to the long haul. I deserve your wholehearted love and loyalty. I won't risk my heart or Allie's for anything less. That is the very least I will agree to."

"You know I won't take the chance. What if I can't do it? I won't hurt you. I'm no better than your ex-husband. When things get too tough to face, I'll be gone. Just like him. I've done it before. I'll do it again."

"You're still punishing yourself for something that isn't your fault. Mike's in a wheelchair because of a choice that he made, not you. Your way of atoning is to remain uninvolved emotionally with anyone you might feel something real for. That translates into a wife and family for you. I can see that you care about Allie and I think you care about me, too. I've spent a long time not trusting my judgment about men. You got past that wall. You're a better man than you give yourself credit for."

He didn't look at her. Her heart ached for him but she had to get through to him. Make him start really living again. He deserved it. She loved him enough to do that and send him away if she had to.

"You can't create someone else's happiness by being unhappy. You can't fix what happened to Mike. Even if you had been wrong. What you can do now is try to be a better friend than you were back then.

"The problem is you have run from and hidden from the issue too long. You've left the subject alone so long that it has grown and festered to a point it's out of control in your mind. Based on what I saw from Mike the other night, he feels no animosity toward you. To me it sounded as if he just misses his friend. Face it, clean the ugliness away then you can see yourself for the person you are. Good, kind, loving, protective and caring. It's time for you to like yourself.

"I hope that one day you realize that and find someone to share your life with. It can't be Allie and I." Those last words almost killed her to say.

His chair scraped across the floor as he pushed it away from the table. He pinned her with a pointed look. His eyes were dark with sadness and something else. Anger? "Are you through?"

She nodded. She was sure she wasn't going to like what came next.

"I have issues, but you do, too. You carry a chip on your shoulder, Laura Jo. In the past nine years you have finished school on your own, raised a wonderful, happy child and started and helped to run a shelter for women, but still you feel you need to prove yourself to the world. You don't need your father and mother's or anyone else's approval. It's time to quit being that girl who had to show everyone she could do it by herself.

"You let your ex overshadow your life to the point it took me using a sledgehammer to get past your barriers. Laura Jo, not every guy is a jerk and doesn't face up to their responsibilities."

"Like you have?"

Mark flinched. She'd cut him to the core. But she had to get through to him somehow.

"I think I'd better go." He stood and started toward the door.

Shocked at his abrupt statement, she said, "I think it's for the best. Goodbye, Mark."

CHAPTER NINE

THE ONLY TIME Laura Jo could remember feeling so miserable had been when she'd taken Allie home from the hospital, knowing the child would have no father or grandparents to greet her. The pain had been heartbreakingly deep. She'd believed the scar had been covered over enough that she would never return to those emotions. But she'd been wrong.

They had rushed in all over again when Mark had walked out the door. The overwhelming despair was back. The problem this time was that it was even more devastating.

Looking back, she could see her goal when she'd been nineteen had been more about breaking away from her parents, standing on her own two feet and discovering what she believed in, instead of following their dictates. Turned out she'd let pride stand in her way all these years. It hadn't been fair to Allie, her parents or herself.

She appreciated Mark's fears, even understood where they came from, but she couldn't accept anything less than full commitment. Allie deserved that, and even she wouldn't settle for anything less.

Experience had shown her what it was like to have a man in her life who didn't stay around. She refused to put Allie through that. If she felt this awful about Mark leaving after they had known each other for such a short time, what would it have been like if they had been together longer?

The past had told her that the only way to survive disappointment and heartache, and in this case heartbreak, was to keep moving. It was Monday morning and Allie had school, she had to work.

Was Mark working the early shift? Moving around his big kitchen dressed only in his shorts? With them hung low on his hips? Bare-chested?

He'd called a couple of times but she had let the answering machine get it. If she spoke to him it would be too easy to open the door wide for him to come into her life. She just couldn't do that.

She groaned, afraid there would be no getting over Mark. She needed to stay busy, spend less time thinking about him. Forcing herself to climb out of bed, Laura Jo dressed for the day, making sure to have Allie to school on time.

Allie asked her during breakfast, "Why're you so sad, Mama?"

Laura Jo put on a bright smile and said in the most convincing voice she could muster, "I'm not sad. Why would I be sad?"

Allie gave her a disbelieving look but said nothing more. For that Laura Jo was grateful. She worried that she'd break down in tears in front of her daughter.

At midmorning, after just releasing a patient home from the ER, Laura's cell phone buzzed. Looking at it, she saw it was Marsha calling. It was unusual for her to call while Laura Jo was working. Something must have happened with the shelter.

"Hello. What's going on?"

"Someone has bid against us for the house. It's far over what we have and I don't see any way for us to come up with that amount of money."

Marsha told Laura Jo the figure. They were doomed. The new house wasn't going to happen this time. "You're right."

"What we'll have to do is use the money we do have to refurbish the place we're in now and start looking for another place to buy. Sorry my call was bad news."

"Me, too, but I was afraid this might happen when the city opened it for bids. I'd prepared myself for it. We'll start making plans this evening when I get home."

Laura Jo hung up. The sting had been taken out of the loss of the house by the loss of Mark. With him no longer in her life, it made everything else feel less important. She and Marsha would deal with this setback somehow.

A week later, her heart was still as heavy as ever over Mark. If she could just stop thinking about him and, worse, dreaming of him, she could start to heal. But nothing she did except working on the shelter, seemed to ease the continuous ache in her chest.

She and Marsha had just finished meeting with a contractor about ideas for changes at the shelter when Laura Jo was called to the front. There a man dressed in a suit waited.

"Can I help you?" she asked.

"Are you Laura Jo Akins?" The man said in an official manner.

"Yes."

"I was instructed to personally deliver this to you."

He handed her an official-looking envelope. Was this some sort of summons?

Laura Jo started opening the letter and before she could finish the man left. What was going on?

Printed on the front was a name of a lawyer's office. Why would a lawyer be contacting her? She opened the envelope and scanned the contents. Her heart soared and her mouth dropped open in disbelief. She thought of telling Mark first, but he wasn't in her life anymore.

"Marsha!" she yelled.

Her friend hurried down the hallway toward Laura Jo. "What's wrong?"

She waved the letter in the air. "You're never going to believe this. My father has bought the house the city was selling and he has deeded it over to me!"

That night Laura Jo wondered about her parents' generosity. Had they had a change of heart years ago but she wouldn't let them close enough to say so? She had been surprised at the krewe dance to discover they knew some of what had been going on in her life. Had they been watching over her? There had been that school scholarship that she'd been awarded that she'd had no idea she'd qualified for, which had covered most of her expenses. Had that been her parents' doing?

She'd told Mark that people had the capacity to change. Had her parents? After speaking to them, she'd certainly seen them in a different light. She'd also told Mark that people could forgive. Maybe it was past time she did.

On Saturday afternoon, Laura Jo pulled her car into the drive of her parents' home. Allie sat in the seat next to her. Laura Jo had told her about her grandparents a few days before. She had asked Allie to forgive her for not telling her sooner, and had also told Allie that they would be going to visit her grandparents on Saturday. Later that evening, Laura Jo had called the number that she'd known from childhood. Her mother had answered on the second ring. Their conversation had been a short one but during it Laura Jo had asked if she could bring Allie to meet them.

"Mama, what're we doing?" Allie asked.

"I'm just looking, honey. I used to live here." That was

true but mostly she was trying to find the nerve to go further. The last time she'd been there, hurtful words had been spoken that had lasted for years.

A few minutes later, she and Allie stood hand in hand in front of her parents' front door. Allie rang the doorbell. Her mother must have been watching for them because the door was almost immediately opened by her mother herself. Not one of the maids. Her father was coming up the hall behind her.

"Hello, Laura Jo. Thank you for coming." Her mother sounded sincere.

"Mother and Daddy, this is Allie."

Her mother leaned over so that she was closer to Allie's level and smiled. "Hi, Allie. It's so nice to meet you."

Her father took the same posture. "Hello."

Allie stepped closer to Laura Jo. She placed a hand at Allie's back and said, "These are your grandparents."

Both her parents stood and stepped back.

Her mother said in a nervous voice Laura Jo had never heard, "Come in."

It felt odd to step into her parents' home after so much time. Little had changed. Instead of being led into the formal living room, as Laura Jo had expected, her mother took them to the kitchen. "I thought Allie might like to have some ice cream."

Allie looked at Laura Jo. "May I?"

"Sure, honey."

"Why don't we all have a bowl?" her father suggested.

When they were finished with their bowls of ice cream her mother asked Allie if she would like to go upstairs to see the room where Laura Jo used to sleep. Allie agreed.

Laura Jo looked at her father. "I don't know how to say thank you enough for your gift."

"We had heard that you were looking for support to buy it."

She should have known it would get back to them about why she'd been at the dance.

"It's a good cause and we wanted to help. Since we weren't there for you, maybe we can help other girls in the same position. I know it doesn't make up for the struggle you had."

It didn't, but at least she better understood her parents now. She had to share some of the fault also. "All those calls I made to Mom—"

"We thought we were doing what was best. That if we cut you off then you would see that you needed us and come back."

"But you wouldn't talk to me." She didn't try to keep the hurt out of her voice.

"We realized we had been too hard on you when you stopped calling. I'm sorry, Laura Jo. We loved you. Feared for you, and just didn't know how to show it correctly."

"You saw to it that I got the nursing scholarship, didn't you?"

He nodded. "We knew by then that you wouldn't accept if we offered to send you to school."

"I wouldn't have. It wasn't until recently that I realized that sometimes what we believe when we're young isn't always the way things are. You were right about Phil. I'm sorry that I hurt you and Mom. Kept Allie from you."

"We understand. We're proud of you. We have kept an eye on you both. You've done well. You needed to do it the hard way, to go out on your own. It took us a while to see that." Her strong, unrelenting father went on, with a catch in his voice, "The only thing we couldn't live with was not having you in our lives and not knowing our granddaughter."

Moisture filled her eyes for all the hurt and wasted opportunities through the years on both sides. Laura Jo reached across the table and took her father's hand. Forgiveness was less about her and more about her parents. A gift she could give them. "You'll never be left out of our lives again, I promise."

Three weeks after the fact Mark still flinched when he thought of Laura Jo accusing him of being a jerk and not living up to his responsibilities. The plain-talking Laura Jo had returned with a vengeance when she'd lectured him.

She was right, he knew that, but he still couldn't bring himself to talk to Mike. That was the place he had to start. He'd spent over ten years not being able to face up to Mike and what had happened that night. Could he be a bigger hypocrite?

He'd looked down on Laura Jo's ex, taking a holier-than-thou approach when he'd been running as fast and far as Phil had when the going had got tough.

Every night he spent away from Laura Jo made him crave her more. He wasn't sleeping. If he did, he dreamed of her. The pain at her loss was greater than any he'd ever experienced. Even after the accident. He wasn't able to live without her. He'd tried that and it wasn't working.

He'd tried to call her a couple of times but she hadn't picked up.

Mark thought about Laura Jo's words. Didn't he want a family badly enough to make a change? Want to have someone special in his life? More importantly, be a part of Laura Jo's and Allie's world?

He'd been running for so long, making sure he didn't commit, he didn't know how to do anything else. It was time for it to stop. He had to face his demons in order to be worthy of a chance for a future with Laura Jo, if she would have him. How could he expect her to believe in him, trust him to be there for her, if he didn't believe it for himself? He had to get his own life in order before he asked for a permanent place in hers. And he desperately wanted that place.

Mark picked up the phone and dialed the number he'd called so many times he had it memorized by now. He'd been calling every day for a week and had been told that Mike wasn't available. Was he dodging Mark, as well?

He'd made his decision and wanted to act on it. It was just his luck he couldn't reach Mike. The devil of it was that he couldn't return to Laura Jo without talking to Mike first. She would accept nothing less. For his well-being as well as hers.

The day before, he'd received a call from Marsha. She'd told him how they had missed out on the house but then an anonymous donor had bought it outright and gifted it to them.

Mark was surprised and glad for Laura Jo. At least the dream she'd worked so hard for had come true. Marsha went on to say that she and Laura Jo no longer required a board but planned to have one anyway. Marsha wanted to know if he was still willing to serve on it.

"Have you discussed this with Laura Jo? She may not want me on it."

"She said that if you're willing to do it she could handle working with you on a business level. I think her exact words were, 'He's a good doctor and cares about people. I'm sure he'll be an asset.'"

Panic flowed through his veins. Laura Jo was already distancing herself from him. The longer it took to speak to Mike, the harder it would be to get her to listen.

Marsha said, "Look, Mark, I don't know what happened between you two but what I do know is that she's torn up about it. I love her like a sister and she's hurting. She can be hardheaded when it comes to the ones she loves. The only way to make her see reason is to push until she does."

"Thanks for letting me know."

The next day, when Mark had a break between patients, he tried Mike's number again. This time when a woman answered he insisted that he speak to Mike.

"Just a minute."

"Mark." Mike didn't sound pleased to hear from him.

"I was wondering if I could come by for a visit," Mark said, with more confidence than he felt.

"It will be a couple of days before I have time." Mike wasn't going to make this easy but, then, why should he. "I've been out of town and have some business I need to catch up on."

Mark wasn't tickled with having to wait, but he'd put it off this long so did two more days really matter?

"How does Thursday evening at seven sound?"

"I'll be here." Mike sounded more resigned to the idea than cheerful about the prospect. Mark couldn't blame him. His jaw tightened with tension from guilt and regret at the thought of facing him. He felt like a coward and had acted like one for years.

The next day an invitation arrived in the mail. It was to a garden party tea at the Herrons' mansion on Sunday afternoon. It was a fund-raiser for the new shelter. Had Laura Jo taken his advice and cleared the air with her parents? He looked forward to attending.

Two evenings later, Mark drove from Fairhope over the bay causeway to Mobile. Mike lived in one of the newer neighborhoods that Mark wasn't familiar with. He hadn't slept much the night before, anticipating the meeting with Mike, but, then, he hadn't slept well since the night he'd had Laura Jo in his arms. He drove up the street Mike had given as his address during their phone conversation. It was tree-lined and had well-cared-for homes. He pulled up alongside the curb in front of the number that Mike had given him. It was a yellow ranch-style home, with a white picket fence surrounding the front yard. Early spring flowers were just starting to show.

Mark sat for a minute. He'd prepared his speech. Had practiced and practiced what he was going to say, but it never seemed like enough. If Laura Jo were here, she would say to just share what was in his heart. To stop worrying. Taking a deep breath and letting it out slowly, he opened the car door and got out. Closing it, he walked around the car and up the walk.

He hadn't noticed when he'd pulled up that there were children's toys in the yard and near the front door. Mike had a child?

Mark winced when he saw the wheelchair ramp and hesitated before putting a foot on it to walk to the door. His nerves were as tight as bowstrings. He rang the doorbell. Seconds later, Tammy opened the door.

"Mark, how nice to see you again." She pulled the door wider. "Come on in. Mike's in the den with Johnny."

She closed the door and Mark followed her down an extrawide hall to a large room at the back of the house.

Mike sat in what could only be called the most high-tech of wheelchairs in the middle of the room. A boy of about three was handing him a block and together they were building a tower on a tray across Mike's knees. "Mark. Come on in. Let me introduce you to my son, Johnny."

Mark went over to Mike, who offered his hand for a shake. "Good to see you again."

Mike dumped the blocks into a bucket beside his chair and then set the tray next to it. "Come here, Johnny, I want you to meet someone."

At one time Mike would have introduced him as his best friend. By the way he acted he wasn't even a friend anymore.

The boy climbed into his father's lap and shyly curled into Mike. He looked up at Mark with an unsure gaze.

"Johnny," Mark said.

"I think it's is time for someone to go to bed." Tammy reached out and took Johnny from Mike. "We'll let you two talk."

Mark watched them leave the room and turned back to Mike.

"I admire you."

"How's that?"

"Having a wife and family. The responsibility. How do you know you're getting it right?"

"Right? I have no idea that I am. I make the best decisions I can at the time and hope they are the correct ones. Tammy and I are partners. We make decisions together." Mike looked directly at him. "Everyone makes mistakes. We're all human and not perfect. We just have to try harder the next time."

Was that what he'd been doing? Letting a mistake color the rest of his life? If he couldn't be sure he'd be the perfect husband or father then he wouldn't even try.

Before Mark could say anything more, Mike said, "Take a seat and quit towering over me. You always made a big deal of being taller than me. Remember you used to say that was why you got the girls, because they saw you first in a crowd."

Mark gave halfhearted grin. Had Mike just made a joke?

Taking a seat on the edge of the sofa, Mark looked around the room.

"Why are you here, Mark? After all these years, you show up at my house now," Mike said, as he maneuvered his chair closer and into Mark's direct sight line.

He scooted back into the cushions. “Mike, I need to clear the air about a couple of things.”

“It’s well past time for that.”

Those words didn’t make Mark feel any better. “I’m embarrassed about how I acted after the accident. I’m so sorry I left without speaking to you and have done little to stay in touch since. Most of all, I’m sorry I put you in that damn chair.” Mark looked at the floor, wall, anywhere but at Mike.

Moments passed and when Mike spoke he was closer to Mark than he had been before. “Hey, man, you didn’t put me in this chair. I did. I was drunk and not listening to anything anyone said.”

“But I was the one going too fast. I’d driven that part of the road a hundred times. I knew about that ninety-degree turn. I overcorrected.” Mark looked up at him.

“You did. But I wouldn’t have been thrown out if I’d worn my seat belt. I don’t blame you for that. But I have to admit it hurt like hell not to have your support afterwards. I can’t believe you did me that way.”

Mark’s stomach roiled as he looked at a spot on the floor. “I can’t either. That isn’t how friends should act.” He looked directly at Mike. “All I can do is ask you to forgive me and let me try to make it up to you.”

“If you promise not to run out on me again, and buy me a large steak, all will be forgiven.”

Mark smiled for the first time. “That I can do.”

“And I need a favor.”

Mark sat forward. “Name it.”

“I need a good general practice doctor to oversee an experimental treatment that I’m about to start. Do you know one?”

“I just might,” Mark said with a grin. “What’s going on?”

“I just returned from Houston, where they are doing

some amazing things with spinal injuries. With all these guys coming back from war with spinal problems, what they can do has come a long way even from nine years ago. I will have a procedure done in a few weeks and when I return home I need to see a doctor every other day to check my site and do bloodwork. My GP is retiring and I'm looking for someone to replace him who Tammy can call day or night." He grinned. "She worries. Doesn't believe me when I tell her what the doctor has said. Likes to hear it from the doc himself."

"I'll be honored to take the job. I'll even make house calls if that will help."

"I may hold you to that."

For the next forty-five minutes, he and Mike talked about old times and what they were doing in their lives now. Mike had become a successful businessman. He had invented a part for a wheelchair that made it easier to maneuver the chair. As Mark drove away he looked back in his rearview mirror. Mike and Tammy were still under the porch light where he had left them. Tammy's hand rested on Mike's shoulder. That simple gesture let Mark know that Mike was loved and happy.

Mike had a home, a wife and child, was living the life Mark had always hoped for but was afraid to go after. All Mark owned was his car and Gus. He'd let the one special person he wanted in his life go. Ironically, Mike had moved on while he had stayed still. And he had been the one feeling sorry for Mike, when he had more in life than Mark did. He wanted that happiness in his life too and knew where to find it.

If he could get Laura Jo to listen. If she would just let him try.

CHAPTER TEN

LAURA JO COULDN'T believe the difference a few weeks had made in her life. It was funny how she'd been going along, doing all the things she'd always done, and, bam, her life was turned upside down by her daughter having a skinned knee. She'd worked Mardi Gras parades before but never had she had a more eventful or emotional season.

She scanned her parents' formal backyard garden. There were tables set up among the rhododendrons, azaleas and the dogwood trees. None were in full bloom but the greenery alone was beautiful. The different tables held canapés and on one sat a spectacular tea urn on a stand that swung with teacups surrounding it. People in their Sunday best mingled, talking in groups. The eye-popping cost to attend the event meant that the shelter could double the number of women they took in. Her parents had convinced her to let them to do this fund-raiser so that she could get the maximum out of the grant. She'd agreed and her mother had taken over.

How ironic was it that she had rejected her parents and they were the very ones who were helping her achieve her dreams? Her anger and resentment had kept her away from her parents, not the other way around. Forgiveness lifted a burden off her and she was basking in the sunshine of having a family again. She only wished Mark could feel that way, as well. She still missed him desperately.

Allie's squeal of delight drew her attention. Laura Jo located her. She was running down the winding walk with her new dress flowing in her haste.

"Mark," she cried, and Laura Jo's stomach fluttered.

She'd thought he might be here, had prepared herself to see him again, but her breath still stuck in her throat and her heart beat too fast. Each day became harder without him, not easier.

Already she regretted agreeing to let him remain on the board. Now she would have to continue to face him but he was too good an advocate for the shelter to lose him. At least, that was what she told herself. Somehow she'd have to learn to deal with not letting her feelings show.

When Allie reached Mark he whisked her up into his arms and hugged her close. The picture was one of pure joy between them.

Laura Jo had worked hard not to snap at Allie when she'd continued to ask about where Mark was and why they didn't see him anymore. Finally, Laura Jo had told her he wouldn't be coming back and there had been tears on both sides.

Mark lowered Allie onto her feet and spoke to her. Allie turned and pointed in Laura Jo's direction. Mark's gaze found hers, even at that distance. Her heart flipped.

He started toward her.

A couple of people she'd known from her Mardi Gras court days joined her. They talked for a few minutes but all the while Laura Jo was aware of Mark moving nearer.

He stood behind her. She'd know anywhere that aftershave and the scent that could only be his. Her spine tingled.

As the couple moved away Mark said in a tone that was almost a caress, "Laura Jo."

She came close to throwing herself into his arms but she had to remain strong. She turned around, putting on her best smile like she'd been taught so many years ago. "Hello, Mark, glad you could come."

"I wouldn't have missed it."

His tone said that was the truth.

"Marsha told me that you got the house after all. That's wonderful. With the grant and all the money you've raised, you'll be able to furnish it."

"Yes. My father was the one to outbid us. He then gave it to me."

His brow wrinkled. "You were okay with that?"

"I was. The women needed it too badly for me to use my disagreement with my parents against them. It really was a gift to me anyway. He wanted to make amends by helping other women going through the same experience I had."

Mark nodded. "It sounds like you and your parents worked things out."

"I wouldn't say that it's all smooth going. But I've forgiven them. We're all better for that. They want to see their granddaughter and Allie needs them. I don't have the right to deny any of them that."

"Mama, look who's here," Allie said from beside her.

Laura Jo hadn't seen her approach, she'd been so absorbed in Mark. She turned. "Who—?"

Allie held Gus's leash. Behind the dog sat Mike and next to him stood his wife. She looked back at Mark.

He smiled and turned toward the group. "I brought a few friends with me. I hope you don't mind?"

Did this mean what she thought it did? Mark had taken what she'd said to heart and had gone to see his friend.

"Hello, Mike and Tammy. Of course you're welcome. I'm glad to see you again."

"We're glad to be here. This is some event. And I understand it's for a very worthy cause. I think we'll have Allie show us where the food is." Mike winked at Mark. "We'll see you around, buddy."

Laura Jo looked between them, not sure what the interchange meant.

"You're busy. I think I'll get some food also." Mark captured her hand. "When this is over, can we talk?"

A lightning shock of awareness and a feeling of rightness washed through her simultaneously. "It'll be late."

"I'll wait."

Mark sat in Mr. Herron's den, having a cup of coffee while he waited for Laura Jo. Her father was there, along with Allie and Gus. Mr. Herron had apparently noticed Mark was hanging around after the other guests were leaving and had taken pity on him by inviting him in for coffee and a more comfortable seat.

The longer Mark sat there the more nervous he became. Would Laura Jo listen to what he had to say? Would she believe that he had changed? Would she be willing to take a chance on him? He broke out in a sweat, just thinking about it.

She and her mother finally joined them. He stood. Laura Jo looked beautiful but tired. Had she been getting as little sleep as he had?

As if her mother knew Laura Jo needed some time alone with him, Mrs. Herron said, "Why don't you let Allie stay with us tonight? We can get her to school in the morning. She can wear the clothes she wore from home to here today."

"Is that okay with you, Allie?" Laura Jo asked.

"Yes. Can Gus stay, too?"

"I think you need to let your grandparents get used to having you before you start inviting Gus to stay," Mark said with a smile.

Ten minutes later, he and Laura Jo, with Gus in the backseat, were leaving her parents' house. She had touched her seat belt when he'd looked.

"Old habits are hard to break," he said in explanation.

"Not a bad habit to have," she assured him in a warm tone. That was one of the many things he loved about Laura Jo. She understood him.

"I hope you don't mind me taking Gus home. I don't want you to think I planned to lure you to my house. I just thought Allie would be glad to see him. I didn't think it all the way through."

"She was, and I don't mind riding to your house."

As they traveled through the tunnel Laura Jo remarked, "I've never known my parents to let a dog in the house."

"Gus does have that effect on people."

She went on as if more in thought than conversation, "Come to think of it, I've never seen my father invite another man into his private space."

"Maybe that's his way of giving me a seal of approval."

She pieced him with a look. "Are you asking for a seal of approval from my father?"

"No, the only seal of approval I'm looking for is from you."

She studied him for a minute before asking, "Are you going to tell me about Mike and Tammy or keep me in suspense?"

"It took me a while to admit you were right. Actually, I knew all along that you were. I just didn't want to admit it."

"So what made you decide to talk to Mike?" She had laid her head back and closed her eyes.

He hadn't planned to go into this as they traveled. But as usual Laura Jo had a way of surprising him. "Why don't you rest and I'll tell you when we get to my house?"

"Sounds like a plan."

By the time Mark pulled into his drive, Laura Jo was sleeping. Here he was, planning to bare his heart to her after weeks of being separated, and she'd fallen asleep. He let Gus out of the car and went to open the front door.

Going to Laura Jo's door, he opened it, unbuckled her and scooped her into his arms. She mumbled and wrapped her arms around his neck, letting her head rest on his chest. He kicked the passenger door closed and carried her inside.

He loved having her in his arms again. After pushing the front door closed, he went to his favorite chair and sat down. She continued to sleep and he was content just having her close.

Sometime later Laura Jo stirred. He placed a kiss on her temple and her eyelids fluttered open.

"Hello," she mumbled against his neck. Then she kissed him.

The thump-thump of his heart went to bump-bump.

Her lips touched the ridge of his chin, while a hand feathered through his hair near his ear.

His hopes soared. His manhood stirred. Had she missed him as much as he'd missed her? "Laura Jo, if you keep that up, talking is the last thing that will happen."

"So talk," she murmured, before her mouth found the corner of his. "I'm listening."

"Maybe we need to go out on the deck."

"Mmm, I like it here." She wiggled around so she could kiss him fully on the mouth.

His length hardened. If he didn't say what he needed to say now, he wouldn't be doing so for a long time.

"I can't believe that I'm doing this…" He pushed her away until he could see her face. She blinked at him and gave him a dreamy smile. "Why did you agree to talk to me? Was it because you saw me with Mike? You haven't answered any of my phone calls in the past few weeks."

"I hoped…"

"Hoped what? That I had changed my mind? Hoped you'd gotten through to me? Hoped there was a chance for us?"

"Yes," she whispered.

"Do you want there to be?"

By now she was sitting a little straighter and her eyes had turned serious. "Tell me what made you decide to go talk to Mike. When you left my place I didn't think you ever would."

"I went because I discovered that I was more afraid of something else than I was of facing Mike."

Her gaze locked with his. "What?"

"Losing any chance of ever having you in my life."

"Oh, Mark. I thought I had lost you forever until I saw you with Mike today. I knew then that you thought we had something worth fighting for. I've been so miserable without you." She took his face in her hands and kissed him. "We've both been running from our pasts. I think it's time for us to run toward our future. Together."

His arms tightened around her. Their kiss deepened. He had to have her. Beneath him, beside him, under him. Forever.

Mark lifted her off him and she stood. He quickly exited the chair. Taking her hand, he led her to his bedroom. Putting his hands on her shoulders, he turned her around and unzipped her dress. Pushing it off and letting it fall to the floor, he kissed her shoulder.

"I've missed you so much it hurt."

"I felt the same."

He released her bra and it joined her dress. There was a hitch in her breathing when he cupped her breasts. She leaned back against him. As his hands roamed, she began to squirm.

She flipped around to face him. "I want you." Her hands went to his waist and started releasing his belt.

"No more than I want you."

With them both undressed, they found the bed and the world that was theirs alone.

Sometime later, Mark lay with Laura Jo in his arms. Her hair tickled his nose but he didn't mind. All was right with his world if she was in it.

Laura Jo shifted, placed a hand in the center of his chest and looked up at him. "Hi, there."

He looked at her and smiled. "Hey, yourself."

For a few moments he enjoyed the feel of her in his arms before he said, "I've worked for years not to become emotionally involved with anyone. I didn't think I could trust myself. Then along came you and Allie. I've been miserable without you both. I've always wanted a family and when a wonderful one was offered to me, like an idiot I turned it down. I won't do that again if the invitation is still open. See, the problem is that I've fallen in love with you."

With moisture in her eyes Laura Jo stretched up and placed a kiss on his mouth. "I love you, too, but are you sure that's what you want? What you can live with? I can't take any chances. It has to be forever. Kids or no kids. Good or bad days. Sickness or health."

Mark leaned forward so that his face was only inches from hers. “Until death do us part.”

“I can live with that.”

Her kiss told him she meant it.

* * * * *

RESISTING HER REBEL DOC

JOANNA NEIL

CHAPTER ONE

'WHAT WILL YOU DO?' Molly stood by the desk at the nursing station, riffling through the papers in a wire tray. 'Will you go to the wedding?' She sent Caitlin a sympathetic glance. 'It must be a really difficult situation for you.'

Caitlin nodded. 'Yes, it is, to be honest. These last few weeks have been a nightmare. It's all come as a complete shock to me and right now I'm not sure how I'm going to deal with it.' She pulled a face, pushing back a couple of chestnut curls that had strayed on to her forehead. Her shoulder-length hair was a mass of wild, natural curls but for her work at the hospital she usually kept it pinned back out of the way. 'I don't want to go but I don't see how I can avoid it—when all's said and done, Jenny's my cousin. My family—my aunt, especially—will want me to be there for the celebrations. I don't want to be the cause of any breakdown in family relationships by not going. It will cause a huge upset if I stay away.'

Yet how could she bear to watch her cousin tie the knot with the man who just a short time ago had been the love of her life? She and Matt had even started to talk about getting engaged and then—*wham!*—Jenny had come along and suddenly everything had changed.

Her usually mobile mouth flattened into a straight line. When she'd opened the envelope first thing this morning back at the flat and taken out the beautifully embossed invitation card, her spirits had fallen to rock-bottom. She'd had a sick feeling that the day was headed from then on into a downward spiral.

Sure enough, just a few minutes later as she had opened the fridge door and taken out a carton of milk, her prediction was reinforced. She'd shaken the empty carton in disbelief. One of her flatmates must have drained the last drops of milk and then put it back on the shelf. She'd stared at it. No coffee before starting work? It was unthinkable!

'I can see how awkward it is for you.' Molly sighed, bringing Caitlin's thoughts back to the present. 'Families are everything, aren't they? Sometimes we have to do things we don't want to do in order to keep the peace. I just wish you weren't leaving us. I know how you feel about working alongside Jenny and Matt but we'll miss you so much.'

'I'll miss you too,' Caitlin said with feeling. Molly was a children's nurse, brilliant at her job and a good friend, but now, as Caitlin looked around the ward, she felt sadness growing deep inside her. She'd been working at this hospital for several years, specialising as a children's doctor, making friends and getting to know the inquisitive and endearing children who had come into her care.

It would be such a wrench to put it all behind her, but she knew she had to make a fresh start. She couldn't bear to stay while Matt was here. He had betrayed her and hurt her deeply. 'We'll keep in touch, won't we?' she said, putting on a bright face. 'I won't be going too far away—Buckinghamshire's only about an hour's drive from here.'

Molly nodded. She was a pretty girl with hazel eyes and dark, almost black hair cut in a neat, silky bob. 'Are you going to live at home? Didn't you say your mother needed to have someone close by her these days?'

'Yes, that's right. Actually, I thought it would be a good chance for me to keep an eye on her now that she's getting on a bit and beginning to get a few aches and pains. It's been worrying me for quite a while that I'm so far away.' She smiled. 'I think she's really quite pleased that I'll be staying with her for a while, just until I can sort out a place of my own.'

She started to look through the patients' charts that were neatly stacked on the desk. Her whole world was changing. She loved this job; she'd thought long and hard before giving in her notice, but how could she go on working here as long as Matt was going to be married to her cousin? And, worse, Jenny was going to take up a job here too.

She shuddered inwardly. It was still alien to her to think of him as her ex. They'd been together for eighteen months and it had been a terrible jolt to discover that he'd fallen out of love with her and gone off with another woman.

'I shall have to look for another job, of course, but

there are a couple of hospitals in the area. It shouldn't be too difficult to find something. I hope not, anyway.' She straightened up and made an effort to pull herself together. No matter how much she was hurting, she knew instinctively that it was important from now on to make plans and try to look on the positive side. She had to get over this and move on. She glanced at Molly. 'Perhaps we could meet up from time to time—we could go for a coffee together, or a meal, maybe?'

'Yeah, that'll be good.' Molly cheered up and began to glance through the list of young patients who were waiting to be seen. 'The test results are back on the little boy with the painful knee,' she pointed out helpfully. 'From the looks of things it's an infection.'

'Hmm.' Caitlin quickly scanned the laboratory form. 'It's what we thought. I'll arrange for the orthopaedic surgeon to drain the fluid from the joint and we'll start him on the specific antibiotic right away.' She wrote out a prescription and handed it to Molly.

'Thanks. I'll see to it.'

'Good.' Caitlin frowned. 'I'd like to follow up on him to see how he's doing, but I expect Matt will take over my patients when I leave here. I'll miss my little charges.'

Caitlin phoned the surgeon to set things in motion and then went to check up on a four-year-old patient who'd been admitted with breathing problems the previous day. The small child was sleeping, his breathing coming in short gasps, his cheeks chalky-pale against the white of the hospital pillows. He'd been so poorly when he'd been brought in yesterday and she'd been desperately concerned for him. But now, after she had listened to his chest and checked the monitors, she felt reassured.

'He seems to be doing much better,' she told his parents, who were sitting by his bedside, waiting anxiously. 'The intravenous steroids and nebuliser treatments have opened up his airways and made it easier for him to breathe. We'll keep him on those and on the oxygen for another day or so and you should gradually begin to see a great improvement. The chest X-ray didn't show anything untoward, so we can assume it was just flare-up of the asthma. I'll ask the nurse to talk to you to see if we can find ways of avoiding too many of those in the future.'

'Thank you, doctor.' They looked relieved, and after talking with them for a little while longer Caitlin left them, taking one last glance at the child before going back to the central desk to see if any more test results had come in.

'There's a phone call for you, Caitlin.' The clerk at the nurses' station held the receiver aloft as she approached the desk. 'Sounds urgent.'

'Okay, thanks.' Caitlin took the receiver from her and said in an even tone, 'Hello, this is Dr Braemar. How may I help?'

'Hi, Caitlin.' The deep male voice was warm and compelling in a way that was oddly, bone-meltingly familiar. 'I don't know if you remember me—it's been quite a while. I'm Brodie Driscoll. We used to live near one another in Ashley Vale?'

She drew in a quick breath. Brodie Driscoll! How

could she possibly forget him? He was the young man who had haunted her teenage dreams and sent hot thrills rocketing through her bloodstream. Just hearing his name had been enough to fire up all her senses. He had been constantly in her thoughts back then—and to be scrupulously honest even now the sound of his voice brought prickles of awareness shooting from the tips of her toes right up to her temples.

Not that she'd ever let on that he had the power to affect her like this—not then and certainly not now! Heaven forbid she should ever fall for the village bad boy, let alone become involved in any way with him. He was a rebel, through and through, trouble with a capital T… But who could resist him? His roguish smile and his easy charm made him utterly irresistible.

'Oh, I remember,' she said softly. She couldn't imagine why he was calling her like this, out of the blue. Not to talk about old times, surely? Her pulse quickened. Maybe that wouldn't be such a bad idea, after all…?

'That's good, I'm glad you haven't forgotten me.' There was a smile in his voice but his next words brought her out of her wistful reverie and swiftly back to the here and now. 'I'm sorry to ring you at work, Caitlin, but something's happened that I think you need to know about.'

'Oh? That's okay…what is it?' She'd no idea how or why he'd tracked her down, but he sounded serious, and all at once she was anxious to hear what he had to say.

'It's about your mother. I'm not sure if you know, but I moved into the house next door to hers a couple of weeks ago, so I see her quite often when she's out and about on the smallholding.'

She hadn't known that. Her mother was always busy with the animals and the orchard; knowing how friendly she was with everyone it was easy to see how she and Brodie would pass the time of day with one another. Her mouth curved. It was good that she had someone nearby to take an interest in her.

'What's happened?' she asked. 'Are the animals escaping on to your property?' Her mother could never resist taking in strays and wounded creatures and nursing them back to health. 'I know the fence was looking a bit rickety last time I was there. I made a few running repairs, but if there's a problem I'll make sure it's sorted.'

'No, it isn't that.' There was a sombre edge to his tone and Caitlin tensed, suddenly alert. 'I'm afraid it's much more serious,' he said. 'Your mother has had an accident, Caitlin. She had a fall and I'm pretty sure she's broken her hip. I called the ambulance a few minutes ago and the paramedics are transferring her into it right now. I'll go with her to the hospital, but I thought you should know what's happening.'

Caitlin's face paled rapidly. 'I— Yes, of course. I… Thank you, Brodie. I'll get over there… I need to be with her.' She frowned. 'What makes you think she's broken her hip?' She added tentatively, 'Perhaps it's not quite as serious as that.'

'That's what I was hoping, but she can't move her leg and it's at an odd angle—it looks as though it's become shorter than the other one. I'm afraid she's in a lot of pain.'

'Oh, dear.' Those were typical signs of a broken hip. The day was just going rapidly from bad to worse. 'Will they be taking her to Thame Valley Hospital?'

'That's right. She'll go straight to A&E for assessment.' He paused as someone at the other end of the line spoke to him. She guessed the paramedic had approached him to say they were ready to leave.

'I'm sorry, I have to go,' he said.

'All right…and thanks again for ringing me, Brodie.' She hesitated then said quickly, 'Give her my love, will you, and tell her I'll be with her as soon as I can?'

'I will.' He cut the call and Caitlin stood for a moment, staring into space, trying to absorb what he'd told her.

'Are you all right?' Emerging from one of the patients' bays, the senior registrar came over to the desk and looked her over briefly. 'You're as white as a sheet,' he commented. 'What's happened? Is it something to do with one of the patients?'

She shook her head. 'My mother's had an accident—a fall. A neighbour's going with her to the hospital—it sounds as though she's broken her hip.'

'I'm so sorry,' he said with a frown. 'I know how worrying that must be for you, especially with her not living close by. You'll want to go to her.'

'Yes, I do… But are you sure it's all right?' She wanted to jump at the chance to leave but she had patients who needed to be seen.

'It's fine. I'll take over your case load. Don't worry

about it. I'm sure Molly will fill me in on some of the details.'

'Thanks,' she said, relieved.

She left the hospital a short time later, walking out into warm sunshine. The balmy weather seemed so at odds with what was happening.

She picked up an overnight bag from her flat. The news was dreadful and she was full of apprehension about what she might find when she caught up with her mother. It was a relief at least to know that Brodie was with her. She must be in shock and in terrible pain but it would be a comfort to her to have someone by her side. Caitlin would be eternally grateful to Brodie for the way he had responded to her mother's predicament.

Guilt and anxiety washed over her. She should have been there; somehow she should have been able to prevent this from happening… She tried as best she could, but it wasn't always possible for her to get away every week, with shift changes and staff shortages and so on. It was frustrating.

Her heart was thumping heavily as she drove along the familiar route towards her home town. She had the car window wound down so that she could feel the breeze on her face, but even the heat and the beautiful landscape of the Buckinghamshire countryside couldn't distract her from her anxiety.

How bad was it? Being a doctor sometimes had its disadvantages—she knew all too well how dangerous a hip fracture could be, the complications involved: perhaps a significant amount of internal bleeding and the possibility of disabling consequences.

She gripped the steering wheel more firmly. Think positively, she reminded herself. Her mother was in good hands and she would be there with her in just a short time.

A few minutes later she slid the car into a parking bay at the Thame Valley Hospital and then hurried into the Accident and Emergency department, anxious to find out how her mother was getting on.

'They've been doing some pre-op procedures, X-rays and blood tests and so on,' the nurse said. 'And as soon as those are complete the surgeon will want to talk to her. Mr Driscoll thought maybe you might like to have a cup of coffee with him while you're waiting. He asked me to tell you he's in the cafeteria.' She smiled and added good-naturedly, 'If you leave me your phone number, I'll give you a ring when it's all right for you to see your mother.'

'Okay, thanks, that'll be great.' Caitlin wrote down her number on a slip of paper and then hurried away to find Brodie.

He caught her glance as soon as she entered the cafeteria. 'Hi there,' he said with a smile, coming to greet her, his blue gaze moving fleetingly over her slender figure. She had discarded the hospital scrubs she'd been wearing and had on slim, styled black jeans topped with a loose, pin-tucked shirt. 'It's good to see you, Caitlin.'

'You too.' Her voice was husky, her breath coming in short bursts after her rush to get here. That was the excuse she gave herself, but maybe the truth was that it was a shock to see Brodie in the flesh after all these years.

The good-looking, hot-headed youth she remembered of old was gone and in his place stood a man who simply turned her insides to molten lava. This man was strong, ruggedly hewn, his handsome features carved out of…adversity, she guessed, and…success? There was something about him that said he had fought to get where he was now and he wouldn't be giving any ground.

He was immaculately dressed in dark trousers that moulded his long legs and he wore a crisp linen shirt, the sleeves rolled back to reveal bronzed forearms. His hair was black, cut in a style that added a hint of devilishness to his chiselled good looks. Tall and broad-shouldered, his whole body was supple with lithe energy, his blue eyes drinking her in, his ready smile welcoming and enveloping her with warmth.

'Come and sit down,' he said, laying a hand gently on the small of her back and ushering her to a seat by the window. 'Let me get you a coffee—you must be ready for one after your journey.' He sent her a quick glance. 'I expect you've been told that your mother is having tests at the moment? The surgeon's going to see her soon to advise her about what needs to be done.'

She nodded. 'The nurse told me.' She sat down, her body stiff with tension. 'How is my mother?'

'She's okay,' he said cautiously. 'She's been conscious all the while, and the paramedics were with her very quickly after her fall, so that's all in her favour.'

'I suppose that's something, anyway.'

'Yes. The doctor who's looking after her gave her a pain-relief injection so she's comfortable at the moment. She's had an MRI scan to assess the extent of the injury—it's definitely a fracture of the hip, I'm afraid.'

She winced. 'Will the surgeon operate today, do you know?'

He nodded. 'Yes. I was told it will probably be later this afternoon—the sooner the better, in these cases. Luckily she hadn't had any breakfast to slow things up. You'll be able to see her before she goes to Theatre.'

'That's good.' She finally relaxed a little and when he saw that she was a bit more settled he left her momentarily to go and get her a coffee.

Caitlin glanced around the cafeteria. It was a large room, with light coming in from a wall made up entirely of windows. The decor was restful, in pastels of green and cream, and there were ferns placed at intervals, providing a touch of the outdoors.

Brodie came back to the table with a loaded tray and handed her a cup of coffee. It was freshly made, piping hot, and it smelled delicious. 'I thought you might like to try a flapjack,' he said, putting a plate in front of her. 'Something to raise your blood sugar a little—you're very pale.' He took a small jug and a bowl from the tray and slid them across the table towards her. 'Help yourself to cream and sugar.'

'Thanks.' She studied him thoughtfully. She couldn't imagine what it would be like having Brodie as a neighbour. 'How is it that you came to be living next door to my mother?' she asked.

He sat down opposite her. 'I'd been staying in a

room at the pub,' he said, 'while I looked around for something more permanent. Then the place came on the market as a suitable property for renovation. The old gentleman who owned it found the upkeep too much for him when his health failed. He went into a nursing home.'

'Lucky for you that the opportunity came your way,' she murmured.

He nodded. 'It's a substantial property—an investment project, possibly—and I thought it would be interesting to do up the house and sort out the land that goes along with it.'

'An investment project?' It didn't sound as though he was planning on staying around for too long once the place was renovated. 'Does it mean you might not be staying around long enough to make it a home?'

He shrugged negligently. 'I haven't really made up my mind. For the moment, I'm fed up with living in rented accommodation and wanted something I could renovate.'

'I see.' She picked up one of the golden-brown oatcakes and bit into it, savouring the taste. 'I didn't get to eat breakfast this morning,' she explained after a moment or two. 'Someone emptied the cupboards of cereals and bread.' She spooned brown-sugar crystals into her cup and sipped tentatively, all her regrets about missing the first coffee of the morning finally beginning to slip away. He watched her curiously.

'You were right,' she murmured at last. 'I needed that.' She told him about her flatmate drinking the last of the milk. 'It had to be Mike who was the culprit. Neither of the girls I share with would do something like that. He probably finished off the cornflakes as well.'

Brodie grinned. 'I guess he's down for a tongue lashing at some point.'

Her mouth twitched. 'Definitely, if only so I can vent…not that he'll take any notice. He never does—why should he when he leads a charmed life?' She took another sip of coffee. It was reviving and she savoured it for a moment or two before her thoughts shifted to her mother once more. 'Can you tell me anything about what happened this morning with my mother? I'm guessing you must have been outside with her when she fell.'

He nodded. 'I was about to head off for a meeting. Your mother usually feeds the hens first thing, and then checks up on the rabbits, and we say hello and chat for a minute or two. Today she seemed a bit preoccupied—she was worried a fox might have been sniffing around in the night—so she didn't say very much. She started to pull a few weeds out of the rockery and I went to my car. Then I heard a shout and when I looked around she had fallen on to the crazy paving. I think she must have lost her footing on the rocks and stumbled.'

Caitlin winced. 'I've told her to leave the rockery to me. I see to it whenever I'm over here. This is why I worry about leaving her on her own for too long. She's not so nimble on her feet these days, but she's always been independent, and if something needs doing she'll do it.'

'You can't be here all the time. You shouldn't blame yourself.'

She sighed. 'I do, though. I can't help it. I love her to bits and I often think I should never have taken the job in Hertford. It seemed like such a good opportunity at the time.'

He nodded agreement. 'Jane told me you're a children's doctor; she's always singing your praises. She's very proud of your achievements, you know.'

Caitlin smiled. 'She's always been the same. She sees the best in everyone.'

'Yeah.' Brodie gave a wry smile. 'She was the only one who ever saw any good in me. Of course, she'd been friends with my mother since they were at school together, so that must have helped.'

'Yes, I expect so.' Sadly, Brodie's mother had died in a car accident when he was a teenager. That was probably another reason why Jane Braemar had taken him under her wing. Caitlin had lost her father and there had been an immediate bond between her and Brodie because of their shared circumstances. They had each understood what the other had been going through, and in their own way had tried to comfort one another. It had given them a unique closeness, and it had also been good, a source of consolation, that her mother had looked out for Brodie in his darkest times. She'd stood by him all through his unruly, reckless phase.

She hadn't been able to do anything to stem the tide of hostility that had grown among the locals with Brodie's exploits, though.

After a whirlwind period of rebellion—of cocky, arrogant defiance, trespass, petty vandalism, and a 'love 'em and leave 'em' way with girls—even Brodie must have realised he'd gone too far and that he'd worn out any vestiges of goodwill people might have felt for a motherless boy. He'd finally used up all his chances. On his eighteenth birthday, his father had kicked him out of the family home and Brodie had had to hunt around for somewhere to live. He'd stayed with various friends, Caitlin recalled, before he'd left the village a year or so later. At the time, she'd been broken-hearted. She'd suddenly realised she didn't want him to leave.

Her phone trilled, breaking into her thoughts and bringing her sharply back to the present day. 'My mother's back on the ward,' she told Brodie after a second or two. 'The nurse said she's a bit drowsy from the pain medication but I can go and see her.'

'That's good. It might help to put your mind at rest if you can spend some time with her.'

She nodded. 'Thanks again for looking after her,' she said softly, her grey eyes filled with gratitude. 'I owe you.'

'You're welcome any time, Caitlin.' He stood up with her as she prepared to leave. He reached for her overnight bag. 'Let me help you with that,' he said.

'Thank you.' She watched him lift the heavy bag effortlessly. In it, she'd packed everything she thought she might need over the next few days, including her hairdryer, laptop, make-up bag and several changes of clothes.

'Have you thought about what will happen when your mother leaves hospital?' he asked as they set off for the orthopaedic ward. 'She'll need a lot of help with mobility. Perhaps she could go to a convalescent home for a few weeks?'

She shook her head. 'That won't be necessary. I'd planned on coming back to live in the village in the next week or so—this has just brought it forward, that's all.'

He frowned. 'You're leaving your job?'

'Yes. I'll have to find something else, of course, but I'd made up my mind that it was something I needed to do.'

'Are you doing this for your mother's sake or for some other reason?'

'A bit of both, really.' He was astute—she should have known that he would suspect an ulterior motive. 'I have some personal reasons for wanting to leave.'

'There wasn't a problem with the job, then?'

'Heavens, no.' She looked at him wide-eyed. 'I love my work. I just hope I can find something as satisfying to do here.'

They approached the lift bay. 'Hmm. Maybe I could help you out there,' he said. 'No promises, but I've just taken over as head of the children's unit here and I'm fairly sure I'll be able to find you a position.'

She stared at him in disbelief. 'You're a doctor?' Not only that, he was in charge of a unit. How could that be?

He nodded, his mouth quirking. 'I know that must seem strange, with my background, but thankfully I managed to get my head together before it was too late. I used a legacy from my grandfather to put myself through medical school. I didn't know anything about it until the lawyers contacted me but as far as I was concerned it came in the nick of time.'

She was stunned. 'I can't get used to the idea—you were an unruly, out-of-control teenager. You were always playing truant, going off with some friend or other to spend time in the woods.' She shook her head. 'Are you making this up?'

He laughed. 'No, it's all true. I took stock of myself one day and realised I was going nowhere fast. For all that I missed out on some of my schooling, I managed to get through the exams without too much bother, so when I made up my mind what I wanted to do it wasn't too difficult for me to get a place at medical school.'

They stepped inside the lift. 'What made you decide you wanted to be a doctor?' She still couldn't get her head around it.

His mouth flattened. 'I think my mother's accident had something to do with it, although I didn't consciously think of it in that way until some years later. I did some work with troubled teenagers and then I spent some time helping out in a children's home, supervising leisure activities and so on. I suppose that's what guided me towards a career working with young children. They aren't at all judgemental and I think that's what I liked most. They accept you for what you are; I find I can get along with them.'

The lift doors pinged and opened out on to the floor where the orthopaedic ward was housed. Brodie walked with her to the doors of the ward and then handed over her bag. 'I'll leave you to go and spend some time with your mother,' he said. 'Perhaps you'll think over what I said about the job? We always need paediatricians and even though I'm fairly new to the hospital I'm sure the bosses will accept my judgement on this.'

'I will give it some thought, of course—though I can't help thinking you're taking a bit of a risk offering me something like that when we've only just met up.'

'I suppose some might think that. Actually, though, I know your boss in Hertford. Jane told me you were part of his team and I knew then you must be good at your job. He's a decent man; he picks out good people.'

Her mouth curved. 'It sounds as though my mother has been giving you my life history.'

'Like I said, she thinks the world of you.' He scanned her face briefly. 'In fact, your boss actually mentioned you to me once. He said he had this dedicated young woman, Caity, working with him—though at the time I didn't realise he was talking about you.' He was thoughtful for a moment or two, then added, 'If you like, if you're stuck for something to do while your mother's in Theatre, you could maybe come over to the children's unit? The surgery will take a few hours and rather than you waiting about I could show you around. I'm on duty, but you could tag along with me, if that doesn't sound too off-putting?'

She nodded cautiously. 'It sounds fine to me. Perhaps I'll do that.'

He smiled then turned and walked away down the corridor. She watched him go. He was tall, straight backed and sure of himself. He'd always been that way, but whereas once there had been a brash recklessness about him it seemed to have been replaced with a confident, shrewd perception.

He'd made up his mind quickly about her and decided she would be capable of doing the job. She had accepted his explanation but perhaps his decision also had something to do with knowing her from years before.

She didn't know what to make of him. He seemed calm, capable, efficient and friendly—all good attributes. But could he really have changed so completely? Were there still vestiges from the past lurking in his character?

He was certainly impulsive. Was he still the same man who had girls clamouring for his attention? He'd enjoyed playing the field back then; he and his younger brother had caused havoc among the village girls.

She remembered one girl in particular, Beth, who'd been upset when Brodie had broken off their relationship.

He'd told her things were getting too heavy between them. He didn't want to settle down, wasn't looking for anything serious. He was still young and the world was his oyster. He wanted to get out there and explore what was on offer.

Caitlin frowned as she pushed open the door to the ward. What was she to think? Could she work with a man like that?

His personal life shouldn't matter to her, but she couldn't help wondering about him. Was he still the same man at heart—a man who could turn on the charm, make a girl desperate to be with him and then when someone more interesting came along simply cut things dead?

Wasn't that exactly what Matt had done to her when Jenny had arrived on the scene? It had hurt so badly to be treated that way. She had never thought it possible that he could do such a thing.

The truth was, she simply didn't trust men any more. From now on, she would keep her independence and wrap herself around in an impermeable, defensive coat to ward off any attempt to break her down and make her vulnerable again. That way, no one could hurt her.

Even so…she thought about what Brodie had said. A job was a job, after all, and that had to be top of her priorities right now, didn't it? She'd be a fool to turn down his offer, wouldn't she? Maybe she would talk it through with him in a while.

A small shiver ran through her. Right now, all these years later, he seemed like a good man, someone great to have around in a crisis, but you could never tell, could you? Agreeing to come and work with him would be a bit like making a date with the devil…albeit a devil in disguise, maybe. Would she come to regret it before too long?

CHAPTER TWO

'HOW ARE YOU FEELING, Mum? Are you in any pain?' Caitlin sat by the bedside and reached for her mother's hand, squeezing it gently. It upset her to see how pale and drawn she looked.

'I'm okay, sweetheart. They gave me something for the pain. You don't need to worry about me. I'm just so glad to see you, but I'm sorry you were pulled away from your work.' Her mother tried to stifle a yawn and closed her eyes fleetingly. 'I don't know what's happening to me... I'm so tired.'

Caitlin smiled reassuringly. 'I expect there was a sedative in the injection you had. The nurse told me it won't be too long now before you go for your operation. That's good—they seem to be looking after you really well. I'm very pleased about that.'

Her mother nodded, causing the soft brown waves of her hair to flutter gently. 'They've all been so kind, explaining everything to me, telling me to take it easy and saying how I shouldn't fret. I can't help it, though—I keep thinking about the animals back home.' She frowned and Caitlin could see that she was starting to become agitated. 'They need to be fed and the crops have to be watered. It hasn't rained for a couple of days. With this warm, sunny weather everything will dry out.'

'I'll see to all of that,' Caitlin promised. 'You don't need to stress yourself about any of it. All you have to do is concentrate on getting better.'

'Oh, bless you—but there are so many things…' Her mother's brow creased with anxiety. 'You don't know about Ruffles' sores. He's the rabbit—someone brought him to me after they found him wandering in their garden.' She sighed. 'He needs a special lotion putting on his back. I should have collected it from the vet—I forgot to bring it home with me the other day. And the quail needs his claws clipping—he's another one a neighbour brought to me in a bit of a state. I was going to see to the clipping today—' She broke off, her breathing becoming laboured.

'It's all right, Mum,' Caitlin said in a soothing voice. 'Don't worry about it. I'll see to all of it and if anything else comes up I'll deal with that too.' She couldn't help but respect her mother for the way she coped with the smallholding, seeing to repairs, harvesting the crops and looking after various animals. Her mother had had a lot to cope with since she'd been widowed when Caitlin was a teenager, but she'd accepted the way things were, set to and got on with it. She was an incredible woman. 'Trust me,' Caitlin murmured. 'I just need to know that you're all right. Everything else will be fine.'

Her mother smiled wearily but she seemed comforted. 'I'm so glad you're home, Caity. I mean, I'm sorry for the reason for it—for this trouble with Matt, that must be so hard for you—but it'll be wonderful to have you close by.'

Caitlin patted her hand. 'Me too. I'm glad to be with you.' Even so, a faint shudder passed through her at the mention of Matt's name. She didn't want to think about him, and did her best to push him from her mind, but it was difficult.

She watched her mother drift in and out of sleep. It was worrying, not knowing how the surgery would go… It was a big operation… She'd already lost her father to a heart attack and she didn't want to lose her mother too.

She shook off those unreasonable fears. After the surgery her mother would need physiotherapy and would have to use crutches or a walker for some weeks or months.

'Oh, is she asleep?' A young porter came over to the bedside and spoke softly, giving Caitlin a friendly smile.

'She's drowsy, I think.'

'That's okay. It's for the best. It's time to take her to Theatre.'

Caitlin nodded and lightly stroked her mother's hair. 'I'll be here when you wake up,' she murmured, and the young man carefully wheeled his patient away.

'The operation could take up to three hours,' the nurse told her. 'You might want to take a walk outside, or go and get something to eat, if you don't want to go home. I can give you a ring when she's back in the recovery room, if you like?'

'Oh, thanks, that's really kind of you. I do appreciate it,' Caitlin said. She thought for a moment or two. What should she do? There might be time to go home. But perhaps she ought to follow up on Brodie's invitation… It was important that she found work quickly, though how she would manage her mother's day-to-day care when she was back home was another problem.

Decision made, she glanced at the nurse once more. 'Actually, I think I'll go over to the children's unit for a while. Dr Driscoll—the man who came in with her—said he'd show me around.'

'He's a doctor?' The girl's eyes widened. 'He must be new around here. I thought I knew most of the staff in the hospital. Wow! Things are looking up!'

Caitlin smiled. That was probably a fairly typical reaction from women where Brodie was concerned. He'd always turned heads. Perhaps she'd better get used to seeing that kind of response all over again. Of course, she knew how these women felt. Try as she might to resist him, she wasn't immune to his seductive charm.

She made her way to the children's unit, uneasily conscious of the quivering in her stomach now that she was to see him again. It was hard to say why he had this effect on her, but it had always been the same. There was something about him that jolted all her senses, spinning them into high alert the minute she set eyes on him.

The children's wards were on the ground floor of the hospital, a bright and appealing place with colourful walls, decorative ceiling tiles and amusing animal designs on the floor. There were exciting murals created to distract the children from the scariness of a hospital environment, and she noticed that the nurses were wearing patterned plastic aprons over their uniforms.

'Hi there.' The staff nurse came to greet her as she walked up to reception. 'I saw you admiring our wall paintings. They're very recent additions—Dr Driscoll brought in artists to do them the first week he started here.'

'Really?' Caitlin was astonished by that piece of news. 'My word, he doesn't let the grass grow under his feet, does he?'

'Too right. I heard he'd been talking with designers while he was working out his notice at his previous hospital. We all love the changes he's made. It's only been a few weeks and everything's so different here.' She paused by the entrance to the observation ward. 'You must be Caitlin,' she said with a smile. 'Am I right?'

'Well, yes…' Puzzled, Caitlin frowned. 'How did you know?'

The nurse's bright eyes sparkled. 'Dr Driscoll asked me to look out for you—he said I wouldn't be able to miss you. You had glorious hair, he said, beautiful auburn curls, and he told me what you were wearing. He's with a patient in Forest right now but he said to send you along.' Still smiling, she led the way. All the wards, Caitlin discovered, were divided into bays with names derived from the environment, like Forest, Lakeside, Beechwood.

'Ah, there you are,' Brodie murmured, looking

across the room, his mouth curving briefly as Caitlin entered the ward. 'I'm glad you could make it.'

She smiled in acknowledgment. He looked good, and the muscles in her midriff tightened involuntarily in response. He was half sitting on the bed. One long leg extended to the floor, the material of his trousers stretched tautly over his muscular thigh; the other leg was bent beneath him so as not to crowd out his small patient, a thin boy of around two years old.

'This lady is a doctor like me, Sammy. She's come to see how we're doing.'

Sammy didn't react. Instead, he lowered his head and remained silent, looking at the fresh plaster cast on his leg. Brodie sent him a quizzical glance. He silently indicated to Caitlin to take a seat by the bedside.

'His mother's with the nurse at the moment,' he said quietly. 'She's talking to her about the break in his leg bone and advising her on painkillers and so on.'

Caitlin nodded and went to sit down. She felt sorry for the little boy. With that injury perhaps it was no wonder the poor child didn't feel like responding.

Brodie turned his attention back to Sammy. 'Do you want to see my stethoscope?' he asked, showing it to the infant, letting him hold the instrument. 'If I put the disc on my chest, like this, I can hear noises through these earpieces...see?' He demonstrated, undoing a couple of buttons on his shirt and slipping the diaphragm through the opening. The little boy watched, his curiosity piqued in spite of his anxieties.

'Oh,' Brodie said, feigning surprise, 'I can hear a bump, bump, bump. Do you want to listen?'

The boy nodded, leaning forward to allow Brodie carefully to place the earpieces in his ears.

His eyes widened. Brodie moved the diaphragm around and said, 'Squeaks and gurgles, gurgles and squeaks. Do you want to listen to your chest?'

Sammy nodded slowly and, when Brodie carefully placed the disc on the boy's chest, the child listened, open-mouthed. He still wasn't talking but clearly he was intrigued.

'Do you think I could have a listen?' Brodie asked and he nodded.

Brodie ran the stethoscope over Sammy's chest once more. 'Hmm. Just like me, lots of funny squeaks and crackles,' he said after a while, folding the stethoscope and putting it in his pocket. 'Thanks, Sammy.' He picked up the boy's chart from the end of the bed and wrote something on it, getting to his feet and handing the folder to the nurse who was assisting.

A moment later, he glanced back at the child. 'The nurse will help you to put your shirt back on and then you can lie back and try to get some rest. Your mummy will be back soon. Okay?'

Sammy nodded.

Caitlin followed as Brodie walked away from the bed and spoke quietly to the nurse. 'There's some infection there, I think, so we'll start him on a broad-spectrum antibiotic and get an X-ray done. He's very thin and pale,' he added. 'I'm a bit concerned about his general health as well as the injury to his leg—I think we'll keep him in here under observation for a few days.'

'Okay.'

He left the room with Caitlin but at the door she turned and said quietly, 'Bye, Sammy.'

The infant looked at her shyly, not answering, and as they walked out into the corridor Brodie commented briefly, 'He seems to be very withdrawn. No one's been able to get a natural response from him.'

'How did he come to break his leg?'

'His parents said he fell from a climbing frame in the back garden. He'll be in plaster for a few weeks.' He frowned. 'The worry is, there was evidence of earlier fractures when we did X-rays. He was treated at another hospital for those, but the consultant there brought in a social worker.'

She looked at him in shock. 'Do you think it might be child abuse?'

'It's a possibility, and the fact that he's so quiet and withdrawn doesn't help. I'd prefer to make some more checks, though, before involving the police.'

She shook her head. 'I just can't imagine why anyone would hurt a child. It's unbearable.'

'Yes, it is. But Sammy's parents do seem caring, if a little naive, and at least he'll be safe here in the meantime.'

They went back to the main reception area and she tried to push the boy's plight to the back of her mind as Brodie began showing her around the unit. Each ward was set out in a series of small bays that clustered around a central point housing the nursing station. He stopped to check up on various patients as they went along.

'It's a beautifully designed children's unit,' she remarked some time later as they stopped off at the cafeteria to take a break for coffee.

'That's true,' he agreed, 'But I think there are things we can do to make it even better for the patients and their families. There are some children—like Sammy, perhaps—who need more than medicine and good nursing care to help them to get well. I want to do what I can to help them feel good about themselves.'

She sent him an oblique glance. 'That's a tall order,' she murmured, but perhaps if anyone could do it he could. He certainly seemed to have the determination to set things in motion. But then, he'd always had boundless energy and drive, even though he might have used it to the wrong ends years ago when he was a teenager.

'Well, if I'm to be any good at my job, I need to feel I'm making a difference,' he said. 'It's important to me.'

She studied him thoughtfully. He was an enigma—so focused, so different from the restless, cynical young man she had known before. 'That must be why you've come so far in such a short time. Your career obviously means a lot to you.'

'Yes, it does…very much so. I've always aimed at getting as far as I can up the ladder. I try to make all the improvements I can to a place where I work and then move on—at least, that's how it's been up to now.'

So he probably wouldn't be staying around here once he'd made his mark. She frowned. But this time he'd bought a house and he planned to do it up—would that make a difference to his plans? Probably not. Houses could be sold just as easily as they'd been bought.

He finished his coffee and then glanced at the watch on his wrist. 'I must go and look in on another young patient,' he murmured in a faintly apologetic tone.

'That's okay. I've enjoyed shadowing you, seeing how you work.'

He looked at her steadily. 'So, do you think you might want to work with us?'

She nodded. 'Yes—but only on a part-time basis to begin with, if that's possible. I'll need to be close at hand for my mother when she's back at home.'

He smiled. 'I can arrange that.'

'Good.' Her phone rang just then, and after listening for a while, she told him, 'My mother's in the recovery ward. I need to go and see how she's doing.'

'Of course.' He sent her a concerned glance. 'I hope she's all right. I know how worried you must be about her.' He went with her to the door of the recovery ward. 'Perhaps I'll see you later on, back at home?'

'I expect so.' She wasn't planning ahead, just taking one step at a time. It seemed like the best way to proceed at the moment. 'Thanks for showing me around, Brodie,' she said. 'Your children's unit is a really wonderful place and everyone involved with it is so dedicated. If children have to be in hospital, I think they're lucky to be here rather than in any other unit.'

'I'm glad you think so.' He smiled at her, pressing the buzzer to alert a nurse to release the door lock. 'It's been good meeting up with you again, Caitlin.' Somehow they had ended up standing close together, his arm brushing hers, and her whole body began to tingle in response. She didn't know how to cope with the strange feelings that suddenly overwhelmed her. It was bewildering, this effect he had on her. She loved Matt. How could she be experiencing these sensations around another man?

As soon as the door swung open she moved away from him, going into the ward. 'Thanks for coming with me and showing me the way,' she murmured, sending him a last, quick glance.

At last she could breathe more easily… But she hadn't been the only one to be affected by their momentary closeness to one another; she was sure of it. His awareness was heightened too. She'd seen it in his slight hesitation, the way his glance had lingered on her, and now she felt his gaze burning into her as she walked away from him.

How was it going to be, having Brodie living nearby? Part of her was apprehensive, worried about how things might turn out. After all, it was one thing to contemplate working with him, but having him as a neighbour could end up being much more than she'd bargained for.

She couldn't quite get a handle on what it was that bothered her about the situation, exactly. Over the last few weeks her world had been shaken to its foundations by the way Matt had behaved. She was unsettled, off-balance, totally out of sync. In her experience having Brodie close by could only add to her feelings of uncertainty. He was a spanner in the works, an unknown quantity.

She frowned. Perhaps the neighbour dilemma would only last for a short time, while her mother recovered from surgery. After that she could find a place of her own, away from Brodie, but near enough so that she could keep an eye on her mother and at the same time maintain her independence.

The nurse in charge of the recovery ward showed her to her mother's bedside. 'She's very drowsy, and unfortunately she's feeling nauseous, so it might be best for you to keep the visit short. She'll probably be more up to talking to you in the morning.'

Caitlin nodded. 'Okay.' She asked cautiously, 'Did the operation go well?'

'It did. The surgeon placed screws across the site of the fracture to hold everything in place and that all went quite satisfactorily. Your mother will need to stay in hospital for a few days, as you probably know, but we'll try to get her walking a few steps tomorrow. It seems very soon to get her on her feet, I know, but it's the best thing to do to get her on the mend.'

'All right. Thanks.' It was a relief to know that the major hurdle was over. Now the hard work of rehabilitation would begin.

Caitlin went to sit by her mother's bedside for a while but, as the nurse had said, she was very sleepy, feeling sick and wasn't up to saying very much. 'I'll leave you to get some rest, Mum,' Caitlin said after a while. 'I'll come back to see you tomorrow.'

She took a deep breath and left the hospital. At least her mother had come through the operation all right.

That was a huge relief. She could relax a little, now, knowing that she was being well looked after.

On the way home she called in at the vet's surgery to pick up the lotion that her mother had mentioned earlier.

'It's a mite infection,' the veterinary nurse told her after looking at the notes on the computer. 'You can't see the mites on the rabbit's skin, they're so tiny, but you might see dander being moved about.' She made a wry face. 'That's why the condition's sometimes known as "walking dandruff".'

Caitlin pulled a comical face at that, accepting the box containing the lotion that the nurse gave her.

'The vet gave Ruffles an injection,' the nurse said. 'But you need to put a few drops of the lotion on the back of his neck to get rid of any mites that are left. I think Mrs Braemar forgot to take it with her when she came here yesterday. He'll need another injection in eight days' time. Meanwhile, you could comb him to get rid of any loose fur and dander.'

'I'll do that. Thanks.'

Caitlin drove home through lanes lined with hedgerows, eventually passing over the bridge across the lock where brightly painted narrowboats were moored by the water's edge. Soon after that she came to a sleepy, picturesque village, a cluster of white-painted cottages with russet tiled roofs and adorned with vibrant hanging baskets spilling over with masses of flowers.

Her former family home was about half a mile further on, a rambling old house set back from the road, protected by an ancient low brick wall. There was one neighbouring property—Brodie's—but otherwise the two houses were surrounded by open countryside, giving them a magnificent view of the rolling hills of the beautiful Chilterns.

Trees and flowering shrubs surrounded the front and sides of her mother's house, adding glorious touches of colour around a lush, green lawn. Caitlin gave a gentle sigh of satisfaction. She always felt good when she returned home. Here was one place where she felt safe, sheltered.

Her old bedroom was just as she'd left it the last time she'd been here, about three weeks ago, except that her mother had laid a couple of books on her bedside table in readiness for her homecoming. Caitlin's mouth flattened a little. That had been unexpectedly brought forward by her mother's fall. She'd talked to her boss about it and he'd said she could take compassionate leave instead of working out her notice. It was a relief to know she had no worries there, at least.

She went into the farmhouse kitchen and made herself a snack of homemade soup from a tureen she found in the fridge, eating it with buttered bread rolls. The soup was made from fresh vegetables that her mother grew in the large kitchen garden out the back, and as she ate it Caitlin was filled with nostalgia. She had loved growing up here, having her friends to stay and her cousins to visit.

It was sad, then, that her cousin Jenny should be the one to steal the man she loved. Her fingers clenched on the handle of her spoon. How could things have turned out this way, leaving all her hopes and dreams cruelly shattered?

She pushed away her soup bowl and started to clear the table. Keeping busy was probably the best thing she could do right now. She made a start on various chores around the house, seeing to the laundry and collecting a few clothes and necessities to take into hospital for her mother. When she had done all she could in the house, she went outside to water the crops, and after that she made a start on the animal feeds.

True to form, as with everything that had happened so far today, she discovered from the outset things weren't going quite to plan. As she approached the hen house there was a sudden honking sound, an awful shrieking that made her cover her ears and look around to see what on earth was going on.

A trio of buff-coloured geese came rushing towards her, flapping their wings and cackling loudly. The male bird—she assumed he was male, from his aggressive manner—hissed at her and made angry, threatening gestures with his beak, while the other two kept up a noisy squawking.

'Go away! Shoo!' Her counter-attack made them stop for a second or two, but then the threats started all over again and she looked around in vain for a stick of some sort that she could wave at them. The way things were going, they weren't going to let her anywhere near the hen house.

'Get back! Shoo!' She tried again, frantically trying to keep them at bay for the next few minutes.

'Are you having trouble?' To her relief, she saw Brodie striding rapidly down the path towards her. Perhaps he would know how to stop the birds from attacking. 'I heard the racket they were making, so I came to see what's happening.'

'I don't think they want me around,' she said, concentrating her efforts on warding off the gander. 'In fact, I know they don't.'

'They're protecting their territory. Flap your arms at them and hiss back… You need to show them who's boss.'

She did as he suggested, waving her arms about and making a lot of noise. Brodie joined in, and to her amazement the geese began to back off. The gander—the male bird—was the last to give way, but eventually he too, saw that she meant business.

'Well done!' Brodie said approvingly when the birds had retreated. 'They're not usually an aggressive breed, but the males can be bullies sometimes, and you have to show them you're bigger and more fierce than they are. I'd say you've won that one!'

'Well, let's hope I don't have to go through that palaver every time I want to feed the hens. At least I'll be prepared next time.' She was breathing fast after her exertions and she was sure her cheeks must have a pink glow to them. 'I'd no idea Mum had bought some new birds.'

'She liked the idea of having goose eggs and thought the geese might sound a warning if any foxes came sniffing around.'

'Ah. I guess they're doing what she wanted, then. They're guarding the place.'

Perhaps he saw that she'd had enough of trouble for one day because he came up close to her and gently laid an arm around her shoulders. 'It hasn't been the best homecoming for you, has it? How about you finish up here and then come over to my place for a cold drink?'

'I...I don't know...' She was suddenly flustered, very conscious of his long body next to hers, yet at the same time strangely grateful for the warm comfort of his embrace.

He'd changed into casual chinos and a short-sleeved cotton shirt that revealed his strong biceps. The shirt was undone at the neck, giving a glimpse of his tanned throat.

'I...um...there's a lot to do; I still have to find the quail and clip his claws.' She pushed back the curls that clung damply to her forehead and cheek. 'I've never done it before, so it could take me a while to sort things out—once I manage to catch him, that is.'

'I can do that for you. He's in with the hens; your mother pointed him out to me a few days ago. She said wherever he came from, he hadn't been able to run around and scratch to keep his claws down, so that's why they need doing. It's not a problem. I know where she keeps the clippers.'

'Oh.' That would be a terrific help, one less problem for her to manage. 'Okay, then, if you're sure you don't mind?' Her excuses obviously weren't going to pass muster with him. Anyway, a cold drink was really, really tempting right now when she was all hot and bothered. She wiped her brow with the back of her hand.

'Good, that's settled, then. I do a great watermelon

and apple blend. I remember you used to like that.' He released her, but her skin flushed with heat all over again at the memory of hot summer days spent with her friends in flower-filled meadows.

Brodie and his brother had often come with them as they'd wandered aimlessly through the fields and by the river. They would stop to share sandwiches and drink juice or pop they'd brought with them. They had been fun days, days of laughter and innocent, stolen kisses in the time before Brodie had unexpectedly, disastrously, gone off the rails.

Together, they finished off the feeding then she watched as Brodie deftly caught the quail and carefully set about trimming the tip of each claw. 'These little birds get stressed easily,' he said, 'So it's best to get them used to being handled.' He placed him back down in the pen and the bird scampered off as fast as he could. 'He'll be all right now. I doubt he'll need clipping again now that he has a solid floor to run on and plenty of scratching litter.'

'Thanks for that.' Finished with all the chores for now, Caitlin locked up the pen and together they walked over to his house. It was a lovely big old property with a large, white-painted Georgian extension built on to an original Tudor dwelling. The walls were covered with rambling roses and at the side of the house there was an overgrown tree badly in need of pruning. The front lawn was dotted about with daisies and unkempt shrubs sprawled over the borders.

'I need to get the garden in order,' Brodie said ruefully, 'But I've had other priorities up to now, at work and back here.' He led the way along the path to the back of the house. 'In estate agent jargon, "in need of some renovation"; that can be interpreted in lots of ways,' he said with a wry smile.

She nodded, sharing the joke. 'I've always loved this house,' she said, glancing around. 'I expect it will need a lot of care and attention to restore it to its former glory, but it'll be worth it in the end.'

He nodded. 'I think so too. That's why I was so pleased when it came on to the market. I took to this house from a very early age. When I was about ten my friends and I used to climb over the wall and steal the apples from the orchard, until one day old Mr Martin caught us. We thought we were in big trouble, but he surprised us. He invited us into the house, gave us cookies and milk, then sent us on our way with a basket full of fruit.'

'He was a kind old man.'

'Yes, he was.' He showed her into the kitchen and she looked around in wonder.

'You've obviously been busy in here,' she said admiringly. 'This is all new, isn't it?'

'It is. It's the first room I worked on. I looked into different types of kitchen design and decided I wanted one where there was room for a table and chairs along with an island bar. This way, I can sit down for a meal and look out of the window at the garden; or if I'm feeling in a more casual mood, I can sit at the bar over there and have a cold drink or a coffee or whatever.'

She smiled. 'I like it, especially the cream colour scheme. You have really good taste.' She studied him afresh, surprised by the understated elegance of the room.

'Good taste for a rebel whose idea of fun was to spray graffiti on any accessible wall?' He laughed. 'I'll never forget that day you let rip at me for painting fire-breathing dragons on your mother's old barn. You handed me a brush and a pot of fence paint and told me to clean it up.'

'And you told me to forget it because the barn was old and rotting and ready to fall down—but later that night you came back and painted the lot.'

His brow lifted in mock incredulity. 'You mean, you've known all along who did it?'

She laughed. 'I never thought you were as bad as people said. I knew there was a good person struggling to get out from under all that bravado.' She'd understood him, up to a point, knowing how much it hurt to lose a parent. She'd turned her feelings inwards but back then Brodie had become more confrontational and forcefully masculine.

Smiling, he filled a blender with slices of apple and watermelon and added ice cubes to the mix. He topped that with the juice of a lime and then whizzed it up. 'That looks ready to me,' he said, eyeing the resulting juice with satisfaction. 'We'll take this outside, shall we?'

She nodded and followed him through the open French doors on to a paved terrace where they sat at a white wrought-iron table looking out on to a sweeping lawn. This was part of the garden that he had tended to, with established borders crowded out with flowering perennials, gorgeous pink blossoms of thrift with spiky green leaves alongside purple astilbe and bearded yellow iris.

He poured juice into a tall glass and handed it to her. 'I hope you still like this as much as you used to.'

She put the glass to her lips and sipped. 'Mmm... It's delicious,' she said. 'Thanks. I needed that.'

'So, what's been happening with you over the last few years?' he asked, leaning back in his chair and stretching out his long legs. He glanced at her ringless left hand. 'I heard you were dating my friend, Matt, until recently.'

She pulled a face, bracing herself to answer him. 'Yes, that's right. We were going to get engaged,' she said ruefully. 'But then things went wrong. Disastrously wrong.'

It was still difficult for her to talk about it but at the hospital where she had worked with Matt everyone knew the situation and it had been virtually impossible to escape from the questions and the sympathy.

He frowned. 'I'm sorry. Do you want to tell me what happened? Do you mind talking about it?'

'It still upsets me, yes.' She hesitated. 'He met someone else.'

Brodie studied her, his eyes darkening. 'I knew about that but I never understood how it came about. Matt and I haven't seen each other for quite a while. Was he looking to get out of the relationship?'

'No...at least, I don't think so.' She thought about it and then took a deep breath. 'It started about a year and a half ago. My cousin Jenny's car broke down one day and when Matt heard about it he offered to go and pick her up. Apparently she was in a bit of a state—she'd missed an appointment, everything had gone wrong and she was feeling pretty desperate. So he took her along to the nearest pub for a meal and a drink to give her time to calm down. Things just went on from there—he was hooked from that meeting. It was what you might call a whirlwind courtship.' She frowned. 'You knew Matt from school, didn't you? I suppose you know they're getting married soon?'

He sent her a cautious glance. 'I received an invitation to their wedding this morning.'

'Yes, so did I.'

'It was short notice, I thought. They must be in a hurry.' A line creased his brow. 'How do you feel about it?'

She exhaled slowly. 'Pretty awful, all things considered.' She picked up her glass and took a long swallow. The cold liquid was soothing, and she pressed the glass to her forehead to cool her down even more. 'They wanted to get married before the summer ends and the vicar managed to fit them in.'

He was thoughtful for a while. 'How are you going to cope with the wedding? Will you go to it? Yours has always been a tight-knit family, hasn't it? So I can see there might be problems if you stay away.'

'I don't know what to do. I feel hurt and upset. The thought of it makes me angry but, like you say, my family has always been close and if I don't go there could be all sorts of repercussions. I keep thinking maybe

I'll develop a convenient stomach bug or something on the day.'

He winced. 'I doubt you'll get away with that.'

'No.' She pulled a face. 'You're probably right.' She sighed. 'My mother's already upset because she might not be well enough to attend. Jenny's her sister's child. My mother and my aunt have always been very close. I suppose it all depends how well her recovery goes.'

'Let's hope it all goes smoothly for her.' On a cautious note, he asked quietly, 'Did Jenny know about you and Matt—about you being a couple? If she did, she must have known it would cause problems with your family.'

She shook her head. 'Not until it was too late. I was upset, devastated, but I tried to keep the peace for my aunt's sake and my mother's. But it's been hard, keeping up a pretence. I'm not sure how I'll get through the wedding without breaking down.'

She didn't know why she was opening up to him this way. It was embarrassing; she'd been humiliated and her pride had taken a huge blow. But Brodie was a good listener. He seemed to understand how she felt and she was pretty sure he wouldn't judge her and find her wanting.

'We could go to the wedding together,' he said unexpectedly. 'I'd be there to support you and we can put up a united front—show them that you don't care, that you're doing fine without him.'

'Do you think so? That would be good if it worked,' she said, giving him a faint smile. 'I'm not sure I could pull it off, though.'

'Sure you can. I'll help you. We'll make a good team, you and I, you'll see.'

She might have answered him, but just then a noise disturbed the quiet of the afternoon—the sound of footsteps on pavement—and a moment later Brodie's brother appeared around the back of the house.

'Hey there. I've been ringing the front doorbell but no one answered. I felt sure you were around somewhere because I saw the car.' He glanced at Caitlin and did a double take. 'Hi, babe,' he said, his voice brimming over with enthusiasm. 'It's good to see you, Caitlin. It's been a long time.'

'Yes, it has.' She was almost glad of the interruption. Anything and anyone that could take her mind off Matt was welcome. 'Hi, David. How are you doing?'

He was a good-looking young man in his late twenties with dark hair, brown eyes and a lively expression. 'I didn't know you were living in our part of the world,' she said. 'I thought you were settled in London.'

'I am, mostly, but we're doing some filming down here for the latest episode in the TV drama series *Murder Mysteries*—I'll bet you've seen it, haven't you? It's been on the screens for over a year. It's turned out to be really popular, much more so than we expected.'

She nodded. 'I've seen it. It's good—you've certainly found yourselves a winner there.' She studied him briefly. He too had come a long way in just a few years. 'I see your name on the credits quite often. So, am I right in thinking you write the screenplay?'

'I do.'

Brodie pulled out a chair for him and David sat

down. 'Do you want a drink?' Brodie asked, lifting the jug of juice.

'Sure.' He glanced at the pink liquid in the jug. 'It looks great, but is there a drop of something stronger you could put in it?'

'I can get you something from the bar if that's what you want.' Brodie sent him a thoughtful glance. 'Do I take it you're not planning on driving anywhere after this, then?'

David shook his head and sent Brodie a hopeful look. 'I was wondering if I might be able to stay here for the duration—while the research and the filming is going on.' He frowned, thinking it through. 'It could take several weeks, depending on what properties we need to rent, though the actual filming won't take more than a few days. Would that be all right?'

'Of course.' Brodie sent him a fleeting glance. 'You don't want to stay with Dad, then, at the Mill House?'

David sobered. 'Well, you know how it is. I love the old fellow but he's not much fun to be around lately. At least, not since…' He trailed off, his voice dwindling away as he thought better of what he was going to say.

'Not since he heard I was back in the village…is that what you were going to say?' Brodie made a wry smile. 'It's okay. I know how it is.' He pressed his lips together in a flat line. 'Things are still not right with us after all this time…' He shrugged. 'What can I do?' It was a rhetorical question. Caitlin sensed he didn't expect an answer. 'I've tried making my peace with him over the years, and again these last few weeks, but he doesn't seem to want to know. That's okay; I accept things as they are.'

Caitlin watched the emotions play across his face. Things had gone badly wrong between Brodie and his father and no one had ever known why. It had been the start of Brodie's resentment and rebellion; nothing had gone right for him for a long time after that.

'I'm sorry, Brodie,' David said. 'I'm sure he'll come around eventually.'

'Do you really think that's going to happen after all these years?' Brodie gave a short laugh. 'I wouldn't bet on it.'

'Maybe he'll get a knock on the head and develop amnesia. You'll be able to start over.' David grinned and Brodie's mouth curved at the absurdity of the situation.

'I guess we can see how you came to be a screenwriter, brother. You have a vivid imagination.'

David chuckled and turned his attention back to Caitlin. 'I'm sorry about that. You don't want to have to listen to our family goings-on. I can't tell you how great it is to see you again.' He looked her over appreciatively. 'You're absolutely gorgeous, even more so than I remember, and you were stunning back then. Are you going to be staying around here for long? That's your mother's place next door, isn't it?'

She nodded. 'I'm coming back to the village permanently. I'll be living with Mum until I can find a place of my own…for a few months, at least. That should give me time to find somewhere suitable.'

'Wow, that's fantastic.' He moved his chair closer

to hers. 'We could perhaps get together, you and I—go for a meal, have a drink, drive out to a nightclub in town. It'll be fun; what do you say—?'

'Don't even think about it, David,' Brodie cut in sharply, perhaps with more force than he'd intended. His eyes narrowed on his brother. 'I saw her first—way back when we were teenagers and now since she's come back to the village. Besides, she deserves someone with more integrity and staying power than you possess.'

'Oh yeah?' David's dark brows shot up. 'And since when were you the man to offer those things? You—the man who never settles with one woman for more than a few months at a time. I don't think so, bro. Get ready to move aside, man. Brother or no brother, this is a fair fight and Caity's a jewel worth fighting for. This is war.'

'Uh...do you two mind? Have you quite finished?' Caitlin looked from one to the other, deciding it was time to butt in before things got out of hand. 'I'll decide what happens where I'm concerned, and right now neither of you is in the running. From my point of view, you're probably both as bad as each other. So back off, both of you!'

David stared at her, looking reasonably chastened. 'Sorry, Caity.'

He soon recovered, shaking himself down and saying cheerfully, 'I think I'll go and hunt out a bottle of something from Brodie's bar, if that's okay?' He glanced enquiringly at his brother.

'That's fine.'

David left them, taking himself off into the house. Brodie looked back at Caitlin, a trace of amusement in his expression.

'You were always one to speak your mind,' he said. 'I like that about you, Caitlin. It's the barn incident all over again. You've never been prepared to put up with things you're not happy about.'

His smile was crooked as he added softly, 'Years ago, you told me we were a pair of hooligans on the rampage, David and me, not to be trusted. You weren't ever going to date either one of us…me especially, you said.' His face took on a sober expression. 'No matter how hard I tried, you'd never let me persuade you otherwise.'

'So the message was received and understood.' She smiled at him as she took a long swallow of her drink.

'Perfectly.' He returned her gaze, his blue eyes glinting. 'Of course, it's always been out there between us as something of a challenge. I know you like me and there were times when you might have been tempted to go against your better judgement. You do realise, don't you, that my feelings towards you have never changed?'

'Oh, you can't be sure about that,' she said. Even as she tried to make less of it, a tingle of excitement ran through her. 'It's been a long time… Perhaps you only want what you can't have.'

'I don't know, Caity. Perhaps you're right. Things happened when I was a teenager, things that made me question who I am and what I could expect out of life. I always wanted you, that's for sure. I just wasn't certain that I deserved you. I still have doubts, but seeing you again has brought all those feelings back to the surface.'

The breath caught in her throat but she ran her finger idly around the rim of her glass to give herself time to think. Why would he feel he didn't deserve her? Was it because of his behaviour back then, because it had been out of control?

Surely now, more than ever, she had to guard her heart against being hurt?

She said slowly, cautiously, 'It isn't going to happen, I'm afraid. I think we both know that. I'm totally off men right now. They're far too fickle for my liking.'

'Hmm.' He studied her, taking in the faint droop of her soft, pink lips. 'We'll have to see about that.'

CHAPTER THREE

'I KNOW IT's going to be terribly difficult for you this afternoon,' Caitlin's mother said worriedly. She was sitting in a chair by her hospital bed; now she shifted uncomfortably, wincing at a twinge of pain in her hip.

'Yes.' Caitlin's answer was brief. The day of the wedding had come around all too soon for her liking. Her emotions were all churned up inside her, though it wasn't only the forthcoming nuptials that bothered her. A fortnight had gone by since her mother had first come into hospital and after a brief spell at home she had been readmitted. It was distressing.

'Your aunt's desperate for everything to go off smoothly. She's been stressed about one thing and another for some time now.' Her mother's grey-blue eyes were troubled. She winced again, moving carefully as she tried to get comfortable. Small beads of perspiration had formed on her brow. 'She keeps saying how you and Jenny used to be so close.' She frowned. 'I wish I could be there to give you some support.'

Caitlin nodded, acknowledging her anxieties. 'I know.' Soothingly, she dabbed her mother's brow with a damp cloth. There was no way she could leave hospital, let alone go to her niece's wedding.

Instead of making good progress in the last couple of weeks, a nasty infection had set in around the site of the surgical incision, causing her mother a lot of pain and discomfort. Caitlin was worried about her. The consultant had inserted tubes in the wound to try to drain away the infected matter but it was turning out to be a slow process. No one knew how the infection had started but Caitlin suspected it had crept in when the dressing was changed.

'I'm pretty sure Jenny hasn't told her family that Matt and I were already a couple when they met,' she commented softly.

Her mother's brows rose in startled disbelief. 'Oh, you don't think so? Heavens, that hadn't occurred to me. It's probably the general stress of the wedding that's getting to her.'

Of course, if Caitlin didn't turn up for the celebrations this afternoon, her aunt would soon realise something was badly amiss and would want to know what was going on, wouldn't she? Caitlin felt more despondent than ever. Even more reason why she should go along to the event—yet all her instincts were clamouring for her to stay away.

She pushed her own problems to one side and sent her mother a quick, sympathetic look. 'It's rotten for you to be stuck in hospital today of all days. I know you were looking forward to seeing Aunty Anne and having a good chat—but she did say she would come and see you as soon as she could get away.'

'Yes, I'll look forward to that.' Distracted momentarily, her mother patted the magazines that littered the bed. 'At least I have plenty of reading material to keep me occupied in the meantime. Thank you for these.' She smiled. 'So how's the new job going? It was good of Brodie to set you on, wasn't it?'

'It was…' He'd been nothing but kind and helpful so far, but Caitlin couldn't help but think he had an ulterior motive. Hadn't he more or less said so that afternoon in his garden? He wanted to change her mind about men—and about him in particular. Could he do that? A tingle of alarm ran through her at the prospect. Of course he couldn't. That would be unthinkable. Talk about jumping from the frying pan into the fire. When he'd left the village years ago, she'd tried to forget about him, put him from her mind. It had been far too upsetting to dwell on what might have been.

'It's going all right so far, I think,' she said. 'The unit runs very smoothly—everyone knows their job and we all seem to work well together. I'm sure a lot of it's down to Brodie being in charge. He's very organised and efficient, and extremely good with people. Somehow, he always manages to get them to do what he wants.' It was remarkable how people responded to his innate charm.

Her mother nodded agreement. 'I'm amazed how well he's doing. Whoever would have guessed he'd turn his life around like that? I mean, I always liked him, but when he went so completely off the rails as a teenager it was upsetting. His poor mother didn't know where to turn.'

'Hmm.' Brodie's problems had started some time before his mother's death and Caitlin had never been able to find out the root cause. 'Maybe leaving the village was the making of him. He had no choice but to fend for himself, and I suppose that was bound to make a man of him. Of course,' she added with a wry inflection, 'Discovering he had an inheritance must have been a huge boost.'

Her mother nodded. 'True, but he could have gone the other way, you know, and squandered it. Instead, he put it to good use. I think he turned out all right. He seems to be a good man, now, anyway.' She frowned. 'Though I have heard he's still restless, still can't settle.' She sighed then hesitated, sending Caitlin a quick look. 'Does he mind that you keep coming up here to see me in the middle of your work?'

Caitlin shook her head. 'No, not at all…in fact, he's encouraged me to come to see you. He wants to know how you are. He's very fond of you. Anyway, I use my break times to slip away from the unit, so there's no real problem.' She glanced at her watch and gave her mother a rueful smile. 'In fact, I should be heading back there right now. I've a couple of small patients I need to see before I can go home.'

'All right, love. You take care. I'll see you later.'

'Yes. Try to get some rest.' Caitlin gave her a hug and hurriedly left the room.

Brodie was checking X-ray films on the computer when she returned to the children's unit a few minutes later. He shot her a quick glance as she came over to the desk to pick up her patient's file. 'How is your mother?'

'She's not feeling too good at the moment, I'm afraid…though she'll never complain.' She pulled a face. 'The site of the incision's still infected and she's feverish. The doctor's prescribed a different course of antibiotics and some stronger painkillers, so all we can do now is wait and see how she goes on. This setback isn't helping with her rehabilitation.' She sighed. 'It's all been a bit of a blow. We were hoping she'd be able to come home in a couple of days' time but that's definitely not on the cards now.'

'I imagine she's upset about missing the wedding?'

'Oh yes, that too.' Her mouth made a crooked line. 'I think she's secretly hoping I'll be her eyes and ears there. I imagine she'll want to see a video of the highlights on my phone—though she won't come out and ask.'

He smiled. 'It would probably help her to feel better about not being there, but I'm sure she's more concerned about your feelings.'

'Mmm. Maybe.' Even at this late stage Caitlin was desperately looking for a way out. Perhaps she could manufacture a sudden headache that would incapacitate her? Or maybe her car would develop an imaginary mechanical fault at the last minute?

Matt and Jenny were being married mid-afternoon, so as to accommodate relatives who were travelling from some distance away, and Caitlin was becoming more and more twitchy as the morning wore on. In a way, she was glad she'd chosen to come into work for a few hours to keep her from thinking too deeply about the situation. From when she'd woken earlier today, her whole body had been in a state of nervous tension.

She skim-read the notes in her four-year-old patient's file. 'I have to go and look in on the little boy who has pneumonia,' she told Brodie. 'I sent him for an X-ray before I went to see Mum and I'm hoping the results are back by now. He's not at all well: breathing fast, high temperature... He's on antibiotics and supplemental oxygen as well as steroid medication. Hopefully, it should all start to have an effect soon.'

'You're talking about Jason Miles?' Brodie brought up the boy's details on the computer. 'Here we are. Radiology have sent the films through.'

Laying the file down on the table, she studied the images on screen and frowned. 'That looks like an air-filled cyst on his lung, doesn't it? No wonder he's uncomfortable, poor little thing.'

'It does. What do you plan to do?'

'I'll leave it alone for now—it's best to avoid surgical intervention, I think. I'll put him on intravenous cefuroxime and see if that will do the trick. As the pneumonia improves, the cyst should start to disappear.'

He nodded. 'Good. I think you're right. That's probably the best course for now.' He sent her a sideways glance. 'Is he your last patient for today?'

'I just want to look in on Sammy to see how his fractured bone is healing. He went home for a while, didn't he, with a social worker overseeing things... but he's back in today for a check-up?' She frowned. 'Do you still think the other earlier fractures are suspicious? I know the social worker pushed for police action and Sammy's parents are distraught… They're overwhelmed by all the accusations being laid at their door. They're due to appear in court soon —he could be taken into foster care. Yet they do seem to be a genuine couple to me.'

He was silent for a moment or two, thinking it through. 'You could be right about the parents. I've spoken to them about taking extra precautions with him, though they insisted they were already being really careful.' His brow creased. 'I'm beginning to wonder if we aren't dealing with some underlying disease that could cause the bones to fracture more easily than most. I think we should get a blood sample for DNA testing along with a small skin biopsy and send them off to the lab. We'll need to keep an eye on the boy in the meantime—have him seen in the clinic on a regular basis.'

'Okay. I can set that up before I leave.'

'Good.' He leaned back in his chair and studied her. 'So, I'll come and pick you up after lunch, shall I—around two-thirty? Then we'll head off to the church?'

'Um…' She ought to have been expecting it but the reminder still caught her off guard. 'I…um…well, you know, I was thinking… It might be embarrassing for Jenny to have me there. I know her mother dealt with a lot of the invitations, so I'm not necessarily Jenny's choice as a guest.'

She wriggled her shoulders slightly. 'Perhaps it would be for the best if I were to send a message to say something's cropped up—an emergency at the hospital or some such. I mean, it's true, isn't it? Jason's very poorly—maybe I should come back here to keep an eye on him?'

He shook his head, his mouth quirking a fraction. 'You know that won't work, Caitlin, don't you? You're not an emergency doctor and we have people here who will take excellent care of him. You're trying to find excuses, when instead perhaps you should be facing up to things. You need to deal with this, once and for all, instead of running away.'

Her grey eyes narrowed on him. Coming on top of all her worry and apprehension, his comment seemed a bit like a reprimand.

'Are you saying I'm a coward?' After everything she'd been through, the thought irritated her, and she reacted in self-defence. 'Why should I be the one who has to suffer? *They're* in the wrong. Why do *I* have to pay the price for what *they* did?'

'Because you won't be able to live with yourself if you don't,' he said in a matter-of-fact tone. 'Sooner or later, you have to face up to the fact that it's over between you and Matt. He's in love with someone else. See it and believe it. Isn't that what you're running away from? The truth?'

'How can you be so heartless?' Her voice broke and she stared at him, frustration welling up inside her. 'Do you have no feelings? Is that all relationships are to you—off with the old and on with the new?' A muscle flicked in his jaw but he remained silent and she went on. 'What about the aftermath? It's so easy for you to shrug things off, isn't it?'

Resentment grew in her and all her past dealings with him came bubbling up to the surface. 'No wonder Beth was so hurt when you finished things with her. You didn't care too much, though, did you? Not deep down. As far as you were concerned it was just one of those things that happened from time to time. You changed your mind about her, didn't like getting in too deep, and decided to call a halt. It didn't matter to you how she felt, did it? You were ready to move on and you weren't about to look back.' She stared at him. 'How could I ever have believed you might have changed?'

'So this is all about me, now, is it?' His dark brows lifted. 'I don't think you can get out of it that easily, Caitlin, by turning everything around. You're the one who has the problem and the best way you can deal with it is to put on a brave face and go to the wedding.' His voice softened a little. 'I'll be there with you,' he said coaxingly. 'Show Matt you've found someone else, that it doesn't matter what he's done—that you and I are a couple, if that will make you feel any better.'

She looked at him aghast. 'You think I can do that with you—pretend that we're together, that we care about each other?' She gritted the words out between her teeth. 'I don't think so, Brodie. I'm not that much of an actress.'

To her surprise, he flinched, his head going back a fraction at her sharp retort. Obviously her dart had struck home.

'Is it such an alien concept? I'm sorry you feel that way,' he said quietly. 'Finding you after all this time, I was hoping we might be able to put the past behind us and move on, get to know one another all over again. I've always had feelings for you, Caitlin, and I thought this might be a chance for us to get together.'

Still upset, she said tautly, 'Did you? That's unfortunate, because it isn't very likely to happen. We're all out of fairy godmothers right now.'

She picked up Jason's file from the table and walked away from him. For her own peace of mind, she needed to put some distance between them. Her nerves were stretched to the limit. Deep down, though, she knew she'd gone too far, knew she'd said too much.

As she drove home some time later, she warred with herself over the way she'd behaved, over what she ought to do. Through it all she was still trying to find ways out of the mess she was in. How could she get out of going to this wretched wedding?

Back at home, it was some time before she could bring herself to admit that maybe Brodie was right. She couldn't keep running forever, could she?

She fed the hens and tried to think things through as she scattered corn and dropped a couple of carrots into the rabbit's run. By now the geese had learned to accept her and were grateful for a bucket of greens and a bowl of food pellets.

Why was she so convinced she could bury her feelings by pushing them aside, by hiding them away? Matt was marrying someone else. He didn't love her any more. Perhaps he'd never truly loved her because, if he had, surely this would never have happened? What was it Brodie had said? *Was he looking to get out of the relationship?* Perhaps Matt hadn't been consciously looking but somewhere a chink had opened up in the wall and opportunity had crept in.

She went back inside the house. She had to face up to this once and for all: go along to the wedding or berate herself for her weakness for the rest of her days.

Besides, no matter how bad she felt for Caitlin's dilemma, her mother would be desperate for pictures… She rolled her eyes, looking briefly heavenward. Then she took a deep breath and went upstairs to get ready. She'd burnt her boats with Brodie but somehow, when she met up with him at the church later on, she would have to do her best to put things right.

She'd bought her dress especially for the occasion, hoping it might help to boost her confidence. It was knee-length with a ruched bodice and a crossover draped skirt that fell in soft folds over her hips. A small scattering of spangles embellished the thin straps at the shoulders.

She pinned up her hair so that a few errant curls softened the line of her oval face then carefully applied her make-up, adding a touch of lipstick to her full mouth. A final spray of perfume and she was ready.

The doorbell rang as she came down the stairs. Her eyes widened as she opened the door to find Brodie standing on the doorstep.

He whistled softly. 'Wow!' he said in a breathless kind of way. 'You look beautiful. Are you quite sure there isn't a fairy godmother lurking around?' He peered into the hallway as if searching for the mythical figure. 'How else could you have made such a stunning transformation in such a short time?'

'Well, maybe she turns out for the odd emergency.' She smiled at him. 'You look terrific,' she murmured, giving him an appreciative glance. His grey suit was immaculate, finished off with a silk waistcoat and matching grey silk tie. 'I didn't really expect to see you here this afternoon after what I said to you earlier.'

He made a vague gesture with his shoulders. 'I guessed you were under a bit of a strain. We all say things we regret sometimes. Anyway, I was pretty sure you would change your mind about going.'

'What gave you that idea?'

'Keeping the family peace is important to you. Besides, I knew you wouldn't let your mother down, not when she's in hospital wanting to know what's going on.'

She laughed. 'You're right about that. Thanks for turning up.'

He gave her a crooked smile. 'We'll put in an appearance, then, if only to eat the canapés and drink the wine?'

'That sounds okay to me.'

'Good. The taxi's here already.'

She collected her bag and a light jacket then went with him to the waiting cab. 'Will your brother be coming to the wedding?' she asked. 'I haven't seen him around.'

He nodded. 'He's at the studios going over the screenplay for *Murder Mysteries* but he'll come straight from there.'

They arrived at the church in time to be seated by the ushers; in the hushed atmosphere, Caitlin's gremlins came back in full force. She had to steel herself against a rising tide of panic. She would not faint, she would not be sick, she wouldn't make a fool of herself by breaking out in a sweat… No way…this couldn't be happening…

Brodie reached out to her, covering her fingers with his palm. 'It's okay, you're doing fine,' he said softly. His voice and that reassuring touch of his hand on hers helped to calm her. 'Just think how many generations of families have married in this church. Weren't your parents married here?'

She nodded. 'Were yours?'

'Yes.' He looked around, frowning at something, and she saw that his brother had entered the church. The usher was showing Brodie's father and him to a seat a few rows behind theirs. She felt Brodie stiffen.

'You still haven't managed to make up with your father?' she asked in a whisper.

'No.'

'I'm sorry. I thought you might have had a chance to talk by now. Maybe you could have another go at the reception? A family occasion like this might be the ideal time for you to get together and patch things up.'

'Maybe, though I think it'll take more than a patch to mend things between us.'

The wedding service passed in a blur for Caitlin. Jenny looked beautiful in ivory silk, and Matt was tall and elegant in his tailored grey suit and silver cravat. Watching them, she felt a lump form in her throat, a sadness welling up in her for what might have been. A sick feeling burgeoned inside her.

Brodie clasped her hand firmly as they stood to sing the hymns. He wasn't about to let her sway or lose control and she would be eternally grateful to him for that.

At last the service was over and they went outside to pose for photographs. She gulped in a lungful of fresh air. Brodie's arm went around her waist and she glanced up at him briefly, reading the intent, unmistakeable message in his gaze. He would be there for her. She was safe. She gave him a faint, answering smile and, when she looked away a moment or two later, feeling calmer, she saw that Matt was watching her, a bemused, quizzical expression on his face.

Yes, it was perfectly true, she was safe…for now, at least.

They went on from the church to a hotel where a wedding banquet had been prepared for them. Everything was beautifully set out with lovely flower arrangements as centrepieces on the dressed tables and soft floor-length drapes at the windows reflecting the silver-and-lilac colour scheme.

'Have something to eat…you'll feel better for it.' Brodie wasn't listening to any excuses about not being hungry as they sat down at their allotted table. He tempted her with delicate morsels of crispy confit duck and delicious forkfuls of beetroot carpaccio flavoured with lemon, dill and finely chopped red onion. He held them teasingly to her lips until she capitulated.

'All right, all right,' she laughed. 'I'll eat.' She

glanced at all that was on offer. 'It looks wonderful,' she admitted.

David and Brodie's father were seated close by but, although the brothers spoke to one another in a relaxed fashion, the tension between Brodie and his father was noticeable. The older man was straight-backed, uncomfortable, speaking in monosyllabic tones, while Brodie for his part seemed guarded. He tried several times to open up a conversation with his father but the result was stilted and went nowhere. Caitlin watched them cautiously, slowly sipping her red wine.

Eventually, to her relief, the dinner and the speeches were over and it was time for music and dancing. Matt and Jenny started things off with the first waltz then Brodie took Caitlin's hand in his and led her on to the dance floor.

He drew her into his arms and held her close. 'I've been wanting to do this, it seems, like for ever,' he murmured. 'You're gorgeous, Caity, irresistible. And you've been so brave—I wanted to hold you tight and tell you everything was going to be fine. You're doing really well.'

She was glad of his embrace just then. It saved her from thinking about Matt and Jenny whirling around the dance floor locked in each other's arms. 'I couldn't have done any of this without you,' she said with a rueful frown. 'I think I'd still be at the hospital with Jason, if it wasn't for you.'

He made a wry smile. 'I'm sorry if I upset you back then. Matt's a fool for going off with someone else. I can't imagine why he would behave that way—you're beautiful and fun to be with and I can't think what went wrong between you to make him do that. I hate to see you hurting, Caitlin, but I wanted to shake you out of your negative state of mind. You wouldn't have felt right if you'd backed off.'

'Maybe not.' She gave in to the flow of the music and succumbed to the lure of his arms as he swept her around the dance floor. He held her easily, close but not too close, their bodies brushing tantalisingly as they moved to the rhythm of the band.

Perhaps it was the warming effect of the wine but it wasn't long before she found herself relaxing, wanting more, wanting to lean in to him and feel the safety of his arms wrapped even more securely around her.

'I think you should let me take a turn around the floor with Caity,' David said, coming over to them as the musicians took a break. He looked his brother in the eye. 'You've had her to yourself for long enough.' He glanced back at the seating area. 'Besides, it's time you had another go at talking to Dad.'

Brodie frowned, giving way reluctantly to his younger brother. 'Two minutes,' he said. 'That's all you're getting.'

'As if.' David's retort was short and to the point.

'Wow, what it is to be popular,' Caitlin said with a smile as David took her hand in his. The music changed to disco style and they moved in time to the beat opposite one another. She shot a quick look to where Brodie and his father stood side by side. 'I don't understand what went wrong between them. They were always uneasy with one another, I know that, but it was so much worse when he turned fifteen. And then, after your mother died, the animosity spiralled out of control.' She shook her head in bewilderment. 'Do you think they'll ever sort things out?'

'I suppose it's possible, now that Brodie's come back to the village to stay—at least for a while. He's never been one for putting down roots, has he? But that's probably down to the way things were back when he was a teenager. In a way, he's out of sync with the world and he can't seem to find his place in it. He can't settle but he can't move on because nothing feels right.'

She shook her head. 'None of that makes any sense to me.'

'No, well, it's up to Brodie to explain, I think. I wouldn't want to step in and cause even more chaos by trying to fathom what goes on in his mind. All I know is things won't be right with Brodie until he and Dad find some kind of closure.'

They danced for a while then David offered to go and get her a glass of wine from the bar. A late-evening buffet had been set out and there was a mouth-watering selection of food on display. Suddenly hungry, she chose a selection of West Country beef, mixed salad and warm, buttered new potatoes.

'You're feeling better, I see,' Brodie murmured, coming to stand alongside her and filling his plate with savoury tart, a charcuterie of meats, prosciutto, duck liver pâté and sausage, along with ricotta cheese.

'Yes, much better,' she said, surprised at herself. 'It's all down to wine, good food and the company, I expect.'

His gaze moved over her. 'Especially the company, I hope?'

She smiled. 'Of course.' She dipped her fork into a summer-berry meringue and revelled in the combination of sweet and tart flavours as the dessert melted on her tongue. They chatted for a while, enjoying the food, drinking wine and sharing reminiscences with David when he returned to the buffet table.

'I'm supposed to go and dance with the bridesmaids,' David said, draining his glass and placing it down on a tray. 'Jenny's orders. I think the blonde has the hots for me…except it could be simply that she's hoping to get a part in *Murder Mysteries*.' He squared his shoulders. 'Ah, well; a man has to do what a man has to do…'

They laughed and watched him go. 'Shall we go outside and get some air in the garden?' Brodie suggested when they had finished eating. 'I've been to a function here before—the terrace is lovely at this time of night. You can wander along the pathways and breathe in the night-scented flowers.'

'Okay, that sounds good.' She walked with him to the open doors that led out on to the balustraded terrace. It was, as he said, lovely, with soft, golden lighting and the fragrance of wisteria that bloomed in profusion against the wall. Further away from the building, alongside the pathways, were occasional trellises covered with honeysuckle and flowerbeds where sprawling nicotiana gave up its perfume.

As they walked, he put his arm around her and she loved the feeling of closeness. The night air was warm and full of promise. It would be all too easy to fall for Brodie, she conceded. He was attentive, supportive and he had the knack of boosting her confidence when she needed it most. But he wasn't the staying kind, was he? He'd never been one for commitment.

'How did you get on with your father?' she asked. 'I saw you talking to him. He seemed to have lightened up a bit.'

'He's had a drink or two. I guess that's the key to loosening him up and getting him to overlook my shortcomings, although he's never going to feel for me the same way he feels for David. He always favoured him.' He said it without rancour, as a statement of fact. 'When David came along the world was a brighter place and my father expected me to watch over him and keep him safe.'

She sent him a quick look. 'You didn't seem to mind doing that.'

'I didn't, not at all. We fought sometimes, we got into scrapes, but we were brothers. I think the world of him and I'd do anything for him.' His expression became sombre. 'My one regret was that I had to leave him behind when I left home. David didn't forgive me for a long time. He hated that I'd left.'

'I liked the way you took it on yourself to watch out for him. I'm sure he knew you weren't left with much of a choice but to go away, back then.'

She looked up at him as they stopped in the shade of a spreading oak tree. Moonlight filtered through its branches, casting them in a silvery glow. She leaned back against the broad trunk of the tree and he stood in front of her, sliding one arm around her waist.

She'd always liked him—wanted him, even—but always there had been this wariness whenever she was with him. Perhaps it was her youth that had held her back from him in those far-away days, the knowledge that he was at odds with the world, always in trouble, yet he didn't seem to care… There had been that element of danger about him. There still was. Being with him set her on a path of uncertainty—a path that could surely only lead to heartbreak because she still yearned for him. Even as she gazed up into his eyes and read the desire glittering in their fiery depths she recognised the folly of what she was contemplating.

'Caity,' he murmured, lifting a hand to brush her cheek gently. 'You're so lovely. You take my breath away.'

He bent his head towards her, his face so close to her that his lips were just a whisper away from hers. She longed to have him kiss her but she was confused, her emotions a maelstrom of doubt and insecurity. This day had started off with so many echoes of unhappy feelings, she didn't know how she could have come so far to wanting this…

A soft sound drifted on the night air, a footfall on the path just a short distance away, and as she looked out into the shadows she became aware of Jenny and Matt walking along the path, talking quietly to one another. They paused and stopped to gaze up at the moon.

Caitlin closed her eyes to shut out the image and then looked back at Brodie. His gaze was dark with yearning, smoky with desire; in that instant she lost herself, caught up in the flow of that heated current. She needed his strength right then, his powerful arms around her, everything that meant shelter and protection from the outside world. She ran her fingers up over his chest, lacing them around the strong column of his neck.

His kiss was gentle, coaxing, a slow, glorious exploration of everything she had to offer. His lips brushed hers, the tip of his tongue lightly, briefly, tracing the full curve of her mouth, seeking her response. She kissed him in return and in a feverish surge of passion he drew her close, easing her into the welcoming warmth of his taut, muscular thighs.

Her soft curves meshed with his hard, masculine frame and a ragged sigh escaped her, breaking in her throat. He kissed her thoroughly, desperately, his hands moving over her in an awed, almost reverent journey of discovery.

'Brodie…' She didn't know what she wanted to say…just his name was enough. She wanted him, needed him, longed for him to make her his.

And yet…wasn't he too strong, too male, too much of a driving force that would sweep her up and carry her along with him until he had done with her and was ready to move on? Perhaps she had always cared too much… She'd cared for Matt and he'd walked all over her; she cared for Brodie and he would eventually push her away. Could she handle that rejection, that awful nothingness that was bound to come?

But, then again, why shouldn't she experience once

and for all the joy that was his to give, theirs to share, a memory to cherish for all time? She needed him, craved his touch. Somehow in these last few heated moments she had lost all sense of caution, thrown inhibition to waft on the night breeze.

'Caitlin?' He spoke softly, urgently. 'I want you; you know that, don't you?'

She nodded, her gaze fixed on him, intent. 'Yes. I want you too.' It was a whisper.

A soft gasp escaped him. 'I don't want you to regret anything that happens between us... Do you understand what I'm saying?'

'Of course.' Her eyes widened, becoming luminous with unshed tears. 'Of course I understand. But why are you saying this?' Why was he bringing it out into the open, making her think about what she wanted to keep back?

'I know you only kissed me because Matt was there on the path with Jenny,' he said. 'I know why you did it and that's all right. I'm okay with that. I can handle it—at least, I think I can.'

He cupped her face lightly in his hands. 'And I know that you want me too, if only for the moment. But I need you to be sure about what you're doing. I have feelings too, you know. You mean too much to me, and I don't want to ruin what we have by sweeping you off your feet and then having you regret it.'

'I didn't set out to do this.' Her hands were trembling as she drew them back down his chest. 'I didn't mean for it to happen. I'm sorry,' she whispered brokenly. Tears trickled down her cheeks. 'Have…have they gone?'

He nodded. 'They've gone.'

'I'm sorry,' she said again. 'I don't know what I was thinking. I'm so sorry, Brodie.'

'Maybe there's a chance you could change your mind?' His dark eyes were brooding.

'No, there isn't.' She looked up at him, her whole body shaking. 'I can't do this.'

He pulled in a deep breath and seemed to steel himself. 'It's okay. Come on, then. I'll take you home.'

CHAPTER FOUR

THE KNOCK AT the door came as Caitlin was getting on with some chores upstairs before getting ready for work on Monday morning. She wasn't due to start her shift until later that day so up till now she'd been taking things at a fairly relaxed pace. Now, though, as the knocking came again, she frowned. It couldn't be Brodie wanting to see her, could it?

She wasn't ready to face him yet. She was still in shock from the way things had turned out on Saturday evening at the wedding reception. How could she have let things get out of hand that way? But wasn't she secretly, deep down, wishing she'd made a different decision? Why couldn't she have let things take their course, see where they led? The longing haunted her.

She hurried downstairs to answer the door. She would have to see him and try to work with him once more as if nothing had happened. How was she going to do that?

It would be so difficult…though how much worse would it have been if she'd given in to her feelings for him? Would she have regretted it the next morning?

Maybe not. A wave of heat surged through her. The more she thought about it, the more she had to admit that she really had wanted him for himself and not just because Matt had been there to muddle her thinking. Brodie had been wrong when he'd thought that; in truth it was Brodie who had managed to turn her world upside down, not Matt.

And how could that be? Matt was the one she was supposed to care for. He'd been the love of her life, hadn't he? Or had he? The truth was beginning to dawn on her and it was much harder to handle than she might have expected.

Could it be that Matt had been the consolation prize, the runner-up, the one she'd turned to because wanting Brodie all those years ago had been an impossible dream? She groaned softly in frustration. Why did Brodie have to come back into her life and confuse her this way?

The knocking came again, getting louder, and she called out, 'Okay, I'm coming.'

She opened the door, half-expecting to see Brodie standing in the porch, but instead she looked down to see a young girl of around ten years old. She recognised her from the village.

'Hello, Rosie. What can I do for you? Is everything all right?' Rosie didn't look all right. She was breathing fast, as though she'd been running, and her expression was anxious.

'Oh!' Rosie seemed put out. 'I thought you'd be Mrs Braemar.' The girl shook her head at her mistake. 'Hi. It's just—she always looks after the animals.' Rosie frowned and tried to gather her thoughts. 'We found a dog, see, a girl dog—along the lane—my friend and me. She stayed with it, Mandy did. We were playing in the fields, looking for wild flowers on our way to school—there are some summer activities going on there. I think the dog might be hurt.' She pulled a face. 'She doesn't want to move. Will you come and look at her?'

Caitlin thought quickly. The best place for an injured dog would be at the vet's surgery but that was way across town and she had to be at work this morning. Even so, if the animal was injured…

'Give me a minute, Rosie. I'd better call on the doctor next door and see if we can borrow his pick-up truck to go and fetch her.' Old Mr Martin had left the truck behind when he'd sold the house to Brodie and from what she'd heard it was still in working order. Brodie had used it to take unwanted bits and pieces of furniture from the house when he'd moved in.

'Okay.' Rosie prepared to wait patiently.

Caitlin rang Brodie's doorbell, more than a little apprehensive about meeting up with him once more. She'd not seen sight nor heard sound of him since the early hours of Sunday morning when the taxi cab had dropped them both off at home. It had been a moment fraught with tension and Brodie had acknowledged that, reaching for her, wanting to hold her once more. To her everlasting regret, she'd made an excuse and turned from him in a panic.

Now, though, he wasn't answering his door, so she

pressed the bell again more firmly until eventually she heard him padding down the stairs.

'Hi there.' Brodie was frowning as he opened the door, concentrating on rubbing at his damp hair with a towel. 'What's the problem?' Caitlin guessed he'd hastily pulled on trousers and a shirt after his shower. His black hair glistened and his skin was faintly damp where his shirt was open at the neck. He looked… He was breathtaking… She swallowed hard.

'Um…I…I wondered if…'

'Oh…hi, Caitlin.' He blinked, collecting himself, as if seeing her clearly for the first time. He straightened, suddenly alert, heat glimmering in his blue eyes. 'Come in.' He stood back to allow her access but frowned when she hesitated. 'Is something wrong? Is it your mother?'

'No…no, it's not Mum.' Though that was a worry in itself. She'd spent some time with her mother at the hospital yesterday and she'd not seemed well at all.

He looked beyond her, saw Rosie and frowned again. 'Has something happened?'

'Rosie's found a dog. She thinks it's hurt; I wondered if I could borrow the pick-up truck to go and get it. I don't know how badly it's injured.'

'Sure. Uh—give me a minute and I'll come with you. You may need a hand to lift it.' Brodie went along the hallway to dispose of the towel and grab his keys from a hook in the kitchen. Almost as an afterthought, he said, 'I'll get a blanket,' and took the stairs two at a time. A moment later he was back, saying, 'Okay, let's go, shall we?'

He smiled at Rosie and helped her into the cab of the truck, waiting while Caitlin climbed into the cab alongside the girl. 'Away we go, then. Show us where you found the dog, Rosie.'

'It's along the lane, near a lay-by,' Rosie said. 'We were playing by the stile. I don't think the dog belongs to anyone in the village—at least, I've never seen it before.'

They drove the short distance to the lay-by then they all piled out of the truck to go and see where the dog lay on its side in a wild-flower meadow by the stile. Rosie's friend was sitting down beside the animal, a golden-haired terrier, gently stroking its head.

'Hi, Mandy,' Caitlin said, going to sit beside her on the dew-misted grass. 'How's she doing?'

Mandy shook her head. 'She hasn't moved.'

'Poor thing, she looks exhausted.' Caitlin checked the dog over. 'Heavens, she's pregnant. Quite heavily pregnant, I'd say.'

Brodie knelt down beside them, lightly running his hand along the terrier's flank. 'She's very cold,' he said. He carefully examined the skin at the back of her neck, adding, 'And from the way her skin reacts she's dehydrated as well.'

Caitlin frowned. 'There's no name tag or anything to identify her. I wonder if she was abandoned in the lay-by last night? She must have wandered around for a while before settling down here.'

'More than likely. Of course, she may be microchipped—the vet will be able to tell us that. We'll get her home and warm her up—see if she'll take a drink—

and then decide what to do from there. I can't see any injuries anywhere but she'll need to see the vet as soon as possible.'

He lifted the dog on to the back of the pick-up truck and Caitlin clambered up beside her, wrapping her in the blanket and doing her best to soothe the panting, distressed dog. 'Good girl,' she murmured softly. 'You're doing okay. We'll look after you.'

Rosie and Mandy were standing by, watching everything and looking worried. 'Will she be all right?' Mandy asked.

'I think so,' Brodie answered. 'She's cold and worn out—very stressed, I imagine—but we'll take good care of her.'

'Thanks for letting us know about her,' Caitlin said with a smile, preparing to jump down from the back of the truck. Brodie held out a hand to her, helping her to the ground, and for a lightning moment as their bodies meshed a spark of stunning awareness flashed between them. Caitlin caught her breath and tried not to show that she'd been affected by his touch… Not easy, when she was tingling from head to foot. Did Brodie feel the same way? His smoke-blue gaze lingered for an instant longer on the pink flush of her cheeks before he reluctantly let go of her hand and turned back to the girls.

'Perhaps you should get yourselves off to school now,' he suggested quietly. 'You did well, both of you.'

'Okay. Can we come and see her later on?' Rosie's glance went to the back of the truck.

'Of course. Any time—though she might have to stay at the vet's surgery for a while.' Caitlin smiled.

'You saved her—you're bound to want to know how she's doing.'

The girls went on their way at last, chatting animatedly, and Caitlin climbed into the cab beside Brodie. 'I ought to stay with her until she shows signs of getting better,' she said. 'I don't know if she could cope with the journey to the vet right now. Will you be able to get someone to cover for me at the hospital if I'm a bit late?'

'Yes, don't worry about it. We need to be sure she's all right.'

'I can't imagine how anyone could abandon a dog like that. It's bad enough if it's a strong and healthy animal but a pregnant bitch… It's unbelievably cruel.'

'Yeah.' He was silent for a moment or two, deep in thought as he drove back along the lane towards the house. Caitlin noticed he drove slowly, carefully, so as to make a smooth journey for the ailing dog.

'You've always loved animals, haven't you?' she said now, thinking back to when he was a teenager. 'I remember once you found a rabbit that had been caught up in a snare and you nursed it back to health. You kept it in an outbuilding, didn't you, until it was time to set it free?'

'That's right.' He gave a wry smile as he pulled the truck into the driveway of his house and cut off the engine. 'It never did want to leave. I ended up taking it with me to medical school.'

She laughed. 'You're making it up.'

He gave her an exaggeratedly earnest look. 'Am not.

He listened to so many of my tutorials on the computer he could have taken the exam for me.'

They both chuckled then she said thoughtfully, 'There were other animals too: a stray kitten…and you kept pigeons in a shed at one time, didn't you?'

He nodded briefly. 'Until my father made me send them away. It was after my mother died. I don't think he would have done it before then because she always encouraged me in whatever I wanted to do. He said they were too messy, too noisy and there were too many of them.' He pulled a face as he sprang down from the cab. 'I suppose that last was true, in the end. More and more birds wanted to join the flock.'

'You must have found some comfort in looking after animals,' she said musingly. 'Perhaps it was because, when everything else was going wrong in your life, you always had them to turn to.'

He gave her a quick, half-amused look from under his lashes. 'You noticed that, huh?'

She nodded, being serious. 'Well, you used to come to my mother for advice on how to care for them. I could see how different you were around them. You were gentle, relaxed… Not the angry, hot-headed young man that everyone else saw.'

He smiled. 'Pets can be very calming. I was thinking of introducing pet therapy on the long-stay children's ward. It could do wonders for morale—if we bring in the right kind of animal, of course. They would have to be vetted for temperament.'

'Wow!' She stared at him. 'You amaze me, sometimes. I'd never have thought of it. But you could be right…'

He unclamped the back of the pick-up. 'We'll have to think of a name for this one. We can't keep calling her Dog or Girl, can we?'

She gave it some thought. 'How about Daisy, since we found her in a field full of them?'

He moved his head slightly, mulling it over. 'Okay,' he said at last then lifted the lethargic dog into his arms. 'Where shall I put her?'

'There's a kennel round the back…a proper one, with purpose-made quarters. I'll show you.'

She led the way to the kennel and he carefully laid Daisy down in a rigid plastic bed with half the blanket tucked under her for warmth. She didn't stir, but her brown eyes followed him and then flicked to Caitlin. 'You're safe now, Daisy,' she told her.

'I'll get another blanket,' Brodie said. 'Maybe she'll take some water.'

Caitlin stayed with her while he went to get what he needed. 'You'll be all right,' she murmured soothingly, stroking the dog. 'Good girl. I'm sorry you're in this state, but you'll be fine. Good girl.'

Brodie returned with the second blanket and gently laid it over the dog, tucking it in around her. She wouldn't take any water from the bowl he brought, and all they could do was stay with her and wait for her to warm up. Eventually, she accepted sips of water from Caitlin's hand.

After a while, Brodie glanced at his watch. 'I have to get to the hospital,' he said. 'I'm sorry to leave you, but at least she's a bit more responsive than she was half an hour ago. She's starting to look around a bit. Maybe she'll be strong enough for the journey to the vet now.'

'Yes. I'll take her. I'll give the vet a ring and warn him that I'm on my way.'

Brodie stood up and handed her the keys to the pick-up. 'She might as well stay in the bed. I'll carry it out to the truck.'

He made sure that Daisy was settled in the back of the pick-up once more and then glanced at his watch. 'I must go. I'll see you later. Good luck.'

'Thanks.'

She drove carefully into town, unused to the truck, and very conscious of the ailing dog in the back. It wasn't just one dog she had to worry about: the welfare of the unborn puppies was paramount too. Who could tell when Daisy had last eaten, and surely her blood pressure must be way down?

'Ah, we'll keep her warm and get her on a drip right away to replace the lost fluids and electrolytes,' the vet said, examining Daisy a short time later and giving Caitlin a friendly smile. 'She's young—around a year old, I'd say—so that's in her favour. There's no microchip, unfortunately, so we don't know who she belongs to. Anyway, leave her with us for a few hours and we'll see if we can get her to eat something. The pups seem to be okay—I can hear their heartbeats. I'd say she has a few days before she's due to give birth. I'll give you a call later to let you know how she's doing.'

'Thanks. It's such a relief to know that she's in safe

hands.' Caitlin stroked Daisy once more and said softly, 'I'll come back for you later. You'll be okay, I promise.'

She went from the vet's surgery straight to the hospital, keen to get started on her day's work. Luckily, she wasn't late, so she wouldn't feel guilty later at taking a break to go and look in on her mother.

'We've admitted an infant, three months old,' the staff nurse told her when she went over to the desk. 'He's feverish, with a swollen jaw and bouts of irritability and crying. I've spoken to the mother, and she's obviously distressed, so I'm going to get her a cuppa, calm her down and talk to her in the privacy of the waiting room.'

'That's great, thanks, Cathy. I'll go and take a look at him now.' It wasn't surprising that the mother was upset. Babies couldn't tell you what was wrong with them and it was heart-breaking to see such tiny little things miserable and in pain.

Caitlin held the baby in her arms and rocked him gently, trying to comfort him, and gradually he seemed to settle. 'I'll give him a quick examination—listen to his chest, check his ears and so on,' she told the nurse who was assisting her. 'But I'm going to need to do blood tests and get an X-ray to make a proper diagnosis.'

She worked as quickly and efficiently as she could, holding the child once more when she had finished, soothing him. 'I'll send these samples off to the lab,' she said. 'We should get the results back fairly soon.'

After that, she looked in on all her small patients, checking their progress and making sure they were comfortable and cheerful. Youngsters were resilient, she found, and recovery could come about sooner than expected. Four-year-old Jason, suffering from pneumonia, was sitting up in bed watching a DVD. She smiled, pleased he'd found the strength to take an interest.

'You should go and take a break,' Brodie said, coming over to her at the desk mid-afternoon. 'You haven't stopped since you got here.'

'I wanted to make sure I pulled everything in,' she told him. 'Working part-time gives me room to manoeuvre, but I worry about fitting it all in. The wards are at full capacity right now. We're very busy.'

'You're not on your own here,' he said. 'Don't try so hard. You're doing great.'

'I hope so.'

He nodded. 'Is there any news from the vet?'

She nodded. 'He rang to say I can pick Daisy up on my way home. She's a lot better in herself now—still a bit lethargic, but at least she's taking a little food and responding to people.'

He smiled. 'That's good. I'll look in on her later, back home, if that's okay with you?'

'Of course it is.' She glanced at him, a little anxious, uncertain how they would go on together. He'd made no mention of what had happened between them at the weekend but that kiss was seared on her memory for ever... The feel of his hands on her body was imprinted on her consciousness for all time.

He placed a file in a tray on the desk and she looked at those hands—strong, capable, yet at the same time gentle, seeking, magical...

'I...um...I'll grab a sandwich and go and find out how Mum's doing,' she said hurriedly, needing to distract herself. 'She seemed to have some kind of lung problem coming on this morning, so I'm hoping they've managed to sort it out.'

'Uh-huh.' His glance moved over her, slowly, considering, but she couldn't tell what he was thinking. Had he been able to read her thoughts? Surely not? Her cheeks flushed with heat. She was in enough of a quandary already, with her emotions all over the place.

Then he said softly, 'Maybe we'll find some time to talk things over...sort things out between us...? I care about you, Caity—I always have done—more than I can say.' He pulled in a sharp breath. 'Things were super-charged for you on Saturday—I knew that—and I should have taken heed. I shouldn't have let things get out of hand. It was my fault. But maybe we can move on from there?'

'Maybe.' The word came out as a whisper, but immediately she was filled with self-doubt. What was she doing even contemplating getting together with him? 'I don't know... I don't know what I was thinking...' She'd been hurt before—she wasn't about to put herself through that heartache all over again, was she? In the cold light of day it seemed like sheer folly to go from a broken relationship straight into Brodie's arms. What was she, some kind of masochist? 'I should go...'

She hurried along to her mother's ward and sat with her for a while, calming herself down, slowing the churning in her stomach by eating one of the sandwiches from the pack she'd bought.

'You seem stressed,' her mother said, watching her from her bedside chair. 'Is…everything all…right?' She reached for a paper hanky. She sounded as though she was out of breath and Caitlin's head went back a little in alarm.

'I'm fine.' She frowned. 'Mum, what is it? Are you…?' She stood up quickly as her mother began to cough and small flecks of blood appeared on the tissue.

Swiftly, Caitlin drew the curtains around the bed and called for a nurse. 'My mother's not well,' she told her as soon as she hurried forward. She quickly explained what had happened. 'I'm concerned this is a new development. Will you ask the consultant to look in on her, please? I understand he's still here in the department.'

The girl nodded. 'He ordered scans—they were done earlier this afternoon. I'll page him right away. He's on the next ward, doing a round of his patients.'

'Thanks.' Caitlin turned back to her mother, doing her best to make her comfortable. 'It could be a chest infection,' she told her, though she thought that unlikely with all the antibiotics she'd been given for her hip problem. A stronger possibility was that a blood clot had formed in her thigh because of her mother's enforced lack of regular activity. That clot could have broken up and spread to her lungs, where an embolus would cause a blockage. That could be very bad news, depending on how large it was.

The consultant appeared at her mother's bedside within a few minutes. 'I was going to look in on you very shortly, Mrs Braemar,' he said, 'but it looks like things are taking a bit of a turn. We'll get you started on some supplemental oxygen right away.' He indicated to the nurse to set that up then continued, 'I've had a look at your scans and I'm afraid there are a few small blood clots in your lungs. That's what's causing the pain in your chest and it's why you're having difficulty breathing.'

'Is it bad?' Her mother took short, gasping breaths, clearly worried.

'Not at the moment, my dear—not as bad as it might have been. The clots are small, you see, so we can start you on medication rather than having to do any more surgery.'

'Tablets, you mean?'

'Well, we'll give you intravenous heparin to start with, because that acts quickly. It will stop the clots from getting any bigger and will prevent any more from forming. At the same time I want to start you on warfarin tablets. They take two or three days to work and once they've kicked in we can stop the heparin.'

'So the clots won't get any…bigger but they'll…stay in my lungs?' Her mother looked bewildered and Caitlin hurried to explain.

'Your body will dissolve the clots gradually,' she said. 'You should start to feel better soon.'

The consultant patted her mother's hand. 'At least your hip infection is clearing up,' he said with a reassuring smile. 'That's one blessing.'

'True.' She made a weak smile. 'Bring on the rest.'

Caitlin stayed with her while the medication was started but left a little later when she saw her mother needed to sleep. The consultant had put a light slant on things but it was one more thing that Caitlin would worry about. Her mother had always been so active and healthy prior to these setbacks. It was upsetting to see her like this.

She was subdued as she went back to the children's unit. Her mother would be all right, she told herself; the clots weren't huge and although she was uncomfortable she was in no immediate life-threatening danger.

Brodie was tending a small patient with feeding difficulties when she went to check up on the lab results for the baby she'd seen earlier. He was in a nearby bay, setting up a drip feed so that the infant would receive nourishment after an abdominal operation. The baby cooed gently, enjoying the attention as Brodie made funny faces and wiggled his fingers.

Caitlin watched them for a moment or two, her heart full. He was a natural with children. Why, oh why, did he make her care for him so much?

He, in turn, glanced at her; he must have sensed that something was wrong because his expression was quizzical.

'Something wrong with your mother?' he asked.

She nodded, not wanting to talk about it right now. She needed to keep a firm grip of herself so that she could do her job properly. Instead of saying anything more, she turned away and went to look through the lab reports.

'How is your little fellow doing?' Brodie asked later on as she went to check on the baby she'd seen earlier. He looked down at the crying infant in the cot and held out a hand to him. The baby grabbed one of his fingers and pulled, wriggling his legs. Brodie smiled.

'He's not too happy right now,' she answered. 'He's been on indomethacin to alleviate the pain and try to reduce the swelling in his jaw but I think I'll add a corticosteroid to get things working a bit better.'

'Sounds good. Have you had the test results back yet?'

She nodded. 'They showed an elevated erythrocyte sedimentation rate and raised alkaline phosphatase among other things. After seeing the X-ray films, I think we're dealing with Caffey's disease.' She grimaced faintly. 'There are changes in the bones of his jaw and his thigh bones are wider than you would expect.'

'That was well spotted, Caitlin.' He looked at her with renewed respect. 'From what I know of it, it's a rare, not very well-understood disease—with a genetic basis, I believe?'

She nodded. 'It may be passed down through a parent, or it could be through a gene mutation. Of course, it may be rare simply because a lot of cases go undiagnosed in infancy.'

'Yes—they tend to resolve themselves in early childhood.'

'True. At least I can tell his parents that the disease is generally self-limiting and the bones should remodel themselves in a few months.'

She organised the new drug regime and then checked her watch. Her shift was coming to an end and she needed to go and collect Daisy and get her settled at home. She would need to buy tins of dog meat, kibble and maybe supplements to sustain the pregnant dog—hopefully the vet would be able to advise her on what to get. A comfy, padded base for the dog bed would come in handy too.

'You're off home?' Brodie walked with her to the exit doors.

'Yes, in a few minutes. I have to drop these lab forms off in pathology first. I thought I would take a shortcut through the quadrangle.'

He walked with her, stopping by the bench seat in the dappled shade of a silver birch. 'I'm due a break,' he said. 'Do you have time to sit for a minute and tell me what's going on with your mother? I've been to see her, but she always says she's fine, and I know she isn't.'

'Oh...of course, I'm sorry. You must be worried about her too. I keep forgetting how close you were back when...' Her voice trailed away. He wouldn't want to keep being reminded of the time when his life had taken a nosedive. 'She has some pulmonary emboli that are causing her problems—they're not too large, and the consultant's starting her on anti-coagulation therapy, so that should help things to get better.' They sat down beside one another on the bench.

'I'm sorry, Caity.' He wrapped an arm around her shoulders. 'I could see you were upset when you came back down to the unit. If there's anything I can do to help you, tell me—it must be a shock, everything that's happening.'

She nodded wearily. 'Things seem to be going from bad to worse. I thought I'd have her at home by now,

Brodie.' She gazed up at him in despair. 'She was always so active, into everything; it feels so strange, seeing her the way she is now.'

'Her consultant's a good man. I'm sure he'll soon have her on the mend.' He ran his palm down her back in a comforting gesture. 'She'll be back home with you before too long, you'll see. She's a fighter, your mum. Things will soon be back to how they were.' He smiled. 'You were always such a loving family unit—you, your mum and your dad.'

'Yes, we were.'

He sighed. 'I'm almost ashamed to say I envied you back then—you seemed to have everything I was missing out on.'

She looked at him in surprise. 'I'm sorry.'

'There was always something not quite right between me and my dad.' He shrugged. 'I think your mother recognised that and that's why she took me under her wing—David too, of course, after Mum died, though somehow he seemed to cope a bit better than I did. Yet your mother must have gone through agonies when your dad passed away.'

'Yes, it was bad. It was very sudden, a heart attack that took him before we could realise what was happening. But she managed to hold things together. I think she felt she had to, for my sake...and yours. David's too.' She glanced at him. 'My father's death helped bring you and I closer together, didn't it? It gave us a stronger bond...and my mother sensed that. I think she was pleased that we talked a lot because she knew we could be good for each other. She knew you were deeply troubled—not just about your mother—and she wanted to help.'

'We needed all the support we could get. She's a lovely woman. She was like a mother to me after my mum passed away. I always felt I could talk to her. She listened—she didn't always offer advice, but she was there for me whenever I was wound up, wanting to hit out, needing to offload because of some new quarrel with my dad. She usually managed to calm me down somehow.'

Caitlin frowned. 'What did you argue about, you and your dad? I never understood it. You were the oldest child, the firstborn—I'd have expected things to be very different. But, like you said, you and your father never seemed to get on.'

His mouth flattened. 'No, we didn't. I was never sure why, but nothing I did was ever good enough for him. The one, constant feeling he showed towards me was…irritation. In the end I learned to be guarded around him, I suppose. I tried to toe the line…until, one day, we had a terrible argument and everything came to a head and boiled over. I'd had enough at that point and I decided I wasn't going to put up with his hassle any more.'

She studied him, her grey eyes troubled. 'What happened? I wish I could help, Brodie. You never spoke about it, so it must have been something major. Can you talk to me about it? Whatever it is, I promise, I'll keep it to myself.'

'I know.' He idly caressed her shoulder, drawing her to him. He moved his head so that his temple brushed her cheek and the breath caught in her lungs. She wanted to hold him to her. He said quietly, 'I trust you, where I wouldn't trust anyone else—except my brother.'

She loved the closeness, the warmth, that came from him but after a moment or two he straightened and she felt the loss acutely. Pulling herself together, remembering their surroundings, she said cautiously, 'What was the argument about?'

He gave a wry smile. 'Actually, it was about David… or, at least, me looking after him. Dad was at work on the Saturday morning—Mum had a bad headache and was lying down. I was supposed to take David to a football training session but it was damp and drizzly and on the way there he said he didn't want to go. He was never that much into football. He said he was going to hang out with a girl instead, someone we met up with along the way. He said he didn't want me tagging along—he was barely twelve and they were just pals from school, nothing more. She wanted to listen to music back at her house, so I said it was okay.'

'But it didn't work out like that?'

He shook his head. 'A bit later on they apparently decided to go for a walk by the brook. Like I said, it had been raining earlier. David was a bit overambitious—showing off, I expect—and managed to slide down a steep slope, straight into the water. It wasn't deep but he fell in and finished up soaked through and muddy. Dad caught him before he had time to change his clothes. After that it was all hell let loose. I was the one in trouble because I hadn't been with him to watch out for him.'

Caitlin was puzzled. 'But that's the kind of thing most youngsters get up to. Why would it cause such a big problem, one that lasted for years to come? Did you both overreact?'

'We certainly did—big time. Dad said I was totally irresponsible…couldn't be trusted to keep my brother out of trouble. Of course I became defensive and argued back, asked why was it all down to me…why was he putting his job on to me? He was the father, wasn't he? Not that he'd ever been a decent father to me like he had to David, the favoured one… Et cetera, et cetera; I expect you know how it goes.'

'So you went too far?'

'Oh, yes…and he lost it completely. Said I wasn't his son so why would he care about me? He didn't give two hoots about me, just put up with me for my mother's sake.'

Caitlin gasped. 'Oh, Brodie… I'm so sorry. Was it true, what he said, or had he made it up on the spur of the moment?'

Brodie moved his arm from around her and brought his hands together in his lap, clasping his fingers together. It was as though he was totally alone in that moment; she wanted to reach out, wrap her arms around him and comfort him. He was rigid, though, his whole manner isolating himself from everyone and everything.

'Oh, yes. It was true. I asked my mother and she eventually admitted it to me. She was pregnant with me when she married my father, she said. He knew… He didn't like it, because she was having someone else's child, but he married her all the same. He just never wanted me and when I came along he couldn't bring himself to make a bond.'

Caitlin reached out and laid her hand over his. 'Did your mother tell you who your real father was?'

He shook his head. 'She didn't want to talk about him; said it was a fleeting thing—she made a mistake with a man who was never going to stay around for long. He was ambitious, wanted to go back to the city where he lived, wanted to make something of himself. She was a home bird, a country girl, and she didn't think she would ever be part of his world.'

'No wonder you went off the rails. You must have been so bewildered.'

'I was angry… Not with my mother—I could understand how she might have fallen for someone and how she turned to my dad when this man went away. She was always loving towards me, and there were endless rows between her and Dad over the way he treated me. He loved her, I'm sure, but he couldn't get beyond the other man who had figured in her life and things were never easy between them. We weren't what you'd call a contented family.'

She ran her hands lightly over his forearms. 'I wish I'd known at the time. Perhaps I could have helped, instead of being mad at you for the way you behaved. I knew there was a reason but I couldn't fathom it and I didn't know how to reach you…the real you.'

He gave a crooked smile. 'That's because he went

missing for a while.' His expression was sombre. 'Perhaps part of him is still beyond reach.'

She shook her head. 'You don't mean that.'

He looked at her, taking in the vulnerable curve of her cheek and the soft fullness of her pink lips. 'I don't know—I'm still unsure about a lot of things—but it makes me feel good to know that you wanted to reach out to me.'

'I'm glad about that.' She wanted to say more—to go on talking with him, get him to open up to her—but someone stepped out into the quadrangle and they moved apart. 'I should go,' she said and he nodded.

'Me too.'

CHAPTER FIVE

'YOU'VE BEEN BUSY.' Caitlin's mother looked at the basket of fruit Caitlin had brought for her. 'That's not all come from home, has it?'

'It has, actually.' Caitlin was proud of the amount of fruit she'd managed to harvest. It was mostly being sold at the local market but she'd gathered together an assortment for the gift basket. There were early fruiting James Grieve apples, a few pears, pink-skinned Victoria plums and some of the later varieties of strawberries. 'I thought it might help to cheer you up.'

It had also given her something to do, had helped keep her occupied outside of work. It gave her less time to dwell on situations that were fast running out of her control. Brodie had given her a lot to think about with his revelations about his father. His background meant that he probably still had a lot of self-doubt and she wondered if he would ever be able to make a proper commitment to her. She was falling for him all over again but for her own self-preservation she knew she should guard against losing her heart to him.

'Bless you, it's wonderful; a real treat.' Her mother

smiled. 'Oh, it makes me long to be back home. I can't wait to get back there and see how everything's going on.'

'I'm sure it won't be too long now,' Caitlin agreed, trying to give her some encouragement. 'You're certainly looking a bit brighter. There's colour in your cheeks and you seem to be breathing a little easier.'

'I am. I'm managing to get a bit further with the walking frame now before the lack of breath stops me.'

'That's good to know.' Caitlin smiled. 'And there's a bit of news I thought you'd want to know about—David has asked if the film unit can use the smallholding as one of their sets for an episode of *Murder Mysteries*. He said they would pay well, so I said I'd ask you. I didn't really think you'd have any objection. They promise they won't leave a mess, and the filming will all be done over two or three days. I think they especially want to use the barn and the area around the hen hut.'

'Oh, how exciting! Yes, of course that's okay. It'll be so interesting to see our home on the television, won't it? I wonder what they'll make of it? Oh, I can't wait!'

Caitlin chuckled. 'I thought you'd be all right with it. David's asked if we'll be extras and take part in the filming—Brodie and me—along with some of the villagers. Brodie's a bit wary but apparently the villagers are all really keen to get in on the act.'

'I'll bet they are…' Her mother started to cough, overcome with anticipation, and Caitlin frowned. She was looking better and it was all too easy to forget how ill her mother had been.

'Don't try to talk,' she said now. 'Just rest. I'll fill you in on what's been going on.'

'Yes…' Interested to know what was going on, her mother ignored her suggestion not to speak. 'Tell me about the dog you found. How is she?'

'She's doing fine. Rosie's mother drops by whenever she can while I'm at work to make sure she's okay. She and Rosie are helping to take her for walks.'

'Isn't she about due to give birth?'

Caitlin nodded. 'Could be today, according to the vet, so Rosie said she'd keep a special eye on her. I'm not sure what to look for, except the vet said something about temperature changes—she'll get a rise in temperature and then it will drop when she's about to go into labour.'

'You'll know when she's ready.' Her mother paused, getting her breath. 'She'll probably be restless.'

'I'll look out for that. I hope she's okay.' She glanced at her mother, making sure she was all right. 'She's such a sweet-natured dog. Here, I took a picture of her on my phone…' She showed her the photo of the shaggy, golden-haired terrier and told her how the vet had said to feed her on puppy food because it was higher in nutrients and therefore good for her while she was pregnant.

'Brodie comes over every day to see her and she follows him everywhere. At least, I think it's Daisy he comes to see.' She couldn't be altogether sure. They'd taken to sharing the occasional snack supper together of an evening, alternating between the two houses. He'd not pushed anything when it came to starting any kind of relationship with her but she had the feeling he was finding it hard to stay away. She was glad about that. She liked having him around.

A wave of heat ran through her at the direction her thoughts were taking and she quickly forced her mind back to the dog.

'She's fixated on him ever since he tucked the blanket around her and offered her a pull toy and a biscuit. I think she would up sticks and go and live with him if she could.' She made a mock-peeved expression. 'I'm not certain how I feel about that—I think I'm quite put out about it.'

Her mother laughed. 'He always did have a way with the girls.'

'True.' Caitlin didn't want to go too deeply into that. Despite her misgivings she'd come closer to him in these last few days than ever before and it invoked all sorts of exhilarating and tummy-tingling sensations inside her that she'd never experienced before—not even with Matt. But falling for Brodie was definitely not on the cards, was it?

'Are you and he getting on all right?' her mother asked.

'Yes, fine.' She sent her a guarded look. 'Why wouldn't we?'

Her mother shrugged lightly. 'I know how he used to look at you and how you kept putting up barriers—you didn't want to get involved with someone who kicked against the establishment and who seemed happy to play the field. I doubt he's changed that much. He doesn't go with the crowd or let the grass grow under his feet. He has his own ideas and likes to follow through.'

She paused, pulling air into her lungs. 'As to the rest, I've seen him with the nurses when he's come to visit me… They all think the world of him and the single ones are ripe for the picking. I really like him but I don't want to see you get hurt.'

A quick stab of jealousy lanced through Caitlin at the mention of the nurses, but just then a bout of coughing caught her mother out. Caitlin stood up and quickly handed her the oxygen mask that was connected to the wall-mounted delivery system close by.

'Here, breathe in slowly, steadily. Take your time.'

After a few minutes her mother was feeling better and she put the mask aside. 'I'm fine now,' she said. 'I just need to rest for a bit.'

Caitlin nodded, giving her an assessing look. 'Okay. I should be getting back to work, anyway. I've a new patient coming in and I need to look her over.' She gently squeezed her hand. 'I'll be back to see you later.'

She went back to the children's unit, pleased to see that a trio of small children who were able to get out of bed for short periods had gathered around the brand-new aquarium tank that Brodie had introduced to the ward. They were pointing, talking and smiling a lot.

'I see your tropical fish tank is a hit with the youngsters,' she told Brodie at the desk as she read through her patient's file.

He smiled. 'Yes, I noticed one or two of them going up to the glass and watching what was going on. They seem to like the shipwreck and submerged treasure chest, and the fish are colourful.' He brought up some CT scans on the computer screen. 'The next step for me, I think, is to develop a rehab garden outside so that children like Jason and maybe Sammy, who are recovering, can get their strength back by walking about outside on good days.'

'That sounds like an interesting idea.' She looked at him curiously. 'What did you have in mind?'

'Different levels. Nothing too high but raised flower beds, pathways, short flights of wide steps—providing the children have physiotherapists or parents with them to help them negotiate the obstacles. I thought maybe scented flowers and herbs, or different colours and textures, would go down well.'

'Something to attract wildlife, like birds and squirrels, would be good,' she said. 'So maybe you could put up a bird table and plant a variety of shrubs that have the right kind of berries.' She broke off, studying him once more. 'I think you have some great ideas, but where's the funding coming from?'

'There are hospital charities keen on helping out,' he answered. 'And I'll think about putting some of my own money into it. It all depends if I decide to stay here for the long term.'

She frowned at that. Was he really thinking of moving on?

He brought up X-ray films on to the screen of his computer then he frowned and pointed to the images. 'Have you seen these?'

'No. Whose are they?'

'They're films we had done recently to check

Sammy's progress. Along with the results of his DNA and collagen tests, I think we finally have an answer. We're dealing with a specific bone disease—*osteogenesis imperfecta*.'

She winced. 'Poor Sammy,' she said softly. The diagnosis, otherwise known as brittle bone disease, meant that his body didn't make enough collagen—the main protein building block of bone—so his bones and connective tissue, such as tendons and ligaments would suffer as a result. 'So his bones are thin and liable to break more easily than others.' She studied the films on screen carefully. 'It's difficult to detect from the X-rays alone.'

'But the bones are definitely thinner than normal—perhaps his case is mild and he's been unfortunate up to now.'

'Well, let's hope so. The physiotherapist is working with him because of the fracture but it'll be good for him to have ongoing therapy to help him regain his strength and mobility—safe exercise and activity to develop his muscle control.'

He nodded. 'His parents will need advice on nutrition—we can't replace the collagen, but we can make sure his muscles and bones are as strong as possible. Bisphosphonates are the mainstay of drug treatment as far as that goes.'

'I'll get things organised.' She gave a faint smile. 'The one good thing to come out of the diagnosis is that it means the parents are off the hook. It's going to be difficult for them to take it on board—a bittersweet experience.'

'But they'll have an answer at last and so will Social Services and the police.'

'Yes.' Caitlin hurried away to make several phone calls and to get the next phase of Sammy's treatment started. This was a case where she didn't want to waste any time. The parents had been weighed down by doubt, uncertainty and recriminations for long enough; perhaps now Sammy would truly start to make a recovery. It was hardly any wonder the child was quiet and withdrawn.

The rest of the day passed quickly. A little girl, Janine, was admitted with an infection and Caitlin ordered tests to find out what they were dealing with. 'I'll prescribe a broad-spectrum antibiotic,' she told the staff nurse. 'But when we get the results back from the lab we can prescribe a more specific drug.'

'Okay, I'll see to it,' the staff nurse said.

'Thanks.'

When her shift ended Caitlin was more anxious than usual to get home. Brodie came out of one of the bays where he had been examining a child and sent her a quick glance as she went to collect her jacket. 'You're off home, then? You look anxious. Are you worried about Daisy?'

She nodded. 'I am, a bit. Rosie's mother phoned to say Daisy was quite restless, so I'm expecting things to kick off any time soon.'

'I'll come and join you as soon as I finish here. I could pick up a Chinese takeaway on my way home, if you want? I know you like it and that'll be one less chore.'

'Ah, my favourite food…' she said with a smile. 'Beef and green peppers in black bean sauce—yum—and sweet-and-sour chicken. Oh, I'm hungry already at the thought of it.'

'Me too.' He said it softly, his gaze moving over her, lingering; somehow she had the feeling his mind wasn't simply dwelling on the prospect of food.

It was only after she'd left the hospital and was driving home along the country lanes that she wondered about the wisdom of spending too many of her evenings with him, especially this evening, when they were planning to share a mutual treat. It was one thing to throw a sandwich together out of expediency—quite another to make a date. Because that was what it seemed like, all at once. Things were moving too fast. It wasn't too long ago that she'd been looking forward to spending her free time with Matt and look where that had left her. She frowned. What was it about Matt that had made her think he was the one for her, when he so obviously wasn't?

Brodie turned up at the house a couple of hours later as dusk was falling. Caitlin had been watering the plants in the kitchen garden but now she turned off the tap and put the hose away.

'How is Daisy?' Brodie asked. 'Is anything happening with her?'

Caitlin nodded. 'She's definitely not herself. She's a bit agitated, so I brought her into the house—she's in the utility room. Her bed fits in there nicely under the worktop, and it's shaded from the sun during the daytime. She seems to like it there, anyway, so I'll probably let her stay. I left her rearranging her blanket. Come and see.'

She led the way into the house and Brodie put his packages down on the kitchen table. The appetising smell of Chinese food wafted on the air.

She hastily set plates to warm in the oven and then they looked in on Daisy. She looked up at them from her bed, panting, her tongue lolling eagerly.

'She looks happy enough, anyway,' Brodie commented, stroking the dog's head then heading back towards the kitchen. He washed his hands at the sink then helped Caitlin to set out the food.

'Has David said anything more about the filming?' Caitlin asked a while later as she nibbled on a hot spring roll.

He nodded. 'It's all going to start in a couple of days—they have the weekend marked up for it. He's even roped Dad in. Heaven knows how he managed it, but he's going to be kitted out as a farm worker, by all accounts.'

'You're kidding?' It was hard to believe that Colin Driscoll would ever have agreed to it. 'How do you feel about that?'

He lifted his shoulders briefly. 'I'm not sure. I suppose anything that gets us together is a good thing. We're both adults now and it's about time we sorted out our differences. He may not have wanted me around, but he brought me up from when I was a baby, so you'd think he'd have found some feelings for me along the way.'

He frowned. 'But then things happened... I started

acting up, and after I turned eighteen I stayed away, just coming back to see David whenever I could. It seemed for the best.' He raised his dark brows a fraction. 'Maybe, after all this time, Dad might be able to come to terms with the circumstances and finally find acceptance, though I think that's a tall order—for both of us.'

Caitlin mused on that. 'He was never the easiest man to get along with. Not in later years, anyway. He'd come over here to buy produce from my mother, but he was often brusque, and wouldn't want to stay and chat.' She dipped her fork into delicious fried rice and said thoughtfully, 'Have you tried to find your real father?'

He nodded. 'There's no father named on my birth certificate. Dad said he was a Londoner, someone who was setting up his own business, but he didn't know his surname or very much about him. I think he and Mum made some kind of pact not to talk about him. So finding him has always seemed like a non-starter.'

'I'm sorry. I can't imagine what that must be like, not knowing your parents.'

'You learn to live with it.' He speared a tender shoot of broccoli and rolled it around in the spicy sauce. 'There's always a part of you that's missing; when you do something or think something odd or slightly different from usual, you wonder if that's come from your absent parent. Genetics suddenly seem ultra-important, but there's not a thing you can do to find out the truth, so you have no choice but to bury the frustration inside.'

'David says you can't settle and you can't move on—

perhaps, like your dad, you need to find acceptance of some sort.'

He gave a short laugh. 'That's easy to say but not so easy to do in practice. David knows who he is, where he comes from. He's content with his life as it is. It's reasonably orderly and he doesn't need to think too deeply about what he wants from life. He assumes he'll have a great time now and settle down when he finds the right person. He seems to be fairly certain that will happen some day; I'm glad for him.'

'But you're not so clear about that for yourself?'

He shook his head. 'I've seen how people mess things up—I'm a direct result of that—and I don't want to be part of causing it to happen to anyone else. Perhaps I don't believe in the happy-ever-after. I wish I did. I wish it was possible.' He sent her a quick, almost regretful glance. 'For myself, I think I prefer to live in the here and now, and take things as I find them. If I can have fun along the way, that's great, but I don't make any long-term plans because I don't know what's around the corner.'

'That's what you were trying to tell me the other day, isn't it? I shouldn't look for anything more from you.' She studied him, her grey eyes solemn. 'I'm sorry about that—I can't help thinking it's a pity you can't put as much meaning into your personal life as you do into your work.'

He gave her a rueful smile. 'You're right. I do concentrate most of my energy in my work. That's important to me.' He frowned. 'I can't seem to help myself,

Caitlin. Maybe I don't want to think too deeply about anything else.'

'I thought that might be the reason.' Her mouth turned downwards briefly. 'But I suppose all the hard work is paying dividends. I've seen what you've managed to achieve at the hospital. The patients are well looked after, the parents are fully involved in their care and the staff are focused. I'm not surprised you've become head of a unit so early in your career.' She sent him a quizzical glance. 'This won't be your last stop, will it? You'll do what you need to do here and then move on to improve things at some other hospital.'

His blue gaze meshed with hers. 'I don't know about that. Right now I'm concentrating on the job here.'

They finished their meal and went to check on Daisy. There had been no sound coming from the utility room but now, as they looked in on the dog, they heard soft licking noises.

'Oh, my word, look at that!' Caitlin gasped as she saw two wriggling, sleek little puppies suckling at their mother's teats. Too busy to notice that she had visitors, Daisy was intent on licking them clean and only stopped when a third pup began to put in an appearance.

'Well, who's a clever girl?' Brodie grinned as he knelt down beside the dog bed. 'Look at you—you've managed it all by yourself.' Caitlin crouched down beside him and he put his arm around her, drawing her close. 'She's a natural,' he said. 'And there was me thinking we might have to help out, or call the vet if she got into difficulties.'

Caitlin was overwhelmed as she watched Daisy deliver a fourth then a fifth puppy, all perfect, all hungry and vying for a place where they could suckle. 'It's wonderful,' she said, thrilled to bits to see that they were all healthy and strong looking. She turned her head to look at Brodie and he smiled back at her.

'It is,' he agreed. He moved closer to her so that his lips were just a breath away from hers—then he kissed her, hard and fast, a thorough, satisfying kiss. She was so taken by surprise and caught up in the joy of everything that was going on that she kissed him back, loving the feel of his arms around her, loving the fact that they'd shared this momentous occasion together.

They kissed and held on to each other for what seemed like a blissful eternity, until there was a sharp rapping at the kitchen door and David was calling out, 'Anyone at home? Caitlin? Brodie?'

They broke away from one another as they heard the outer door open; David stepped inside the kitchen and came looking for them. Sure that her cheeks were flushed with heat, Caitlin looked back at the dog and her wriggling pups.

'We're in here,' Brodie said. 'We've had some new additions to the family.'

'Hey, that's great.' David came to look at the proud mother, kneeling down to stroke her gently and admire her offspring. 'Well done, Daisy. Are you all done, now? Is that it…five altogether? Wow!'

They watched the tableau for a while and then David

asked, 'Is that Chinese food going spare in the kitchen? Only, I haven't eaten for hours.'

'Help yourself.' Caitlin stood up. 'I'll get you a plate.'

'Cheers. You're an angel,' David murmured. 'Oh, and at the weekend, I thought you might want to play the part of a farm girl feeding the hens—Brodie can be hoeing the kitchen garden. I talked it over with the producer and he's okay with that. You don't have to say anything, just do the actions.'

Brodie followed them into the kitchen, frowning. 'So what's the scene all about?'

David took a seat at the table and helped himself to stir-fried noodles and chicken. 'It'll be mostly centred around the barn—the detective is looking for a suspect and asks the farmer if anyone's been hiding out in the barn overnight. The farmer says no, but then they find a bloodstain in the straw and after that the forensic team is brought in.'

'That's it?' Brodie raised his brows expressively.

'Yeah. It's an essential part of the drama. Someone was there, see, but the body has been moved.'

'The plot thickens.' Caitlin chuckled. 'What does your father have to do in the scene?'

'He'll be delivering foodstuff for the animals—unloading it off a lorry. I suppose Brodie could go and give him a hand—yeah, that would be good. It'll fit in with the red herring we planned: he looks like the man who drove the getaway car—our prime suspect.'

Caitlin smiled. 'What a pity the drama spans the TV watershed; the youngsters in the children's unit will be missing a treat—their favourite doctor on TV. Unless, of course, their parents let them stay up for the first half.'

Brodie's eyes narrowed on her. 'Please don't tell them. I'll never hear the last of it.'

She chuckled, but David said quickly, 'I think most people roundabout will know, sooner or later. The press will be on hand for the filming—you know the sort of thing: "*Murder Mysteries* will be back on your screens for the autumn. Filming is taking place now in the peaceful, picturesque village of Ashley Vale, Buckinghamshire. Local doctors have given over their properties for the recording..."'

Brodie groaned. 'Why did I ever agree to this? We'll have the local newshounds all over us as well as the national.'

Caitlin lightly patted his shoulder. 'Look on the bright side: you'll be out at work most of the time. Unless they follow you and find you there, of course...'

He groaned again, louder this time, and they laughed.

The film crew arrived early in the morning on Saturday to allow time for costume, make-up and setting the scene. David had the bright idea of putting Daisy and her puppies in a wooden feed trough in the barn. They would be written into the scene, he said—a means whereby the victim of the story was drawn to the barn. 'It'll be a sweet moment in the drama,' he said, 'Seeing them all golden-haired and snuggled together.' They were certainly thriving, getting bigger every day.

Dressed in jeans and a T-shirt, Caitlin duly went out to scatter corn for the hens. There was a moment of aggravation when the geese decided they needed to ward off the visitors, but after a few minutes of chasing about, she and Brodie managed to grab hold of them and shut them in one of the outhouses.

'I'll give them a feed of leftover vegetables and pellets to keep them happy,' Caitlin said, breathless after her exertions. 'I hope we haven't disrupted the filming too much.'

'I think they're used to happenings like that on set,' Brodie murmured. 'Besides, it's given you quite a glow—you'll look great on camera.'

So she was flushed and harassed already—not a good start. One of the extras was wheezing heavily as he walked by the barn to the lorry but she decided perhaps that was the part he was meant to play. Anyway, Brodie was with him, unloading sacks of grain, his shirt sleeves rolled up, biceps bulging.

She looked away, her own lungs unexpectedly dysfunctional all of a sudden. She began to spread corn over the ground, trying not to show that she'd been affected in any way by his sheer animal magnetism.

For his part, Brodie's father stood by the lorry and helped to unload the sacks. He and Brodie spoke briefly to one another in undertones as they worked, but their expressions were taut, businesslike. Brodie heaved another sack from the lorry and walked with it on his shoulder to the barn.

'Okay, thanks, everyone. That's a wrap on this scene!' the director said after a while. He went over to the film crew. 'We'll move on down the lane in half an hour and do the accident scene. David, you need to come along with us—I'm not sure the script works too well where the policewoman finds the overturned car with the woman at the wheel. She's on her way to meet her daughter at the farm but I'm not sure her feelings of anxiety are fully shown. Maybe you can tighten it up a bit.'

'Okay.' David winced briefly but he didn't seem too bothered by the request and Caitlin guessed he was used to being asked to make last-minute changes.

'An overturned car?' Brodie shot David a piercing look. 'You didn't mention that part of the script when you told me about the episode.'

David pulled a face. 'It was something the producer wanted written in to heighten the drama. There are only the main members of the cast involved, so I didn't think you'd need to know the details.'

Brodie's expression was taut. 'Don't you have any problem with it?'

David's mouth flattened. 'Of course I do—but it's my job, Brodie. I don't have a choice but to go along with things. You understand that, don't you?'

Brodie didn't answer. His jaw flexed and his eyes glittered, bleak and as hard as flint.

Caitlin watched them, two brothers deep in earnest conversation, and knew something was badly wrong. A car accident had featured heavily in their young lives—it had been the cause of major tragedy for both of them. Was that what was causing the tension between them now?

David glanced at her. 'I should have said something before this,' he murmured. 'It was bound to come as a shock…a reminder of what happened. I've had time to get used to it because I've been working on the original script for some weeks.' The director was on the move, briskly calling for the crew to follow him, and David looked back at his brother. 'I have to go. Will you be all right?'

'Of course.' Brodie's answer was curt but David clearly wasn't convinced. Once more, he looked at Caitlin and made a helpless gesture with his hands.

She gave an imperceptible nod. 'Brodie, let's go and get a coffee, shall we? And I need to let the geese out of prison as soon as the crew have gone.'

'They're all packing up and moving out along the lane. It shouldn't take them too long. I imagine it will be safe soon enough.' He walked over to the barn, calling out, 'I'll get Daisy and her brood.'

His father had already left, Caitlin noticed, and she wondered if that bothered him too. She'd invited Colin to stay behind for coffee and a snack earlier, but he'd declined the offer, saying he had to get back to Mill House. He was having problems with his roof.

Brodie installed Daisy and the puppies—three male, two female—back in their new home in the utility room and then came into the kitchen. Caitlin poured coffee into a mug and slid it across the table towards him. 'I see you let the geese out,' she murmured, glancing through the kitchen window. 'They've taken up position by the gate, just in case anyone tries to come back.'

He made a faint smile at that. 'It's good to know we

don't need a guard dog. I'm not sure Daisy would be up to the job right now.'

'I don't know about that. Wait till the pups are wandering about. I expect she'll be very protective of them—the mothering instinct will take over.'

Brodie's expression tautened and she quickly sat down opposite him at the table, placing her hand over his in a comforting gesture. 'What's wrong, Brodie? Do you want to tell me about it?'

'Nothing's wrong.' He stiffened, sitting straight backed, his gaze dark.

'Your mood changed as soon as you heard about the car scene. Perhaps it will help to talk about it.'

'I don't see how. Anyway, it was all a long time ago. It shouldn't…' His voice trailed off and Caitlin gently ran her hand over his.

'Did you ever talk about what happened? This is about your mother, isn't it? Why don't you bring it out into the open once and for all? Tell me what you're thinking. It might help.'

Angry sparks flared in his eyes. 'Don't you think David suffered just as much as I did? He lost her too, you know, and he was younger than me. She was a huge loss to all of us.'

'I know. But there's something that's been burning inside you ever since it happened. I saw it in your face after the accident. I knew there was something you weren't telling me…something you kept locked up inside. What is it, Brodie? Why can't you tell me what's wrong?'

He wrapped his hands around his coffee cup and

pulled in a deep breath, bending his head so that she wouldn't see his face. When he spoke, finally, it was almost a whisper. 'It was my fault,' he said.

She frowned. 'How could it be your fault? You weren't there. It was dark and there was a rainstorm—the roads were treacherous. She went into a skid on a bend in a country lane and the car overturned. How was that your fault? How could you even think it?'

'I was sixteen. I'd stayed out too long in town—way past when I was supposed to be home—and the buses weren't running. I didn't have the money for a taxi, so I phoned home and asked for a lift.'

His voice was low so she strained to hear what he was saying. He took a shuddery breath and went on, 'Dad answered the phone. He was furious because I'd been irresponsible and he told me to walk home in the rain. It was twelve miles, and I argued with him, kicked up a fuss, which made him worse. He was going to put the phone down on me but my mother came on the line and wanted to know where I was. She came out to fetch me because he refused.'

His hands clenched into fists. 'It was my fault she died,' he said. 'I should have walked home. In the end, the police came and found me and told me what had happened. My dad didn't speak to me for days.'

A small gasp escaped her. 'I didn't know…about the row, I mean. I'm so sorry, Brodie.' She stood up and put her arms around him. 'It was an awful thing to happen, but it wasn't your fault. Lots of teenagers get into scrapes and cause their parents hassle. You can't go on blaming yourself.'

'But I do.' He pulled a face. 'Logically, I know all the reasoning, the explanations—but in my heart I feel the guilt all the time. I don't feel I have the right to be happy. I didn't know how to handle it when I was younger, but later I decided to try to make some kind of reparation by going into medicine. It doesn't appease my guilt but it helps, a bit.'

'Believe me, you've done everything you can. And now you have to put it behind you. Your mother wouldn't want you to go on blaming yourself. She wouldn't want you to waste your life feeling guilty.'

His brow creased. 'No, perhaps not.'

'Definitely not. She was always there for you, Brodie. She loved you. She would want you to be happy. And I think she would have wanted you to make up with your dad.'

She rested her cheek against his. 'She would have hated the way your father reacted afterwards, not speaking to you, but have you ever thought that maybe, once he was over the initial shock, that he felt guilty too? You asked him to come and get you and he refused—maybe, if he'd been driving, he'd have handled the road conditions differently. Perhaps that's why you and he can't get on—you both feel that you're equally to blame for what happened.'

He sighed heavily. 'I know… I know…you're probably right. I've been over and over it in my mind. But I don't see how we can resolve things after all this time. I stayed away because I wasn't wanted but now I've come back here to work, he does his best to avoid me.'

'Does he? Are you sure about that?' She straightened, letting her arms fall to her sides. 'Why did he take part in the filming today? He didn't have to do it. He could have found an excuse and stayed away. But he didn't, Brodie. He came along, knowing you would be here. It isn't much, but it's a start. Don't you agree?'

'I suppose so.' His mouth made a crooked, awkward line. 'The truth is, I'm not actually sure I want to make up with my dad. He treated me harshly and it left a scar.'

'You've both been scarred. It's time to start the healing process.'

He gave her a long, assessing look. 'When all's said and done, I think that's what I like about you, Caity. You've always made me look at the big picture, made me face up to what I'm doing with my life; shown me what a mess I'm making…even if it's not what I want to know at the time.'

'Maybe I do it because I care about you,' she said softly. 'I don't think you're making a mess of things—you're doing the best you can in the circumstances. I want to help you. I don't want to see you hurting.'

And maybe she did it because she loved him…because she'd always loved him, though she hadn't always recognised it.

His revelations had shocked her to the core, but now she understood why he had so many doubts about himself. Perhaps this tragedy of his childhood, together with the uncertainty of his parentage and the difficult relationship with his father, were all part of the reason why he couldn't commit to love.

For herself, she had come to realise that her feelings

for him went very deep, far more than she had allowed herself to acknowledge until this moment. He might not feel the same way about her, didn't even know what he wanted right now, but she would look out for him all the same. She couldn't help herself.

CHAPTER SIX

'I HAVE TO go over to the hospital to deal with a couple of things that have cropped up,' Brodie said. It was Sunday morning; he'd surprised Caitlin by appearing on her doorstep some time after breakfast.

She was dressed casually in a short-sleeved shirt and pencil-line skirt that faithfully outlined her curves. She was inwardly thrilled that he appeared totally distracted for a moment as he looked at her, until he shook his head, as though to clear it.

'Uh, something...something's happened with one of your patients—a reaction to the medication she was prescribed—and I wondered if you want to come with me. It's Janine, the five-year-old with the chest infection.'

'Heavens, yes, of course I'll come with you.' She was appalled by the news and immediately on the alert. 'Is she all right?'

'I believe so. It looks as though she's allergic to the penicillin she was given this morning. Her throat swelled up, she was wheezing and she has an all-over rash. The registrar acted quickly to put things right, but obviously the parents are upset, so I want to go and talk to them.'

'Okay.' She made sure Daisy and the puppies were safely ensconced in the utility room and grabbed her jacket, going out with him to his car.

The roads were fairly clear of traffic but Brodie drove carefully as usual and appeared to be deep in thought. 'You're very quiet,' she commented. 'Are you worried about the situation at the hospital?'

He shook his head. 'These things happen. It's no one's fault, and the little girl is all right.'

'Okay.' She glanced at him, noting the straight line of his mouth. Was he dwelling on what they'd talked about yesterday, about his problems with his father? 'Is it your dad, then? Are you going to try to sort things out with him this afternoon when the film crew set up again?'

He shrugged. 'I haven't given it much thought. I prefer not to think about it.'

It was clear he wasn't going to talk about it and she was disappointed. Maybe that was selfish on her part, but she couldn't help feeling that sorting out the problems from his past was the key to his chance of true happiness for the future.

Would that future include her? Something in her desperately wanted to keep him in her life but, at this point in time, who could tell if it would come about? More importantly, would any relationship last? He had more than enough problems to overcome and, as for herself, she'd been through a lot of heartache; she didn't want to put herself through any more. Caring had been her downfall. Somehow, she had to be strong, put up defences and guard herself against being hurt.

And right now they both had more pressing matters to deal with. Of course he was right to stay focused.

At the hospital, Brodie showed Janine's distraught parents into his office and invited them to make themselves comfortable in the upholstered chairs. The room was designed to put people at ease—carpeted underfoot and fitted out with pale gold beechwood furniture.

'Unfortunately, Janine had an allergic reaction to the penicillin,' he told them. 'It's fairly unusual, but luckily the doctor on duty caught it quickly and gave her an injection of adrenaline. We'll give her steroid medication as well for a short time, and obviously she needs to have a different antibiotic.' He frowned. 'The allergy wasn't noted before this on her records, so I'm assuming this is the first time she's had a reaction like that?' He looked at the parents for confirmation.

The girl's mother nodded. 'She's always been healthy up to now and not needed penicillin. We were just so shocked when we saw what was happening to her.'

'That's understandable.' Brodie was sympathetic.

'I'm so sorry this happened to her,' Caitlin said. 'We hoped that the penicillin would resolve the problem of her infection but clearly she'll need to avoid it in any form from now on.'

'We'll inform her GP,' Brodie said. 'And a note will be made in the records. This shouldn't happen again but you'll need to tell any medical practitioner of the allergy if they plan on prescribing antibiotics for her.'

'We'll do that,' the father said. 'Thank you both for taking the trouble to come and talk to us. It's been a worrying time.'

'I know it must have been very distressing for you,' Brodie said. 'But I've spoken to the registrar and you can be reassured that Janine is all right. She won't suffer any long-lasting effects and the rash will fade in a couple or so days.'

They spoke for a little while longer then, as they were leaving the office, the staff nurse took Caitlin to one side. 'I have a mother here who is worried about her baby,' she said quietly. 'Seeing that you're here, would you have a word with her?'

'Of course.'

'You might as well use my office,' Brodie said. He lightly touched her arm in a gesture of reassurance. 'I expect this thing with the mother is something you can sort out easily enough.'

Caitlin hoped so too.

'I have to go and meet up with my animal therapy volunteer,' Brodie said. 'She rang me earlier to say she'd like to come in—but I'll catch up with you later.'

'Okay.'

The nurse handed her the baby's thin file and she skimmed the notes quickly. By the time the young mother arrived at the office with the infant in her arms, she was fully prepared.

'How can I help you?' she asked with a smile, inviting her to sit down in a comfy armchair.

'It's just that the surgeon tried to explain things to me, but I don't really understand what's happening to my baby.' The young mother held her baby close to her, wrapping her more firmly in her shawl and looking anxiously at Caitlin. 'Olivia's only five weeks old—she keeps being sick and she's losing weight. I'm really worried about her. Why can't she keep her milk down?'

'I know this is upsetting for you, but really, it's a simple, straightforward operation,' Caitlin answered kindly. 'I'll get some paper and a pen and see if I can draw it for you.'

Swiftly, she drew the outline of a baby's stomach, showing the opening into the intestine. 'Usually, see, the opening is wide enough to let the milk pass through—but sometimes the muscle here is thick and causes a blockage. When that happens, the milk can't get from the stomach to the intestine and the baby brings it back up. It's a forceful, projectile vomiting, as you've discovered, rather than a gentle regurgitation of excess milk.'

'How will the surgeon put it right? Is it a big operation? Will it leave a scar?'

'The incision will be very small, near the belly button, and there shouldn't be much of a scar at all, once it's all healed up. The surgeon will cut the muscle and that will cause the opening to be wider.'

'Okay, I get that, I think.' The young woman frowned. 'The doctor said she would be admitted to hospital today but they wouldn't operate until tomorrow. What does it mean? Will you be doing tests and so on?'

'Mainly for the next few hours we'll be making sure that she's not dehydrated—that's our biggest concern, so she'll have a fluid line inserted in a vein. It won't hurt her, but the repeated vomiting means she's lost a lot of fluid and it needs to be put right, along with minute traces of sodium and potassium and so on that might be out of balance. We'll need to do some blood tests to check that all's well.'

'All right.' The woman nodded, seemingly reassured. 'Thanks for explaining it to me.' She gently rocked the baby in her arms, soothing her. 'How long will she need to be in hospital?'

'Until about two or three days after the surgery to make sure she's feeding properly and that her temperature and blood pressure and so on are normal.'

The girl looked troubled. 'Will I be able to stay with her?'

'Yes, we have a room where you can sleep and still be close to Olivia. The nurse will show you where you can put your things—and if you think of any more questions, just ask. We're all happy to help.'

'Thanks.'

A nurse came to show her where the baby would be looked after and Caitlin, relieved that she'd been able to help, went in search of Brodie. He was in one of the patients' bays.

He smiled as Caitlin entered the room. A woman was with him, a slim, middle-aged woman with a kindly face, and she had a calm-looking yellow Labrador on a lead by her side.

Caitlin watched as the woman introduced the dog to the children. They patted and stroked him and Brodie was smiling, looking totally relaxed. Maybe a dog was good therapy for Brodie too, she mused.

'He's like a giant, cuddly teddy bear,' Jason said, laughing in delight. The four-year-old was getting on well now, off the oxygen for the most part, but having brief sessions with the nebuliser every few hours. He was sitting in the chair by his bed with his parents looking on.

The other little boy, Sammy, two years old and still with his leg in a cast, was much more reticent. He was in hospital briefly for further tests. He too was seated; now he cautiously reached out to touch the dog's head but pulled his hand back when the dog turned to look at him with big, brown eyes.

'It's all right, he won't hurt you,' the dog's owner told him. 'He loves children and he likes being stroked.' She crouched down to his level and demonstrated.

Sammy seemed to take to her. 'What's his name?' he asked in a timid voice.

'Well, we call him Toffee, because he's such a gorgeous toffee colour. I think it suits him, don't you?'

Sammy giggled. 'Toffee,' he said and giggled again. 'Toffee…' He bent over, laughing, as if he found that hilariously funny. Recovering himself, he looked at the Labrador once more and tentatively reached out to stroke him. 'Toffee's a sweetie, what you eat,' he said, chuckling.

Toffee's owner smiled and Sammy's mother said cheerfully, 'Well, he is a bit of a sweetie, isn't he? He's lovely.' She looked at the woman and then at Brodie. 'I'm so glad you brought him in to see us. It's been the best thing for Sammy—for Jason too, from the looks of things.'

Both boys were patting the dog now, their troubles forgotten for the time being. Caitlin relaxed, seeing her young charges happy and on the mend.

'That worked out really well,' she commented to Brodie when they went for lunch in the cafeteria. 'I'm glad we came in this morning.'

'So am I. Anyway, I wanted to be here when the dog was brought in. I think he'll be a great hit with the children. He certainly brought Sammy out of his shell.'

'He did. We'll have to try the dog with children who are in wheelchairs—there won't be any danger of them being accidentally nudged and he'll cheer them up no end.' They filled their trays with a Sunday roast dinner—beef, Yorkshire puddings with roast potatoes and an assortment of vegetables—and went to sit at a table in the far corner of the room.

Brodie glanced at Caitlin as he started to eat. 'I meant to tell you, I heard from Matt the other day.' His gaze was thoughtful, pondering. 'He phoned.'

'Oh yes?' She stared at him, suddenly very still.

'He's been back at work for a while now and he was asking about you. He wondered how you were doing.' She nodded slowly, taking that in, and he went on, 'He said to tell you the little boy you were treating—the one with the infection in his knee—is completely better now and fully mobile. He came to the outpatients' clinic the other day.'

'I'm glad about that.' Molly must have told him she wanted to follow up on the boy. She looked at Brodie guardedly. Matt hadn't phoned only to update her, had he? 'What did you say to him?'

He lifted a dark brow in query. 'About how you were doing?'

She nodded, not trusting herself to speak. She hadn't thought about Matt recently but now, at the mention of him, her palms were clammy and her mouth was dry. Her hand trembled a little so she laid down her fork and rested her fingers beside her plate. Brodie's blue eyes followed the action.

'I told him you were doing fine—no thanks to him, since he'd treated you so badly.'

She gave a small gasp. 'You said that? But Brodie, he's your friend…'

He shrugged. 'I couldn't say too much to him about it at the wedding—it was the wrong time—but I wanted him to know that I didn't like the way he'd behaved towards you.'

She shook her head. 'You shouldn't have done that—it was between me and him.'

His blue gaze was steady. 'He was my friend, yes, my best friend, so I could be straight with him. I didn't like it in the first place when I heard he'd started dating you; all kinds of bad feelings swept over me… jealousy, for the most part…but when he took up with Jenny I had mixed feelings. I was glad it was over between you because it meant you were free—but I was concerned for you.'

Her eyes widened a fraction. He'd been jealous? 'I'd no idea you were keeping tabs on me.'

'I've often enquired after you—talked to people

I know, kept in touch with your mother from time to time.' His mouth flattened. 'Anyway, I told Matt you were getting on well in your new job, that it was great living next door to you and I wished I'd moved in sooner. It's all true, of course.' His gaze meshed with hers.

She smiled faintly at his admission. It made her feel better, knowing he liked being near to her, and she expelled her breath in a soft sigh. 'I thought I was in love with him, that we would get married, but I had it all wrong, didn't I? How is it possible to make a mistake like that? It's left me so that I don't know if I can trust my feelings any more.'

'Yes, I know. But you could have ended up in a bad marriage. So maybe you had a lucky escape.'

She tried a smile. 'Then again, we could have been okay. Marriage is what you make it. It depends what you put into it.'

He shook his head. 'You'd both have had to work at it, and Matt obviously wasn't prepared to do that. Something must have been out of sync for him to go off with Jenny the way he did.'

'Yes, you pointed that out once before.' She pressed her lips together, trying not to let her emotions show. After all this time she was still on fragile ground, and she sensed that Brodie was pushing things, testing her to see if she would stumble.

'Have you given it any thought?'

She nodded. 'I have but I'm still not exactly sure what happened,' she said cautiously. 'All I can think is...' She took a deep breath. 'I've always tried to handle situations by myself the best way I can. Ever since my dad died, I've tried to be independent, to make sure Mum was all right. But Jenny was never like that. She needed help—with her car, with her state of mind. Things had gone wrong for her and she was a damsel in distress. She's often needy and I think that must have appealed to Matt. Perhaps he needs to be with someone who will rely on him for support. She brings out the protector in him, whereas I... Perhaps I don't have that same vulnerability.'

Brodie mulled it over as he slid his fork into green beans. 'I don't know about that—the vulnerability thing. I'd want to make sure you were okay, no matter what.' He ate thoughtfully for a second or two. 'You could be right, though. Matt does tend to want to take control.' He studied her as she picked up her own fork once more and began to eat. 'He's a fool, if he doesn't see what he let go.'

'Thanks for that. But perhaps it was for the best. I suppose it wouldn't have worked out for us in the end. I wouldn't want to be in a bad marriage. My parents were always good together, and their kind of relationship is what I want for myself.'

'I can understand that. That's probably why I've never felt the urge to try it. I don't want to make a mistake like my mother did with my real, my natural, father and then again with my dad. If it had been a good marriage, he would have handled things differently.'

'Perhaps...but they stayed together, so they must have had something pretty strong going for them.'

He seemed to be mulling that over. 'I suppose so. I've been looking at things from a different angle.'

She tasted the medium-rare roast beef, savouring it for a moment on her tongue. His troubled background would always affect the way he felt about relationships. 'Obviously, when it comes to marriage, you're afraid,' she said eventually. 'That's why you flit from woman to woman without making any commitments.'

His eyes narrowed in mock jest. 'Who's been talking?'

She gave a wry smile. 'My mother, for one, and the hospital grapevine is rife with rumour as usual.'

He laid down his fork. 'Your mother I can't account for, and I won't argue with her because I'm really very fond of her. But I can tell you now that whatever you've heard on the grapevine is pure conjecture. I haven't dated anyone since I came back to Ashley Vale.'

She looked at him steadily. 'Maybe you've been too busy.'

He gave a short laugh, returning her gaze with a penetrating blue glance. 'Yes, maybe. Perhaps I've found someone special...someone who cares about me and makes me feel I might actually be worthy.'

The breath caught in her throat as she met his gaze. If only she could believe what he was saying. 'That sounds...wonderful...something to be working on.'

'I'm glad you think so.' Smiling, he returned his attention to his meal.

Caitlin finished her main course and reached for her dessert, a Bramley apple pie topped with creamy custard. She didn't know what to think. He was making out he was perfectly innocent but she knew him of old. He was a wolf in sheep's clothing. He would lure her into a false sense of security then when she was completely ensnared he would devour her and move on in search of new prey. Didn't she know better than to fall for his charm? She'd already been hurt badly by Matt. She was feeling stronger now but surely she shouldn't make herself vulnerable again if she could help it? All the same, she was so, so tempted.

'Hey, you two, have you seen the pictures in the papers? You've even made the nationals—look.'

Cathy, the staff nurse from the children's unit, came over to their table. 'Am I interrupting?'

'No, of course not,' Caitlin said. 'Are these the pictures from *Murder Mysteries*?'

Cathy nodded. 'Yes, look. I bought the local paper and the *Tribune*. You're both splashed over the TV feature pages—it's mostly the main characters they're showing, but you two are there as well. I can't wait to see the series when it comes out. I'll be watching out for your scenes all the way through.'

Caitlin and Brodie glanced through the papers. 'Oh,' Caitlin said, 'They filmed the geese when they ran up to the camera!' Brodie was in the shot, smiling as he looked at the startled cameraman. 'I thought they would edit those shots.'

'They probably have in the TV version—but the press will choose whatever appeals, I suppose.' Brodie was amused. 'Thanks for showing us these, Cathy.'

'You're welcome. I expect they're in all the papers. All the nurses are talking about them.'

She went off to join her friends, leaving Caitlin and Brodie to finish their lunch. Afterwards, they went to spend some time with Caitlin's mother.

'The doctor says I should be well enough to leave here in a few days,' her mother said, looking happy. Her cheeks were flushed with anticipation. 'I'm so pleased. I can't wait.'

'It'll be good to have you home,' Caitlin said, giving her a hug.

They stayed for half an hour then left to meet up with the film crew once more back at the smallholding. David was already there, organising things. Caitlin had given him access to the house and grounds.

'I thought Daisy and her puppies would like to be out in the sunshine for a bit,' he said, coming over to greet them, 'so I've put them on the lawn. They won't be going anywhere,' he added with a rueful grin. 'The geese are keeping an eye on them. At least they're leaving the camera crew alone today. They're too busy guarding the newcomers.'

Caitlin smiled, seeing the geese gently nudging the puppies back on to the grass whenever they wandered near the edge of the lawn. They were just beginning to find their feet, but Daisy seemed happy to let the birds shepherd her flock while she simply lazed in the sunshine and gathered her strength. Thanks to good food and plenty of love and care, she was thriving, and her shaggy coat was beginning to take on a healthy glow.

The film crew spent some time working around the house and outbuildings, and then moved off to concentrate their attention on the wooded area around the smallholding. A couple of villagers acted as extras, wandering along the footpath that led from Brodie's property to the copse beyond. The same man who'd been wheezing the day before was there. Caitlin stood and watched them go.

'I think they've finished with us for now,' Brodie said as he walked with her to the back of her house. He gave her a long, appreciative look. 'It looks as though I have you all to myself at last.'

'Is that what you want?' she murmured.

'Oh yes,' he said. They came to a halt on the terrace overlooking the lawn and in the privacy of a jasmine-covered arbour he leaned towards her.

'I never seem to get you alone, what with David being around, the film crew and whoever else decides on a whim to drop by.' He slid his arm around her waist and tugged her towards him. 'You've had all sorts of creatures demanding your attention: a rabbit, the quail, Daisy and the pups, three terrifying geese—and for all I know a motherless kitten could turn up at any minute to distract you. I'm all for moving in on you while I can.'

She smiled and lifted her face to him, rewarded instantly when he bent his head to hers and claimed her lips. She was ready for his kiss, wanting it, needing it, craving the feel of his arms around her. He eased her against the rustic trellis, supporting her with his forearm, raining kisses over her cheek and throat, nuzzling the creamy velvet of her shoulder beneath the loose collar of her shirt. 'Do you think we could be together, you and I?' he murmured. 'A couple? Could we give it a go?'

The sweet fragrance of white jasmine filled the air as she moved against him, pressing her soft curves into his muscular frame. 'Oh, yes…yes.'

She heard his gasp, revelled in his strength, and lost herself in his kisses, running her hands up over his chest, delighting in the swift intake of his breath as his body tautened against her.

'Ah, Caity…you've made me so happy. I want you so badly. You know it, don't you?' His voice was roughened, the words thick against her cheek, her lips. 'When I saw you first thing this morning, it took all I had to keep my hands off you.' He kissed her again, hungrily. 'You're so lovely, so perfect, Caity. You're everything I could ever want.'

'Mmm… I want you too, Brodie,' she murmured. She snuggled up against him, loving the way he needed her, exhilarated by the feel of him, by the delicious stroking of his hands as they moved over her curves, filling her with feverish excitement. If only it was true, what he was saying. Could she really be everything he could ever want? 'I want you so much…'

She was seduced by him, by the heady perfume of jasmine that wafted on the air, the warmth of the sun on her bare arms and legs and by his wonderful, coaxing hands that seemed to know instinctively how to make her body yearn for more. Why shouldn't she accept what he was offering, let him take her on that tantalising, breathtaking voyage of discovery?

'Let's go inside the house…' His voice was husky,

urgent, ragged with passion; she was more than willing to go along with him.

'Okay.' She didn't want to break away from him and neither, it seemed, did he want to move away from her. He kept his arm around her as they walked the short distance to the kitchen door.

But before they made it as far as the kitchen, they heard David's voice calling to them from across the garden. 'Are you there, bro? I need to talk to you. Brodie?'

The geese started cackling at the intrusion and Caitlin gave a slow, heavy sigh, her fizzing, shooting senses coming back down to earth with a bump. Beside her, Brodie stiffened.

'One of these days…' Brodie said, gritting his teeth. 'He's my brother,' he said under his breath, 'and I'm very attached to him, but there are times, I swear, I could…' He didn't finish what he was saying.

David came around the back of the house. 'There you are. I thought I saw you both in the garden a minute ago. There's a problem with the look of the back of the house—your house, Brodie. It's too neat. The director wants to know if we can put some plants there in place of yours—shrubs and so on—to make it look straggly and overgrown. We'll put everything back how it was afterwards.'

'Sure. That's fine.' Brodie's answer was brisk and to the point. 'Why don't you go and see to it right away?'

'Hmm. Am I sensing something here?' David looked from one to the other. 'The thing is, I would go away…but you need to come and talk to the director and see what he wants to do. There are papers you need to sign.'

'You can sign them for me.' Brodie's impatience was showing and David studied him thoughtfully.

'Sorry, no can do. Anyway, you did say you'd be available to deal with any queries that came up today.'

His glance went to Caitlin, who was waiting edgily through this back-and-forth chitchat. She was coming to realise how very close she'd come to burning her boats with Brodie.

'He seems anxious to be rid of me,' David commented. He raised his brows in a silent question that she decided to ignore. 'I'm hugely jealous,' he said, his dark eyes glinting with mischief. 'You know that, don't you? You always said you wouldn't lose your heart to either of us because we would trample all over it.'

'Leave it off, David,' Brodie warned, his whole body tense. But David merely smiled, for all his worth playing the part of the irritating younger brother. He glanced at Caitlin, as though expecting an answer.

'Did I say that?' She sounded breathless, even to her own ears. 'That was a long time ago.'

'Yes, well, nothing much has changed. Except I'm the one you should go for.' Again, that imp of devilment appeared in his eyes. 'I'd make you happy.'

'You're right,' she agreed. 'Nothing's changed, has it? I ought to know better than to listen to either of you. My father used to warn me about you two. "Pair of young rascals," he said. "Full of testosterone, looking for conquests and moving on."'

She'd been very young when her father had died—

fifteen years old and emotionally insecure. But her father had loved and cherished her; she knew that. He'd wanted the best for her and she'd missed him so much after he died. Perhaps his loss was the reason she'd tried so hard not to fall for Brodie…then and now. It hurt so much to lose someone you loved. Was she making the biggest mistake of her life?

David smiled. 'Your father had a point. We were very young and immature.' He started to move away across the terrace. 'See you in a minute or two, bro.'

Caitlin turned to Brodie with a rueful smile. 'Perhaps you should go and sign your papers. I think that motherless kitten has arrived.'

'I guess he has.' Brodie gave her a long, steady look. 'Another time, then,' he said quietly. 'I've already waited a lifetime…what does a little longer matter?'

'I don't know about that, Brodie,' she said equally softly. 'I don't know if I'm making a mistake.'

'He was just teasing you.'

'I know. But perhaps it's a good thing that I have time to think. I've just finished one relationship. Maybe this is the wrong time to be stepping back into the fray.'

'And, then again, it might be the perfect time. Sometimes you need to follow your instincts.'

She nodded. 'Okay,' she said softly, still troubled.

'We'll be fine,' he said. 'I promise.' He gently brushed her mouth with his and then went off in the direction of the camera crew.

She watched him go, the memory of his kiss imprinted on her lips. David's comments played over in her mind, though. He had given her food for thought and taken her right back to when this had all started. Brodie had pursued her since they were teenagers. He'd never faltered, taking up where he'd left off as soon as they'd met up again. He couldn't resist a challenge.

Perhaps to him she was simply the one that got away and that was why he persisted in going after her.

CHAPTER SEVEN

CAITLIN WAS NEARING the end of her shift on Monday afternoon when the staff nurse asked her to look in on baby Olivia. 'Her mum's worried—she had her operation first thing this morning, and she started taking small feeds six hours later, but the poor little thing's still vomiting.'

'Okay, Cathy. Bless her—I'll go and see her now. She's still on a fluid drip until her full feeding regime is restored, so there aren't any worries on that score.'

She hurried away to go and look in on the mother and baby. She and Brodie had been busy all day and hadn't really had a chance to talk. Even at lunchtime he'd been involved in meetings with chiefs from the local health authority.

Now she went to see Olivia, checking the heart and respiration monitor, glad to find that all was well there. The infant looked reasonably content, squirming a little in her mother's arms; every now and again her pink rosebud mouth made little sucking movements.

'Hi,' Caitlin said, going to sit down beside them. 'I hear she's having a bit of a problem?'

'That's right.' The mother's brow creased with anxiety. 'She keeps being sick. Does it mean the operation hasn't worked?'

'Not at all. The surgeon reported that everything went very well. This type of surgery is very low risk.' She stroked the baby's palm and felt the infant's fingers close around hers. 'She's lovely, isn't she?' A quiver of unforeseen, overwhelming maternal instinct ran through her, melting her insides.

The mother nodded and smiled. 'Yes, she is. She's so precious to us and this is all very upsetting.'

'It *is* upsetting, but it's quite usual for a baby to be sick after this kind of surgery. It happens because there's often a bit of swelling after the operation, but that will soon go down and she should be able to feed normally after that. I'll ask the nurse to check how often she's being fed and how much, and to work with you on that. Things should soon settle. She just needs tiny feeds for the time being. I'm sure she'll be fine.'

'Thanks.' The girl looked relieved. 'I'm sorry to be such a pain…'

'No, you're not being a pain at all. I'm sure all new mums worry. It's natural.'

Maybe one day she would be holding her own child in her arms, looking down at him or her with such love and tenderness. She already knew how good Brodie was with children; she'd seen him in action with children and animals and he was wonderful with them all. Did he want to have a family of his own? Would he ever contemplate taking that step? She'd dearly love to have children with him. He'd be a fantastic father.

A rush of heat rippled through her. She'd never once contemplated having a family with Matt, even when they'd talked about getting engaged. It was very odd but it simply hadn't occurred to her.

She met up with Brodie as he was getting ready to leave the hospital for the day. 'They're filming at the village pub this evening,' he told her. 'David said he hoped we would both be there.'

'Yes, he mentioned it to me.'

'How do you feel about it? Do you fancy going along? We don't have to do anything—the camera crew will be filming the actors and we'll be in the background somewhere with the rest of the pub's customers.'

'Yes, okay. I'd like to go.'

He smiled. 'Good. It's a date, then. He said to come early—he wants me to meet someone, something to do with one of the photos that appeared in the papers. He says it's important, but he didn't go into details. I can't imagine what that's about.'

'Perhaps a talent scout saw you on camera and wants you to do a hero doctor drama series,' she said with a smile.

He laughed. 'Of course, why didn't I think of that?'

She walked with him to the car park and her expression sobered. 'Are you and David getting on all right now? I was a bit concerned after the way you were sniping at one another yesterday afternoon.'

'We're fine. It's just banter—on his part, especially.' He gave a wry smile. 'David was a demon for trying to wind me up when we were younger…you probably remember that?'

She nodded. 'He hasn't changed much, has he?' she said with a smile.

He shook his head, sending her a sidelong glance. 'Though I suspect yesterday's comments came about because he has a big crush on you.'

She shook her head. 'No, he doesn't. He may have fancied his chances years ago, but now it's all bravado—designed to get a response from you, I think. He only makes a play for me when you're around. That's a definite hangover from the old days.'

'Maybe.' They parted company as they reached their cars. 'I'll call for you in about an hour and a half,' he said. 'And we'll stroll down to the pub together…is that okay?'

She nodded. 'It's the last of the filming sessions today, isn't it? I heard they'd arranged a celebratory buffet meal for everyone in the lounge bar for when it's all over.'

'Sounds good to me.'

Caitlin rushed through her chores as soon as she arrived back at the house, feeding the animals and making sure Daisy and the pups had a run outside before quickly getting ready for the evening. She showered and dressed in slim-fit jeans and a layered top. Leaving her hair loose to flow in burnished chestnut curls to her shoulders, she applied a swift dab of make-up to her face, finishing off with a light spray of perfume.

Brodie sucked in his breath when he called for her a short time later. 'You look beautiful,' he said, his eyes darkening with appreciation. He stepped inside the house and moved towards her. 'Shall we give the pub a miss and stay in?'

'Behave yourself,' she admonished him with a laugh. 'Anyway, you know David will only come and find you if you don't turn up—or else the director will decide it's a good idea to do a final scene outside your house.'

'I don't care. I'm prepared to risk it,' he murmured, walking further into the hallway and sliding his arms around her. As an afterthought he pushed the front door shut with his foot to give them some privacy then he lowered his head and stole a kiss.

Instantly, in an intuitive, innate response, her lips softened beneath his and she kissed him tenderly, wanting him, loving him, yet at the same time warring with herself about what she was doing. It had hurt so badly to be rejected when she'd been with Matt; she couldn't help feeling she was storing up trouble for the future by getting ever more deeply involved with Brodie. The trouble was, she couldn't help herself.

Brodie deepened the kiss, tugging her closer to him so that she could feel the passion burning in him. There was no mistaking his desire for her. His hands moved over her, making sweeping forays over all the curves and planes of her body, shaping her, tantalising her with his gentle, knowing expertise; all the while his lips teased the softness of her mouth and made gentle trails over the silken skin of her throat.

His fingers slid beneath the flowing hem of her top, slowly gliding upwards until he found the soft swell of her silk-clad breasts and lingered there. A shuddery, satisfied sigh escaped him. 'Ah, Caity, you're so lovely…'

A muffled gasp caught in her throat. His touch was heavenly, sensual, luring her into a state of feverish euphoria. It was pure seduction, taking her to heights of ecstasy she'd never known before, making her want ever more. She groaned softly, heat intensifying inside her as he moved against her. She felt the brush of his thigh against hers, his hard, muscular body driving her to distraction.

And then came the jarring, insistent bleep of a mobile phone and she blinked in bewilderment, her body recoiling in a spasm of shock.

'What is it? Who can it be…?' She stared up at him, dazed, uncomprehending. Her whole being was in a state of traumatic distress.

He shook his head. Perhaps he managed to recover his equilibrium faster than she did because he said cautiously, 'It's not my phone. It must be yours.'

'Oh…are you sure?'

He nodded.

Befuddled, she searched in her jeans pocket with shaking hands and drew out her phone. It was the hospital calling and immediately she was on alert, worried. Was something wrong with her mother? Had she taken a turn for the worse?

She listened carefully to what the nurse had to say. 'Thank you. Thanks for letting me know,' she said quietly at last.

She cut the call and looked up at Brodie. 'My mother

can come home tomorrow—if her blood pressure, pulse and so on are okay. Her blood oxygen level is fine now, apparently. The consultant just paid her a quick visit while he was there to see another patient.' She gave a rueful smile. 'I think, actually, she probably badgered him into it.'

'That sounds like your mother—she likes to get things sorted. She must be feeling a lot better.'

She nodded, looking at him, not knowing quite what to say. The mood had been totally disrupted. Now that she was thinking clearly again, making love right now didn't seem like such a good idea. She might love him and want children with him but she wanted the whole package: love, marriage and a vow of eternal devotion. Was he even capable of that?

'I guess we ought to head for the pub,' he said reluctantly, gauging her reaction. 'I suppose you were right earlier. David's quite likely to come looking for me. He seemed particularly anxious for me to meet this person.'

'A man?'

'A woman, I believe.'

She frowned. 'Do I need to be jealous?'

'Would you be?' He sounded almost hopeful and that surprised her a little. Didn't he know how she felt about him?

'Oh yes, very much so. I want you all to myself.'

'Good. I'm glad about that.' He opened the door and she stepped out onto the porch with him.

'The trouble is, I never quite feel safe with you, Brodie...emotionally, I mean. I'm never sure if you'll decide to look around and see if the grass is greener somewhere else.'

They started to walk along the country lane. 'Have I ever given you any reason to doubt me?' he asked. 'Nowadays, I mean…since I came back here?' He studied her, his expression suddenly brooding. 'Surely I'm the one who needs to be on his guard? After all, you're still hankering after Matt, aren't you? How do I compete with him?'

She shook her head. 'You're wrong about that. I don't even think about him any more. It's over.'

He made a short, dismissive sound. 'I don't believe that's true. His name came up the other day when we were having lunch and your hands were shaking. I don't think you're over him at all.'

She sent him a troubled look. 'It was a shock, that's all: what he did; the way he finished with me… Everything in my life changed overnight. It was just a reaction to what had been a harrowing episode in my life.'

'Well, when you can be with him or think about him without trembling, maybe then I'll believe you. Till then, it's all up in the air.'

Caitlin pressed her lips together briefly. No matter what she said, she had the feeling he wouldn't believe her right now. Yet, deep inside, she truly wondered why she'd ever thought she was in love with Matt. He was a good man—pleasant company, supportive—but he'd never made her feel the way she did when she was with Brodie.

'You don't need to worry about Matt,' she said.

He reached for her, holding her briefly, his hands

cupping her arms. 'I want you, Caity. I want you all to myself, and I'll do whatever I can to drive him from your mind. I'll prove to you that I'm good enough for you, that I won't let you down.'

Brodie made her insides tingle with longing, he made her blood fizz with excitement, and he made her yearn for him when he wasn't around. If she explained that to him it would more than likely incite him to launch a full-scale, bone-melting sensual assault on her body and mind, no holds barred, right here in the lane. Much as she'd love that, she wasn't at all sure she could handle the consequences.

She loved everything about him: the way he helped out around the smallholding without a care; the way he was there for her before she even knew she needed him; even the way he accepted her for what she was, without wanting to change her.

'Ah, you made it. Good.' David looked pleased to see both of them when they walked into the pub's lounge bar and several of the villagers who were seated nearby or standing by the bar nodded acknowledgement. In the background the camera crew were setting up, getting ready for filming, and the actors were going over their scene in readiness.

'Heard you're doing good things up at the hospital,' one of the men at the bar said to Brodie. 'My sister's little girl had to stay there for a day or so—they were very impressed.'

'I'm glad to hear it, Frank. We aim to please.'

Frank Brennan had been one of Brodie's arch accusers way back when Brodie had been an annoying teenager. He'd been subjected to trespass and minor vandalism and he'd borne the brunt of Brodie's talents as a graffiti artist on his various outbuildings. Caitlin looked on and smiled at how things had turned full circle.

'Also heard you had the offer of another job in London,' Frank went on. Caitlin frowned at that, sending Brodie a quick, sharp glance. He returned her gaze fleetingly, looking slightly uncomfortable.

This was the first she'd heard about any forthcoming new job. If it was true, it meant Brodie had kept his cards very close to his chest, and it seemed as though all her fears were coming to fruition. She felt a painful, involuntary clenching of muscle in her abdomen. He wasn't going to be staying around, was he? He was prepared to go all out after her, make her care for him beyond reason, then he would calmly leave as though it didn't matter at all. Being with her was simply a ripple on a pool.

She looked at him once more. Perhaps it was just a rumour. Ought she not at least give him the benefit of the doubt?

Brodie sent Frank a quizzical glance. 'News travels fast around here. How did you come to know about it?'

He wasn't denying it, then. Caitlin let out a slow, fraught breath. Her nerves were in shreds.

'Through my father-in-law. He works in admin at the hospital. Said the bosses at the local health authority were well taken with the way you'd changed things and wanted you to do the same thing at one of the London hospitals.' He gave Brodie an assessing look. 'So, what are you thinking? Will you be taking them up on the offer?'

So that was why he'd been involved in meetings at lunchtime. They must have been discussing the new role and the opportunities it presented.

'I don't know yet, Frank,' Brodie said. 'I've only been at this hospital for a short time and the new contract isn't due to start for a few months. I'm still thinking about it.'

'Well, whatever you decide, from the sound of things you'll go far.' Frank laughed. 'I never thought I'd hear myself saying that.'

'Likewise.'

Brodie went to the bar and bought drinks, sending Caitlin a cautious glance as he handed her a glass of sparkling wine. 'I was going to tell you,' he said, reading her thoughts accurately. 'I was just waiting for the time to be right.'

'When would that have been, I wonder?' In the background, she was conscious of the filming taking place, but at least the cameras weren't pointed her way.

He shrugged awkwardly. 'I knew you would be concerned about me moving on—but the offer came out of the blue very recently and out of respect for the bosses I have to give it some thought.'

She was distressed, certainly, and she might have said more, but Brodie's father came and stood next to them, looking uneasy.

He nodded towards Caitlin and then turned his narrowed gaze on Brodie. 'I couldn't help hearing what you and Frank were saying. So you're thinking of going away again in a few months? You don't like to stay still, do you? You've only just come back here.' There was almost a hint of accusation in his tone.

'It's more that I like to feel I'm achieving something,' Brodie answered carefully. 'I didn't go looking for the job offer. They came to me with it.'

'You'd call it being headhunted, I suppose?' His father's manner was gruff.

'I suppose.' Brodie took a swallow of his drink. He sent his father an odd, questioning look. 'I didn't think you'd be bothered.'

Caitlin nudged him. Despite her unhappy mood right now she felt she ought to remind him of the conversation they'd had a while ago. 'Remember what we talked about?' she said in an undertone.

His father might well care more for Brodie than he liked to admit. He could be carrying a burden of guilt that he hid from everyone. She only hoped Brodie would cotton on to what she was getting at. 'You don't always see things the way others do,' she murmured.

'No, that's true.'

David decided to join in. 'If Brodie took the job in London he'd get to see more of me, most likely,' he said, giving an exaggerated smile and showing his teeth. 'What better reason could he have for going there?'

'Like I said, I haven't made a decision yet.' Brodie looked at Caitlin then back at his father. 'Anyway, if I did make up my mind to accept it, it's only an hour and a half by car. I could easily get back here, the same as David does.'

'Sure. I get back here often enough,' David agreed. He was about to expand on that when he saw someone heading towards the bar and excused himself. 'I have to go—I'll be back in a minute or two.'

Brodie's father shifted awkwardly. 'I know you well enough, Brodie. You'll do what you want, I don't doubt. You always did.' He turned away to take a long gulp from his drink; Frank Brennan took him to one side to talk to him about the repairs going on at Mill House.

'I hear you're thinking of having the roof fixed,' Frank said. 'I can match up the slates for you, if you want. I know they're special—a particular kind.'

Caitlin didn't hear Colin Driscoll's muffled reply. She was uneasy.

'An hour and a half may sound like nothing at all,' she told Brodie, 'But it's a three-hour commute in the day and he knows it wouldn't be too long before it turned into a long-distance relationship.' She blurted out what was on her mind then took refuge in sipping her drink.

'You're not just talking about my father and me, are you?' Brodie asked, his gaze moving over her curiously. 'You're thinking about the way it might affect our relationship—yours and mine?'

'It applies equally well to both—though, yes, I'm thinking about you and me. It's hopeless, though, isn't it? If you're planning on going away it looks as though it's even more unlikely that you and I will ever get together in any meaningful way, doesn't it?'

'You could always come with me.' His blue eyes were suddenly dark and impenetrable like the sea.

'Could I?' She looked at him and inside her heart wept. 'You don't really think that's a possibility, do you? You know I wouldn't want to be too far from Mum now that she's had a fall. I couldn't leave her to fend for herself. I'd always be worrying about her.'

Besides, it would take more than a casual offer of 'why don't you tag along with me?' to make her go with him, wouldn't it? Where was the love, the cherishing, the for-ever promise that she desperately needed?

'It doesn't have to be a major problem,' Brodie insisted. 'We could work something out.'

Her heart lurched at the prospect. Could they? Was it possible?

He took a step back from her as David came over to them, bringing with him an attractive girl who looked to be in her late twenties. Caitlin knew the chance of pursuing the conversation was lost for now, and she resigned herself to putting it on the back burner.

'This is the young woman I wanted you to meet.' David introduced the woman to both of them. 'This is Deanna.' To Deanna, he said, 'This lovely girl is Caitlin, and this is my brother, Brodie.'

Deanna smiled at both of them. She had mid-length dark hair and grey eyes; she looked at Brodie as though she was especially thrilled to be meeting him.

'I just had to come and see you,' she said, gazing up at him eagerly, her eyes shining. 'I saw your picture in the paper and I knew I had to get in touch with the film company.' She hesitated. 'I hope you don't mind?'

'I don't think I mind,' Brodie said, smiling at her enthusiasm. 'Is there any reason why I should?'

'It's this picture, you see.' She pulled a sheet of newspaper from her jacket pocket and opened it out. Brodie was in the picture, looking straight into the camera as he attempted to rescue the cameraman from the goose intent on pecking his leg.

'Okay...' he said slowly. 'That's me.' He looked at her questioningly.

'There's another picture you should see.' This time she opened up her handbag and carefully took out an envelope. 'Take a look at this.'

She waited with bated breath. Brodie gave her a puzzled look but opened up the envelope and drew out a glossy photograph. He stared at the photograph for several seconds and then looked back at Deanna. He passed the photo to Caitlin. When he spoke, his voice was cracked, almost a whisper, as though he was in shock.

'Who is this?' he asked.

Deanna pulled in a deep breath. 'He's my father,' she said. 'That photo was taken when he was a young man. When I put the two pictures together, I knew I had to come and find you. You're exactly alike, aren't you?'

Caitlin looked at the photo and sucked in her breath, her mind racing, while Brodie appeared to be struggling to find words. 'Is he...does he...does he know about me...about the picture in the paper?'

Deanna shook her head. 'He's not seen it yet. He's been busy lately—he had to go out to Sweden to sort out a new order for his company.' She glanced at her watch. 'He was flying back today—in fact he should have landed at the airport a couple of hours ago. Anyway, I wanted to talk to you before I showed him.' She hesitated. 'It's a bit awkward. He never mentioned having a son—apart from my younger brother, Ben, I mean. But there's such a strong likeness between the two of you, I can't help thinking there's a connection between you. I had to come and find out if there's any history, any kind of background that we didn't know about—'

She broke off, floundering a bit. 'Do you understand what I'm trying to say? I don't know if my father had a relationship with a woman before he met and married my mother, but if he did…I think you could be my half-brother.'

Brodie dragged in a deep breath and Caitlin wanted to wrap her arms around him and hug him. This must be an incredible moment for him. Instead, being in a public place, she reined in her instincts and contented herself with sliding an arm around his waist, trying to show him some silent, unobtrusive support.

He looked at her fleetingly and a wealth of understanding passed between them. Then he braced himself.

'You've obviously spoken to David, about this,' he said, glancing at David for confirmation, then back to Deanna. 'So you must know something of my background.' David acknowledged that with a slight movement of his head.

'Yes, I have,' Deanna said excitedly. 'That's what made me think there could be something in it. David told me your mother's maiden name—I want to ask my father if he ever knew her.' She looked at him searchingly. 'How do you feel about that?'

Brodie was silent for a moment or two. Then he said guardedly, 'It depends... Obviously I want to know the truth, but I'm not sure how he might react, or whether his response is going to cause trouble for your family—for your mother and your brother. They're bound to have strong feelings about this—and in the end they might have more to lose than I do. I've always wanted to know who my father is but I don't want to cause heartache for his family.'

Deanna relaxed. 'My father's an easy-going kind of man, a very fair-minded person. And I've already sounded my mother out about any previous relationships. She said there was a woman in Dad's life before they were married but it was over when she met him.' She gave Brodie a steady, assessing look. 'I'd really like your permission to ask my father about this.'

Brodie exhaled slowly. 'You don't need my permission. But you have it anyway. Go ahead and ask him.'

Deanna still seemed to have something on her mind.

'What is it?' Brodie asked.

'Um... I could phone him right now?' She said it in a questioning way.

Brodie nodded, taking a deep breath. 'Okay. Go ahead.'

'Perhaps it'll be better if I go outside, into the garden to make the call. Why don't you come with me? It will be quieter out there and we can find a more private place to call him.'

'Okay. But I want David and Caitlin to come along.'

'All right.'

Caitlin had been afraid she would be left out of this major event but her spirits soared when Brodie included her. He put his arm around her waist and led her to the paved seating area outside.

They sat at a bench table in a far corner, brightened by a golden pool of light that spilled out from an overhead lamp. Deanna phoned her father and, after chatting to him briefly about his trip abroad and his flight home, she told him about the item of news featured in the paper and gently sounded him out about his life before he met her mother.

'Did you ever know a woman called Sarah Marchant?' Deanna asked.

Caitlin didn't hear what he said but Deanna listened, glanced at Brodie and then said, 'So you were involved with her for a while?' The conversation continued and after a while Deanna said, 'Dad, I think there's something you should know...someone you should meet.'

It was a fairly lengthy conversation; when it eventually came to a close, Deanna put down her phone and looked at Brodie. 'He'd like to see you. He suggested that either he could come here or you could meet in London?'

Brodie gave it some thought. 'I'll go to London,' he said. 'After all, it isn't just my father I have to meet. It looks as though I have to catch up with a whole new family I knew nothing about until now.'

Deanna hugged him. 'I'm so glad I saw that picture in the paper,' she said. 'I can't describe to you what a shock it was. I was certain you must be related to me in some way.'

Brodie hugged her in return then after a few minutes they all trooped back into the bar. The filming was finished and the landlord was busy setting out the food the production company had asked him to provide.

It was a wonderful buffet, colourful, tasty and beautifully presented; Caitlin duly tucked in alongside Brodie, his brother and newfound half-sister. They were all in a happy mood, smiling and cheerful.

She couldn't help thinking, though, as she let Brodie tempt her with filo prawns with sweet chilli dip. and mozzarella and sunblush-tomato bruschetta, that this celebratory meal was the exact opposite of what she was feeling.

She didn't feel like making merry, because Brodie was going to London to meet his new family—what were the chances he would be tempted to stay there with them? He was more than keen to go and it didn't call for a lot of working out to know that the prospect of taking up a new job there would absolutely complete the picture for him.

'I could go over there next weekend,' Brodie said to her, smiling as he helped himself to a selection from the cheese board. 'Will you come with me?'

'I'd love to,' she said, but frowned, thinking about the practicalities. 'But I don't know if I should leave Mum alone so soon after she's home from hospital. And there are the animals to see to: she won't be up to it for quite a while, with her mobility problems. It'll be some time before she's walking unaided.'

'I'm sure we could find somebody to help out, if only for a short time.'

'I suppose so,' she agreed. 'She has friends in the village who would be glad to help.'

'But something else is bothering you, isn't it?' He studied her, his gaze shifting over her thoughtfully. 'I can read you, Caitlin. What is it?'

'Nothing.' She smiled at him, not wanting to spoil the moment for him. 'I'm really, really happy for you, Brodie. This is what you've wanted for so many years and it's wonderful that you have the chance of some kind of closure.'

'But? There is a *but*, isn't there?'

Clearly, he wasn't going to leave it alone. She lifted her hands in a helpless gesture.

'I'm just worried about how things will work out in the long term—for us, I mean. I can see you wanting to move away now that you've found your family. It's natural you'll want to be with them and, with the job offer, how could it have worked out better? It's bound to affect us, though.'

She looked at him unhappily, taking in a deep breath. 'I want to be with you, Brodie, but I came back to Ashley Vale to make my home here—I don't think I want to uproot myself again.'

He frowned. 'The truth is, you came back here because Matt was getting married to Jenny.'

'Initially, that was the reason, yes, but then things changed. My mother had an accident. That made things different.' He had her on the defensive now and she didn't like it. She was confused—about him, about everything. Her emotions were tangled and for the life of her she couldn't sift her way through them.

'Are you putting up excuses, Caitlin? Don't you want to be with me?' His dark eyes narrowed. 'I can't help thinking I was right all along, that you can't make up your mind to be with me because you're not over Matt yet. You can't move on. There won't be any future for you and me while he's there between us, will there?'

His jaw clenched. 'Maybe I should take up this offer of a job and give you time to decide what you really do want?'

'Are you trying to make me choose?' Her voice broke and she looked at him with tears shimmering in her eyes. 'Matt doesn't come into it. He never did, where you were concerned. I always cared for you, but you weren't around, Brodie. What was I supposed to do? You left. You stayed away for years. And now you want me to choose between going away from here or staying—between being with you or losing you.'

She gulped in a quick breath. 'I don't want to choose, Brodie, and I don't want to persuade you to do something against your best interests. You're the one who has to decide. Stay or go.' She pressed her lips together briefly to stop them from trembling. 'I've made my decision, for good or bad, and I'll live with it.'

CHAPTER EIGHT

'HOW DID YOU get on in London this weekend?' Cathy was keen to know how Brodie and Caitlin had fared when he'd gone to meet his father for the first time.

'It went well, on the whole,' Caitlin answered. 'But I think Brodie found it all a bit strange.' As she finished writing up the prescription for Jason's medication, she glanced across the desk at the nurse. 'He said he didn't expect to feel quite the way he did. It was a bit overwhelming.'

'I can imagine it would be. After all, from what I've heard, his natural father is a complete stranger to him. He didn't know anything about him, his life or his relationship with his mother. Brodie said it was like a bolt from the blue, learning that he was around and that he wanted to meet him.'

Caitlin nodded, handing her the prescription. Young Jason was finally being discharged from hospital today and the medication was to tide him over until his GP saw him next. The little boy was doing really well now, gaining in strength every day. She was glad to see him going home but she would miss him, she acknowledged. Sammy too, was being allowed home on a new regime of medication to help strengthen his bones. He was another one she would miss—he'd started to come out of his shell and was a favourite with all the staff.

'It's true,' she said now, thinking about Brodie and his new family. 'He didn't know they existed. I'm not sure what he expected, really, going to see them… I don't think he knew himself what might come of it but for a first meeting it turned out better than he imagined. We met his father in a pub to start with, so that we could talk in private.'

His natural father had been astonished to find that he had a son he knew nothing about. Brodie's mother had apparently said nothing to him, probably thinking he wouldn't want to know, but he was horrified to learn that she'd kept her pregnancy to herself. He would have stood by her and his son, he'd said.

But Caitlin didn't say any of that to Cathy. It seemed too private, too personal, and it was up to Brodie if he wanted to share that with anyone else. 'Anyway, then he took us to his house and we had a meal together—the whole extended family. It was…surreal.'

They'd all got on well together. His half-brother and half-sister especially had encouraged him to accept the promotion he'd been offered and go to live closer to them so they could keep in touch regularly. Even so, Caitlin still didn't know what he planned to do.

He seemed to be keeping his options open and, much as she longed for him to stay here in Ashley Vale with her, she couldn't blame him for looking further afield. He'd always worked hard to succeed—everything he did was designed to further his career—and it looked as though his efforts were paying dividends.

'Are we ready for the little girl?' Brodie strode briskly into the children's unit and checked his watch. A twelve-month-old girl was being brought in from the hospital where Caitlin used to work for specialist treatment. 'She'll be here in about ten minutes.'

Caitlin nodded. 'We're all set.' Cathy left them, hurrying over to the pharmacy to get Jason's prescription filled.

'Good. I want this transfer to go smoothly. If it all goes well she'll be able to have the operation tomorrow morning.' He glanced at her, his dark eyes brooding. 'Are you okay with everything? You're prepared?'

'You mean because it's Matt who's bringing her here?'

'Yes, that's what I mean.' His tone was unusually curt.

'Of course. You don't need to worry, Brodie, I'll be fine.' She frowned. 'Look, I know you must have things you need to do, meetings to go to and so on… You can leave everything to me. There won't be a problem. Matt and I are both professionals, after all.'

'Hmm.' His mouth flattened. 'That isn't exactly what's bothering me. I think you know that.'

'I told you, I'm over him.' She didn't try to argue the point any more. This was a difficult time for Brodie, she recognised that; if he was unusually tense right now it was probably to be expected. His mood wouldn't have darkened simply because of Matt's impending arrival, would it? Matt was his friend and they kept in fairly regular contact with one another. They must have smoothed things over with one another by now.

No, his taut, preoccupied manner surely had more to do with discovering the existence of his real father after all these years of believing it would never happen. It had been a profound experience for him and it was bound to be unsettling.

For now, whatever state their emotions were in, they had to put all that to one side and concentrate on their work. The tot who would be arriving here any minute now had been suffering from symptoms of chest pain, bouts of fainting and shortness of breath. After specialised tests she'd been diagnosed with a narrowing of the pulmonary valve in her heart. This narrowing was causing a problem with the flow of blood to her lungs.

'They're here.' Caitlin heard the faint clatter of a trolley and hurried to meet her new small patient. Greeting Matt with a brief nod, she concentrated her attention on the baby. Connected up to various monitors that recorded her heart rhythm, respiration and blood oxygen, she was wheeled in to the ward and between them Caitlin, Brodie and Matt set about transferring the child to her new temporary home. She was a tiny, vulnerable little thing, and Caitlin wanted to pick her up and cuddle her. 'Hello, Emily,' she said softly. 'We're going to look after you now. We'll make sure you're going to be absolutely fine.'

'Her parents followed us here,' Matt said. 'They should arrive within a few minutes.'

Brodie nodded, acknowledging his friend and listening as he outlined her condition. 'We'll do what we can to get her settled and then I'll go and talk to the parents. It's a straightforward procedure she'll undergo tomorrow, a balloon valvuloplasty; she should be fine afterwards.'

Matt agreed. This hospital was a centre of excellence for catheterisation procedures; if everything went well and her vital signs were satisfactory the little girl would have treatment to widen the valve. Afterwards she should be able to live a normal life. There wouldn't even be much of a scar, because the catheter would be inserted in a vein at the top of the infant's leg and the thin tube would then be passed up to the heart. Once there, a balloon would be inflated to widen the valve. When that was done to the surgeon's satisfaction, the balloon would be deflated and would be removed along with the tube.

Brodie supervised the infant's admission to hospital but, once Caitlin had sorted out the baby's medication, he left the ward and went in search of the parents.

Caitlin saw him glance back once briefly in her direction—that same dark, brooding look in his eyes that she'd seen earlier—but then he continued swiftly on his way. It occurred to her at that moment that she hadn't realised quite how much Brodie kept his feelings locked up inside him. Perhaps the relationship she'd shared with Matt was one more seed of doubt that made him feel unworthy in some way. Maybe she ought to try to do something to get him to open up to her more.

'I heard your mother was back home after the problems with her hip and the emboli in her lungs,' Matt said, walking with her to the cafeteria a short time later. The paramedics who had accompanied the child were in there, taking a break before the journey home. 'How is she?'

'She's feeling much better, thanks.' Caitlin smiled, amazed at how relaxed she was in his company. 'She's using crutches to get about at the moment, and she has physiotherapy every day, but she seems to be doing very well. She's determined to get out and about to see to the animals and so on, so at the moment I'm having to make sure she doesn't overdo things. Of course, the puppies keep us on our toes. They're into everything.'

'I heard about the new additions to the menagerie. She'll be in her element.'

'Oh yes, she is. She's even contemplating keeping a couple of the puppies, though we've managed to find people who want to take care of them when they're old enough to leave their mother.'

'Well, if she's taking a keen interest in things it sounds as though she's going to be all right in the long run. We were worried when she didn't make it to the wedding.'

Caitlin nodded. She expected to feel a pang of dismay at the mention of the big event, but nothing happened, and she felt an immense lightening of her spirits. 'Yes, it was difficult for her.' She glanced at him. 'I thought it all went off very well.'

'Yes, it did.' He bought two coffees and a couple of buns and started to carry the tray over to the table where the paramedics were seated. 'I'm glad you came along on the day,' he told her as they walked across the room. 'I was worried about you. I know I treated you badly…but things just sort of slid out of my control.'

'I know. It doesn't matter. Forget about it.'

'Are you sure?' He studied her, his expression solemn. 'Do you forgive me?'

'I do. It's all water under the bridge. I hope you and Jenny will be very happy together.' She meant it. It was as though a weight had been lifted off her.

He smiled. 'Thanks, Caity. I think I needed to hear you say that.' He pulled out a chair for her and said quietly, 'Brodie's been telling me what a fool I've been and how badly I treated you. I knew it, of course. I hated what I was doing to you and I hated that it was ruining my friendship with Brodie.'

'He's had a lot on his mind this last week or so. I wouldn't worry about it too much.'

'I don't know about that. He seems okay, but he's had a problem with me for quite some time. It just got worse recently.'

She frowned. 'I think he was jealous at first because you were with me, and then he was worried because he thought I was hurt.'

He nodded. 'I thought it might be something like that.'

She smiled as they approached the table. 'You've always been good friends. I'm sure things will be fine between you from now on.'

They sat opposite one another and chatted for a while, sharing the conversation with the paramedics, who were already well acquainted with Caitlin from her time at St Luke's.

After a while, Caitlin's pager bleeped and she made her apologies. 'I have to go and check up on a patient,' she said. 'I'm sure I'll see you all again before too long. Take care.'

She hurried along to the ward to look in on the youngster who had some time ago suffered an allergic reaction to penicillin. 'How are you doing, Janine?' she asked the five-year-old. 'Nurse tells me you've been feeling a bit breathless?'

Janine nodded. 'My chest feels a bit tight.'

'Okay, sweetheart. I'll have a listen, shall I?' Caitlin ran her stethoscope over the little girl's chest then went over to the computer at the desk and brought up her recent X-rays on the screen. They'd been done that morning to see if the infection was clearing.

'I think we'll give you some extra medicine,' she said, returning to the child's bedside after a while. 'Something you can breathe in to make your chest feel better.'

'All right.' The girl settled back against her pillows while the nurse went to sort out the new medication.

Brodie met Caitlin at the entrance to the patients' bay. 'Is there a problem?' he asked.

'It looks as though she has a bit of scarring on the lungs from the recent infection. I'll ask the physio to come and show her how to clear her chest and do breathing exercises. As long as she has antibiotic treatment for recurrent infections she should be okay.'

He nodded. 'So how did it go with Matt?' he asked. 'I thought you might still be with him, catching up on things.'

'No, I left him in the cafeteria when I was bleeped. Haven't you spoken to him?' She was surprised. 'I'd have thought he would have caught up with you again before he left.'

'I'm sure he will but he's not likely to tell me how he left things with you, is he?'

'Things are the same as they ever were,' she told him. Her gaze was thoughtful. His self-doubt was coming to the fore once again. 'I think you worry too much. He's married now and he only has eyes for Jenny. But you know that, don't you?'

'It's your feelings towards him that concern me,' he answered, but his pager bleeped before he had time to say any more. He checked the text message and immediately became businesslike. 'I have to go and assess a new patient.'

'Okay.' It was nearing the end of her shift and she said quickly, 'Will I see you back at the house tonight? You could come to supper if you like?'

He frowned. 'Thanks but I'm not sure if I can make it—I promised Dad I'd go and see him at Mill House. He seems to be anxious to put things on a better footing between us lately.' He lifted a dark brow. 'I guess you were right about him all along. He's fighting his own demons.'

She was disappointed she wouldn't be seeing him but she tried not to let it show. If he'd wanted to spend time with her, he would have found a way, wouldn't he? 'That's fine,' she said, trying to inject a note of nonchalance into her voice. 'I'm glad you and he are getting on better. When all's said and done, he's the one who brought you up. There must have been good times as well as bad.'

'Yes, there were. I think my memories were coloured by the way I found out he wasn't my real father and by the way he acted towards me when Mum died. He was angry and then he shut me out. I suppose that spurred me on to rebel against him all the more. We were both hurting and we lashed out at one another.'

She reached out and lightly touched his arm. 'I hope you can work things out between you.'

He made a wry face. 'I think we will. We're both up for it, now that we've finally squared up to the truth and realised our shortcomings.'

'Good luck, then.'

'Thanks, Caity.'

Caitlin finished her shift, checking on all her young charges and making sure they were comfortable and happy before she left the hospital.

Then she drove home, taking a route through town and along the country lanes, letting the quiet beauty of the Chilterns soothe her. She wanted to spend time with Brodie but, if he preferred to stay away, what could she do? Maybe she would have to get used to the idea that he wouldn't be around for much longer. David had already gone back to London. Was Brodie planning on joining him there in a few months' time?

'Sorry to love you and leave you, Caitlin,' her mother said shortly after she arrived home. A car horn sounded outside on the drive. 'My friend's arrived to take me to the book club meeting—did you remember it was on for tonight?'

'I remembered, Mum. Enjoy yourself.'

'I will. You'll get yourself something to eat, won't you? Because I'll be eating at Freda's house. There's the makings of a ploughman's lunch in the fridge and I made a batch of scones earlier. You could have them with some of that strawberry preserve.'

'Thanks, Mum. Don't worry about me. I'll have a shower and change and then I'll sort something out.'

'Good.' Her mother looked at her closely. 'You're looking a bit peaky. I hope you're not coming down with something.'

'I'm fine, really.'

'Hmm.' Her mother wasn't convinced. 'Is it Brodie? Is he the problem?' She frowned. 'I wish you and he could sort yourselves out. I thought when he bought the house next door he was all for settling down—but now that's all up in the air again with this job in London on the cards.'

Caitlin flicked her a glance. 'He told you about it?'

'Oh, yes. He said it's a fantastic opportunity. They've told him he can have carte blanche to make changes and there's even an executive house that goes with the job.'

Caitlin's heart sank. It sounded too good to be true and he was obviously impressed with the terms of the contract. Why would he even think of turning it down?

After her mother left with her friend, Caitlin showered and changed into jeans and a fresh, pretty top, then took Daisy for a walk along the quiet lane by the house. The terrier was happy to be out and about, fully restored to health with a shining, shaggy coat. She explored the grass verges, her tail wagging the whole time. Caitlin let her sniff and forage for a while, until finally she said, 'Come on, then, Daisy. It's time we were heading for home. I expect the puppies will be wanting their mum back.'

Daisy eagerly started back along the lane. She was unusually happy to hurry home and Caitlin had no idea what had brought about that enthusiasm until they rounded a bend in the road and saw a lone figure up ahead. He was coming towards them.

'Brodie?' Caitlin's eyes widened. 'I thought you'd be up at Mill House.'

He walked towards her, long and lean; his body was supple, his legs clad in dark chinos, his shirt open at the collar. 'Hi there. Yes, I was. I talked to Dad for a while and then told him I had an invitation for supper at your place. He seemed to think I should take you up on it.'

'And you were okay with that?'

'Oh, yes. I told him I was hoping he'd say that.'

She laughed, letting Daisy off the lead now that they were close to home. 'You got on well with him, then?'

'Yes, it was good. I think we smoothed a lot of things out. We'll be okay.'

The dog ran up to him, fussing around him delightedly, rapturous at finding her favourite person in all the world so near at hand, and Brodie stroked her silky head in return. 'I thought I'd find you both out on a walk along here,' he said.

'Mum's out at her book club meeting and I haven't started supper yet,' Caitlin told him. 'I thought I might make a pizza. What do you think?'

'Sounds good to me. I'll prepare the topping if you want to do the base?'

She nodded. 'Fair enough. There's cheese and ham and sun-dried tomatoes. Does that sound all right to you?'

'Perfect.'

They went into the house together. Daisy went off to find her offspring while Caitlin washed her hands at the sink and started to get organised for supper. She sent Brodie a quick glance. 'Did you catch up with Matt at the hospital before he left? I wondered if you and he had a chance to talk?'

She switched on the oven to warm and then gathered together the ingredients for the pizza, setting them out on the kitchen table. 'He seemed to think you had a problem with him.'

'So he said. Yes, we talked, for a short time. We're all right.' He started to chop ham and then grated the cheese she had put out on a board. 'I guess I just need to get over the fact that he dated you for what seemed like for ever.'

Her brow creased. 'That seems to have bothered you quite a bit.'

'It did. A lot.'

She shook her head. 'I'm sorry but I don't really understand.' She paused in the middle of putting together the mix for the pizza base. 'That all started a long while ago—Matt and me. Why would it worry you? You weren't around.'

He pulled a face. 'Maybe…but I wanted to be.'

She'd started to roll out the pizza base but now she

hesitated once more. 'I don't think I follow what you're trying to say.'

He moved his shoulders awkwardly. 'That's probably because I'm finding it hard to say it. I'm not used to baring my soul, Caity, but I suppose it's about time we had this out in the open.' He started to pace around the kitchen.

She frowned. 'Okay.' She spread sun-dried tomato paste over the pizza base and added the grated cheese and ham. 'What is it you need to tell me?' She slid the pizza into the oven and set the timer. 'Perhaps you should stand still and tell me before I get dizzy from watching you walking around.'

He gave a rueful smile at that but stood still. 'I always thought there was something missing in my life, something I was searching for. I thought I felt that way because I didn't know who my father was. I couldn't settle. I thought if I found him, found my natural father and discovered who I really was, that would resolve everything. But then I realised that wasn't the problem at all.'

'It wasn't?'

'No.' He shook his head. 'You see, it was you I wanted, Caity. It was you I wanted all along. You were the one who was missing from my life. I wanted you when we were teenagers but you weren't having any of it… I went away thinking I'd get over you, I'd make a new start…but it didn't happen. I never found anyone who could make me happy.'

He drew in a long breath. 'For a long time, I thought I didn't deserve to be happy. I believed I couldn't make you happy. Back when we were teenagers I wasn't good enough for you… I was so confused and out of sorts. I spent years thinking I wasn't good enough, that I was lacking in some way, not to be trusted. And then I heard you were with Matt and I knew I had to make one last effort to see you again, to see if things might change.'

He started to pace again and Caitlin stared at him, not daring to believe what he was saying.

'Is it true, Brodie? Do you mean it?'

He came over to her and wrapped his arms around her. 'It's definitely true, Caity. I came back here to Ashley Vale for one reason and one reason only. I wanted to be near you. I knew you would come to stay with your mother from time to time, so at least I would see you.'

He frowned. 'Knowing you and Matt were together drove me crazy. I'm ashamed to say I wanted to break things up between you. I couldn't stand the thought of you and him being together. In fact, I didn't want to think of you being with anyone other than me.'

'But you didn't say any of this to me.' She looked up at him, hardly daring to believe him, yet inside her heart was soaring. He'd missed her, he wanted to be with her and he'd come back to Ashley Vale to be near her.

She lifted her hand to his cheek, tracing the line of his strong jaw with the tips of her fingers. 'Why didn't you tell me?'

'How could I, when you seemed to be so much in love with Matt?' He bent his head and rested his cheek against hers. 'I'm sorry, but I was glad when you broke up with him. I thought maybe, in time, you'd come to see me in a different light, that you might come to love me as I love you.'

'Do you…love me?'

'I love you, Caity, more than anything. Being with you since I came back here just confirmed what I believed all along: that you're the only woman for me; my soulmate; my true love.' He held her close and kissed her and she clung to him, hardly able to breathe because she was so full of joy and love for him.

After a while, he reluctantly broke off the kiss to say raggedly, 'When you said you were unhappy because I left Ashley Vale, that you turned to Matt because I wasn't around, I began to hope there was a chance for you and me to be together. I hoped I could prove to you that I'm strong now, that I'm capable of true, heartfelt love, and that I can give you what you need. Tell me I'm right, Caity.'

'Brodie, I love you. I've known it for a long time now.' She kissed him fiercely, passionately, wanting to show him how much she cared for him.

'I think I turned to Matt because he was safe—he was steady and responsible—but as soon as you came back here I knew I'd made a huge mistake. I was in such a state of turmoil. I never felt for him, or for any man, what I feel for you. I always hankered after you but I was afraid to act on my feelings. I was so scared of being hurt, of loving you and losing you. Can you understand that? I think it all goes back to when I lost my father. It was so painful—I didn't want to risk you not loving me in return.'

'Ah, Caity…' He kissed her tenderly, his mouth achingly sweet as he explored the softness of her lips. 'I love you and I'll never let you down. I want you to know that. I'll always be here for you. All you have to do is say you'll marry me—say the word and everything will work out fine. We'll stay here and look after your mother and they can find someone else to take the job in London. It's not important. You're what matters to me, more than anything. I want you to know that you mean everything to me.' He gazed at her, his eyes dark with passion. 'Say you'll marry me, Caity?'

'Yes, Brodie. Yes. Yes, I will.' She was laughing now with happiness, brimming over with it, still hardly daring to believe this was happening. Was it all a dream? Would she wake up and find it was a fanciful, wonderful fantasy?

But then the buzzer from the oven rang out, signalling that the pizza was cooked, an all too real sign that she was well and truly awake, and that someone would have to do something about it. Then they were both laughing, wrapped up in each other's arms, kissing and hugging, neither one wanting to let go of the other.

Daisy came in from the utility room to see what the noise was all about. She gave a short bark and nudged Brodie's leg.

'I think she wants me to stop the buzzer and get the pizza,' he said with a smile. 'You can tell who's going to be the boss in our house, can't you? A small, raggedy-haired dog with a tail that wags ten to the dozen.'

'"Our house",' Caitlin repeated with a smile. 'I love the sound of that.'

Brodie switched off the alarm and kissed her again, tenderly, thoroughly. 'So do I. Our house—a family home filled with love. Maybe even, some day, if you want it too, our own small brood of children.' He gazed down at her, holding her close.

'Oh, I do,' she murmured. 'It sounds absolutely perfect.'

* * * * *

COMING SOON!

We really hope you enjoyed reading this book. If you're looking for more romance, be sure to head to the shops when new books are available on

Thursday 24th January

To see which titles are coming soon, please visit

millsandboon.co.uk/nextmonth

MILLS & BOON